DANCE OF THE ELEMENTS BOOK I

IGNITED
A.M. DEESE

RADIANT
TEEN

IGNITED
(Dance of the Elements, #1)
© 2018 A. M. Deese
www.amdeese.com

www.radiantcrownpublishing.com
An Imprint of Radiant Crown Publishing

Deese, A. M.
Ignited (Dance of the Elements, #1) / by A. M. Deese 1st ed.

Available as an eBook with exclusive content
ISBN-13: 978-1-946024-12-1 (Trade Paperback)
Library of Congress Control Number: 2017958520

Editing by Leah T. Brown
Map by Tiphaine Leard
Cover design by Desiree DeOrto Designs
Book design by Inkstain Design Studio

Printed in the United States of America
First Edition: March 2018
10 9 8 7 6 5 4 3 2 1

This book is dedicated to Lorraine,
who read it first and supported me always.

TH

LA'NOR

SAMR

FYKK

THE R
THE

O R E R R A M
S E A

TIRDRAKOR

SCIM

ARENA

ELEK

LS'LE'SPAR
(AINA)

B A R I

THE WORLD OF JA

ONE

JURA

Jura *imagined it sounded like* rain. The steady tap of grains of sand pounding against the glass walls and ceiling was almost musical. The sands were still untamed but she was safe from the dangers of the earth.

No, death was more likely to come from inside—and she was late.

Her robes were on backwards. The last several hours plotting what to say and just how she would say it had all been a waste of time. It was doubtful the Thirteen would take a young woman seriously, especially if she wasn't even capable of dressing herself. The gold and purple stitching on the formal black court robe was only slightly different in the front than the back. *Would anyone notice?* Jura could feel their eyes watching her, swore she could hear the occasional chuckle thrown in her direction. She wanted to run, she wanted to die from embarrassment right on the spot.

Don't panic. You don't have time to change; just breathe. She inhaled sharply, letting her breath slowly leak out between clenched teeth. *Had the justice dome always been so tall?* She felt dwarfed by the massive walls towering around her. She lifted her thick maiden's braid as a trail of sweat escaped from the nape of her neck to drip down the stiff collar of her robe. She sidled to a pillar on the least populated side of the dome and pressed her back against the cool marble.

The members of the Thirteen milled about the concave room, flitting in and out of conversation and tossing distrustful glances at one another. No one else was wearing the traditional court robes, and Jura suddenly remembered they were only used on voting day or when foreign diplomats were present. She bit her bottom lip, blood rushed into her cheeks. Wearing the robes now proved her inexperience; wearing them backwards showed she was an inexperienced idiot. Her spectacles slid down the bridge of her nose. She sighed as she shoved them back up. Why had she even worn the flaming things? The glasses, not the robes. Although they were both giving her trouble. She scanned the room and noticed that almost all of the Thirteen had arrived. The council meeting would start in a matter of minutes.

If the council didn't accept her, her house would lose everything.

Kader, Eighth of the Thirteen, was making his rounds with refreshments. The members of the Thirteen took turns serving one another, and Jura was grateful that she didn't have to add the duties of serving girl to her growing list of anxieties. Kader stopped in front of her, offering water from his silver serving tray. She reached for a glass and was about to bring it to her lips when she became aware of the Eighth's beady black eyes following her movement. She paused, her hand faltering in mid-air. Water was the standard beverage during council meetings. Not only was pure water a nod to the Thirteen's stature, it was also the most difficult liquid to poison without detection.

Jura rolled the glass in a slow circle, watchful for any residue that might have stuck to the clear goblet as it tilted. *Was he watching to see if I'll drink it or just curious because I shouldn't be here?* She raised her eyebrows and forced the corner of her lips to tilt upward. Kader inclined his head politely before turning to offer water to another council member. She deliberately set the glass down on the floor beside her. She wouldn't drink from it, just in case.

Jura frowned as a woman entering the room caught her attention. *There isn't enough water in the world to make me wear something so scandalous.* Not only was Denir, Fifth of the Thirteen, flirting prettily, but she also wore a low cut golden gown that clung to her figure. She smiled up at Jabir, the Seventh, a tall narrow man in neutral shades of gray with dark curly hair and a devilish gleam in his eye. He leered down at the Fifth.

He's married, isn't he? Jura couldn't remember, and honestly, it didn't seem to matter. She struggled to place a name for a few of the others but couldn't recall any except Ahmar, the Third, and father of her closest friend. He was deep in conversation with a man who seemed impossibly wide for his short stature. The fat man's jowls quivered as he spoke, and he leaned back from the Third nervously, his hand hovered just above his sheathed dagger. It was forbidden to have one's *Arbe* in attendance, but nearly everyone carried a weapon. The dagger seemed to be the favored choice, although Jura noticed a few scimitars and even an assegai strapped to the back of a tall, skinny man in pale yellow robes. Jura fingered the whip holstered at her waist. No one, aside from Kader, had even acknowledged her presence. If she had acted when she first had the thought, she might have been able to sneak away before the—

"Daughter of the First, good evening. I almost didn't see you there, skulking away in the corner as it were." Velder, Second of the Thirteen, lifted a hand and twisted his fingers into the complicated gesture that signified a greeting as he walked toward her.

"Making a new fashion statement, I see?" He raised his eyebrows.

Jura muffled a groan, of course he'd noticed her fashion faux pas. She grimaced before intertwining her fingers and wriggling her thumbs in reply.

"Councilman Velder. How good to see you."

"Indeed. And how very odd it is to see you, *alone*. Where is the First? It's nearly time to start the session." The councilman's long, tapered fingers stroked his thin gray mustache.

This was the moment she'd been dreading. Council meetings were closed to all except the voting members of the Thirteen families; everyone knew that. Jura was not the voting member; her father was and had been for the last twenty years, but now they were stuck with her. Her worst nightmare had come true.

"Yes. I mean, no. That is, the First is…indisposed."

Velder frowned down at her. "Is that so? His presence is needed to preside over the council meeting."

"I understand," she mumbled. Father hated when she mumbled. If he was here, he'd have pulled her by the ear and given her a lecture on leadership and her responsibility to the family name. Leaders didn't mumble. Her fingers flew up to her throat, as if scratching at her tender skin would send the words pouring forth. She just had to spit something out, anything.

Anything but the truth.

"Councilman Velder, the First is—"

4

"Absent for the second day in a row." Velder's dark eyes narrowed. "The people of the Republic cannot rule themselves. The First—"

"The First is indisposed!" She had not meant to shout. She lowered her eyes, frowning at her shoes. *People would stare.*

"He is unwell," she said in a softer voice. Her tongue darted out to moisten lips gone impossibly dry. She considered drinking Kader's offered water, even poison was better than this.

"I will judge in his stead." There. The words were strangled, but she'd said it.

Velder barely concealed his chuckle beneath his hand. "With all due respect, the Thirteen will never approve."

"The Thirteen? Or you?" Velder had never liked her. He didn't seem to like anyone. Jura bit the inside of her cheek to keep from screaming. Her hands were shaking, so she squeezed them into fists by her sides. She was seventeen years old, hardly a child. She could do this, she *had* to do this.

Father will never forgive me if I cause the house to lose Rank.

She pushed her dangling spectacles up the length of her nose and glared at the councilman. At least, she thought she was glaring, it felt like she was squinting up at him, and she hoped she appeared stern. She felt ridiculous.

"I am the only heir to house of the First." He didn't respond, and she took the opportunity to raise her voice and address the room. She flinched when her voice came out as a high-pitched squeak. "It is my duty to serve as interim First if my father is incapable. His sickness—" She frowned, correcting herself. "His minor illness has forced me to step forward and fulfill my duty as his heir. Who will oppose this law?"

"Not I," chimed out Fatima. Jura rewarded her with her best smile.

Fatima currently held a low Rank, she was from the House of the Eleventh or Twelfth. Jura could never keep the Rankings of the lower houses straight, they were never stagnant and the bottom three didn't even have a vote when it came to Rank. The councilwoman probably thought her quick approval would secure her position when the next vote occurred.

"I second it," Ahmar boomed. He was the Third and father of Amira, Jura's closest friend. He was her best bet at gaining quick acceptance from the Thirteen. The giant of a man tossed a curious smile in her direction.

Jura hid her sigh of relief behind her grin. His approval was all she needed; the others would follow.

Velder stepped back, bowing low. His face was apologetic, but his tone dripped with sarcasm as he straightened and said, "Of course I, as a humble servant to the laws of our great Republic, would not have a place to question it. I will, naturally, accept your ruling. It's such a shame his Greatness is too ill to issue the proclamation himself…" He trailed off, raising a bushy brow.

She let out a sigh and squared her shoulders, glaring up at Velder. This time she was *sure* it was a glare. If she didn't appear tough, the vultures at court would peck at her. It was only a matter of time before someone discovered her secret.

"The council has spoken." *Thank the Everflame.* She shot another smile in the direction of Fatima and Ahmar. "Consider this matter closed and call the council meeting to order." She brushed past him and hurried up to the dais before he called her bluff.

She struggled to keep her pace normal, the result was an awkward cross between a jog and a shuffle as she made her way across the dome to her father's chair. She stumbled into the seat.

It was the duty of the Second to call out the beginning of the session, and Velder did so as Jura straightened in the imposing glass throne meant for her father. Like most of the palace, the massive throne was made entirely out of glass. This late in the day, the setting sun shone through the crystal clear domed ceiling, casting out prisms of pale pink and dusty orange that shone down on her and created a natural spotlight. Jura clasped the seat of the throne, squirming against the rigid glass. She tried to ignore the fact that all eyes were on her. They probably all saw her as a little girl playing dress up. Well, she had more important things to think about. For instance, how was she to lead a meeting she had never attended?

As acting head of council, she was granted four votes. The house in the number two Rank held three votes, the Third house held two votes and the six remaining houses held one. The bottom three council members had no vote at all. The First also had final say on any crime worthy of a death sentence and in all matters of war. Though they held weekly meetings, the council only voted on the rankings of the council members once a month. Today was not a voting day. At least something was going her way.

The Thirteen seated themselves in a neat row of chairs lined against a long stone table ahead of her, and Velder took his position just to the right of her father's throne. The first citizen was called for judgment. After a few minor issues were judged, Jura began to relax. The session was going smoothly and there were only two citizens left to place judgment.

The first was a complaint between two merchants. One merchant argued the other was poaching on his district by setting up a stand of pottery not far from his own and selling duplicate wares. The other potter argued that his product differed. Jura granted the second merchant a stake of property in a neighboring province but placated him by giving him more property than he'd had before. Easy. Velder called in the final citizen.

"This is Tylak," Velder sneered, "citizen of Ish." His voice dripped with condemnation. Ish was the poorest of the thirteen provinces, probably because its leadership was held by the Thirteenth, a position that was never stable.

Tylak, a slave name, and yet he had citizen status. Interested, Jura leaned forward. It was rare for a slave to gain enough wages to purchase his freedom and even rarer for a slave to be granted such freedom from his owner.

"Tylak is charged with thievery," Velder paused, meeting her eye. "The council suggests execution."

Jura squeezed her father's chair so tightly it was a wonder the glass didn't break off in her hand. It was true that execution was the maximum punishment, but it was seldom carried out. Especially not for a crime as petty as thievery.

"I see," she whispered.

Velder smiled, revealing teeth stained brown from tobacco.

She cleared her throat. "What did the accused steal?"

"Fire." He paused, his gaze sweeping over the seated members of council before settling on Jura. "From the Everflame."

Impossible.

"Is this true?" Jura looked down at the young man, his appearance was unkempt, but he appeared strong rather than haggard. His dark hair was greasy and hung in lank locks over his pale face.

The man shrugged.

Velder's eyes burned into her. She looked up at him. "What proof stands against the accused?"

"He was captured within the walls of the glass tower, carrying a torch, and he is no Fire Dancer. Where else would he have acquired it? He has stolen Fire from the Everflame and as such has stolen from the Republic. This is unnatural magic at work. This man is clearly dangerous. Not to mandate an immediate execution would make the Republic seem weak."

Jura understood his implication. The Second was testing her. *Pompous, manipulating worm.*

If she did not order this man's execution, *she* would appear weak and she would lose any footing she'd gained today. But how could such a man, how could anyone besides a Fire Dancer, have done such a thing? Unless…she squeezed the throne tighter to keep her hands from shaking in excitement. After all this time, was she finally being faced with some tangible evidence? What did this man know? She leaned forward.

"Tylak, was it? Tell us how you accomplished such a feat. Answer me truthfully and you will be spared." She ignored Velder's glare. *Tell me, please.*

The young man lifted his face up to her, and she resisted the urge to gasp. The man had gray eyes that cut into his chiseled features and smoldered with hate. A pale, jagged scar traced from beneath the corner of his left eye down to the edge of his lips. He was beautiful. He was terrifying. Jura swallowed against the massive lump in her throat.

"I didn't steal anything. But kill me; I don't care." He spat at her feet.

Velder backhanded the man and he fell to his knees, head bowed. He said nothing else. "Greatness, his insolence must be punished."

Jura could not take her eyes off the man. He was dirty and poorly dressed but he didn't look like a crazed villain. And yet, according to Velder he was entirely too dangerous to be allowed freedom. A man that could accomplish what this man was accused of was more than just an idle threat to her family's Rank, he was a threat to the entire Republic. He was also her only chance. What kind of person would dare steal from the Everflame? Could she really sentence this man to his death? Did she even have a choice? She needed more time.

She nodded. "See that it is done." The prisoner was escorted from their judgment hall. Jura watched him leave.

"Was that all?" She couldn't wait to get out of there.

Velder nodded.

Jura stood up, wishing nothing more than to run to her chambers and tear off the insufferable robes. "Velder, call the session to a close."

She hurried from the auditorium and was jerked to a stop so quickly her glasses flew from her nose.

"Flames," she mumbled, stooping down to pick them up. She pulled her arm from the stubborn grasp of her friend Amira.

If the circumstances were different she would have been happy to see the friendly face. Amira was opinionated, tall, and beautiful; she could have befriended anyone in the court. Yet despite her busy social calendar, she had chosen Jura, who normally preferred to spend her time alone. If not for Amira, Jura would spend all of her free time gardening or reading in her room.

"I thought I saw you enter the judgment halls," her friend squealed. It was a trait that bothered Jura in most people but on her best friend it was endearing. "Tell me everything! And how did—wait, are your robes on backwards?"

Stalling for time, Jura adjusted the delicate frames of her spectacles and once again perched them on her nose, only to have them slide down the bridge and dangle precariously. She should have left the flaming things in her room.

"What's going on?" Amira pressed.

Immediately, Jura wanted to tell her. Amira had just returned from a tour with her father. It was the first time the Third had opted to take his daughter along and the two hadn't had alone time in weeks. There was so much to tell her.

She wanted to fall into Amira's arms and cry to her that she had just killed the one man who might hold the answers she'd been searching for. That she didn't want the position she was thrown into. That she was worried for her father.

But she couldn't tell her anything.

"My father is ill," she said slowly, working out what information was safe to share. "It was my duty to attend council in his stead."

Amira's khol lined eyes widened. "I can't believe you did that!" She was squealing again. "Well, tell me everything. How was it? What happened? Your father must be on his deathbed to allow you to attend the session."

Amira had always wanted to attend a session, but anytime her father went away on a business trip he'd always chosen her younger brother as his representative. Her eyes narrowed and her lips drew into a pout in the tell-tale sign that she was jealous.

"Nothing serious. I'm sure he'll be back in no time at all. He'll definitely be back by next week's meeting." Jura forced a smile as years of conditioning kicked in. The histories contained countless stories of houses that had fallen simply because they'd thought to confide in a friend. Her father would want this kept a secret.

None of the Thirteen could be trusted. No one could, except maybe Markhim.

Her *Arbe* stepped up behind her and Jura started at their arrival, still not used to their presence. Unable to attend the meeting, the four bodyguards had been forced to wait outside the Justice Dome's imposing double doors. They appeared now, a silent towering mass. Grateful for their intrusion, Jura excused herself to flee to her rooms. Amira would have to wait.

She entered her chambers and dismissed her house staff immediately, needing to be alone. She ripped off the robes. They landed in a heap on the cool stone floor. She sank down beside them and let the hot tears slice down her cheeks. She had just killed a man. He'd known that she would, and he'd hated her for it. And she'd given the orders to end his life. The knowledge was crushing.

She drew in a shaky breath and wiped at the tears. They served no purpose and even though she never wanted for water, she knew better than to waste it. Father hated when she cried. She'd never seen him cry, not even when mother had died. She could just imagine the disappointment in his eyes if he saw her now.

She shouldn't have allowed Velder to bully her into the execution. If she talked to the prisoner, convinced him to admit how he'd done it, she might be able to reduce his sentence before his execution was carried out. And although she didn't want the man's death on her conscience, she had to admit that questioning him served another purpose. If the man truly did know how to accomplish the impossible, perhaps he held other secrets. Maybe he held the key to the answers she'd been searching for all this time.

It was unlikely she could maintain control of the Thirteen for very long. It was only a matter of days before someone would demand to see the First. What would she do then?

She knew she was alone in her salon, but she thoroughly checked again to be sure. The room was sparsely decorated. Despite their vast family wealth, her father believed they should live a frugal lifestyle. Jura didn't mind, her only luxuries were found in her books. She had hundreds of the leather-bound pages resting on shelves that lined the stone walls of her chambers. She frowned down at the weathered, ornate floor rug before pulling it back to reveal a heavy trap door. The door was large and imposing. It took all her strength to pull it open. She descended the small ladder into the darkness, blinking to adjust her eyes.

The man inside was bound and gagged, he stared up at her with furious dark eyes. He tried to speak, but the gag prevented it. Jura knelt down beside him, careful not to get too close.

"Hello father."

TWO

JURA

"I'm going to remove the gag, but you mustn't alert the guards. Can you promise this?"

Her father narrowed his eyes but nodded. She pulled down the cloth that covered his mouth and offered him some water, which he gulped down greedily. Water dribbled down his chin and she flinched at the waste.

"I've brought you some dates as well. Do you want them?"

He said nothing but allowed her to feed him. It reminded her of a few years before when she'd dislocated her shoulder after a strenuous training session. Jura hadn't cried out, but her father had known she was injured and had called the session to an immediate close. Later that night he'd fed her honeyed dates spread with goat cheese. Jura hadn't even realized he'd known they were her favorite. She fed the dates to him now but, after he'd eaten a few, he turned away from her and sat back against the stone wall, as far away from her as possible. She pulled the gag back into place with trembling fingers. She couldn't blame him for hating her.

"You know I can't let you out. Not yet. You're not well."

He said nothing. Could he even understand her?

"I've told the Thirteen that you are ill. I've been covering for you. I even attended council meeting today and judged in your stead."

Her father's eyes narrowed. Apparently he *could* understand. She'd known that information wouldn't make him happy. He was probably horrified that she had stepped in. Timid little Jura, trying to lead the entire Republic. Even *she* knew the notion was ridiculous.

"I had to," she continued. "It's for the good of the Republic. I'm doing this for you." She paused. "I think you would want me to, if you were more yourself."

Without meaning to, her eyes fell down to the delicate gold chain that dangled from his wrist. It was as beautiful as it was deadly.

A blood chain, a relic from more dangerous times. Once attached to its captive, the tiny chain used some sort of magic to render its captive under its complete control. The person controlling the chain controlled the person who wore it. Her father was nothing more than someone's puppet, and Jura was determined to find out who his puppet master was.

She couldn't understand where the blood chain had even come from. She hadn't even known they actually existed. Someone had gone through a lot of trouble to find one. Jura raked her brain, desperate for an answer. As the First of the Glass Palace and leader of the Republic, her father had any number of enemies, he always had. And now, so did she.

"If you could just tell me who did this to you. I know you're still in there, father, somewhere. Please. Please? Tell me. Who's done this to you?"

15

She wanted to reach out and shake his shoulders, but she kept her arms by her side. Her father hated to be touched, even when he was himself.

Still, the First said nothing, closing his eyes and leaning his head back as though to sleep. Jura sighed. She would have to find answers on her own.

Three days ago, her life had been very different. She had been in the gardens when it happened. She often spent her mornings surrounded by the lush greenery in the courtyard. It was a frivolous waste of water maintaining the gardens, but her mother had loved them. There was a vast assortment of ferns and palm fronds which bordered the fountain in sturdy clay pots. Several squat fig trees and a few dwarf citrus trees dotted the perimeter. There were several different varieties of flower, but Jura favored the delicate petals of the white Jasmine. They had been her mother's favorite, and the fragrant flowers reminded Jura of her mother's presence and of happier times. As was her habit, Jura had spent the morning tending to her flowers when she'd heard the strangled cry.

She'd turned, only to find Akkim, her personal bodyguard, lying in a pool of his own blood. A spear protruded from his back. A spear that she quickly realized had been meant for her. Standing above Akkim was her father, fury in his eyes as he reached down and yanked the spear from Akkim's still twitching body. The feeling of terror was still branded in her brain, and yet the finer details of the moment were lost to her. She only remembered that her father's movements had seemed languid. She would never forget the look of the frightening sneer that had rolled over his thin lips.

She still couldn't quite understand how she'd managed to defend herself. She was half his size and the attack had been so unexpected. If she hadn't been carrying her tiny garden trowel, she'd have been unarmed. She accredited her survival to years of Akkim's training in self-defense. Her father, like every parent who was a member of the Thirteen, had required it as part of her studies, and she was grateful for the training that allowed her to reflexively swing the tiny shovel at her father with all her might.

She'd hit his temple and he had crumpled immediately at her feet. Horrified, she'd knelt beside her father, praying for a pulse. She'd found one, along with the blood chain on his wrist. At least, that's what she suspected it was. She'd never actually seen one before. It matched the descriptions she'd read about in the histories, and it would explain her father's uncharacteristic attack.

It had been easy enough to summon her father's personal *Arbe* to cover up the mess in the courtyard. An *Arbe* would never share their secret, *couldn't* share such secrets, and Jura would protect her house at all costs. It was what her father would expect from her.

Akkim had died saving her life. She would never forget his sacrifice, the way his blood had pooled at her feet. The pain of his loss caused tears to form in her eyes and snapped her back to the present. She was crying for the second time today and that was unacceptable. She brushed the salty liquid away and took her father's face in her hands, forcing him to look at her. She didn't care that he didn't like to be touched; he needed to listen.

"I know you. I know this isn't your fault. I will find who has done this to you. And I will make them pay."

He lunged at her then, and she cried out as she fell back out of harm's way. The chains that bound the First were sturdy and gave little room for him to move about. He snapped at her like a wild animal, as though he meant to tear her in half with his teeth. With a strangled cry, she scurried out of the crawl space, slamming the door behind her. Safe back in her chambers above, she sat heavily on the floor staring down at the trap door, struggling to regain some normalcy to her breathing. She began counting to still the rapid beating of her heart.

She started at the gentle knock on her chamber doors. "Just a moment," she called out. She hurriedly replaced the rug and stood on top of the door, calling out that the knocker may enter. *Had she remembered to gag him? Could she hear her father calling to be freed or was that her imagination?*

Velder stood in her doorway and offered a smile that bordered on leering. Jura realized that her robes still lay in a heap on the floor and that she was wearing nothing but a thin shift.

Sandstorms. Is there no end to my humiliation today? Velder noticed everything, but she hoped he would at least have the decency not to mention it.

At least all her clothing was modest, even her underwear. Thank the Everflame she was still covered from neck to toe, though the material was indecently thin for outerwear. She crossed her arms over her chest.

"Greatness, you left the session so quickly I didn't have a chance to commend you on your excellent leadership skills."

Jura resisted the urge to openly roll her eyes. "Thank you, Second." She smiled, taking small pleasure in the fact that serving under her must irk him.

Velder grinned in response, and Jura wondered why the mere sight of his teeth made her skin crawl. Jura lifted her chin under the scrutiny of his predatory eyes and cleared her throat.

"Surely you could have waited to speak to me of this tomorrow. I assume you had another reason for disturbing me in my private chambers?"

"Of course. Your presence is needed in the Great Hall. That is, the presence of the First. I would summon your father, but as you say, he is indisposed." Velder's smile deepened.

"Indeed he is," Jura replied. "I'll be right there."

Velder bowed low and left. Jura shut the door after him and released a pent-up sigh. Velder had the most to gain from her father's incapacitation. As the second of the Thirteen, he would be the next in line if anything were to happen to herself and the First. Not that her death was needed for Velder to move forward in Rank. A simple voting at the next session could accomplish that, but her father *had* tried to kill her. If the commander of the chains had meant for her father to kill her and then himself, Velder would have been the one with the most to gain. Jura put him at the top of her list of suspects.

She pushed thoughts of conspiracy aside for the moment and wondered instead what had occurred. *Why was she being called back to the Justice Dome not even an hour from her earlier departure?* Opting for a simpler day robe instead of the heavy ceremonial ones she'd worn earlier, she hurriedly got dressed. Not too quickly though, as she double checked to make sure nothing was backwards or inside out.

Her *Arbe* waited for her outside the door and for the second time that day she was thankful for their presence. *Arbe* was the top line of defense for the ruling and influential. Trained from infancy in martial arts and espionage, there were none better. Except of course the Shadow Dancers. The Shadow Dancers were said to be a secret group of assassins, thieves, and spies. There was no proof of their existence, and many believed the guild was nothing but a story to frighten children. *You just saw a blood chain that's not supposed to exist,* she reminded herself. *If they do exist, they could help with father.*

Unlike the rumors of Shadow Dancers, there was no disputing the existence of *Arbe*. Anyone who could afford to purchase an *Arbe*, had one. In fact, it was common to have more than one, and some felt that the more men they had as bodyguards, the more it displayed their power. Jura's father had never agreed with this practice, he argued that any man who needed more than four men protecting him was weak, nothing more than a fool flaunting his wealth. Because everyone had one, *Arbe* were no more than accessories to the upper class. Jura imagined that each *Arbe* knew more secrets than the supposed guild of spies.

Of course, Shadow Dancers weren't required to cut out their own tongue like the men handpicked to join the *Arbe*.

Her own *Arbe* followed her, never more than five paces behind, and she found their presence distracting. Her father had gifted them to her on her tenth birthday, and she'd never cared for them, preferring instead the singular company of Akkim. Akkim, the man who had told her bedtime stories of far off lands as a little girl. Now, with him gone and her father locked away, she was utterly alone, and her *Arbe* was vital to her safety.

Still, she was grateful that her father didn't believe in the practice of keeping two *Arbe*; she couldn't imagine what she would do with eight men in tow. In Jura's mind, the glass halls of the palace were more than enough protection. The only stone in the palace was found in bedchambers, and that was only for privacy's sake. The glass served its purpose well. It was near impossible to sneak up on a council member when every hall was made of clear, paper thin glass. A few days ago, Jura had felt safe enough to travel the glass halls on her own, oblivious to the open stares she'd received from the other twelve families. After recent events, Jura didn't judge those who felt the need for extra precaution, and she was thankful for the quiet presence of the massive men that guarded her. They never let her out of her sight.

Was there a way for them to spill her father's secret? The four men were more than aware that she kept her father locked away in her cellar. *What did they think of her? Would they tell?* Without a tongue or the ability to write, that would be hard. The members of her and her father's *Arbe* were heaped on her growing list of anxieties.

She entered the large auditorium where she'd been little more than an hour ago and was startled to find the golden banners displayed. *Why hadn't Velder specified the reason she'd been summoned?*

The gold banners were only shown when foreign rulers or embassies were present. The entire delegation of Thirteen were already seated on their benches. They were all wearing their ceremonial robes. Once again, she was dressed as an outsider, and once again she had no time to run back to her rooms and change. With a soft sigh, Jura took her seat on the glass throne.

"Announcing His Royal Highness Sto' Ne, Grand Wave Master and Admiral of the Three Oceans," The crier bellowed out, and Jura's eyes were drawn to the imposing figure who entered the hall.

He was massive, tan, and bare chested with white blonde hair with colored stones braided in that fell down past his shoulders. He strode across the hall followed by a dozen men and women with the same flowing hair and transparent silk garments that fell in waves of silken fabric. Their sheer clothing and exposed skin made Jura blush. No one in the Republic went about in such an uncovered state. The Sea King and his people did not even have anything covering their bare feet. She gripped the edges of the glass throne, steeling herself to gaze the Sea King in his face. It did *not* matter that his was the first bare chest she had ever seen, and she refused to notice the ripple of thigh muscles underneath his sheer trousers. She bit her bottom lip and kept her eyes trained above his head.

The Sea King stopped in front of her and bowed low. "I hope I'm not intruding upon a time of mourning. The First…"

"Is indisposed." Jura bit the inside of her cheek. The excuse was sounding repetitive, even to her.

"I am Jura, heir to the Sand Sea and Speaker of the Dunes."

The Sea King smiled. "Of course, I met you once before, though that was years ago and you were just a girl hanging on her mother's robes. You look the spitting image of her. Same tiny stature, same long black hair and amber eyes…I was very sorry to hear of her passing."

He looked away, and Jura was aware of the compassion in his green eyes. It was rare to find such lightly colored eyes in the Sand Sea, and for a moment she couldn't look away. Her own eyes, amber flecked with gold, were an anomaly and a source of Amira's random spurts of jealousy. She shook her head and forced herself to follow society protocol, wriggling her fingers in the formal greeting.

She didn't know much about the sea people. Most of her knowledge came from the extensive histories she'd read on the Tri-Alliance. She knew they were a proud race, their religion deeply rooted in everything they did. The colored stones tied in his hair twinkled in the waning sunlight, and she wondered at their significance. She hoped she wouldn't insult the King. She offered him her best smile.

"I apologize my father could not meet with you in person. I hope you will allow myself to stand in his stead."

The Sea King smiled again, "Certainly. My own daughter, hellion that she is, would do the same. At least I hope she would." His face turned serious.

"Am I free to discuss serious matters of politics?"

Jura caught Velder's watchful eye and inclined her head, knowing he'd overheard. The hall cleared out save for the members of the Thirteen and the Sea King's entourage. A chair was brought out for the King and placed on the dais beside her. Jura clenched her fist to keep from fidgeting.

"Your Majesty, you're very far from home. What has brought you to the Sand Sea?"

The Sea King looked over to the members of the Thirteen and then back to her. His eyebrows wrinkled in concern. "I'm sad to say this visit was one of necessity and great urgency. Greatness, I've come to discuss matters of war."

Jura's own brows knitted together in response, and she caught her bottom lip between her teeth. "War? I don't understand. The three kingdoms are at peace. The treaty—"

"Is null and void after my people were captured and sold as slaves to Kitoi."

"That's impossible." *Wasn't it?*

"Is it?" The King's voice was low and fierce. "It's common knowledge you land dwellers practice slave trade."

"The slaves are the Chosen people. They—"

The Sea King held up a silencing hand, interrupting her. "While it's hardly my place to question your country's politics, it's always been quite understood that the peoples of my kingdom are off limits."

Jura chose her next words carefully. "Of course. And if Kitoi has breached the terms of our peace treaty, I can understand why you would be upset enough to leave your kingdom and seek answers."

The Sea King sat back in his makeshift throne. "Upset? Greatness, this breach in contract is an act of war. I came here to see if I had the support of the Sand Sea."

"And you will have it. But I cannot condone entering such a war without proof," she paused. *What would father do?* She looked out at the Thirteen and found that each of them watched her intently. Ahmar looked concerned; Velder amused. The First was responsible for deciding all matters of war. *She* was responsible. She couldn't make a decision lightly.

"Do you? Have proof?"

The Sea King stood, fury in his eyes. "Your father is indisposed you say?"

Apparently the Sea King also wondered what her father would do. She had to remain strong, she *had* to, but she couldn't enter a war lightly.

"Your majesty, when and if you can provide proof of Kitoi's actions, you will have the full support of the Sand Sea's soldiers. Until then, my hands are tied."

The Sea King shook his head, but his voice was full of sadness, not anger. "Your father is someone I once considered a friend. I hope that you will come to see the error of your ways. It appears I've wasted valuable time in coming here. I should return to my people. I have much to prepare for."

He turned and swept from the hall, his entourage following in a rush of silk.

Jura fell back against the glass throne, unsure of what had just happened. *Have I made a mistake? Or is it right erring on the side of caution?* Kitoi had never given any indication they were dangerous. They were a small yet powerful kingdom that, while on the border of the Republic, operated entirely on their own. She knew it was best not to act against her neighbors without any proof.

It wasn't fair that she had been thrown into such a position, forced to make decisions in matters of life and death. Unbidden, her eyes turned to the spot where just an hour before she had sentenced a man to his death. *Had he really stolen fire from the Everflame? And if he had, was that truly a crime to be executed for, or should I have questioned him further? I'm making a terrible mess of everything.* She took a deep breath and reminded herself to focus on saving her father, she needed his strength. She needed to question the slave, find out what he knew, if he really had access to secret magics. She had less than a week to come up with a plan.

THREE

ASH

He pulled the heavy volume from its place on the tall shelf and stared down at in with some reverence. The chronicles did not yet include him, but they would. *That was something, wasn't it?* Ash was known as the greatest Fire Dancer of his time. He had known fame that most people could only dream of. The people of the Republic would know his name for years to come.

He hadn't thought his imminent departure from the arena would affect him in such a way. He was surprised to feel the pain was physical; it started in his gut and spread from his belly up into his chest. Or perhaps it was just heartburn from his earlier meal. He didn't like to think just how possible the latter outcome actually was.

There was no place more sacred to him than the arena. He cherished the blood-stained dirt, the acrid scent of blood and gore that inflamed his nostrils, the rush of a screaming crowd.

Retirement won't be so bad. His mantra. He repeated the words to himself, trying to stem the ever-flowing numbness that threatened to engulf him. Never again would he step out onto that dirt. Never again would he hear his name echo on the cries of thousands. He had enough wealth to last until the end of his days and he would never want for water, but his fame…his fame wouldn't last forever. And in the eyes of future spectators, he was already forgotten.

He blew the thick layer of dust off the tome and opened it, careful not to overly disturb the brittle pages. *So many*, he mused. The art of Fire Dancing had been applied to the arena for over a century and there had been many heroes. Each had their moment to bask in the love of the people and each was eventually immortalized in this chronicle.

It was all Ash had left to look forward to, his name in a dust covered book.

He poured over the names of the hundreds that had come before him, some names brought a smile to his thin lips, Lightning and Flash Fire had come years before him but were some of the greats. Ash had even gotten to watch Flash Fire in the arena before Singe had crushed his back. He let loose a soft sigh and raked his fingers through his thinning hair. There were so many he didn't know. *Will I be remembered?*

He heard the trumpet's cry, marking the beginning of an arena battle. He turned toward the sound, his blood singing in response to its call. He must have followed the noise down the sacred halls, because he found himself at the doors that opened up to the arena, unsure how he'd gotten there. He blinked at the doors before him, struggling to remember when he'd left the arena library.

The large metal burned hot from the heat that emanated in waves from within the arena. Two gladiators stood beside them, rolling sore muscles and checking armor before the fight. Ash reached for his own assegai only to remember he'd left it leaning against the doorframe of his bedroom. *Am I losing my memory already? So soon?*

"Still here old man?" Timber grinned. Young, arrogant, and the current favorite in the arena, he was a massive man that towered over Ash's own frame. Ash was not a puny man, but in the shadow of Timber's presence, he felt weathered and stooped. He couldn't believe that he'd left the arena little more than an hour ago. The moment was already as fleeting as yesterday.

"Lay off him," snapped Kindle. She placed a gentle hand on Ash's shoulder. "Come to watch me pummel him into the sand?" Her blue eyes sparkled and the tiny scar over her left eyebrow gave her a dashing appearance before she slipped on her helmet and adjusted her brilliant blue breastplate.

A Fire Dancer's armor covered their shoulders, chest, back and face. The arms and legs were left exposed to allow for maximum movement in the arena. Many Dancer's had their careers ended from a badly timed move that had left their appendages as nothing more than smoldering stumps. Ash's own eyebrows had burned off more than once, and he sported an ugly scar that ran up the entire length of his right arm. He looked down at the scar now, remembering when it had been red and angry. Now it was white and almost forgotten, like him.

Timber snorted, his armor was a deep emerald green, its vivid color a stark contrast to his dark skin. "That would be something to see. Stick around old man, let me show you what we gladiators are doing these days."

Ash nodded, "I'll stay for the match. Give you a few pointers after." Kindle squeezed his shoulder.

Timber grinned, "I saw your little exhibition this afternoon. I think I might have something new for you."

Ash ground his teeth and said nothing. His fingers flexed with the need to knock in Timber's teeth, but he kept his hand trained by his side. Though he was an arrogant ass, Timber was not to blame for Ash's departure from the arena.

Oblivious to Ash's anger, Timber pursed his lips and kissed the air between himself and Kindle, "As for you, stay out of my way. The people came to see a real fight."

"I'd worry more about staying alive and less about running my mouth if I were you," Kindle retorted.

Envious, Ash watched the exchange between Timber and Kindle. If only he'd been able to leave the arena in a blaze of smoke and fire. No gladiator deserved to live so long, and he resented his every breath. It was his right to die young and glorious. His afternoon stint had been nothing more than a farewell show, and apparently everyone knew it. He'd fought Smolder, a massive beast that had killed dozens of Fire Dancers in her prime. Now she was used mostly in the training arena as sparring practice for new cadets. Killing her had been an act of mercy.

The trumpets sounded again, and Ash's body hummed with the excitement of a new battle, the hairs on the back of his neck rose up and shivers raced down his spine. Nothing compared to the thrill that came with the start of a fresh fight.

The battle was starting and he would give anything to be allowed to participate. He tightened his jaw and pushed the feeling aside.

He followed the two dancers through the heavy doors that led into the arena and turned to the hallway just to the side of the arena entry gate. He was no longer allowed in the arena, but he could take a seat in the glass spectator box reserved for the trainers, owners and the upper society of the Republic. He was welcomed there and greeted by a polite smattering of applause and a few handshakes. His name had not died yet.

He'd never watched from the spectator box before, and there was something to be said for the experience. Ash preferred to be out in the open where he could feel and smell the action. The air behind the glass wall was sweet smelling and servants waited in every corner, eager to refill their master's wine and offer fan service against the scorching heat of the flames. Ash took his seat next to Beshar, a member of the Thirteen. Beshar sat on the edge of his seat, clutching at a handkerchief, and Ash noticed the hungry look in the man's eyes. He was probably an owner in the upcoming match.

Beshar shook his hand enthusiastically. "Ash! Ash Fire Dancer. We've met once before, after you slaughtered Reckoning. That was some fight." He continued to work Ash's hand up and down.

Ash wondered what the man's Rank was, although it really wasn't important. He was used to men of all Rank fawning over him, but it still felt good to have the attention of one of the Thirteen.

"Are you working as a trainer now? Beshar's question was polite and mumbled as an afterthought, his eyes now riveted on the empty sand field.

It was common practice for retired Dancers to take on new cadets to train in the ways of the arena. Ash had given it little thought before now. Perhaps Beshar was on to something. He imagined taking on a cadet. Perhaps through training new blood his legacy could live on. Ash smiled at the idea. It was a marvelous solution. He would do anything to get back in the arena.

"Scouting out the competition." Ash had to raise his voice because the spectators in the arena had begun to cheer and shout. Were they chanting Timber's name? He ignored them. "Who have you got today?"

"Wildfire, making her debut." Beshar wiped at his brow with his crumpled, perfumed handkerchief. "She's small, but agile as they come. We might see some blood tonight." His face was hard and eager, an odd expression on his pale round features.

Arena battles could end in three ways. The owner could call an end to the fight to protect his investment, at which point the Fire Dancers would be awarded a win and the owner was allowed to take his beast home to be used for breeding purposes. This was seldom done, as even the owners liked to see the Dancers bring out blood. The second was a fight called off by the Dancers themselves. If a Dancer was feeling overwhelmed, they could concede defeat and take a loss. A loss forced them to remove themselves from the arena and recoup for a minimum of three moon cycles. When and if the Dancer returned, they were almost always out of favor with the crowd. Ash would rather have died in the arena then call for mercy while he licked his wounds. The final and preferred ending to the arena battle was an all-out battle royale. Two Fire Dancers entered the arena with the beast, and in the end, only one dancer or beast remained standing.

The arena trumpets sounded one last time, their tune slightly different from before. The sound announced the entry of the beast. Ash leaned forward in his seat, drumming his fingers against his aching knees. Timber and Kindle began to turn and leap, cartwheeling across the dirt arena, warming up their bodies and exhibiting an exotic display of acrobatics for the restless crowd.

The unmistakable sound of the metal gates rolling back indicated

Wildfire's release. The crowd grew silent in anticipation of her debut.

She stepped out slowly and, as always, the initial sight caused Ash to swallow a lump in his throat.

First to appear was her clawed foot, claws that were capable of shredding a man to ribbons with a single blow. Her head appeared next. It was massive, the size of four men, and her giant eyes scanned the arena, black and feral. Her neck arched as she sniffed the air. Her forked tongue flickered out, tasting her surroundings. She hissed, and smoke curled from her nostrils. Firelight from dozens of glimmering torches danced off her scales and cast prisms of eerie green light on the dancers. As she made her way out from her holding stall, her huge tail uncoiled behind her and caused a furrow of sand several meters tall in its wake.

Once fully emerged she stood still a moment, staring out at the crowd as if daring them to look away from her majesty. Then she leaped from the arena ground and took flight, causing the crowd to roar in delight as she flew up and circled the dome of the arena. The people were not afraid; they were bloodthirsty and ready for the fight.

The spectator box darkened under the shadow of her flight, and Beshar slapped Ash on the back shouting, "Didn't I say she was something?"

He rubbed his hands together, and Ash smiled at the reverent look in the owner's eyes. This wasn't his first dragon, but Beshar was certainly proud of this one. And he should be, Ash thought, admiring the dragon's display as she circled the arena. Her body was a sensuous display of twisting, gleaming scales. She bellowed her fury, a stream of molten fire shooting out against the sturdy reinforced glass ceiling of the arena. There was no escape, and soon, angered, she would land and fight the Dancers.

He knew his knees could never handle another fight with such a young dragon, yet Ash wished he was out there, even if it meant it was his last fight. His death would be beautiful.

Timber and Kindle stood at the bottom. Kindle nervous and hopping from foot to foot; Timber calm and still as a stone.

Wildfire landed on the ground, causing the arena to shake. She turned on Kindle first, propelling a line of fire directly at the young dancer. Kindle leaned back, throwing out her arms as she did and the fire rolled away from her, ricocheting off the glass of the spectator booth. Beshar jumped and Ash chuckled.

Furious, Wildfire flicked her tail around and Kindle leaped over it, somersaulting in the air and landing nimbly on her feet. The crowd roared. Timber made his move. While Wildfire's attention was captured by Kindle, he sprang toward her, his assegai gleaming as it plunged into her chest.

The dragon roared and turned toward Timber, simultaneously swatting Kindle with her gigantic tail. Kindle bounced off the arena floor and lay still. Timber's weapon was stuck in her scales, so he twisted backwards, performing a series of twirling leaps to stay in motion.

To the crowd, the fire just appeared around Timber's twirling form, but to Ash it was a thing of beauty. A Fire Dancer's ability lay in their power to manipulate the flames, to move around them. So long as the Dancer anticipated the moves of the dragon and understood their body, fire was as harmless to them as it was to the dragon. Timber pulled the flames from the dragon and held on, bonding the fire to him. He became a tornado of flames, spinning ever faster, and the crowd screamed in exultation as Timber released the fire at the dragon. The flames wouldn't hurt her and were mostly for show, but what a show it was.

Timber was so seamless that even to Ash it looked as if he was *creating* fire. The notion was impossible, but the thought had Ash grudgingly admitting to himself that Timber was as good as he'd claimed. Better, even. Wildfire spit fire back at Timber in retaliation, and Ash watched him pull it around him and shoot it up toward the dome. The crowd went crazy, stomping their feet and screaming.

Timber leaped forward to retrieve his assegai and yanked it from Wildfire's chest, causing blood to spray across the dirt. The dragon bugled in pain and spit another ball of fire that Timber deflected easily with a twisting leap. The fire curved around him and hit the dirt near Kindle's still form. Timber shook his assegai in the air, and the crowd chanted his name. Ash was so caught up in the fight that he didn't care. Let them call out Timber's name, for in this moment he was a god and Ash was living through him.

The dragon continued to blow fire at Timber, but he had caught the rhythm of her breathing now and she was no match for him. When she raised up on her hind legs, he took the opportunity and plunged his assegai deep into her exposed belly, ripping it open. Blood and gore spilled across the arena floor. Wildfire gave a final cry before collapsing into the dirt. Sand billowed up in a porous cloud around her as the dust settled. Timber straddled the fallen beast and raised his assegai to the chanting crowd. His eyes met Ash, and the retired gladiator suddenly felt impossibly cold and rubbed his arms against the chill.

"She didn't last very long," Beshar mumbled, disappointed.

He stood up to leave and Ash followed him. He didn't want to watch Timber accept his winnings.

FOUR

TYLAK

The incessant *drip drip drip* of water was enough to drive any man insane. He'd been halfway to the mad house before he was brought to this prison, so he decided that it no longer mattered. *I am going to die.* Tylak grinned. The thought should terrify rather than amuse him. He giggled, confirming his descent into lunacy. Yes, he was crazy, and he would die alone and mad in this dank and dirty cell.

He could hear them, the mutterings and groans of those around him. Too long in the darkness and solitude of the dungeons had reduced each of these poor souls to little more than mumbling fools. And he was becoming one of them.

Maybe before everything had happened he would have resisted. *The old me would have been busy plotting an escape. The old me would never give up.* But that was before, when he'd had something worth fighting for. And even if he wanted to fight now, how could he? Once again he was nothing, stripped away from any value he thought to hold. Once again he was Tylak the slave.

His thoughts drifted off to Sykk and the promise he'd made to his mother. Tylak had never known his father, but his mother had been enough. She was kind and good. He could picture her now, worn and tired but ready with a smile for him and his young brother.

"Remember, you are strong. You can make a difference in Sykk's life, in your own. You can shape your destiny." Those had been her final words.

When he was fourteen he'd taken a job as the blacksmith's assistant, eager to do the manual city labor and earn an honest pay. A slave earning an income. He had been so proud. He and Sykk had celebrated the day he'd brought home his first two weeks of pay. He'd earned five water chips and an entire gallon of water. An entire *gallon.* He'd been so shocked he'd almost dropped the priceless liquid. They'd shared a loaf of flat bread and fresh meat and had drank themselves silly. To Tylak, water had never tasted sweeter.

Back then he had still dared to believe that things could improve for him and Sykk. He had dared to have hope. *It was all a joke. People like me can't shape their destinies.* He felt foolish that he'd once held on to the beliefs that he and Sykk's lives could change. All those hopes were gone now. The world was a cruel place, and the rich got richer while the poor stayed poor. A slave would never be any more than a slave.

Never again. He made the silent vow, feeling the anguish of his loss tear through him once more. He pushed all thoughts of Sykk away from his mind. *Don't think about him; not anymore. Give up.*

He lay down on the floor and drank from his glass. How ironic that here in this prison he could have more water at his disposal than he'd ever dreamed possible. The rich and powerful didn't have to worry about when they will have their next drink of the precious liquid. For them, water is only a purchase away. And there was none such display of this opulence than that of the palace. He'd seen the garden on his way to the judgment hall. The lush green and fragrant flowers had disgusted him. And there had been a fountain. A damn fountain! The sheer waste of it all made his skin crawl. He figured his cell was probably beneath the gardens. That would explain the occasional heady waft of flowers and the constant drip of water into his glass. He took another greedy gulp. He might die here in these dungeons, but he wouldn't die thirsty.

The scrape of his heavy cell door opening was deafening, and he jumped to his feet. He hadn't expected for them to come for him now, in the dark of the night. His adrenaline surge was fleeting, and he slumped back against the wall. *What does it matter? If my time is now, so be it.*

Despite the fact that he told himself he didn't care, he still watched the opening door with interest. He couldn't hide his surprise as his captor approached.

"You," he spat. "What are *you* doing here?"

She widened amber eyes. She was probably surprised at being spoken to in such a way. The shock in her face almost made him smile. He would have, if he hadn't been so angry. She and her kind were the reason he was in this mess.

"I've come to ask you some questions. You will answer them truthfully."

Bossy little thing. He frowned at her.

Her voice was low and husky, a surprising feature on her delicate frame and a direct contrast to the squeak he'd heard earlier when she'd sentenced him to be executed. If the situation was different, Tylak might have thought her beautiful. She had delicate features, a slender nose, tiny pouted lips. Her hair, long and black, hung down to the small of her back, shiny as obsidian. Her almond shaped eyes dominated her tiny face, and they were full of wonder and…*Was she frightened? Good, let her be afraid.* He spat again. "What do you want?"

She took a careful step back to avoid the puddle of saliva and clasped her hands behind her back.

She lifted her chin. "I have questions, slave, and you *will* answer them."

She tried to look stern, but her spectacles slid down the bridge of her nose and he laughed.

He stood up, closing the distance between them and taking pleasure when her tiny pink lips parted into a delicate O. Her *Arbe* closed rank around her, yet another reminder of her status. She waved them back.

Interesting. *She's brave. Or maybe she just realized that my chains prevent me from getting any closer.* He narrowed his eyes and scowled down at her.

"I am known as Tylak." He kept his voice steady, even. He was doomed to rot in a prison cell until his execution, but he was not her slave. He stared her in the eye to make sure she saw he was unafraid.

"I am Jura, daughter of Justir, First of the Thirt—"

"I know who you are," he snapped.

She bit her bottom lip and furrowed her brows. Tylak enjoyed watching her squirm and said nothing. *She doesn't know what to make of me. Good.*

"I have some questions for you. If you answer them to my satisfaction, I will see you rewarded."

She was persistent, he had to give her that. Tylak smiled.

"What could you give me that I would want?"

"Well, your life for one." Though her statement was smug, her voice was hopeful and her eyes pleaded with him. "Freedom, perhaps? A chance to start again."

He chuckled. "If it's just the same, I'd rather not accept any favors from one of the Thirteen. Thanks for stopping by, though. I'm sure you can see yourself out." He sat back down on the cool stone floor and turned his back to her, staring at the wall. He took another swig from his glass of water, ignoring the sound of her gasp. He wanted to be left alone.

"You're drinking bath water."

"Excuse me?"

"The water dripping into your cell." Her voice had become lilting and amused. He liked her better when it was laced with desperation.

"I happen to know you're directly under Councilman Beshar's bathing chamber." She wrinkled her nose. "He's very large and sweaty. Though perhaps it's safe. He doesn't seem to bathe often, at least if his odor is any indicator." She shrugged. "I think that's why he favors that floral perfume."

Do not *let her see you're disgusted.* Deliberately he set the glass back down. He sighed, it didn't seem he would get rid of her so easily. "Ask your questions and be gone."

Her smile widened. It was a nice smile, though he would never admit it.

"You're here because you stole from the Everflame."

"That's what I'm told."

"Well," she cleared her throat. "How did you do it? Only Fire Dancers can manipulate fire. So how did you steal it?"

He sighed again and leaned his head back against the wall. He wanted to bash it in and be done with her, with everything. "I didn't steal anything."

"Well then, were you a Fire Dancer once? Relegated back to mere slave after you committed some crime?" Her eyes were earnest, and she ran the tip of her tongue against her pink lips.

"I'm no Fire Dancer and I'm not a slave either. Not anymore." He glared at her. "And I didn't steal fire. Look, I can't explain it to you and there's no point even if I wanted to. I'm being executed tomorrow, why does it matter?"

She frowned. "You're not making any sense. Are you saying that you never had any fire in your possession? That the guard lied or was somehow confused? I don't understand."

"There's nothing to understand. Go away."

She caught her bottom lip between her teeth and shook her head. "I was hoping—"

"Hoping what? Listen, I don't have any evil scheme. I just…what is it? Do you feel guilty? Is that it? I'm a dead man," he growled. "Go back to your palace and leave me in peace. I want to spend my last hours alive in silence."

"N-no. I was hoping you'd tell me where you'd learned to do such a thing, that you could teach me. You could help me with—oh, never mind, this is foolish."

Her outburst was unexpected and he cocked his head to the side regarding her with new eyes. "You want to learn how to steal fire?"

"Yes," her voice was defensive. She frowned down at him.

He couldn't help it. He threw back his head and roared with laughter.

"Enough," she seethed, placing her hands on her hips.

Was she about to throw a tantrum? Oh, he really hoped she was.

"I can't help it," he gasped. "You're as mad an anyone in here. *Greatness*, as far as I know, stealing fire is a feat only done by Fire Dancers. I can't teach you. Why in the name of the Everflame would you want to? Surely you have Fire Dancers in your own employ to help you?"

"Of course I do. It's just that…" She trailed off. She appeared to be blushing though it was hard to tell in the dark cell.

She cleared her throat and continued, "I thought if I could steal fire, that they would have to take me. That they would let me in."

"Who would let you in?" The humble look in her eyes was really quite charming.

"The Shadow Dancers," she mumbled, looking at the ground.

She really *was* mad. Completely and utterly insane. *Why do I always attract the crazy ones?* "The Shadow Dancers don't exist." Tylak rolled his eyes. "And even if they *did,* they wouldn't let *you* in their midst."

"Please," her voice caught in her throat. "I'm desperate."

"Clearly. And more than a little insane."

She nodded. "And it would appear I've wasted my time." She lifted her chin. "I'll leave you to your death then."

She walked back toward the cell door, calling out for one of her *Arbe* to open it for her.

Tylak watched her, battling with himself. Her kind wasn't to be trusted. She was privileged, pampered, and represented everything he hated.

And she was his only chance at survival. Perhaps there was hope for him yet.

"Greatness, wait."

She stopped and turned around, frowning at him.

Tylak heaved a deep sigh and lifted his arms. He couldn't tell her everything, but he was a fool if he allowed himself to stay in this prison waiting for his death. "I may not have been entirely forthcoming with you.

41

I know something that can help."

She tossed her head at one of her silent giants, and the member of the *Arbe* undid his chains. They fell to the floor with a beautiful clamor.

Tylak rubbed his wrists and followed her out of his cell. He couldn't trust her, but he had every intention of using her.

FIVE

KAY

Kay opened both her eyes and smiled. She leaped from her bed, throwing on pants and the tunic from the day before. She pushed the sleep out of her eyes and washed her face and mouth before running outside toward the corral. The morning sun was more pink than orange as it peeked over the puffy white clouds. The clouds hung so low Kay almost felt she could reach out and grab one. Well, if Daddy held her up.

Kay's father was the biggest, strongest and bravest around. Kay knew there was a lot more to the world than her family's acreage, but she never had the urge to explore. Their homestead had everything she could ever want. Daddy had built their home himself with his own two hands. Kay often sat in his lap and stared at those hands. His fingers were long and capable, his palm big and hard. Daddy never minded when she climbed up, not even now that she was seven years old and getting too big for cuddles.

Mama stopped her at the gate and Kay skidded to a halt, annoyed that she hadn't woken up earlier. If she had, Mama might not have caught her.

"Where are you going, young lady?" Mama's face was warm and loving as always, yet she narrowed her eyebrows in an effort to appear stern. Kay knew that Mama meant it.

"I just want to see him. Please, Mama? Just for a moment? I'll be so quick." Kay beamed her full smile, the one she showed her mama and daddy when she wanted them to see just how good of a little girl she was. "Please, Mama?"

Mama remained firm. "Chores first. I can't be expected to do everything myself."

Kay wanted to ignore her mother's wishes but instead thought about all the work Mama would have to do by herself if she neglected her chores. She turned around and headed back toward their house.

There were chickens and rabbits to feed. The garden needed constant care. Kay was in charge of watering the plants as well as harvesting the ripe vegetables. The house always needed a good cleaning, and laundry was in need of a washing. It was mid-morning before Mama announced that Kay had completed enough chores and was permitted to go outside to the corral.

Kay needed no further prompting and ran from the house, kicking up trails of dust as she ran up the dirt road that led to the north barn. The *best* barn. The building was located on the edge of their property atop a large dirt mound that stood out against the otherwise rolling green hills. She stopped short in front of the massive building. Made of shiny metal and wire, the structure leaped from the ground and towered into the sky, two double doors dominated the front of the square building. Eager, Kay opened one of the doors.

She was immediately aware of the blast of heat that hit her skin and her lungs, the tell-tale characteristics inside the north barn. She smiled at the familiar feel and smell of the room.

"Daddy, are you in here?"

Her father appeared from the opposite end of the barn. He smiled and waved her over.

"Be careful now. Rumble has a bit of a temper today."

Kay laughed, "Daddy, you say that about Rumble every day."

The dragon in question lay curled on his side in a roped off corner of the barn. He opened one lazy eye at the mention of his name but didn't move. Too old to still breed, the dragon lived there out of habit more than anything else. Rumble had been in her family decades longer than Kay, then her father even. Kay had asked her father once how old Rumble was. When he'd been unable to answer, she'd decided to demand the answer from Rumble herself. She'd stood atop his magnificent snout and stomped her foot until he'd opened both of his monstrous eyes. The giant black orbs had stared at her blankly. Mama had been so scared she'd wept like a baby, and Daddy had been so mad that, after he'd gotten her safely off, she'd gotten a whooping. She'd been five years old. Kay felt that Rumble would never hurt her, and it appeared the old dragon was content to spend the rest of his days sunbathing in various spots in the surrounding pastures and his nights sleeping, curled into a sinewy ball of scales in the barn.

Kay reached her father and fell into his arms. Daddy swooped her up in the air just as she'd known he would and she laughed.

"What are we doing today?"

Her father was an important man. Kay had grown up seeing a constant stream of people who traveled from all over to trade with her father, people from as far away as the Sand Sea. They gave furs, silver, and gold, or formed pieces of art. Some gave spices or other various assortments of exotic foods. The list of products traded always differed, but the people all came wanting one thing, dragons.

"I caught a new one, sleeping by the lake early this morning. She had her guard down," he pushed back Kay's wild curls. "She's pregnant."

Kay squealed with delight. She loved to watch baby dragons grow. They were born small enough to hold in her hand, and she loved looking at their shiny scales and dark glistening eyes. They grew fast though, reaching Kay's own size after just a week and they were curious and often got into squabbles with each other and their mother, testing their strength and power. They were intelligent too. They understood when feeding times were and they were aware that they had to return nightly for dinner and the security of the barn. Raised in the barn, they seldom ever sought escape, and dragons born at the barn were the easiest to train for breeding, probably because they imprinted with her father when they were still babies.

"Can I see her?" Kay hopped from one foot to the other, twisting her hands in circles. "Oh, may I?"

But Daddy said no and instead ordered her to look after Rumble's breakfast, arguing that the newly captured dragon needed time to adjust. The mother dragon would be chained now, and though distressed at her capture, she would also be nesting and preparing to give birth. Mama had informed both Kay and her father more than once that under no circumstances was Kay to be placed in any dangerous situations. A newly caught mother dragon would fall under the category of such a situation.

More than anything, Kay wanted to watch, but she knew that Daddy would never let her. Probably because he was scared of Mama. Kay didn't know why her father was so frightened of Mama, but she could tell that he was. He never went against Mama's wishes. Kay thought it had something to do with the way Mama would tap her foot and scrunch up her eyebrows. She could look pretty mean when she did that.

Kay fed Rumble, carefully setting down his portion of mixed meat. Today it was several fat pigs and a bird of some sort. Kay suspected it had been a turkey, though without feathers it was hard to tell. Rumble hated feathers. She left his meat as well as several bushels of vegetables in front of the dragon before she leaped far from the pile and shouted, "Now, Rumble!" The dragon lifted his noble head and blew a stream of fire over his offering. Once the food was sizzling and smoking, he devoured his portion, swallowing the meal quickly and sniffing the air around him. Kay was glad that her father had never sold Rumble, because he was her favorite. Kay had heard the terrible stories of what happened to dragons across the Sand Sea and had asked Daddy about it once. His face had looked very angry and his voice was firm.

"It's not our business what happens to the dragons we sell."
Kay had kicked at the ground while she thought over his answer. "But don't you feel sad knowing you're giving the dragons away to people who are just going to be mean to them?"

Daddy had been very firm. "We do not give the dragons away, Kay. We sell them to pay for the things we need to survive. Don't you love all of your toys? Don't you love where we live?"

"Yes, Daddy," Kay had answered solemnly, because she really did love her life just the way it was. But, she just felt bad for the dragons sometimes.

Mama was always particular to Rumble, more so after Kay had provoked him and he hadn't attacked. She saw him as a member of the family and was constantly reminding Kay that she was lucky to have such a friend in Rumble because most people never got to know dragons and no one counted one as a friend.

Daddy suggested that Rumble's natural friendliness toward the family, and particularly Kay, was just because he was so old. And though Mama agreed, it sometimes looked like she wondered.

Kay sat in the dirt beside Rumble, careful to give him plenty of space while he finished his breakfast. She watched him for a moment, smelling her hands and wrinkling her nose at the smell. No wonder dragons had such smelly breath. Finished with his meal, Rumble licked the ground where it had been and then sniffed at the air, flicking his forked tongue in and out before fixing one dark eye on Kay.

She held up her hands, "No more. You'll just have to wait for dinner."

Rumble grunted and twin lines of smoke curled up from his nostrils. Kay watched them, mesmerized. Kay had seen dragons in every color of the rainbow, but Rumble was the prettiest. Rumble was a deep red that Kay imagined must be the most beautiful color in all the world.

"It's the color of rubies," Daddy had once said, showing her a small red stone. Kay had wrinkled her nose at the shiny rock. It was pretty, and while the hue reminded her of Rumble, it did nothing to capture the sparkle in his scale or his richness of color.

"You wouldn't hurt me," she said softly. She stood up slowly, keeping her eyes trained on Rumble's mouth. The dragon stood unmoving. She reached out her arm, unfolding her fingers one by one, careful to keep her breathing slow and normal.

"Easy, Rumble, I'm not going to hurt you."

"He's not worried that you'll hurt him," her Daddy's voice was calm and even. "Come away from him baby."

Kay sighed and did as she was told, turning her back on the dragon and walking toward her father. She could feel Rumble's eyes watching her leave.

"He wouldn't have hurt me, Daddy." Her voice was impatient, but she was careful not to whine when she presented her case. Daddy always said that if she pleaded her case like an adult, she would be treated like one. "Rumble has never been aggressive before. And you even said that when I stood on his nose when I was a little girl he didn't look like he was mad at all."

Daddy smiled, showing his even white teeth. She liked when they peeked out from behind his scruffy beard. "You're still a little girl."

Kay narrowed her eyes, "Daddy I'm presenting a case here."

"Oh, I'm so sorry," he smiled, lifting his arms in surrender. "Please continue."

She cleared her throat. "Because Rumble has never acted aggressive toward me and due to the fact that we have established a relationship," she was pleased to see Daddy's eyes widen at her using such big words, "I propose that I am allowed to try and pet him." *And try to ride him*, she added silently to herself. She knew the importance of picking her battles and instead finished her case with, "Please, Daddy, just let me try one time."

Her father seemed to actually be considering it. That is, he hadn't said no and was staring off at Rumble when an opening door sent in a rush of outside air. The cool air tickled her sweaty skin, and Kay shivered from the goosebumps.

Her father spun around at the open doors and smiled at Mama who stood in the doorway. Though her mother respected Rumble, she would never approve Kay's efforts to get closer. Kay sent pleading eyes to her father, and he squeezed her shoulder before ushering her to the door by keeping a large steady palm in the small of her back.

"Is it time for me to help get lunch, Mama?" She was quick to ask before Mama questioned what they'd been talking about.

"It is. Why don't you wash up?" she smiled at Kay before turning serious eyes to her husband. "There's a buyer here." Her tone was meaningful, and Kay was aware that her parents were silently communicating. She was missing something and she scowled. She hated being left out. She knew better than to ask any questions, however, and instead scampered off to the kitchens, wanting to reach home before her parents in hopes of gaining a clue as to the new buyer.

She raced back home, ignoring her parents calls that she wait, and pumped her tiny legs as fast as they would take her. When she reached their house, she was sweaty and breathing hard. She opened the back door and fell inside, pleased to see the visitor waiting inside their small family kitchen. The kitchen smelled of warm bread, and Kay smiled deeply at the visitor, feeling very satisfied.

"Hello," she said, ripping the corner off the fresh loaf and popping it into her mouth. Mama made the best bread. It was hot and buttery and melted in her mouth.

The buyer looked different than the others. In place of the heavy wool robes, the man wore a light tunic not dissimilar to her own. His pants stopped just under his knee and ballooned slightly at the bottom. She was interested in his odd clothing but was more fascinated by his shiny bald head. The man's dark eyes slanted down at her.

"Hello," his voice was low and musical. "You must be Kay."

Kay smiled. She liked feeling important. She was the daughter of the dragon catcher, the greatest dragon trainer that ever lived. She stood tall.

"I am." She nodded and didn't demand to know the stranger's name, even though she wanted to, because she didn't want to be rude. When he didn't offer it, she cocked her head to the side and thought of what she could say.

"Rumble is my favorite, but he's not for sale."

The buyer's eyebrows lifted and he smiled, "Is that so?"

Kay nodded, feeling braver. "Yup. He's my friend. One day I'm going to ride him and everything."

"Aren't you scared?" The buyer widened his eyes and looked down at her impressed. "What about his big teeth and all that fire?"

Kay shrugged her shoulders. "I'm not scared, Rumble would never hurt me. Besides, if he blows his fire at me, I'll just move it away."

"Kay, go to your room." Her father had appeared and he filled the doorway. He did not look happy.

"Daddy, I—"

"To your room." He didn't even look at her. His eyes were trained on the buyer. She fled from the room but stopped just outside in the hall. She leaned against the wall and took a deep breath, trying not to scream. She wouldn't throw a tantrum. Only babies threw tantrums and she was seven years old.

"What are you doing here?" It was her father's voice. He was asking the buyer.

"Is it true? Does Kay have the gift?"

Kay straightened at the mention of her name and pressed closer to the wall so that she could hear better.

"I asked you what you were doing here." It was Daddy's "don't ask me again" voice, which meant that he was good and angry. The buyer would have to apologize now.

"You know why I've come." The buyer's voice sounded more amused than frightened. Kay frowned and wrinkled her eyebrows, trying to hear what her daddy whispered.

"You can't have her." At least, that's what it sounded like to Kay, but she was already pressed close to the wall and if she moved any closer she would be spotted. If Daddy saw her, she would get in trouble for not going to her room like he'd asked.

"She belongs here, with her family."

"It's her duty. Did you think to hide her from us?" The buyer's voice was angry now. "Did you think we would never find out?"

"You can't have her." Her father repeated, and Kay was suddenly overwhelmed with gratitude. She was sorry she'd ran ahead and she didn't want to know any more about the mysterious man, she only wanted him to leave.

There was a thud and she jumped back from the wall that still vibrated from the impact. Daddy grunted on the other side. Kay suddenly remembered what Mama and Daddy had told her. She was in trouble, and it was time for her to run. She turned on her heel and hurried to her room.

SIX

BESHAR

Beshar, *Tenth of the Thirteen,* tried to stay indoors at night. His life in the arena was demanding however, and this wasn't the first time he had been summoned after hours, nor would it be his last. He was grateful his business there had been concluded within an hour, with any luck he would make it back to his chambers before the sun fully set. Though it was early in the evening, the pits had all been ignited and they cast shadows that flickered and danced on the clay buildings and homes that made up the city. The arena was close to the palace where he made his home, close enough that he'd felt he could walk, Everflame knew he could use the exercise. Now, he regretted his earlier desire to try his hand at fitness.

You should have brought more men. The three Samur that followed flanked behind him and to either side, but even with the security of his Samur, he felt naked and vulnerable. As a member of the Thirteen, assassins were a constant threat. He quickened his pace, gazing sharply from left to right, drinking in the sights around him. The city smelled horrid of course. The rank odor of the poor wafted up to him, attacking his sinuses, and he pressed a perfumed handkerchief to his mouth to ward off the pungent smell. *What was that? Sewage and rotting meat?* He shuddered delicately. He was never walking to the arena again.

The palace rose up ahead of him. Emblazoned by the light of the Everflame, the glass monstrosity twinkled and glowed a brilliant orange against the sandy dunes surrounding it. When he got inside he would enjoy a nice steam and a bottle of wine. Maybe two.

The palace had been his home for the last twenty years, so Beshar did not notice its sparkling brilliance or the fact that the fourteen majestic glass towers were awe inspiring in their size and architecture. Built decades ago, the palace was made by Torches who heated the surrounding sands and manipulated the fine sheet of malleable glass into tall, hollow, twisted peaks. The architecture of the palace was beautiful and unmatched by anything in the world, but Beshar saw none of that. To him, the palace was simply his home. To be more accurate, the Tenth Tower was his home. But the towers were all connected to make one striking unit.

A small group of people, upper class by the look of the fine cotton of their robes, strolled toward the palace. A few took leisurely swigs of water along the way, most likely to flaunt their wealth to any who might observe. *New money. Where are they going at such a late hour?* The palace closed its gate every evening, and no one, aside from the Thirteen, were granted entrance after sunset.

There were four of them, three men and a woman, and Beshar realized that though they were all wealthy to a degree, only one of them had *Arbe* in tow. The four guard men gave Beshar and his men a careful once over.

"I think it's scandalous." The voice came from the woman, and Beshar walked closer, eager to overhear any gossip she might share. There was power in information.

"Where do you suppose he is? It's unlikely he'd tour the cities so late in the season."

One of the men snorted. "He didn't leave for a tour without anyone noticing."

"Then where has he been? He hasn't been seen for two days..."

The people turned down an alley and their voices faded with them. They were more than likely headed to the theater, it was the only source of entertainment this close to the palace. For a moment, Beshar toyed with the idea of following them. He dismissed the thought quickly. It was better not to stay out any later than he had to and he had an excellent vintage waiting for him.

He continued on his trek to the palace, mulling over the conversation he'd overheard. It had been a pitiful excuse for gossip. He was aware, of course, that the First had been missing at court. He hadn't been seen in days. The rest of the imbeciles that made up the Thirteen might have accepted the explanation of the daughter of the First, but Beshar was a man of intellect, and the facts remained that her story didn't add up. The daughter of the First claimed that her father's illness wasn't serious, but if that was the case then why hadn't he attended the council meeting? A minor illness would not keep one from his duty of ruling an entire republic. And yet, if the sickness was serious enough to warrant an absence from council meetings, why then had the First not seen the palace surgeon? Beshar knew that he hadn't. He'd paid handsomely for that knowledge and had the man followed for good measure. The surgeon had not been summoned. The daughter of the First was up to something, and Beshar's mouth watered at the opportunities that arose from her deceit. *What was she up to?* He couldn't wait to find out.

He was almost to the palace, he had only to cross one alley and then he would arrive at its front gates. The gates, while also made of glass, were reinforced several times over and rose nearly twenty feet into the sky.

He hesitated for the briefest of moments in front of the alleyway. It was short and narrow, darkened by the height of the two buildings on either side of it. The courtyard pit did little to light the alley, but Beshar was not afraid of the dark. The absence of torchlight only made things safer.

He strolled forward, ready to relax with his steam and his wine, but he was stopped by a firm grip on his forearm.

He frowned down at the offending appendage before dragging his stare up to meet the imposing figure of Kenjiro. His head Samur shook his head slightly, indicating that there was a potential threat just ahead.

A surge of adrenaline rushed through Beshar. He was no fighter. When trouble arose, he relied on his wit and the power of his wealth to see him out of it. Once again, he wished he'd thought to bring more men. The darkened alley loomed before him. He took a deep breath and steeled himself for the worse.

"Who goes there?" he called out. He was surprised at the deep timbre and authoritative ring to his tone.

A figure stepped forward. It was hard to distinguish features in the light of the distant fire pit, but Beshar assumed it was a woman based on the tiny form of the figure and the unctuous sway to the hips.

"Hello, Beshar." The voice purred over his name as it stepped ever closer.

He was right. It was a woman. She was dressed entirely in black, loose black trousers and tunic, with her hair knotted at the nape of her neck. A black silk mask covered her features.

He dipped his upper half into the semblance of a bow but kept his gaze trained on her face, what he could see of it in any case.

He thought he could detect a slight smile from beneath her mask.

"Such the gentlemen."

"My lady. It appears you have me at a disadvantage. You know who I am, but I am woefully unaware of the beautiful Shadow Dancer who stands before me."

She chuckled, shaking her head at his flattery.

When she made no move to say anything else, Beshar sighed. "Would that I could stand here before your presence for the rest of my days, but alas, a bottle of red calls my name." He took a step forward, Kenjiro and his other men keeping pace.

The woman held out a halting hand. Beshar stopped, his men flanking around him, waiting to hear her words. It galled Beshar to do so, but he would gain no information from simply cutting her down where she stood. Well, ordering his men to cut her down in any case. He eyed the dagger that gleamed from its sheath on her hip.

"You have been summoned."

"I was," Beshar nodded. "It was an invitation, I chose not to accept."

"An invitation was polite. You will not like what happens next." Her voice still purred but she fingered the dagger at her waist, stroking its silver handle.

"I'll take my chances." He could afford to be brave with Kenjiro and the other

57

two standing there. He had wondered how long it would take for the Prince of Shadows to send a messenger when his invitation had gone unanswered.

The woman sucked her breath in sharply, there was a faint whistle as the air blew between her teeth.

"The sands have been quiet. Some have considered them tame."

Beshar took a step forward, intrigued by her words. This was a fact rarely mentioned in public. Nobody liked what it seemed to imply. He muttered her fear aloud, "No one can release the flame."

"Yes, the Everflame. But that is the least of our worries. The daughter is not suited to this role. Some would have her dead and be over with it. Perhaps yet another reason you should seek haste in meeting with my master."

Why the sudden change of tactic? And what did the daughter of the First have to do with anything? "I keep my nose out of politics."

"You are a fool."

Beshar smiled, nodding his acceptance. "So I've been told before. But I think once you get to me know me, you'll find that I'm actually quite smart."

She snorted and turned back toward the alley. She walked several paces before she turned sharply on her heel. She frowned, shaking her head and clucking her tongue in a sound of disapproval.

"You're wrong, you know. Only a fool would defy him. We'll be watching you." She turned and disappeared into the darkened alley.

Beshar watched her walk away, panting hard in an effort to stop the wild beating of his heart.

SEVEN
JURA

The dungeons of the glass palace were a vast labyrinth of hallways and dead ends nestled nearly a hundred feet below ground. Under the escort of her *Arbe* and with Tylak in tow, she had little chance of leaving unnoticed. The slave had kept his mouth shut since leaving his cell and, surrounded by her *Arbe*, he'd done nothing but follow her meekly.

I truly have gone crazy, she thought to herself as she stood at a forked hall. She couldn't remember which way they should turn. *Look left, look right, and praise the light. You are my choice upon this night. Left.* The childhood rhyme had certainly steered her wrong before, but as Jura headed left, she could only hope she'd chosen the way which led to a narrow shaft that opened up outside the palace. The hallway intersected with the palace latrine and as such was always loosely guarded, most of the outskirts of the dungeon were. If luck was on her side, they would be able to leave without anyone detecting them.

She stopped and turned to look at Tylak. He followed just behind. *Time to find out if he can be trusted.* She sent her *Arbe* back to her rooms, thinking that if they stood outside her doors it would appear that she was safe in her chambers. She was probably a complete idiot for doing so, but she couldn't afford to raise suspicion. If anyone in the council suspected what she was up to she would be a dead woman. Better to take her chances with Tylak. She sent a silent prayer to the Everflame that she was doing the right thing. Unable to actually burn the prayer, she could only hope her prayers would be heard.

Once the *Arbe* disappeared from view, she straightened her shoulders and fingered the whip she carried on her side. It was mostly for show. The whip was the chosen weapon for ladies in fashion, and though Jura had managed to twist it into a good snap, she'd had yet to achieve any real aim with it. Aside from her lack of skill with any weaponry, Jura doubted she could hold her own in a fight against Tylak. His body was slim, but wiry with muscle, and her forced training in self-defense would likely be useless. Tylak didn't have to know that, though. Her grip on her holstered whip tightened.

He followed her through the narrow hallway that grew increasingly foul as they traveled south. The pungent odor crept into Jura's nostrils, grasping at her lungs and making her eyes water. She choked back the rush of bile and focused on taking short, shallow breaths. Tylak didn't seem to notice the awful smell. They traveled in silence for several minutes, neither looking at the other until a thin snake slid over Jura's foot. She let loose a startled gasp but stood firm, ignoring Tylak's smile.

"Did you have to take us this way? These sewers are rank."

She hadn't expected him to make conversation, and his choice of topic was startling. *Was he trying to crack a joke?*

"It's the safest way to smuggle you out of here." She angled her body to get a better look at him, but he made no response. They continued on in silence for some time. "Markhim said this was a bad idea." She mumbled to herself.

"Who is Markhim?"

Flames but he had good hearing. "He's my…" What was he exactly? Jura had battled over whether or not she should share her plans with Markhim. There was no one she trusted more, not even Amira. He had balked at her scheme, as she'd known he would. But in the end he'd understood why she felt the need to carry through with her plan, no matter how insane it was. His understanding was what made her love him. She grinned to herself at the revelation. *I love Markhim.*

"He's my friend."

"Ah, your lover." Tylak smirked.

Jura choked as her strangled gasp drew in far too much of the rancid sewage air. "He's not my lover!" She felt the heat rush into her cheeks, and she shook her head so rapidly that her long braid flew over her shoulder. "He's a friend, I—"

She cut off so she could glower at Tylak until he stopped laughing.

"Who he is, is none of your concern." The less Tylak knew about her the better. For all she knew, the criminal plotted her death at this very moment, and she refused to drag any of her friends down with her. Besides, she had yet to confess her feelings to even Markhim, and she certainly wasn't going to divulge her inner most secrets to a former slave turned convict. The awkward silence stretched on, making her uncomfortable.

"What will you do with your freedom, now that you have it?" She asked, desperate to once again break the silence.

He was quiet for so long she thought he wouldn't answer, when he said, "Leave. Leave the republic and never come back."

"Where will you go?" she asked, looking back at him. His eyes were glazed and stared ahead into the darkness.

"Anywhere. The wilds maybe. Or the ocean…I need something from you." He stopped walking and stared at her intently. He didn't look threatening, yet her hand tightened over her holstered whip.

"What do you want?"

"My birthstone…it was taken before the arrest. I'll need it back before I can leave."

"Birthstone? How do you—"

He held up a hand cutting her off. "Shh…there's a noise. Just ahead."

"We're close to the exit. There's probably a guard." She hoped it was guards. She couldn't handle if it was another snake or some other vile creature that lived in the sewage.

It was a guard, and though there was only one, he stood alert at the exit. Jura strode toward him purposefully.

"You, guard. Open the gate."

He jumped at her authoritative voice but hesitated at the gate. "Greatness, that man you are with…he's dangerous."

"I believe you're mistaken. Her Greatness has taken to her chambers for the night." She leaned forward and said to him in her most menacing voice. "Yet if I was her Greatness, I would expect to be served without answering to the likes of you. Now, shut your mouth and open the gates." She was immediately horrified that she'd spoken to someone in such a way and pulled a small canteen of water from within her robes and handed it to the guard. "Pure water from the palace. Several days' worth."

The guard snatched the water from her hands and opened the gates without further protest.

Once outside the gates, Jura breathed in deeply, taking in the freshness of the outdoor air. That was without a doubt the most disgusting thing she had ever done. And the most dangerous. Walking about the darkened dungeons with a convicted criminal, her desperation was turning into insanity. It was better not to think of the danger, she decided. Better to push forward. She squared her shoulders and walked off with purpose, only to be pulled back by Tylak.

She scowled at him. "Don't presume to touch me," she snarled, jerking her elbow from his grasp. Her hand flew back down to her whip.

"My apologies, *Greatness,*" he sneered at the word. On his lips, the word was a far cry from the honorific it was supposed to represent. "But you were going the wrong way."

She wished she was taller, so she could look down her nose at him. As it were, she had to crane her neck just to meet his eyes. *Sandstorms.* She gestured that he take the lead and followed him into the darkness of the city.

The majority of the capital city of the Republic was plunged into darkness with every night's setting sun. The palace could afford to keep torches, of course, and the gladiator dome with its surrounding housing was an emblazoned beacon on the opposite side of the city, yet the rest of the city relied on single bonfires which were lighted nightly. The fire pits were placed in the center of courtyards that were strategically placed throughout the city.

"I can't believe I'm doing this." She looked down at her soiled robes and the blackness around her and felt a thrill tickle her spine.

"It's not too late to change your mind. We can go our separate ways. Nobody has to know." Tylak offered, staring off into the distance before leisurely heading west.

"Don't you want my help?" She slanted her eyes over at him and watched him wipe sweat off his brow with the back of his sleeve. It left a streak of black on his forehead and she winced.

"I don't trust you with it yet."

If I could reach his neck, I would strangle him. He'd said so little on their trek through the underground prison tunnels. All she'd managed to get out of him was that he needed help recovering his lost birthstone, presumably taken into possession by the Republic after his arrest. How he'd gotten one in the first place was a fact he seemed unwilling to share.

Many in society were gifted a family birthstone upon their coming of age. The stone acted as a family crest and opened doorways into polite society. In ancient times, the birthstone was more sacred to the family and the stones were more common. Now, though most of the upper crust of society owned birthstones, they were seldom seen within society's lower classes and certainly not in the hands of a former slave. Often, if a slave was found with one, it would be given to the owner to hold as token. It was common practice to gift birthstones to slaves once they were freed.

Maybe that was how Tylak received his. Her own stone, gifted to her on her sixteenth birthday, lay nestled beneath her robes on a delicate silver chain. Her father was fond of saying the amber coloring matched her eyes. Still, she could see why the stone might hold sentimental value to Tylak, and she'd sworn to help. A small price in exchange for information that might free her father.

"You'll have to trust me sometime," she said pointedly. For some reason, she desperately wanted to know more about him. He reminded her of a character from one of the mystery novels she was fond of reading. Her father hated that she read the stuff. He believed her time would be better spent practicing politics or at the very least reading a book on the subject. There had been many times that Jura had found herself sneaking a quick read from novels her father believed were less than satisfactory.

"We need to hurry." He didn't explain why, just broke into a run, and Jura hurried after him, silently cursing his name. Once she talked to the leader of the Shadow Dancers, she could be done with the infuriating man. Well, after she upheld her end of their bargain. She'd managed to get herself into a real sandstorm.

After running for a good distance, Jura was sure her chest would explode. She was grateful when Tylak came to a stuttering halt outside a curved building.

"Why'd we stop?" she panted loudly, desperately wishing she hadn't given all her water away to the guard.

"We're here."

"Sandstorms."

Tylak's eyebrows shot upward. "The lady curses." He whistled softly.

She rolled her eyes and took a deep breath, staring up at the quiet building. It was little more than a hut, and Jura stared at the baked clay walls with some fascination. She'd never been inside a clay building. She'd read about them, of course, but the palace was constructed entirely out of glass, and aside from the stone walls of her bedroom, she'd never known anything else. She touched the side of the building, surprised that the outside exterior was as hard as stone. *Fascinating.*

Tylak stood with his arms crossed, watching her.

Right, time to go inside.

"Are they," she gulped, "just inside?" *Isn't this what you wanted?* She had the sudden thought that this could be an elaborate trap. *It's too late now,* she scolded herself. She'd trusted Tylak to get her this far. She couldn't doubt him now. Hiring a Shadow Dancer was her only chance of discovering who had placed the blood chain on her father. It was either this or rely on her own skills at sleuthing, and the latter was unlikely to produce a favorable outcome. And if the Shadow Dancers held answers that would help her father, who knew what other secrets they might carry? She just had to speak with a member and offer him water. Surely services were rendered in the manner they were traded in the market.

Please, let this be easy.

Tylak raised a single brow and smirked. He really needed a bath. Clean the man up and he would actually look rather nice. Of course, slaves and the poor couldn't afford to take baths, and she knew the steam rooms open for the public were filthy and unsafe. Most of the people in the lower class could only afford true baths on the rarest occasions. *Had he* ever *had one?* She shook her head. Now was not the time to worry over the cleanliness of those less fortunate. She had come this far, she only needed to go a bit further. She had to trust that Tylak hadn't led her to a trap, that he would still be waiting for her once she went inside.

"I'm not going anywhere," he mumbled, as if reading her thoughts. "Not until I get back what's mine."

Right. The agreement that she would return his birthstone. She only had to find where it was, steal it away, and get it to him without alerting any members of the Thirteen. Easy, she thought wildly. It was a fine assumption of his that one of the Thirteen had it. It was common practice for the Thirteen to take anything of value from those convicted.

But what if it was a trap? What if she walked inside only to be assaulted by more criminals or kidnapped by a slave trader? She shuddered at the thought.

Standing outside imagining the worst isn't going to help. It's now or never. She took a deep breath and opened the door.

Shadows danced on the wall from a fire caged against one smooth wall of the building. There was a fireplace in the palace, and she was impressed at the opulence of what she'd considered a tiny hut. The building was a single story, round room with no windows and a single door. Though small, the room wanted for nothing by the way of luxury and was filled with as many riches as Jura would find in her own chamber, perhaps more. She walked across thick carpet to a man who lounged on a sofa. He waved his *Arbe* away at Jura's approach. Unlike Jura's *Arbe*, the four men were dressed in the same black costume as the man relaxing on the chaise.

"I've been waiting for you." The man did not turn her way, but Jura felt as though she were being watched.

"You knew I was coming?" she asked, feeling foolish. Naturally the leader of an underground league of spies knew everything that happened in the city.

"Of course. I am the Prince of Shadows."

"I've come for your help. I need to know about my father."

The man laughed, his chuckle a rich baritone, and sat up to face Jura. She was surprised to see that the man appeared young, hardly older than Jura's own seventeen years, though it was hard to be sure because he covered much of his face with a stained-glass mask. Firelight reflected off the colored glass mask sending chips of broken colors to twirl about the room with each turn of his head. It was impossible to see the features beneath the stained glass. He wore black pants and a loose tunic in the style worn by Fire Dancers. His dark, shiny hair was cut close to his face and thus not a distraction from the intricately detailed mask.

"Yes, little one. I know who you are and why you have come here," he held up his hands, stretching his palms toward the ceiling. "What I want to know is why you think we would help you?"

Jura bristled at the words "little one" and took a look at the already decadent room. "I'm prepared to offer you great riches. More water than you've ever thought possible."

The masked man laughed, throwing his head back and revealing a neck that was unnaturally pale. The white skin shone bright against the rich black silk of his tunic.

"Silly girl, I have no use for your water. There is nothing more valuable to me than information. I offer an exchange of information, nothing more. You're acting as head of household now." It wasn't a question.

Jura swallowed, the Shadow Dancers really did know everything.

"I assume you'll be able to give me inside information on the Thirteen. I'll expect a full report in exchange for the information you seek."

"Anything," Jura's head bobbed up and down enthusiastically. She sucked in a deep breath, but she couldn't hide her eagerness. "I'll get you whatever you need."

Jura saw the edges of a smile creep out from beneath the prince's mask. "For starters, you can have Tylak come out from his hiding place. I believe he and I have much to discuss."

Jura struggled to maintain her composure as she hurried to the door to do the man's bidding. *Of course the Prince of Shadows knew Tylak by name.* She'd wondered how Tylak had known the location of the Shadow Dancers, and she'd had her suspicions. It appeared he was a member after all. She stepped outside, squinting out into the darkness. The building that housed the temporary headquarters of the Shadow Dancers was in a dark section of the city, and after the warm glow of the firelight, her eyes took a moment to adjust.

"Tylak, where are you? You've been summoned inside." She received no response and she frowned. Her eyes were adjusting and he was nowhere to be found. "Tylak?"

Still nothing. She circled the building placing an unsteady hand where her whip was holstered to her hip. There was nothing but silent blackness around her. *Flames, he'd left her out here. Alone. What would she tell the prince?*

She yanked open the door to the building and stumbled into an empty room. Everything was gone, the fur carpets, the furniture. Everything. Smoke curled around the extinguished fire, the only indication that anyone had actually been there at all.

EIGHT
KAY

She'd grown up being told to run. She could hear Mama's voice in her head. *Baby, if they ever come for you, just run. Run far away. Don't come back.* She shut the door to her room and slid the lock. *I will find you again. Daddy will find you.* She stuffed clothing in a satchel: pants, tunics, socks, and leggings. *Just run.* She put on her boots, the comfortable ones for when she went on hiking trips with Mama.

"Not everyone is like you and Daddy," Mama had once tried to explain. "You two are special."

For the first time in her life, Kay hated being special. Her movements were mechanical and she bit back tears, wiping at her eyes. She stashed the last of her things in her leather satchel and slowly opened the door.

The hallway was empty. Kay slung her satchel around her shoulder and crept along the wall. It was like the games she played with Daddy. Daddy would close his eyes and Kay would have to creep around the room collecting pebbles without alerting Daddy she was near. She pretended she was playing now and only paused when she came to the entry of the kitchen. To her left was the hallway which led to the front door; to her right lay the truth. They were keeping secrets from her, and Kay wanted to find out what. Besides, Daddy might need her. She couldn't leave without stopping to see. She slowly peered around the corner, hoping that she would find her mama and daddy, happy and ready to eat dinner. The strange visitor would be gone. Everything would be as it should.

The kitchen was empty. Kay spun around the room, as if her parents would suddenly pop up from a corner and surprise her like they had on her previous birthday. Where was Mama and Daddy? The door! It was still open a crack, as if someone had kicked it shut at their departure but not with enough force to close it fully.

But where would they go? *Think, Kay. Use your brain.* The barn. It was so obvious. She knew Daddy wouldn't be happy when he saw her. Mama would want her to run now while she had the chance and would probably cry when she saw her, but she had to try, didn't she? Daddy *needed* her help. She was special.

She ran back toward the north barn and found the massive twin doors flung open wide, hot air billowed out in waves. Kay coughed and stopped, knees shaking, while she tried to catch her breath. She had to use her head. She would be no help to Daddy if she barged in and made a scene. This required that sneaky word, what was it? Oh right! Stealth, she thought, standing tall and feeling restored. This job required stealth.

She entered the barn and kept close to the wall, creeping along the west side of the barn. The barn's dome was open to allow for dragons to take flight, but there were darkened alcoves cut into the side that provided individual shelters for dragons. Kay walked in those shadows, keeping her breathing low and even, scouting her surroundings with watchful eyes.

She didn't see anyone at first, and she wondered if she'd been wrong. Maybe they had gone elsewhere, and her being in the barn was not only dangerous, but also a waste of time. But if she was wrong, then where did everyone go? She frowned and was concentrating so fully on being quiet that she almost ran directly into a sleeping dragon. A beam of sunlight reflected off the dragon's scales. Kay noticed Rumble's deep familiar red. She muffled a gasp that tried to escape, but Rumble didn't open his eyes. She carefully scooted closer to him. If she walked around his snout, she would have to step into the light, and if she did that, she risked someone seeing her. Her only advantage was the fact that she would be able to scout out what was happening before she was spotted by anyone. Her only alternative was to crawl over Rumble.

He would never hurt me. She leaned her weight on his neck. He felt smooth and leathery, unlike the feel of jagged metal and glass that Kay had imagined. She pushed her palms down and slid up Rumble's side until she straddled his thick neck. He opened his eyes but didn't move. She slid down the other side and stared up at the dragon. He blinked his giant eye and stared back. She continued creeping in the shadows. Her heart raced. She had touched Rumble! More than that, she had climbed over him. She'd practically rode him! And Rumble had done nothing.

He does like me. He would *let me ride him. Concentrate, Kay. You have to find Mama and Daddy.* She was in the center of the barn, and she could hear voices. She slowed her approach. She felt as though she was barely moving as she crept against the walls.

Sometimes you have to be patient, her father had said when she'd stared down at her first dragon egg. She had been four or maybe five, and she wanted to crack it open to see the baby inside. Daddy had rescued the egg before she smashed it and explained that if she had cracked open the egg the baby would have died. She'd been horrified and had cried and cried. Daddy had hugged her tight and told her everything would be fine. No harm was done, and she had learned that patience was rewarded. A few weeks later she was able to see the tiny baby dragons nursing from their mother.

I will be patient. She pressed herself against the wall. She could finally see them. Daddy had his back to her; her mother struggled in the arms of the stranger.

Kay knew what it meant to use strong words like hate. Mama always said she shouldn't ever use the word because it was powerful and mean. But Kay knew it was the right word for the moment. Kay *hated* that man. She tiptoed away from the wall and crept closer to her father.

"Do you think I'm a fool? I know why you've brought me here. You think to take me to the place you're most powerful," the stranger said. Kay watched as his arm squeezed tight against her mother's throat. Mama cried as she kicked at the air and slapped his arm. Kay felt panic poke in her tummy, and she bit her tongue to keep from crying out. *Patience.*

"Just let her go. Leave our farm and we'll both forget you ever came here. No one has to get hurt." Daddy's hands were in the air. His words were soft and even.

Kay could see him Breathing in the heat, pulling it up from the ground, from the air; Breathing it all in. She paused. Maybe she'd been foolish in coming. Daddy had everything in control, and he would be very angry when he caught her there.

The man laughed, loud and shrill. "I know what you're doing. You're not smarter than me. I can take in the extra heat from the dragons just as you can."

Wait, this was wrong. The stranger was also Breathing! *How could that be?* Kay shook her head. She and Daddy were special, so why was this man Breathing too? The man Breathed in at an alarming rate. Kay could see the heat radiating from him in waves that distorted the air. She hadn't been wrong. Daddy needed her help. She came just in time to warn him.

She Breathed. It was amazing. A sharp searing heat entered her lungs, and she Breathed in deeply, holding the heat tightly in check. Holding in such power was a dizzying sensation. The stagnant energy bounced around inside her, waiting to burst from her fingertips at her command.

"Daddy, look out. —He's Breathing too," she shouted. She Breathed in more, ready to release.

Mama was thrown to the ground. "Get out of here, Kay" she screamed. "Run, baby!"

The stranger released his flame at Daddy just as her father released his.

Mama screamed.

Kay released her flame at the stranger too and scooted close to Daddy. Streams of molten fire blazed from her tiny fingers. She stood just beside her father, using all her strength. Their flames were a wall of fire, and they fanned against that of the stranger's. Neither flame sputtered out. Kay ignored the strength sapping out of her. It didn't matter that she grew tired. Daddy and Mama needed her. She Breathed in more heat.

"No, Kay. Run, now. Do it." Daddy used his "'I mean it'" voice.

Kay's bottom lip quivered and a line of sweat beaded across her forehead. "Daddy, I can help."

"Now, Kay, run. Don't stop." He shoved her away and her concentration broke. She breathed normal, surprised at the steamy heat in the air. Rumble was watching her with solemn eyes.

She knew she was supposed to run away, but she couldn't tear her eyes away from Daddy and the stranger. She had to make sure Daddy and Mama were going to be fine.

Rumble stood up, growling deep in his throat.

The stranger suddenly stopped his flame and leaped to the side, rolling out of Daddy's line of fire. Her father Breathed in deeply and pulled his flame tightly to him. It encircled her father, a tiny tornado of flame that whirled around him. The barn grew dark from the sudden absence of so much fire.

"You're a fool," the stranger cried out from the darkness. "You thought you could live out your days in solitude. Thought your life was your own to grow profitable, lazy in your wealth. She was never yours. Just as your life was not your own." He stood up and Daddy whirled toward him.

The stranger shot out his flame. But not at Daddy.

Mama screamed when the flame shot into her chest. The flame crawled over Mama's body, and she twitched and jerked under it.

Daddy's flame sputtered out. "Kara," he fell to his knees and whispered Mama's name.

Mama! "No," Kay shouted, rushing toward the stranger. She hated him. She would make him burn. She Breathed in, ready to attack.

"Kay?" Daddy turned white when he saw. "I told you to run away."

The other man came from out of nowhere. He was dressed entirely in black and had a silk mask covering his face. His large, strong hands wrapped around her throat.

Where had he come from? She shot a flame at him. It was weak because she was exhausted and he was choking her, but it was enough to make him jump back in pain. He released her, and she struggled to Breathe in more.

She could feel Daddy growing hot behind her. "Daddy?"

"I love you, Baby," he smiled at her, then pushed her away. She fell to her knees and watched as Daddy Breathed in more heat than she thought possible.

"You'll kill us all," shouted the stranger, shooting a small flame out toward her father.

Daddy breathed it in too.

The second man, the one that had sneaked up on her, was running out of the barn. Rumble roared at him when he got too close. Daddy was hotter than should be possible. She worried for him, wondered what it would mean for him to hold so much heat. And Mama…

"Run, Kay!" Daddy's voice was pleading. The air was growing cold around her. Daddy was sucking in all the heat.

Kay ran.

She was exhausted but struggled to pump her legs as hard as she could. Daddy wanted her to run. She would run. The air was cool and crisp outside the barn doors. Rumble came out after her, spreading his wings wide in the evening light. The setting sun reflected off him, and he glowed brighter than any flame.

Kay kept running. She ignored the dragon flying above her. She raced from the barn, bathed in the shadow of Rumble's flight.

She was still running when Kay was pushed from behind and lifted off the ground before she was violently shoved back down into it. She coughed and looked up but could see nothing. Total blackness. She panicked. Ignoring the ringing in her ears, she screamed and wiped at her face. The darkness shifted, and she realized she wasn't blind, just completely covered by Rumble's enormous form, cocooned under his wing.

She pushed her way out from under him. Exalted, she cried out Rumble's name. Then she remembered Daddy. She looked around, dazed. *Where was the barn? Mama and Daddy…*Her mind was a storm. Emotions crashed over her, and she cried out, begging for her parents. Daddy had told her to run. He'd wanted to protect her. The barn…the barn had exploded. Rumble had covered her up to protect her.

"You really wouldn't let me get hurt." She offered the dragon a weak smile before falling to her knees in front of him. She wanted Daddy's arms. She wanted to eat Mama's fresh bread while her mother brushed her hair. *Why? Why had this happened? What had the man wanted?*

Rumble roared and Kay stared at the long stick protruding from his side. He stared at her with his giant black eyes before he collapsed to the ground. Smoke puffed out his nostrils.

"No, Rumble," she screamed out. "No!"

The sneaky man from the barn. *Where did he keep popping up from?*

"Stay away from me," Kay warned, Breathing in what little heat she could. Her head hurt and she was so tired.

"I can help you." The sneaky man smiled.

Kay exhaled and tried to call in more heat. She coughed. "You're a bad man. You hurt me and you killed Rumble." She took a few steps back toward the house, trying to run. Her body felt heavy and she stumbled over her feet.

The man tsked. "Poor little Fyrling, you must be exhausted."

"Stay away from me," Kay tried to shout but the words were choked. She fell to her knees. "Stay away." She continued to crawl further away from him.

He stood over her and reached out his arms. "Come little one, now you belong to me."

NINE
JURA

It disgusted her to do so but Jura chose to return to the palace through the same sewage passages she'd used earlier in her escape. It was better that no one see her sneak back to her rooms. She silenced the guard's questioning stare with narrowed eyes and a quick shake to her head. She was getting good at glaring. Must have been all her practice from her night out with Tylak. Her scowl deepened as she replayed the events of the evening. Once again, she'd been successful at screwing everything up. The palace had never captured a known Shadow Dancer before, and she let him escape. No, she'd led him to his freedom. He'd been so smug. And why shouldn't he be? He'd convinced the most powerful family in the Republic to do his bidding. Sandstorms but if he was here now Jura would strangle him with her whip. Well, she would try to in any case.

She was still lost in her dark thoughts, so she didn't notice the arm snake around the corner and grab her wrist before she was propelled into Markhim's strong embrace.

She immediately recognized his scent, sandalwood and leather, so she didn't cry out and instead rested her head on his chest.

He wrinkled his nose. "You smell as though you—"

"I did." Her face was buried in his chest so the words were muffled, but Markhim let out a quick bark of laughter in reply.

"What are you doing down here?" She pushed away from him so she could stare up into his handsome face. Markhim had skin the color of volcanic glass and warm brown eyes to match. His shiny black hair was ever in need of a hair cut and hung into his eyes, giving him a rakish look. He grinned down at her and a familiar dimple appeared in his left cheek.

His eyes roved over her body and his smile deepened. "You're filthy."

She rolled her eyes and shoved his chest. "You would be too if you'd just crawled through the palace latrine."

"How did it go?"

"Will you spare me the 'I told you so's' if I tell you what the Prince of Shadows looks like?"

"No. You saw him? In the flesh?"

Jura nodded, trying to keep her face from appearing overly smug. There was at least one thing to be proud of. "I did. Very young. Very creepy. He wore a mask made out of colored glass. And then he disappeared into thin air."

Markhim whistled low between his perfect teeth. "And the slave? A man like that is dangerous. Barom said he just appeared beside him, holding the sputtering torch. We still can't figure out how he got inside the palace."

"I don't want to talk about him." Jura snorted in disgust and once again twisted her lips into a scowl. "The point is the Prince of Shadows says he will help me so long as I provide him with information on the Thirteen."

Markhim nodded. "I figured it wouldn't come free. Well at least that's easily done."

"Easy? Spying on a network of families who don't trust anyone in a society where information is power? Yes, you're right. And while I'm at it, I might decide to join the Arena and slaughter a dragon." She sighed. "I can't do this. I'll just have to find some other way to help my father. Maybe if I call a meeting of the Thirteen…"

"No, definitely not. Jura, I'm not even a member of the Thirteen and I know that's a terrible idea. You said yourself, no one can be trusted. Besides, you don't owe them anything. So what if you do a little spying and disclose some secrets. It's not like they don't deserve it."

As always, his tone was bitter when discussing the Thirteen. It was part of the reason Jura had kept their relationship a secret from even Amira. Markhim thought Amira was vapid and selfish. Jura's friendship with her had been the source of more than one ongoing argument between the two of them. Another reason Jura kept their relationship a secret was that Jura had yet to understand the boundaries of their relationship herself. Markhim was her friend but how could she show him that she wanted to be more than friends? Surely he thought of her as something more? She sighed. Markhim hated the Thirteen and she was a member of its First family. Flames, but her life was complicated.

"Well, I suppose it doesn't hurt to try. In any case, I have to figure out something. I can't explain my father's disappearance for much longer. There has to be something I've missed. I found an entire history on the forging of the Tri-Alliance. I bet there are answers there."

Markhim grinned. "That's the Jura I love, confident that all of life's questions can be found answered in a book."

The heat rushed into her face and she looked down at her soiled slippers. *He said love!*

"…about your mother?"

"Hmm?" She snapped her attention back up to his face and tried to focus on what he said.

"I asked if you questioned the Shadow Dancer about your mother? You know, about the—"

"No, I didn't. There wasn't much time before he, well, disappeared. But I have a feeling I won't be getting any information for free. I should get going. I'm exhausted and I still have some reading to do, and tomorrow I have to try and be a spy, and I don't even know the first thing about getting people to talk."

"Let me know how I can help. I'm here for you, whatever you need." Markhim reached down and pushed a stray tendril of her hair back from her face. His hand lingered on her cheek and Jura leaned into it ever so slightly.

"Thank you. You have no idea what it means to me to be able to talk to someone about all of this. I just feel so alone."

"You're not. I'm with you." He leaned forward and Jura closed her eyes. This was it, he was about to kiss her. She dug her fingernails into the palm of her hand to keep her hands from shaking.

"Flames, but you stink."

The moment gone she smacked his chest and turned sharply on her heel. "That's it. I'm going to take a bath, right now."

"Thank the Everflame."

She narrowed her eyes and tossed her braid over her shoulder. "I don't have to take this. I'm going to my chambers."

"Will I see you tomorrow?" His eyes danced and his grin was doing something to her insides.

"If you're lucky," she replied saucily.

His grin deepened. "If I'm lucky, you'll have bathed by then."

"Go ride a dragon." Jura stomped away and his laughter followed her down the stone hall.

TEN

TYLAK

Tylak had been nine years old when it happened. Sykk had been a toddler, an appendage on his mother's hip. They had been walking home from the fair or the market and the sun was dipping behind the dunes, casting the city in an eerie orange glow. Tylak skipped, still full of energy from such an exciting day. His mother worked constantly, long hours that drained the day away so that when she made her way to the hovel they called home she did little more than feed her children before collapsing on her frond mat. This particular day had been a rare treat, and the nine-year-old boy could not remember one better. He loved his mother fiercely and understood the importance of working hard. That's why he helped her at home every day, watching his baby brother and setting snares for hares and lizards that would make supper. He was young but he was the man of the house, and she'd said so when she gave him the stone. It was blue. *Like the color of the ocean,* his mother had whispered dreamily. He had never seen the ocean but he imagined it was beautiful, like his mother.

He held that stone in a leather pouch that hung at his waist. He liked to touch the stone from time to time to marvel at its smoothness. He'd been thinking of his stone and the adventure of seeing the ocean. Skipping ahead, he didn't notice the two men come at his mother from behind. He heard her cry out and Sykk's quiet whimpers. He turned around and found his mother on the ground while two men pawed at her.

He'd been so angry. How dare those men hurt his mother. She was beautiful and full of light, and these men were evil. Tylak remembered his hands shaking. He dropped the stone back into its place in his pouch. The stone was hot to the touch. *He* was hot and the anger burned inside of him as he growled and lunged at the two men.

He landed squarely on the back of one and bit the man's ear hard, soliciting a scream. The second man grabbed him by the throat and ripped him off his partner's back. Tylak gasped for air as the man held him up over the square's fire pit.

Flames shot out, running down the arm of his captor and leaping onto his face. He howled, his expression panicked as he dropped Tylak to the ground. The flames engulfed the man. He flailed wildly, his arms desperately reaching out for salvation. The other man took off running, but Tylak couldn't watch him go, his eyes mesmerized by the burning corpse.

His mother had been fine. She never spoke of the incident again. *Don't think about it,* she'd told him, rubbing his back in calming circular motions. *It never happened.*

And in a way, it really hadn't. Not to him anyway.

Tylak knew they had arrived because he no longer felt nauseous. His throbbing head ache, however, was another story. He'd spent the better part of an hour being hauled around in a rain barrel. He'd probably traveled in the bed of a water cart, though he couldn't be sure because whoever had tied him up had also blind folded him, which meant that it wasn't the palace guards. Though he had a varied list of individuals who hated him, he felt with fair certainty that he knew the identity of his captor. The Shadow Dancers. He was in trouble, deep dragon shit kind of trouble. The unmoving cart told him one thing. He had only a brief opportunity before he was taken into yet another building. His best chance at an escape was to leave now on the open road.

The rain barrel was heaved off the cart with a grunt, and Tylak hit the ground with a jarring thud. Ignoring the pain, he jumped to his feet, kicking out around him. He heard a familiar chuckle before the blindfold was yanked off of him.

"Easy. You should be thanking me."

Tylak looked up into the very amused face of his one-time friend. "Peppik, is that you?" He held his hands out for Peppik to untie. "What did you hit me with?"

Peppik winced. "I thought you'd be mad at that. I was only trying to help," he smiled. "I could see you were in a bit of a sandstorm and I thought I'd see you out of it. I only hit you so I could skip over the explaining part and get to the rescuing part. Which is what I did. It was a daring rescue. You're welcome."

Peppik had attached himself to Tylak once before. Stalked him, was more accurate. He'd been forced to have the simple-minded fellow in tow for the better part of the year before he'd gotten caught up with the Shadow Dancers.

Tylak gingerly reached up to feel the knot on his head. It burned hotter than dragon's breath but it didn't appear to be bleeding. "Where are we?"

Peppik's smile widened and he handed Tylak a skin of water before gesturing his hands wide. "Outside the city gates. On the road that leads to the border of Kitoi. You're free."

"I'm not leaving the Republic." Tylak swallowed another gulp of the tepid water and handed the skin back to Peppik. "Thanks for the rescue. Really. But I need to remain in the capital. I lost something in the palace and I know someone that can help me get it back."

"But the trial. You were arrested. They said you'd be executed." Peppik's voice rose in nervous excitement. "I saw it happen. I rescued you."

"Yes, but that was before I made a deal with Jura. Wait, you were there? What were you doing in the city walls?"

Peppik bowed his head and Tylak remembered how much older his friend was than him. He noted the thinning hairs on Peppik's head and the wrinkles that folded around his dark eyes.

"I was there waiting for you. You told me to wait in the city."

Tylak tilted his head in wonder. "Peppik, that was years ago."

Tylak had been fifteen years old. His mother had died a few years before and Tylak had taken the position as the blacksmith's assistant. The work was long and tedious but he'd made a fair pay, and he and his brother had been happy. Sykk was a quiet boy and never wanted to play with boys in the city, no matter Tylak's encouragement that he do so. He preferred the company of animals and spent much of his free time with his pet goat. He made cheese from the animal, and Tylak could trade it for a canteen of water. His brother asked for nothing, so on the eve of his tenth birthday when he expressed a desire to go to the arena, Tylak had vowed to make it possible.

Olver, his friend and a free citizen blacksmith, had been delighted at the idea. He insisted that Tylak take his tickets to the night's match and sent him and his young brother on their way. Peppik had appeared, following behind them, watching Tylak in his odd way. It'd felt good to take his brother to the fights and he'd looked forward to the evening.

Olver's tickets allowed them access to arena seating, and Sykk was too excited to notice the boys were out of place. He bounced in his seat excitedly while Tylak kept his head down, afraid of making eye contact with one of the men or women of the upper class. While these people were far below the reach of the Thirteen ensconced in their glass box below, none of these people were of the slave race. Sykk and Tylak had more in common with the Fire Dancers than with the people around them. Their elaborate robes and made up faces unsettled him, and though they spoke the same language, their inflections caused it to seem unfamiliar to his ears. He and his brother's seats were a far cry from anything *good,* yet they were surrounded by free citizens of the Republic. Tylak had never before been so painfully aware of his low status.

The trumpets initiated the beginning of the battle, and Sykk stood up in his seat, grabbing his brother's arm and squeezing with surprising strength. "There he is! Look, it's Ash! He's my favorite. He can defeat anything." The last part was breathed out in a reverent whisper, and Tylak smiled at his brother's excitement.

Ash had long been the most popular Fire Dancer and was, by far, his brother's favorite. Tylak was grateful he'd gotten tickets to the night's battle because Ash's battles often sold out early.

The battle was epic. Ash fought the opening fight to get the crowd excited. In it, he fought two leaping animals called jaguars. They were black, stealthy, and attacked with a ferocity that had Sykk gripping his brother's arm in anxiety. Ash defeated the two creatures, and Sykk stood up and cheered as Ash ran off the field. Then a pair of Fire Dancers took to the field and exhibited a grand display of shooting fire. They leapt and danced around it in a way that Tylak found beautiful. Sykk murmured that he thought it had been a good show but when was the dragon coming out? He didn't have to wait long. Ash returned to the field with another Dancer and the two leapt and twirled, demanding excited cheers from the crowd.

The dragon was as magnificent as Tylak thought it would be. More so. The sheer mass of the beast was inspiring, but more than that was the radiance that glimmered off his pearly scales. The regal toss of his head and the sensuous movement of his body was mesmerizing. It was beautiful. Sykk was equally delighted and showed his enthusiasm by pumping his fist in the air and screaming Ash's name.

The deadly dragon had flown out of his containment box jetting a stream of molten fire directly at the unprepared and nameless Fire Dancer in the arena beside Ash. He'd landed in a smoldering heap of soot and dust on the floor. Not wasting the opportunity, Ash had plunged his assegai deep into the dragon's exposed belly. The dragon had shot up to the ceiling of the dome, circling the glass and occasionally growling his displeasure. The crowd hissed and threw things at the dragon, though no one's aim was far reaching enough to hit the monster. He continued to circle the dome, alternately flapping his leathery wings or gliding along wind currents that he had created. The crowd grew restless as the dragon made his ceaseless circles, and they cried out their displeasure. Screaming loudly and stomping their feet, they created a frenzy that Tylak and Sykk were easily swept up in. He could still remember the feel of the warm air rushing at his face when the dragon rose in front of them.

It was the job of the Fire Dancers to distract the dragon if the crowd captured its attention. It was rare, but training procedures were implemented on all new cadets. It's said on that fateful day Ash did all he could to regain the dragon's blood lust, but something attracted him to that particular section of the crowd and he would not be pulled away.

One moment, Tylak screamed and stomped his feet with his brother, and the next moment the dragon was directly in front of them. Tylak saw his horrified expression reflected in the beast's gigantic eye. The dragon opened his mouth in a slow yawn, and Tylak noticed with wonder that the beast held fangs that were as large as the span of his arm. He reached for Sykk's hand and thought of his mother. The fire started in the back of the dragon's throat and gushed forward in a rush of brilliant red.

Sykk had screamed. They all had. But Sykk had thrust out his arms, and when he did, the fire shot back toward the dragon, curving away from the crowd and back at the dragon's face. The dragon roared in fury and swept down to the field; the crowd screamed in excitement.

It didn't take them long to come. Minutes? Seconds? There were three of them, tall robed figures in red that swept his brother up and away from him. Tylak had leapt to his feet, confused and ready to fight. He kept demanding to know what was happening but there was no explanation, he was just held back as his baby brother was escorted away.

"There's nothing you can do." A wrinkled old face had stared at him in pity. "He's been chosen. He's a Fire Dancer. He must begin his training." She shook her head, clicking her tongue in her mouth. "It's a miracle it took them this long to find him. Must be a late bloomer."

He'd ignored the old woman and struggled against the man holding him. It was all so wrong.

"I don't understand. Sykk isn't a Fire Dancer. He's my brother, he—" Tylak fell to his knees confused and suddenly very tired. "What's happening to me?" The robed men had blown smoke in his eyes. They must have poisoned him.

The old woman's dark eyes shone with amusement. "Poor little fool. Your brother never belonged to you."

Tylak shook his head at the memory and stared at Peppik in wonder. "You found me after the guards threw me out of the arena. I woke up in the alley with you. You told me that there wasn't a way to get Sykk back. I didn't believe you."

"This is right. You said you would find a way, that you were leaving. I asked what you wanted me to do and you told me to wait for you in the city. I've been waiting for many years and finally I found you. Only you had been arrested by the palace." Peppik frowned. "Who is Jura?"

Tylak couldn't believe that Peppik had waited for him after all this time.

He knew the simple-minded man had been unbalanced, but for him to wait for so long bothered him. In any case, he was stuck with him now. *Thank the Everflame for his presence,* Tylak thought. *He can help.*

"Jura is the one that is going to help us get my brother back."

ELEVEN

ASH

Ash didn't care for the new rooms he'd been forced to inhabit. Nearly a week later, he was still having a difficult time remembering to turn down the hall that led to his new quarters. He'd tried to stay in his old room, but it simply wasn't done. He was no longer gladiator. His suite in the Fire Dancer headquarters had been given to someone else. *Timber probably*, he thought with bitterness.

His new room was half the size of his old and lay at the opposite end of the citadel. The room was one of seven that stood in a long hallway for retired Dancers that chose to remain living at the arena. The rooms were all empty save his own. The glory of the gladiator was to die young and brave, rich in strength and still full of power. Perhaps that's why so many retired Dancers purchased their freedom and disappeared. It was difficult to live in the shadow of so many.

The memory of the arena fight from the night before still burned in his mind. Timber had been good, better than good. He would never admit it aloud, but Timber rivaled Ash when he had been at his best. Now his knees always ached, he felt a burning sensation in his back whenever he stood up, and he had no feelings in the fingers of his left hand. He could still dance with fire, no one could take that away, yet he wasn't himself if he wasn't dancing in the arena. If he wasn't Ash the great Fire Dancer, who was he?

He had entered a world where his abilities were to be repressed or used in service of the palace only. If he wanted to dance with fire, he could only do so under the strict supervision of the palace. He had two choices really; disappear and allow himself to fade away like his fame, or stay and try to make a new name for himself. He had purchased his freedom long ago, choosing to stay in the arena and continue fighting simply because it was the only life he knew. He could take that freedom granted from years ago and disappear like so many others before him, or he could stay and live out his days in the shadow of others. The decision tore at him, and though his pride begged otherwise, there was only one answer that burned in his heart. He could never leave the arena.

There was only one option that allowed Ash to salvage any happiness. Ash had to find a new cadet that wasn't contracted to another trainer and offer his services. *Surely someone would leap at the chance to work with the great Ash himself? Perhaps one of the houses needed a trainer?* ...Ash wished he'd stuck around the spectator box the night before and found out. He'd wasted a perfect opportunity. The only person he'd even spoken to had been Beshar. At least the councilman had seemed amicable toward him. Perhaps his was in need of another trainer. He left his depressing room and walked as quickly as his aching knees would allow. New cadets were in the sparring field and would be called out to dinner shortly. If Ash hurried he could catch the end of their session.

The training sessions of the cadets had never interested Ash before. They were young, inexperienced, and too weak to be interesting. They were most focused on achieving any control of the flame at all, and their sparring moves were unpracticed and awkward. Ash had never believed himself to have the patience for instructing, but if this was his only chance at staying near the arena he would hold onto it. He quickened his pace, ignoring the jarring pain that pricked at his left knee as he made his way through the twisting narrow hallways. A particularly sharp turn sent spikes of searing hot pain through his lower joints, and he was grateful when he reached the sparring field a few moments later. He stood straight, smiling to himself when he barely felt winded. His joints were falling apart, but he still had his endurance.

The four cadets, all boys, were lined up in the sparring field. *Could there truly only be four?* Ash frowned. In his inaugural year there had been forty-seven. He'd heard the whispered rumors that the power was dwindling, that fewer and fewer were being chosen. This would certainly make it harder for him to acquire a cadet of his own.

Ash had been chosen when he was eight years old. Though not unheard of, it was uncommon for a boy to be chosen before his ninth or tenth birthday. Ash had always been a prodigy. His family had belonged to Ishar, then the seventh house of the Thirteen, and Ash had been called Azukk. Ishar's province was known for producing Dancers, and an average of five to eight children were chosen every year. Like many his age, Ash had looked forward to any change that came to his body, hoping for a clue that would signify he'd be chosen. Though it was nearly forty years ago, Ash would never forget that fateful day.

He was in the city with several boys from his house, sent on an errand of fetching meat and dragon oil from the market. The boys had retrieved the items quickly and were taking their time on their way home, climbing over city monuments dedicated to the Everflame and collecting shiny pebbles and beetles. Ilyakk was turning ten the following week. He had balanced on the edge of the fire pit, boasting that they would discover he was a Fire Dancer in the upcoming week. The boys cheered for Ilyakk, begging him to show off his moves, and the boy obliged, pivoting several times along the pit's edge and causing his peers to cheer in delight.

Ash had been impressed by the boy's display. Though he'd never been to the arena, he loved to hear stories of the bravery that occurred there. Maybe after Ilyakk was chosen he would invite them all to the arena to watch. More than anything in the world, Ash wanted to see a dragon.

This moment, the moment his life changed, would always be seared in his brain. One moment Ilyakk was spinning on the fire pit's edge and the next Ash watched as he slipped and tottered backwards into the flaming pit below.

It was terrifying. Ash had called out and threw his arms out toward Ilyakk, a futile effort to catch his friend, when the most remarkable thing happened. The fire in the pit swept out and toward Ash's arms only to then sweep upward and disappear into the sky. A dazed Ilyakk had hit the soot below and stared at Ash in wonder. Ash had helped his friend out of the fire pit. The boys of his house were all covered in ash and slapping him on the back enthusiastically when the arena scouts appeared.

He'd been so excited to learn that he had been chosen. He had never felt that he held any power, and the knowledge was overwhelming to his young mind. He'd been thrilled to move into the citadel for training, not understanding the full depths of his sacrifice. His mother had come to see him once, crying on the edge of the practice field. He hadn't seen her at all in the two years since he'd been chosen, and at first, his heart leaped at the sight of her. She'd waved and called out, but when she'd started to cry, Ash had felt embarrassed and ashamed. The cadets were taught that crying was a weakness. Water was priceless in the Sand Sea. One must never waste what little the body held. He'd turned away from his mother and focused instead on proper foot placement while he executed his turns. When he'd looked up again, his mother was gone. He ignored the pain of missing his mother. He'd been chosen by the priests of the Everflame. They had scouted his talents and picked him, marked him for greatness. They had brought him home.

Ash would later learn that such scouts stood watch at all major fire sources, keeping a watchful eye for children that displayed any power. When the Everflame sees fit to gift them with power, it is the responsibility of the palace to see that the children are raised to use their power for good. Though many would only train to use their power for the good of the palace, a special few were selected to train in the true art of Fire Dancing. Their power was needed to help vanquish the beasts of evil that ruled beyond the Sand Sea. Dragons.

Ash had never seen for himself, but he'd learned in his studies that the world was a much bigger place than the Glass Palace and its surrounding cities. Beyond the sea of sand lay a steep mountain range, and beyond the mountains a vast jungle of wild creatures. It was there that the dragons made their home. Few traveled outside the Sand Sea and returned to tell the tale, though Ash had heard stories of the kingdom of people that lived in the jungle beyond. Merchants from the distant land traveled to the Sand Sea to make trade with the palace. He'd heard wild stories of people traveling with their own water because it was so plentiful in their land. The people brought exotic metals and creatures in exchange for spices, rugs, and the precious dragon oil that was found plentiful in the Sand Sea.

It was common practice for youths from the palace to travel beyond the Sand Sea in hopes of capturing a wild dragon. Those that returned at all often came back empty handed, but there were a few houses that had made a name for themselves through such an achievement. Many houses owned facilities that worked at breeding the creatures, though that was a deadly practice and only the most gifted Fire Dancers were successful of such a feat.

How had his mind wandered to the breeding practices of dragons? And why the trip down memory lane? Ash shook his head, angered at his nostalgia. He needed to focus.

He snapped his attention back to the sparring field. As expected, the boys were clumsy and awkward with their assegai, tottering under the tall sleek weapons as they went through their forms. One boy stood out. Ash admired his fluidity with the unpracticed movements. He was smaller than the others, yet nimble and quick. He was awkward still, but he had a natural grace that with some guidance could be—

"I see you're admiring my boy," Timber's deep familiar voice startled Ash. He would have whirled around had Timber not placed a crushing hand on Ash's shoulder.

"Yours? Early on for you to take an apprentice of your own. Seeking an early retirement?" Ash shrugged off Timber's grip and turned to meet him head on. He refused to let the man belittle him. Ash wouldn't forget who he was, and he wouldn't allow others to do so either. He was Ash, the greatest Fire Dancer of his time.

Timber smiled, and Ash was surprised to see that the man had dimples. They gave him a boyish quality though his dark eyes glittered dangerously. "I couldn't leave my flesh and blood to the training of the aging relics offered through the citadel now, could I?"

Now that Timber mentioned it, the boy looked incredibly like his father. It was not common practice for Fire Dancers to marry while they still fought in the arena and even more uncommon for a Dancer to sire a child old enough to be trained while he still fought. Ash looked at Timber with renewed interest.

"He has nice lines," he found himself saying.

Timber's smile deepened. "Yes, he has a natural talent. Chosen when he was eight."

That would explain his small size. "How old is he now?"

"Nine and growing every day. He grew up on this arena. He'll be greater than myself someday." Timber smiled politely, and Ash heard the unspoken comment: better than us both.

Seems I will have to look elsewhere for my protégé. "It's sad to see there are only four cadets. I suppose they are all spoken for? Are there any in need of a trainer?" It galled him to ask.

Timber's eyes widened. "You were here scouting? Can't stay out of the game, can you?"

Ash flexed, reminding Timber he still had strength in his old, scarred arms. "I've got a bit in me yet. Though these cadets are disappointing."

Timber nodded grimly. "The smallest class yet. And yes, all spoken for, so you'll need to look elsewhere."

Ash shook his head. "I've already been denied the boy I'd most like to work with." He watched as the child leaped into the air with ease and spun down to his knee thrusting out his training assegai.

"The boy's mother?" He wondered out loud.

Timber's eyes darkened and he scowled down at Ash. "Mind your business old man."

Ash watched him leave, realizing that Timber was a man of many surprises.

TWELVE
KAY

When Kay woke up, her head was foggy and there was a strange buzzing sound in her ears. The muscles in her leg spasmed and her joints begged to straighten, but when she tried to do so her feet hit something hard. Her eyes snapped open and she stared down at her feet, pressed against a wooden crate. The crate was small, no more than a few feet across, and even shorter than it was wide. Encased inside Kay could scarcely move about. Her lips were dry and parched. She licked them in an effort to moisten them but the effort proved little result.

Where was she? She vaguely remembered leaving her home. That man, that horrid sneak of a man, had thrown her into a sack like a wayward chicken and, surrounded by the dark wool, Kay had succumbed to exhaustion. That was the last thing she remembered.

She turned her head to the side to further take in her surroundings. She peered through the large gaps between the wooden slats, squinting in the morning sun. Her crate was on the far side of some sort of cart. She wasn't alone. The cart was full of the wooden crates, and in each of the crates lay a kid. Most appeared to be much older than her, but there were a few that seemed the same age. *How long have I been asleep?* She didn't recognize her surroundings. The rolling hills and woodlands of her home were replaced by sparse yellowed grass that grew in patches and stunted trees that had more branches than leaves.

He's not taking me anywhere. I have to get out of here. She was aware of the intense heat all around her. It was in the ground below, the sun above, it even emanated off the bodies of her fellow prisoners. She shouldn't Breathe in their heat. It was dangerous to do so, and Daddy wouldn't approve. But if it came down to it, she would.

The people in the other crates lay still and quiet. She frowned at them. *Why weren't they shouting to be let out? Had no one tried to escape?* It wouldn't take much. She simply had to Breathe in the heat and blast her way out of the crate. Once she was out, she would jump from the crate and run as fast as she could back toward home. If anyone tried to stop her, she'd blast them too. She didn't feel her strongest but she couldn't waste any more time, each second only took her further and further away from home. She Breathed.

Nothing happened. Despite the heat of the air around her, goosebumps prickled her arm. What was wrong with her? Again, she tried to Breathe in the heat and again nothing happened. She could feel the heat around her, but she couldn't reach it. The harder she tried, the more it seemed to wriggle further out of her grasp. The buzzing in her ears increased, and she began to pant. The air she sucked in seemed thin and smoky. Her thoughts were jumbled and slow, and she tried to piece together what was happening. Was her power gone? The thought didn't make sense. If her fire power was gone, she wouldn't still feel the burning heat around her. This was different. Her power wasn't gone, it was blocked.

In the crate closest to Kay, another girl lay curled up in a ball. She was bigger than Kay by more than a few years, and even though she was in a larger crate, it was still so small around her that her body was pressed into it on all four sides. The crate was close enough so Kay pushed her arms through the narrow slates of her crate and poked at the girl's skin. The girl groaned in response. Her tone was agitated, but Kay refused to give up. She needed answers. She poked her again, digging her nail into the skin of the girl's arm.

The girl lifted her head slightly and glared at Kay. Kay glared back.

"Where are we?" Kay asked.

The girl widened her eyes and shook her head.

"How long have we been here? Where are we going?"

The girl shook her head so violently that Kay wondered how her eyes didn't rattle in her head. She opened her mouth to repeat her questions, but the girl interrupted her with a stream of incoherent babble that erupted from her mouth in a feverish whisper. There was no understanding that; she spoke another language.

Defeated, Kay lay her head back down against the wood. Even her movements felt slow, as though the air around her was made of tree sap. She had just closed her eyes when she heard a soft voice just off to her right.

"Girl. Hey girl. I'm from Tirdrakor too. Can you hear me?"

"Yes, I'm here!" Her heart leaped and she felt a small rush of energy pulse through her. "Where are—"

"Shh." The voice interrupted her. "You must stay quiet. Udo doesn't like for us to speak."

"Who is Udo?" She worried that her voice had dropped too far below a whisper because it was several moments before the voice responded.

"He's a bad man. He's taking us far away. I don't think we'll ever go home again."

No. The voice is wrong. She *would* go home.

"What's your name?"

"I'm Kay. What's yours? How long have you been here? Do you know where we're going?"

"Kay is a boy's name and you sound like a girl. My name is Wallace."

"I *am* a girl," Kay struggled to keep the anger out of her voice. She didn't want to talk about names. She needed answers. "Where are we going?"

"I don't know. We travel east. We've made several stops along the way, but we haven't stopped since we got you. That was days ago. I thin—"

Wallace's voice cut short with a startled yelp and the cart jerked to a stop. Kay twisted around in her crate, struggling to see what had caused the boy's sudden exclamation. The girl in the crate beside her trembled and pressed her head into the floor, murmuring her foreign words at a rapid pace.

"You will be silent," a deep baritone growled.

Kay didn't have to turn about in her crate to see, because the boy was thrown into the dirt beside her. She watched from her crate as Wallace whimpered and crawled in the sand. A horrid man stood over him and kicked Wallace in the ribs. That must be the man the boy called Udo. The boy groaned and cried out from pain.

"There is no talking." Udo drew back his foot and once again shoved it into Wallace's rib cage. Wallace begged him to stop, but the man only grinned and kicked him harder.

"Stop it! Stop it!" Kay shouted.

Udo straightened and left Wallace rolling in the dirt, moaning and holding onto his middle. Udo walked to the cart and stooped so that he was eye level with Kay.

"You ask me to stop?"

Kay had seen many smiles in her life. Daddy had a smile that ate up his entire face. Mama's smile made her eyes sparkle and a fat dimple winked from her left cheek. Udo's smile was the most wicked thing Kay had ever seen. His was no smile. Kay swallowed hard and once again reached for the heat around her. She Breathed…and nothing happened. Her head felt like it was underwater, and her belly turned and rolled itself in knots.

Udo chuckled. "It won't work. Your power is not your own. You cannot hurt Udo. And you cannot escape. You will be mine until I say it is not so." His accent was harsh and guttural, his words clipped and foreign sounding.

He bent down to Wallace and punched him directly in his face. Blood spurted out of the boy's nose and sprayed across the dirt.

"Please," Wallace begged. "Please, no more."

Udo kept his eyes trained on Kay's face. His smile deepened when she gasped at the blow he gave Wallace.

"Leave him alone." Kay didn't want Udo's anger directed at her, but she refused to allow him to lay another hand on Wallace. She pressed her palms into either side of the crate and heaved her body weight from side to side. The crate scarcely moved from her effort, and she screamed in frustration.

"You are weak. I am your master now, and you will obey. There is no talking."

Kay stared down at Wallace. He was sobbing in the sand. He didn't move except for the shake of his shoulders. Wallace had only tried to help her. He didn't deserve this beating. She hated Udo. Hated him more than she'd ever felt anything in her life. He'd taken her away from Mama and Daddy. He'd helped kill them. All so he could take her away. The hate built up inside her, a small inferno that burned in her gut. Though she'd never hated anything with such intensity before, the hate burning inside her felt familiar. She felt as if she could almost... Breathe.

Udo's smile faltered.

The feeling was wondrous. Heat flared up inside of her. She pulled it in from all around. Heat from the air, the burning sun, the hot bodies all around her. Heat from the molten fire hundreds of feet below the ground. She Breathed it all in. The wooden crate burned red around her before it exploded into bits. Shards of broken wood showered all around her and she stood up, pulling in still more heat.

Udo stumbled back, throwing his arms up to shield his eyes from the falling debris.

Kay stood tall. Her muscles were no longer aching. Instead, she felt strong and full of energy. She cradled a ball of fire in her hand. The heart of the flame was already larger than her head. In another moment, she would hurl it straight at her enemy, blowing him up into tiny Udo bits.

She raised her arms and he disappeared.

She leaped from the bed of the cart, chest heaving as she whirled around in search of her enemy. He was truly gone.

But that's impossible. People don't just disappear.

She tossed back her head and screamed up at the sky, hurling her ball of fire up and away. Udo should be lying in a pile of ash. *Where was he?*

Kay knelt down beside Wallace. His face was covered in blood. She touched his shoulder, but he didn't turn toward her. When she found Udo she would make him pay, she would.

—Pain exploded at the black of her head and shot into the back of her eyes. She fell forward, struggling to blink the world back into focus.

She recognized Udo's boot as it came into view, just before it shot toward her chin. She flew backward and landed on her back. She gasped, choking in a strangled breath. *Where had he come from? What...* Udo grabbed her throat and raised her up. She wanted to struggle against him but she was in so much pain that all she could think about was dragging in her next uneasy gulp of air. Udo pressed a wet cloth to her face, covering her mouth and nose. She saw his wicked smile, and then she saw no more.

THIRTEEN
JURA

S *omeone pulled on her leg.* She snapped out of her slumber, her reflexes lethargic as she shook off the last of her dream. The pressure on her leg grew tighter. She looked around the room, seeing no one, yet an ever-widening sense of panic forced her to sit up. There was no one in the room. *What's on my leg?!* She threw the covers away from her body and let loose a strangled gasp at the gigantic snake that was tightly coiled around her leg. She kicked and jerked away from the bed, stumbling for her bedside table in search of a weapon of some sort and calling for help.

Her *Arbe* burst into her room. In a few seconds the snake was dispatched with the flash of a scimitar and she collapsed against her bed frame, breathing heavily.

Someone had put a snake in her room, in her bed. How? Was it poisonous? She asked the question out loud and her *Arbe* shook their heads. She suddenly remembered reading that venomous snakes didn't usually constrict their prey. The fact that it wasn't poisonous did little to calm her. The snake had been nearly as big as she was and if she hadn't woken when she did, she might have had the life choked out of her. She swallowed. Well, it wasn't the first time in the last week that someone had almost killed her, at least this time the effort hadn't come from her father. He was still locked away in her cellar and wasn't responsible for this scare. *So, who was?* Perhaps it was her father's Chain Master or any member of the Thirteen. Maybe it was even Tylak. He'd seen the way she'd reacted over the snake in the dungeon, and his disappearance the other night proved he wasn't trustworthy.

She wasn't mad. She assured the *Arbe* before sending them out to dispose of the vile creature. She'd always hated snakes. But no, she wasn't mad at her *Arbe*. They had saved her. Hadn't they? But that still left the question. How did someone manage to get the snake past them and into her room?

She watched her *Arbe* leave and released a heavy sigh. She should have expected the attack. She had been foolish to let down her guard, even for a second. She was First Interim now. Everyone wanted her dead.

She opened the cellar door to check on her father. He squinted back at her.

"Do you want some bread and some figs? It's my normal breakfast. The kitchens won't send me anything else." *Why am I apologizing?* A man should know his daughter's preferred breakfast. Just as she knew he preferred fried egg and strong tea, foods that were never sent to her chambers. She had tried to bring them from his chambers but had run into too many servants who still had their tongues. She wanted to make sure no one suspected her father was anywhere except holed up in his room. A member of his *Arbe* ate the First's meals throughout the day. It was working for the moment, but people were beginning to talk. Jura had attended every court activity aware of the questioning eyes and the whispering voices.

"Father, please say something. Tell me who's done this to you."

She'd spent the better part of her free time pouring over research books and her great-grandfather's journals in hopes of discovering clues about her father's predicament. She'd learned very little.

Blood chains were created hundreds of years ago by Gregor the Great, or Terrible, depending on which history book you read. The man was responsible for several battles and the start of the Border Wars. The Border Wars were a series of battles over the borders of Kitoi and the seven kingdoms of the Sand Sea. Though none of the books explained how, they all agreed that Gregor originally developed the blood chains for his soldiers. He discovered that a soldier wearing a blood chain did not tire and kept toward his goal with a single-minded obsession. They followed their master's orders to the word. Generals could be hundreds of miles away, and the soldiers would follow their every command. He soon had an army of unstoppable soldiers. Gregor's reign of domination lasted for forty-three years before he was killed by Josper the Usurper, Jura's own great-grandfather.

Though originally known as an usurper, he was also remembered as a bringer of peace. It was Josper who united the kingdoms and Josper who suggested the system of the Thirteen for the seven ruling kingdoms and the six ruling merchants. The kingdom was united, and Josper signed treaties with the Is' Le Sp'Ar islands that were ruled by the Sea King and the kingdom of Kitoi, which sat on the outskirts of the Sand Sea. Her great-grandfather had seen no use for the mighty, unstoppable soldiers and had demanded that all weapons be destroyed in an effort to embrace their time of peace. The histories only outlined the stories of war, and even though her great-grandfather's journals made note of blood chains, there was no mention of what had happened to them. *So how did one end up on father?*

Her father ate her breakfast and drank the water greedily, but he wouldn't tell her anything about blood chains. He wouldn't say anything at all. Jura wasn't surprised by this. He'd been locked up for a week now, and aside from the one time he'd lunged at her, they hadn't had any interaction.

She closed the First back up in her cellar and searched out her spectacles, prepared to spend the rest of the morning going over her research books and Josper's journals. She didn't need the spectacles except for reading but found it easier to keep them on rather than waste valuable time searching for them. She was grateful to find them on her nightstand where she'd left them the night before. *Good thing my Arbe had acted as quickly as they had.* The tiny spectacles would have made a poor weapon against the snake. She shuddered again before perching the glasses on her nose and reaching for an old history book.

There was little extra information on blood chains. One book suggested that her great-grandfather had kept one of the chains for posterity but that could not be confirmed. If it was true, the location of such a chain was gone before Jura had ever been born. Yet another history book was proven to be a dead end.

Her level of anxiety shot upwards. The council meeting was at the end of the week and Jura had just three days to discover who held her father captive. Well, who held him captive aside from herself. The council would not stand for her excuse another week. She knew that they were plotting against her house. She didn't need a snake in her bed to prove that. It was logical. It was expected. Her family had been the First house for two decades, and while some respected her father, he was also hated. The house position as the First was vulnerable, and Jura would be wise to expect attacks until the day of the meeting and next vote.

She had spent much of her time hiding in her room. She hadn't even bothered to seek out Markhim. It was hard to push away the strong sense of disappointment she felt in herself. Father would be aghast. She showed weakness by hiding away. If nothing else, the snake served as a bitter reminder that she was a fool for thinking she'd be safe in her rooms. It was time to put her books aside and take action.

The next three days were full of court social functions. Their purpose was to entreat allies and strengthen or weaken one's position. If Jura continued her stand-off behavior, the house of the First would appear weak and their Rank would be questioned. Jura refused to let her father down and resolved to appear strong over the next few days. In order to do so, she had to drastically change her behavior. She could no longer be a scared little girl hiding in her room behind dusty old history books.

She went to her hall to send for a handmaiden. She frowned in consideration. Her *Arbe* always seemed to sense when she was coming. And yet, they hadn't noticed someone leave a snake in her room. *Did that make them suspect? What had she read about Arbe? It was something useful…* She hated that she didn't have a photographic memory and vowed to look for the passage later.

A handmaiden arrived and helped her dress. Most girls her age wore dresses with sheer floor length wraps that still allowed their intricate dresses to shine. Her own body was woefully disappointing in a dress. She was too short, too thin, and had no curves to speak of, so Jura refused to wear them. Instead, she preferred the simplicity of modest robes. She chose a robe at random. It was a pale, shiny blue with tiny purple flowers sewn along the neckline and at the hem. She paired the robe with soft gray trousers and a blue tunic that was made especially for the robe. Her hair was brushed until shiny and pinned back into its traditional braid, the accepted hairstyle of an unmarried woman in society.

She left her rooms, *Arbe* in tow, just before high noon. The first social function was a luncheon at the home of the Third. Jura was actually looking forward to this function. Hosted by Amira's father, the two were sure to have time alone to catch up, and Jura missed her friend.

She kept a watchful eye out, hoping to catch a glimpse of anything out of the ordinary. She still had to find something useful to present to the Shadow Dancers. Yet another reason she couldn't hide away in her rooms. She was running out of time and failing miserably at her quest. It had been four days since her encounter with the Prince of Shadows and she hadn't learned any gossip or secrets worth repeating. If anything, she was only more confused. *Were they watching, eager to see if I hold up my end of the bargain? And just how did they envision me fulfilling the bargain anyway?* Jura knew they couldn't want her for her skills as a spy. It made more sense to use her position to pass a new law or to gain a new alliance, yet both notions were impossible. Jura failed to hold any real sway over the Thirteen. She was a filler for her father, nothing else.

She arrived at the house of the Third and found that her anxiety rose instead of lessened. She'd been to her friend's house several times before and thought the familiar surroundings would help calm her. Instead, she fought to calm her hammering heart as she felt all eyes on her.

Like her own tower of the palace, the tower of the Third was made up of several large rooms, all with walls made out of the customary thin glass. The rooms were circular, the tower reaching out into the sky and the room was emblazoned by light from the sun. To the far side, a darkened stone hallway extended out, housing the stone rooms of the Third and his two children. Jura's own quarters were identical, with the exception of the large courtyard that housed her gardens. Everyone in the palace had more or less the same home, the palace constructed out of fourteen tall spherical glass towers. They varied in size, Jura's home was the largest while the Thirteenth was the smallest, and at the center was the massive domed tower that housed the Everflame. Council meetings were held off to its side, just to the north of the inextinguishable flame.

The tower was crowded, filled with not only members of the Thirteen, but also merchants and traders from the various provinces of the Republic. Several tables were set out, covered with deep purple linen and laden with food. The Third had even hired acrobats, probably from the arena, and the group of entertainers performed twisting stunts and juggled fire. Jura stood frozen in the doorway. The glass walls gave her no place to hide, and the heavy sun had her in an instant sheen of sweat.

Why is everyone looking at me?

"Wow, you've certainly caught everyone's attention. They must all be wondering where did you get your robes?" Amira exclaimed as she sauntered over. "But I know you'll only tell me," she whispered confidentially.

Jura smiled at her friend and took a deep breath. So, she hadn't just imagined their stares. She'd known this would happen, but had still failed to prepare for the sensation of being watched by all. *Focus, Jura.* She took Amira's hands in greeting and kissed the smooth tan skin of her friend's cheek. She pasted a smile on her face and stepped further into the room.

"Where's your father? I want to thank him for inviting me."

Amira nodded enthusiastically. "He insisted. Father has been great. In fact, he wants to speak with you."

Amira's eye's sparkled mischievously, and Jura found herself grinning back. Amira's joy was often infectious. Amira wore a gown in pale yellow cotton. Tiny stones were beaded along the plunging neckline, and the gown hugged her figure and just barely prevented her bosom from escape. Her eyes were lined with khol and her lips smeared in red. Jura had never actually seen her friend without any makeup on. Jura had tried to line her eyes once. She'd gotten khol in her eyes and they had become red and inflamed. It had been a miserable experience.

Unaware of the scrutiny from her friend, Amira grabbed Jura's hand and dragged her across the room. The girls paused every time someone acknowledged her or Jura. Many called out to her. The sound of "Greatness" or "My Lady First" rang in her ears and Jura struggled to make eye contact with them all. She wanted to appear strong and capable, but with the beautiful Amira tugging her across the room, she felt awkward and clumsy.

Her nerves fluttered wildly, and she felt the familiar pull of hunger that occurred whenever she was anxious. She grabbed a pastry stuffed with leafy greens and goat cheese and stuffed it in her mouth in hopes that it would still her rumbling belly. She immediately regretted the decision. What if she got greens stuck in her teeth? Soup would have been a better option. She frowned over the passing trays laden with food, but Amira yanked her along before she could make any further selections.

Amira's father, Ahmar, stood in the center of the dance hall. Though not a dancer, he liked to be in the center of the action and stood talking to Velder, Dahr, and Geedar. Jura gulped, councilmen from the Second, Third, Fourth, and Sixth, all together.

Ahmar smiled at her warmly. "Amira, I see you've brought your friend." His fingers intertwined and his thumbs wriggled toward her. "Daughter of the First, you grace us with your lovely presence."

The others nodded politely and Jura wriggled her thumbs in response. "Elders you flatter me. My father will be pleased to hear the house of the First has been treated so well during his absence."

"How is your father?" Velder asked, stroking his long mustache and smiling down at her tiny frame.

"Recovering daily," Jura replied with a tight smile. "I have confidence that he'll be himself before the next meeting."

"That's wonderful news," Ahmar put a strong hand on her shoulder and gave it a soft squeeze. "I'm sure I speak for everyone when I toast to his health and pray to the Everflame for his fast recovery." Ahmar raised his glass and the rest of the group followed suit. Geedar and Dahr somewhat awkwardly, while Velder stared at her in appraisal.

Jura inclined her head in thanks and allowed herself to be led off by a chattering Amira. It was nice of her friend's father to stand beside her as he did. He must want an alliance with her house. Jura considered the possibility. It made sense. An alliance to one of the top three houses made her house more powerful and secure in it's Rank. A necessary trait, considering her father's absence and her family's tentative hold as First. Her father would have never felt the need for such an alliance. He oozed power and authority. But Jura needed the strength another house could offer. In fact, an alliance would be to her house's benefit, and Jura was surprised that she was just now realizing this. She could have secured her house's position days ago. Engaging an alliance might spark her father's anger, but it was a chance she was willing to take.

Amira handed Jura a glass of muddled wine and clinked her glass with hers, smiling at her friend. "I have something to tell you."

"Oh? Well out with it then."

Amira shook her head, smiling wide. "I don't know, Jura. It's really supposed to be a secret."

Jura frowned, "So, why even bring it up?"

Jura gestured for a member of her *Arbe*. A tall, silent giant appeared at her side in seconds. She leaned up to whisper in his ear. "Please fetch the red leather book with gold lettering." *The Principals of Alliance*. Jura hoped she had time to study a chapter or so on proper alliance etiquette before she approached the Third.

She watched the member of her *Arbe* walk away and noticed that he stopped for a moment in front of the other members of her *Arbe*. He held up a fist in front of his chest before leaving the room. *Was he saying goodbye? Paying them a sign of respect?* Jura had never seen members of an *Arbe* trying to talk to one another before, but she supposed they did. Perhaps it was something that happened fairly frequently. She really needed to find that book and reread that passage. The idea nagged at her and she was staring off at her silent statues when Amira brought her back to the present.

"—and you don't even care." Amira pouted, pursing her vivid red lips out and stomping a slippered foot.

Jura resisted the urge to roll her eyes. "Don't care about what? Have you ever noticed anything odd about your *Arbe?*"

Amira did roll her eyes and threw her hands up in exasperation. "Father forbid me from telling you and here I go telling you anyway and you don't even respond, so it's like you don't even care!"

"Tell me what?"

"About Antar!"

Jura cocked her head to the side. "Your brother? What about him?"

Amira placed her hands on her hips and shook her head. "You really weren't listening? Father proposes an alliance between our houses. He suggests a betrothal between you and Antar! We'll be sisters in real life!" She grabbed Jura's hands excitedly and hopped up and down. "Isn't it amazing?"

"Antar? Your brother? Antar."

Amira stopped hopping. "What are you saying?"

Jura chose her words carefully. "It's not that I'm opposed to an alliance, the thought had crossed my mind...but Antar still acts like a boy. He's too young. *I'm* too young. Besides, you have to know that I see him as more brother than husband. Surely you can see why I wouldn't want to marry him." *And Markhim. I want to marry Markhim.* Jura knew she didn't have much of a chance of convincing her father to allow her to marry outside of the Thirteen, but she at least wanted the chance to convince him to consider it.

Amira stiffened. "No, actually I don't. He's the son of the Third house. He's from a good family. He's a strong and capable young man."

Father would agree. Jura stiffened. *But father isn't here.* She tried to smile reassuringly, "I'm sure he'll make someone an excellent husband someday. There's someone--"

Amira forced out a laugh. "Right. Someone. Just not you." She shook her head. "I thought you thought of us as sisters. I thought this would make you happy. Do you think you're too good for him? Too good for my family?"

"What? No! Amira, where is this coming from?" She placed a gentle hand on her friend's arm. "I'm sure if you stopped and thought about it you would realize how absurd a marriage between your brother and me is."

Amira jerked her arm away. "Right, because marrying into my family is so crazy. I was wrong about you, Jura." She spun on her heel and hurried out of the room, her *Arbe* close behind.

Jura watched her friend go, unsure if she should run after her. She took a step toward her friend's departing figure and was stopped short by Beshar's large frame. The councilman belonged to the house of the Tenth and was the lowest of the members allowed to vote for Rank among the Thirteen. She suppressed a sigh and nodded in greeting.

"Beshar," she mumbled. Born into the house of the First, Jura was allowed to call any council member by their first name. The honorific Councilman was only used when Jura was trying to be polite.

He squinted at her. "Daughter of the First. Well, you look simply ravishing." He bowed low and wriggled his thumbs. Jura was impressed he was able to move his large frame about so gracefully.

"Thank you, Councilman."

"It's excellent for you to join us today. Trying your hand at politics, are you?" He looked at her thoughtfully. "Your father would be proud."

"The First is proud," Jura answered, carefully forming the words. "He is pleased he has an heir that will see to his Rank while he is indisposed."

"Ah, yes, his illness is improving I pray?"

"Better every day." Jura turned up the corners of her mouth.

"Thank the Everflame." Beshar nodded, leaning against an ornamental cane and wiping his brow with his customary perfumed handkerchief. Jura held her breath until he put it away.

He released a heavy breath. "I notice I never see your family at the arena."

Jura resisted the urge to wrinkle her nose. She hated the bloodshed of the arena and what it represented and made a point to stay far away from there. She had made up her mind after her first and only visit to the arena back when she was a child. Her father had attended a few shows but only for political reasons, and he'd never forced her to attend.

"Nothing better than the rush of excitement, the roar from the crowd, the heat of the dragon, and the feeling of exhilaration as you brush against death."

"I wasn't aware you were a gladiator," Jura said smartly. She immediately wished she hadn't. Rudeness would get her nowhere.

Beshar laughed it off. "I'm not a gladiator by any means, but I have men from my house who fight and I breed a line of dragons for the games. There's a thrill that comes from involvement, gladiator or not. I'd like to invite you to watch tomorrow's games with me in the spectator box."

Jura thought carefully. Beshar was making a risk by inviting her. She was unmarried and acting council member of the First house. Though her position was weak, she was the interim head of council. Beshar was making a play at gaining Rank. She couldn't blame him. It was a low risk involvement. As Tenth in the Thirteen he could gain high reward if her house remained strong in the upcoming weeks.

What would father do? Jura bit her bottom lip. Her father would never be in this situation. Her father was dominant and all powerful. If he was here now, the Rank of the First wouldn't be in question. Even if she did accept an alliance with the Third, and she certainly wouldn't agree to one through terms of marriage to a fifteen-year-old boy, this outing with Beshar could prove beneficial.

"I'd love to attend," she answered with a gracious smile. She really hoped she didn't have greens in her teeth.

Beshar's round face lit up. "That's excellent. I'll send for you tomorrow afternoon." He bowed low and hurried away as though to run off before she changed her mind.

Jura let loose a pent-up sigh. She felt that she'd made the right decision. Next, she had to talk to the Third and cement arrangements with him while politely declining any offers of a betrothal. Then she needed to find Amira. She walked back toward where she'd left the Third but instead found him off in the corner in deep conversation with the Second. Ahmar's back was to her, but she could see the intensity in Velder's eyes. She slowed her approach.

Ahmar noticed her before she could make out what they were saying and waved her over. Both of them gestured their fingers politely, and Velder excused himself, hurrying from the room. Jura frowned after him.

"He seemed upset," Jura noted. Velder couldn't be trusted, and she didn't care for the scheming look in his eyes.

Ahmar lifted one shoulder. "He's received distressing news. I've told him I'm proposing an alliance with your house."

Jura relaxed. "Of course. He wouldn't like that."

Ahmar nodded. "I've already gained some ground within the council. Such an alliance would guarantee at least three votes in my favor when it's time for the vote."

Jura hid her surprise. "You wish to move up in Rank." It wasn't a question. She should have known Ahmar's end game was to move into the Second position.

Ahmar smiled. "Naturally. I trust Amira has let slip my intentions, and that's why you have sought me out?" He looked around. "Where is my daughter?"

Jura frowned. "That's why I had to seek you out." She swallowed. "I think an alliance would benefit both our families, but I cannot accept your terms. I can't agree to a betrothal with your son."

Ahmar nodded, considering. "You love another?"

"No." *Yes.* Jura turned the corners of lips upward in a forced smile.

"No," she repeated. "Nothing like that. I just, well, I would like to think that a marriage for love is still possible. Father has not expressed any desire that I commit to a spouse and especially not one so youthful and, um... inexperienced."

Understanding dawned in his eyes. "You see Antar as a child."

Jura blushed. "I'm sure that he would make an excellent husband, but I—"

"You need explain no further." Ahmar smiled down at her gently. "Might I propose an alliance without the strings of a betrothal?"

Jura sighed in relief. "I would like nothing better."

Things were looking better for her family already.

FOURTEEN
JURA

"There are a few ways* to get rid of a member of the Thirteen. Their family name can be disgraced, causing them to be voted out, or they can be injured to the point they can no longer serve," she stared at Jura pointedly. "Or death."

Jura couldn't help but shiver at Amira's cold smile. "We're not hurting anyone."

Amira's brown eyes widened. "Of course not." She shook her head. "But accidents happen, and a person's *Arbe* can't always be accounted for." She winked. For once, her eyes were unlined with khol. In fact, Amira wore no makeup at all. It was strange and the first thing Jura had noticed upon her arrival. When she'd asked Amira about it, she'd seemed confused and embarrassed, so Jura let the matter drop, eager for their friendship to regain a sense of normalcy.

The girls had made up earlier that morning when Amira had invited

Jura for breakfast. She'd accepted the invitation eagerly, ready to put the fight behind them. She hated when she and Amira were on the outs, which seemed to be more and more often. She had finalized an alliance with the Third during their meal, and the two girls were sitting on Amira's bed discussing strategy.

Ahmar insisted that he had the situation in control and had urged the girls to go off and do whatever it was that girls like to do. Ahmar had trouble grasping a knowledge of anything outside of politics.

The girls sat on Amira's plush bedspread and discussed the various ways the Third would take down the Second. Jura fingered the intricate gold threading while she searched for something to say. *They weren't planning a murder, were they?*

"I think your father makes Velder appear dishonest in front of the council." Jura thought this seemed most logical. As Second of the Thirteen, Velder was nearly as important as the First, and he was expected to live in a way that upheld the moral and ethical codes valued by her countrymen. Preservation of water, honesty and honor, bravery, selflessness, and faithfulness to the Everflame were the most esteemed values held sacred by her people. Unfortunately, as much as Velder made her skin crawl, he was an upstanding councilman who did his job completely.

Amira shrugged. "He is the last of his house. A quick death would be the simplest. A little poison in his wine..."

Jura hit her friend lightly on the shoulder. "You're terrible."

"I'm serious. Poison in one's wine is the easiest way. It's what I would do." Amira giggled but the laughter didn't reach her eyes.

Amira is joking. She has to be. Jura forced a laugh before changing the subject.

"I'm going to the arena this evening."

"What? And you're just now telling me? Are we using your box?"

Jura's attention remained focused on the ornate pattern of Amira's bedspread. "I didn't know my family even had a private box, but I was invited into the spectators box by Beshar."

Amira wrinkled her dainty nose and snorted. "Eww, that roly poly excuse for a councilman? Why?"

"He invited me." Jura bit her bottom lip. "I thought it was a good political move."

Amira's eyes bugged. "In what way? So that everyone would be wondering *why* you were at the games with the Tenth? He's barely a voting councilman." She let out a groan. "You're hopeless. All right, I'll go with you to the arena."

"Oh, no," she shook her head. "That's not what I meant. I can go by myself. In fact, I have to."

Amira narrowed her eyes. "Are you going on a date? You'd tell me, right? Just because you're not marrying into my family doesn't mean that you have to woo the affections of the Tenth."

"No, I'm not trying to woo anyone." She frowned at the bed sheets. "Except maybe Markhim."

"Markhim? The Light Guard?"

Sandstorms. Did I say that out loud?

"Umm, yes. Markhim. But, we're just friends."

Amira stared at her blandly. "Right, just friends. Just a crush. I remember now." She said with a flippant toss of her hand.

"You do?" Jura wrinkled her brow in confusion. She would rather die of thirst than succumb to the embarrassment of willingly admitting her feelings for Markhim. She certainly had never mentioned them before to Amira.

"Of course I remember. We're best friends, right? And best friends tell each other everything." Amira smiled. "I know I tell you everything."

"Yes. Of course." *Surely I must have said something to her and then simply forgotten? That's possible, right?* She pushed the questions out of her thoughts. "In any case, Beshar is not a date."

"Right. It's not a date." Amira squinted down at her in confusion.

Jura rolled her eyes. "It's not a date," she repeated. "I was just going to meet with him. Privately." *Why had this conversation turned so awkward?*

Amira continued to squint at her friend. Finally, she smiled and stood up. "Well, you better head home and figure out what you'll wear." She lifted her brow. "Be sure to stick to jewel tones or else you'll looked washed out."

Jura forced herself to take a deep breath and smiled. "Thanks for the advice. You're always looking out for me."

Amira cocked her head to the side and smiled sweetly. "Of course, Greatness," she winked.

Amira used the appropriate honorific for addressing Jura, but it didn't sound like she meant for it to inflect any honor. *What was with all of Amira's sudden mood changes? And why does she seem mad at me? Again? Does she know I'm hiding something from her?*

Jura waved a farewell and left for her rooms. It wasn't fair that she had to deal with everyone's judgments and plotting. She shouldn't have to hear mockery from her friend as well. She was doing the best she could. She wanted to make her father proud. She strode to her rooms, her *Arbe* squared off around her, keeping step.

Their harmonized movements gave her pause. They always seemed to know exactly when to appear and they were always perfectly synchronized. She knew that *Arbe* were once slave boys in training. That they had once had tongues and friendly conversation. The boys picked for *Arbe* training were the most agile, the tallest, the strongest of their age. *Arbe* trainers appeared after a boy's tenth birthday. They always scouted out the ones they wanted. It was an honor for those chosen. Shortly after the boy's birthday, he was taken from his home and brought to the Everflame before enduring a ten-year training process that included removing one's own tongue on the final day of their tenth year. Then, they are formed into *Arbe* and sold to the elite.

When she reached her door the two men in the rear of her *Arbe* swept into her room to look over it thoroughly while the first two remained at the door. *How had they known who would sweep the room and who would stay at the door? Had that all been defined during their training?* Jura marveled at the realization that there was more than just a physical transformation. Her *Arbe* must have gone through rigorous mental training as well.

The two searching her room were satisfied and left to guard outside in the hall. She noticed they pulled back her covers and checked under her bed. They left without needing to be dismissed. She wondered if anyone else had ever taken the time to study the nuances of their *Arbe*? Or did the majority just view their *Arbe* as a fixture of palace life, the *Arbe* nothing more than silent giants that followed them around to do their bidding? She really needed to search the library again. Maybe she'd missed a book.

…She shook her head in frustration. No, she could not afford to go on a tangent now, she had to stay focused. In just two short days the council would meet again. If her father did not attend, the Thirteen would wonder at the capability of her house to stay in control. Their Rank would be called into question, and it was doubtful they would allow Jura to continue to head council.

She checked on the First, giving him water and staring woefully at the tiny gold chain around his wrist. It was impossibly tiny and yet extremely powerful. She'd tried to remove it that first day. She'd pulled at the clasp with all her might and, sobbing, had commanded the members of her *Arbe* to try. When even the large scimitars of her *Arbe* failed to make a cut, she knew it was the fault of the chain's magic. Without knowing who had put it on him, she had little chance of having it removed. She felt infinite pity for him. The once proud man now shriveled in her cellar chained twice over, by his captor and by his own daughter. He said nothing, just stared off at the distance, waiting for his freedom.

She closed the cellar door slowly, wishing more than anything that she had discovered who had done this to her house. It had to be one of the Thirteen. Who else would have even known of the existence of the blood chain? An old house? One that possibly had records in their own library. She wished the Shadow Dancers had been more help. She hadn't heard a word from them in all these days, and so she was no closer to exchanging information with them. Not that she had any information to exchange.

She rang for a handmaiden and one shortly appeared. The woman was employed by the palace and thus didn't belong to just one house. Though it wasn't uncommon for young ladies to employ their own. Amira had three. Jura had never felt the need for any of her own. She hardly ever needed their services, as they were used only to draw baths and arrange outfits and hair. But Jura wanted to look memorable tonight. Not because she was going to the arena with Beshar, but because she had said as much in front of Amira and her handmaidens. By now, everyone in the palace would know of Jura and Beshar's outing. Amira's handmaidens, like Amira herself, were notorious gossipers. Jura had to appear strong and capable, like a woman in charge, not a scared little girl.

She did choose robes that were jewel tones. The emerald green flashed against her dark hair which hung in a fat braid down her back. As usual, her birthstone was tucked beneath her robe and hung low between her breasts. She gave Tylak a passing thought but quickly pushed him out of her mind. She had enough on her plate without adding the stress of the former slave and his missing birthstone. She focused on her appearance in the mirror and decided to select jewelry to complement the robes. She chose green earrings, emeralds the size of her thumb, and she giggled as their weight settled on her ears. She doubted she'd be able to keep them on for the entire night before she yanked them off. Still, they were very pretty, and they had been her mother's. The handmaiden, Sirikka, chattered easily and exclaimed in delight when Jura put on the earrings.

"You look beautiful, Greatness. You truly look like the Lady of the First."

Jura grinned and blushed at the simpering maid. "Thank you." It felt good to be fawned over, even if it was just by the palace handmaiden.

A knock sounded on her chamber door.

Curious, Jura swung the door wide, knowing that her *Arbe* would never let anyone through who might mean her harm. She got a chastising look from one of them. She decided she would name them, based on their positions around her: North, South, East, and West. They were unable to tell her their true names, but if they were going to hover around her she had to call them something. She smiled back at East, but his disapproving look was gone.

Amira stood in her doorway, looking beautiful in a pale silk dress that clung to her figure and a large white silk scarf that covered barely enough for Jura to consider it an effort to be modest.

"Jura, you look amazing! Truly, I've never seen you look more beautiful. I didn't even know your ears were pierced."

Though Jura had refused to wear a dress, the emerald green robes and silk pants folded around her skin and showed off her features nicely. Jura smiled and touched a hand to her ears.

"They've always been pierced. Mother did it for me when I was baby. These were hers."

Amira's face softened. She had lost her own mother at a young age and it was something the girls had bonded over. "I brought you this." She forced a slender box into Jura's hands.

Inside the box were a pair of gold filigree spectacles. Instead of perching over her nose, the spectacles were meant to be held in place with a thin gold wand. Jura held the lorgnette up to her face and gasped in delight. They were like little binoculars.

"They're beautiful."

Amira smiled and tossed back her thick braid. "I thought you'd like them. I smuggled them back from Kitoi."

That would explain the excellent workmanship of the gold. Jura tried to keep her face impassive as she examined the contraband. Though the country was under the Tri-Alliance, trade between Kitoi and the Republic was technically illegal without any permits. She doubted that Amira had gone through the trouble of obtaining a permit for the elaborate gift.

She must have done a poor job of hiding her reaction because Amira made a face. "Don't worry. No one is going to notice. It's a lorgnette, not a weapon of mass destruction. Besides, you need something nice to wear at the arena. And at court." She hugged Jura, gripping her shoulders tight. "You're my best friend and I really am proud of you. I wanted to apologize. I guess I've been a little jealous lately."

"Jealous?" Jura was shocked. "Of me? Whatever for?"

"Well, you're the daughter of the First. And you're so smart and interesting. And last week you voted in council. I would never be allowed to do that." She let out a deep breath, puffing out her round cheeks. "But I shouldn't have let jealousy cloud our friendship. I'm sorry."

Jura hugged her back. "Thank you, Amira."

Amira laughed and gently pushed her friend away. "You better go. Beshar sent a palanquin for you."

"No."

"Truly. It's just outside. Oh, and I have one more gift for you."

Jura raised her eyebrow, amused by the mischievous spark in her friend's eyes.

"I spoke with your guard and told him all about your little crush. So now you don't have to keep it a secret anymore." Amira's smile widened. "After all, what are friends for?"

FIFTEEN
JURA

When Jura was eight, she climbed to the top of the weapon scaffold despite the protest of Akkim. He'd been there to mend her sprained ankle after, but she would never forget the sensation of falling. She felt that same sensation now. Surely Amira hadn't just said what she thought she said.

"You told him?"

Amira nodded enthusiastically. "Mmm, yes, and I told him if he wants to keep you from dating disgusting old men, he needs to make a stand for you. Oh, here he is now." She winked at Jura. "I'll leave you two alone." Amira turned and left, her shoulders shaking with laughter.

I'll strangle her. Jura squeezed her hands together and took a deep breath before turning to meet Markhim's dancing brown eyes.

"Hello."

"Is that all I get? You send your insipid friend to embarrass me in front of all the Light Guards and all you have to say is hello?"

"I'm sorry?"

He laughed. "Well, that's a start, at least."

Her shoulders slumped in relief. She hadn't realized how tense they had been until that moment. "So, you're not angry with me?"

"No, I'm not angry. A bit confused maybe. I thought we agreed we weren't going to tell anyone about us?"

"But there is an us?"

Markhim stepped forward to take her hand but stopped when he noticed the Seventh and his entourage through the thin glass of the adjoining hall. The Seventh nodded to Jura as he passed. "Of course there is an us. So long as you're not truly trying to woo any old men?"

"No." Jura laughed. "Definitely not. I was hoping I could get some information though. You know, the sort I can use to bargain with."

"Well, be careful. There's rumors surrounding the Tenth. He has the potential to be dangerous."

Jura rolled her eyes. "You think everyone has the potential to be dangerous." She lowered her voice to mock his rich baritone.

"I'm serious. The man is very secretive."

"He's a member of the Thirteen. We're all secretive." Her face softened. "You know I have to do this. Not only for my father but for me. The Shadow Dancers know things. They have access to magic I've only dreamed of. I have to believe they can give me the information I've been searching for. But I promise to be careful. I brought my book on espionage just to be safe."

"This isn't the time to make jokes. Be careful. Promise me."

"I promise."

Markhim nodded, satisfied. "I better get back to my post. There's rumors of an escape from the dungeons. It won't be long until whispers trinkle up through the Thirteen and there's an inquiry."

"Maybe we can find a way to stage his death?" Burn it all, that man was still giving her trouble.

"If I find him back in these glass walls, his death won't need to be staged."

His eyes twinkled, but his voice was laced with a level of venom she'd never heard from him before.

"Your post," she murmured, catching her bottom lip between her teeth.

"The Everflame isn't going to guard itself," Markhim agreed. "Can I see you later?"

Jura nodded. "After I return from the Arena. Meet me in our spot at midnight."

"I can't wait." Markhim smiled and dipped into a low bow before walking briskly down the hall and back to his post.

Now late, Jura tried to keep her running to a lady-like trot as she hurried outside. Beshar really had sent a palanquin, and it sat outside the palace gates with her house's colors and emblem emblazoned on the side, the golden sun shining stark against a purple background. She raised an eyebrow at the richness. *What game was he playing? Had he truly had a palanquin created for her alone?* The litter was carted by eight oiled men. They bowed deeply in nod to her stature. Overwhelmed by the fuss made over her, she entered the vehicle quickly, grateful for the privacy the enclosed box afforded. She called for her *Arbe* to follow, but they had already positioned themselves in their customary square around her. She leaned back against the plush pillows of the litter and enjoyed her trip.

They were slow going, but the steady pace of the men beneath her was soothing and Jura found it easy to close her eyes and let her thoughts drift. She practiced the things she would say when she was approached by members of the council. She would give each a gracious greeting and say, of course she loved the arena (they didn't have to know that was a lie). Then she would ask if they have a man or a beast in the fight. And she would listen. Perhaps this trip to the arena would finally afford her with some knowledge to give the Shadow Dancers. If nothing else, it was sure to help with her political standing.

Lafer's *Politics of the Sand Sea: Tales of Arena and War* suggested that the best way to gain a strong political foothold was to gain the respect of the council, both inside and outside of meetings. That meant attending social functions. And there was nothing more social than the arena. She'd gone once before. Her mother had been alive then, and the family had sat in the public spectator box with the other members of court. Jura hadn't cared for the noise or the bloodshed. She had stayed closed to her mother who had soothed Jura by playing with her hair and entertaining her with fairy tales. She told Jura stories of far off lands and adventures of the brave. Everyone had loved her mother. She greeted everyone by name and responded graciously to every conversation.

Jura missed her mother desperately. If Jaydra was still alive, her family wouldn't be in this mess. She had thrived in society, and people had never called her awkward or shy. Her mother would have known what to do to fix her father. At the very least she would have been capable of maintaining the family's Rank while a solution was found.

I will make them proud, mother and father both. She had only two days, but there was still hope. Jura prayed that by attending the arena today, she would be able to discover a clue about her father. It was one of her last chances, and she was running out of ideas.

The palanquin jostled as if one of the carriers had lost a step. She opened her eyes to find herself staring into the dark eyes of a Shadow Dancer.

SIXTEEN

JURA

*S**he would have screamed but** a gloved hand quickly clamped over her mouth. Jura's eyes widened, and she struggled under the weight of the Shadow Dancer.

Her assailant was larger than Jura, though that wasn't saying much compared to Jura's small frame. Jura suspected she was a woman, because her attacker had remarkably slender wrists. The Shadow Dancer was dressed entirely in black. A loose tunic fit over tight black pants that came to a stop before shiny black boots. Jura's eyes widened when she noticed the long dagger peeking out the top of one boot.

"Don't scream and I'll remove my hand, agreed?"

The woman's voice had a high registry, but her tone was an authoritative growl. Jura nodded.

"How did you get in here?" she asked, wiping her mouth after the woman removed her hand.

The woman's face was entirely covered by a silky black mask. Only her thin lips and chin were visible, and those lips curved up in a smile.

"How does smoke drift in the wind?"

Cryptic. Jura rolled her eyes. The Dancer fell back against the pillows opposite Jura and leaned against the litter wall, staring at her. By her estimation, they had less than ten minutes before they arrived at the arena. Jura intended to make those minutes count. She searched for something to say to break the silence. She needed answers.

"I thought he would send for me sooner."

"You were asked to retrieve information."

"I have," Jura protested.

The woman giggled, and Jura wondered if her assailant was little more than a girl. And sure, maybe she didn't have much information but she had something.

"Geedar and his wife are expecting a baby. There is now a solid heir in foundation for the House of the Sixth. And the Third and I have agreed to the terms of an alliance. We plan to announce it tomorrow evening."

The Dancer snorted. "That's it? In nearly a week's time that is all the information you've been able to gather?"

"Those facts are not yet public knowledge," Jura stammered.

"Nor are they secrets. You were tasked to provide us with information and you've failed."

"N-no," Jura begged, tripping over her words. "Please, I'll get more. I'll be at the arena tonight. Surely I'll learn something new. Please, give me another chance."

The woman held up a hand. "Stop begging. We suspected as much from you. That is why I'm here," the Dancer leaned forward, "to give you some direction. You actually did something good. You're attending the arena tonight with Beshar as your escort. Seduce him."

Jura's eyebrow's shot up. "Excuse me?"

The woman leaned back again, crossing her long, slim legs at the ankle. "You're young and beautiful, and Beshar is an unmarried man. He has needs. Fulfill them."

"But—that is, I—"

The woman let out a sigh. "You're hardly a master at dissemble. You're much too naive. But pillow talk…" She smiled again. "You'd be amazed at what a woman can find out in her lover's bed."

Jura felt the blood rush to her cheeks. "I can't." *Definitely can't.*

"You can and you will. Beshar has many assets, and we want to know more. He knows something that gives him power over the Thirteen. A secret. We need to find out what it is. Find out and we'll help you save your father."

Jura bit her bottom lip and clasped her hands together to keep them from trembling. "We only have two days before the next council meeting."

The litter came to a stop.

"Then you better hurry."

Jura heard the voice, but the woman was gone as quickly as she'd come. Jura frowned. *How did they do that?* The curtains opened, and Jura was assisted down from the litter. Her *Arbe* closed rank around her. *Had they really not seen the Shadow Dancer come and go?* She studied their faces, but they all had the same blank look. Was it her imagination or did North look a bit distracted? She squinted up at him but saw nothing in his eyes that gave anything away. She sighed and allowed herself to be escorted away by

Beshar's footmen; her *Arbe* in tight formation around her.

She had forgotten how large the arena was. She stared up at it in wonder, marveling at the tall walls and rounded dome top that were made entirely out of glass. She never had reason to leave the palace, much less travel across the capital city to watch bloodsport. The arena dome, originally commissioned by Josper, was impressive and second only to the palace itself. Jutting up into the sky, the sun reflected off of the glass and sent prisms of light in every direction, the dome appeared to sparkle and glow. Jura's breath caught in her throat.

"Beautiful, isn't it?"

She hadn't heard him approach, and Jura flinched, startled by his touch.

Beshar immediately dropped his hand from where he'd placed it at the small of her back.

Seduce him. She stared at Beshar's enormous figure, at the beads of sweat that rolled down his pale round face. She swallowed.

"Councilman, thank you for your invitation and the use of your litter." She inclined her head politely. "You're too kind."

"Happy to do so, Greatness," he held out an arm. "May I?"
She gingerly placed her fingers around his. His sleeve was slightly damp and she wondered if he was sweating through his robes. *Don't think about that*, she ordered herself. She concentrated on her father.

"Thank you, Councilman."

"Beshar, please. You look ravishing." He smiled at her, flashing tiny yellowed teeth and looking directly into her eyes. *Seduction. Right. You can do this, Jura.*

"Well then, please, call me Jura." She squeezed his arm.

Beshar's eyes widened. "You honor me," he stared down at her hand. "Shall we go inside?" He swooped out his other arm in a grand gesture.

Beshar led her through the imposing doors to the arena and through a glass hallway behind a gate that held its own *Arbe*. The men waved them through. At the end of the hallway was a single door. When Beshar pushed it open, Jura was pleasantly surprised by the rush of cool air. He led her to a plush seat and she sat down, accepting a baked tart from a slave.

She placed the tart in her mouth, tasting the dried apricot and honey as the sweet textures rolled on her tongue. "It's much..." Jura stammered. She smiled without showing her teeth, bits of tart stuck to them. "Much more refined than I thought it would be."

Beshar nodded. "It's the only way to watch the fight." He waved out at the arena that was already full of screaming citizens and shuddered delicately. "I don't know how they do it."

Jura held her lorgnette up to her face. She felt a prick of pain and frowned down at her finger. A tiny piece of the gold wiring had bent back and pierced her finger causing a tiny drop of blood to appear. *Poison?* She'd heard any number of stories in which poison was administered through a tiny prick on the hand. *No, it's a gift from Amira.* She shoved the wild fear out of her mind before it grew any strength. Politics of the Thirteen were a breeding ground for paranoia. *Still, someone did put a snake in my bed...*

She pushed the wiring back down and popped her finger in her mouth before peering out at the crowd. They seemed crazed with excitement. She forced her thoughts back to her conversation with Beshar. "I suppose I've never known what all the fuss was about it?"

Beshar frowned at her. "Don't know what's the fuss? The Fire Dancer and his battle with the dragon is a time-honored tradition. There is no more noble sport on this planet."

Jura was quick to place a hand on his shoulder. "Perhaps I just don't understand it." She squeezed her fingers lightly. "I need someone to teach me." She hoped she hadn't upset him. She bit her bottom lip in frustration, and Beshar smiled.

"I'd be delighted to teach you." He leaned toward her. "Jura, I must say this blossoming friendship is a welcome surprise."

Jura swallowed and tried not to blush.

"I'm full of surprises," she heard herself saying. *I'm possessed by desperation.*

Beshar's smile widened. "I bet you are. Look, it's the Third."

Ahmar entered with Amira on his arm and Antar on his left. His house was announced and they swept into the box, their *Arbe* close behind. The men looked serious and thoughtful. Amira looked beautiful and sweet. Her braid was twisted around the crown of her head and she wore very little makeup, her eyes only slightly lined with khol and her lips a soft pink. She sent a wink in Jura's direction before seating herself in the back. She snapped her fingers for the attention of a slave carrying a large fan.

Beshar nudged her elbow. "You know Geedar of course," he leaned closer.

"His wife is expecting." Jura nodded.

Beshar's grin widened, "Then you know the baby isn't his?"

"Isn't his?" she stammered. "Then, who is the father?" *Beshar's more of a gossip than Amira.*

Geedar walked over stiffly from across the room and stepped in front of Beshar. He stared down with hatred in his eyes before he reached in his pocket and threw out a small pouch. The pouch landed on Beshar's lap.

Geedar spun on his heel and walked back to his wife. The two sat close together but not touching, and whispered in the back row.

Beshar opened the pouch and smiled down at the water chips inside.

"To me, all that matters is who isn't the father." He handed the pouch to one of his attendants. Jura noticed that all of his slaves still had their tongues. The men who followed the Tenth looked strong and capable, men trained to fight, born warriors. His men looked everything like members of an *Arbe,* and yet every man still had his tongue. Their muscles also appeared to be slathered in some sort of oil that also distinguished them from the other *Arbe. What's the purpose of all that oil? And why was Beshar comfortable enough with men who still had their tongue? What did it mean? Maybe Markhim was right?* She was quickly learning there was much more to Beshar than she'd originally thought.

"Greatness, it is an honor." The voice came from a small, thin man with stooped shoulders and a droopy beard. He bowed low in front of Jura.

She smiled, "Greetings, Zer…"

"Zair of the Thirteenth house." Beshar chimed heartily, thumping the thin man on the back.

The man smiled weakly.

"Please, sit with us." Jura gestured to the seat across from her, and Zair sat slowly, his eyes darting from side to side.

Beshar's raised a single eyebrow at her but said nothing.

"This is my first time to the arena since I was a little girl. Do you have any pointers for me?" Jura smiled at him warmly. *Why does he look so tense?*

"When the bell sounds, get ready for the fight to start. And be ready for the fire. A lot of people are startled when they first see it."

"That's excellent advice. When did your family join the Thirteen?" Jura found name lineage to be the most tedious of studies and could scarcely keep up with the current Thirteen, as in the case with Zair.

Instead of immediately answering the question, Zair sent a sidelong glance at Beshar. The look was exaggerated, his eyebrows raised in inflection.

"Go ahead. Tell her." Beshar nodded.

"I noticed that the house of the Al' Kemar family held only a widow and her heir only a four-year-old boy. I demanded trial by combat, and I won."

Jura stared at him. It was rarely done, but an eligible outsider could claim membership by challenging the Thirteenth. If challenged, it was then up to the strongest to survive. Similarly, a member of the Thirteen could challenge another for his rank, though again, it was rarely done, a tradition that hadn't been practiced with any regularity since the days of her grandfather. Entry by murder was naturally frowned upon. But if the murder wasn't sloppy or couldn't be proven, the council members never gave it a passing thought. However, entering the Thirteen by combating a widow and a child was a political loophole that was heinous, and retribution would naturally be swift. Of course, no councilman would outright do the deed themselves. But as Amira was fond of saying, a person's *Arbe* couldn't always be accounted for. That explained Zair's uneasiness.

Beshar studied her intently so she kept her face neutral. *Why had he called Zair over? Was he truly only offering an introduction to the Thirteenth? Or was he trying to remind her that people were willing to do anything to become one of the Thirteen? It had to be some kind of test.*

Jura smiled. "Welcome to the council."

Beshar seemed to know everyone. He leaned into Jura and gestured to a woman who sat on the bench two rows behind them. She was cloaked in lovely shades of red and gold and four men squared off around her.

"That's Denir, the Fifth," Jura whispered. *Why had she started whispering?* "She's very elusive."

"She's smart. She doesn't interfere. She just watches."

"Isn't that why we have our *Arbe*? To stand watch?" Jura asked.

Beshar shook his head. "Brainwashed strangers standing guard? No, you need to watch."

Jura frowned at him, wondering what he meant. *I'm missing something.* Zair had excused himself at least a quarter of an hour ago and he had yet to return. *I shouldn't feel bad*, Jura reminded herself. He had killed a woman and her child, but still she wondered where he'd gone. By this time, she had greeted everyone in attendance, everyone except for the house of the Third. Perhaps she should have greeted the Third. She said as much to Beshar.

Beshar shook his head. "You're the daughter of the house of the First. It's he that should come to you."

He was right, but only in the most literal form. Jura had grown up with this man as an elder, and she an obedient child. She had not been acting as First long enough to realize she held absolute Rank. She wanted to ignore his warnings, but instead she resisted the urge to look back at her friend and her father. Beshar seemed to know what he was talking about, and she wanted to appear strong in front of the Thirteen. She pretended not to notice when Amira waved her over.

Beshar nodded his approval. She knew Amira would be furious, but Beshar was right. She was the interim First and if she wanted to remain in power she had to hold onto it. *Show no weakness*, she thought to herself. He was telling her to keep an eye out because no one had her back. Some wouldn't stop until they found blood.

She only had two days.

She held court in their seats. The servants lingered to take care of the majority of the crowd, which circled around Jura. Some said they simply wanted to formally meet her, claiming they'd met once before when she was still a child. Others acted like they were meeting her for the first time, no matter the fact that she had just spoke at council meeting the week before.

A giant of a man approached. Though he showed signs of aging, his bare arms were still corded with muscle. Jura blushed.

"Ash, what an honor. I didn't think to see you in the observation deck so soon." Beshar smiled at the man, but Jura noticed that the smile didn't quite reach his eyes.

"Greatness, this is Ash Flame Dancer. He was a legend." Beshar introduced her to the man.

The giant flinched and sank to his knees. "My apologies, Greatness. I didn't realize."

Jura's heart went out to him. "How could you? Please, rise. If you are a legend, then I suppose it's my honor to meet you." She grinned at him.

Beshar smiled as he helped the man up. "I don't think her Greatness would mind if you sat with us. She has a habit of inviting people." He cast a look over at her and wiped at his brow.

Ash took the seat where Zair had sat across from them and leaned toward Beshar.

"Who do you have in the match tonight?"

Beshar looked over at Jura before smiling. "A Dancer in the opening fight. A dragon in the main."

"I'll get to cheer for both sides." Jura batted her eyelashes. At least she thought she did. Ash gave her a funny look, and Beshar didn't seem to notice.

The preliminary horns sounded, and Jura found herself smiling in anticipation of the fight. *This could be fun. So long as things didn't get too bloody.* She leaned forward in her seat.

"I had something I'd like to talk to you about, Councilman." Ash seemed to stumble over the words and his voice was soft as he said them.

Beshar looked distracted. "Not now, Ash. The fights are about to start." There was a hungry look in the Tenth's eyes, and Jura felt swept up with anxious butterflies.

Ash looked disappointed, but turned his attention to the fights. The horns sounded again and two Fire Dancers walked into the arena. They seemed to suddenly appear in front of her. Jura realized they must have walked in from a room directly underneath the observation box. The Dancers strutted around the ring, twirling and flipping across the dirt. Their agility and athleticism was a thing of beauty. She leaned forward in her seat and squinted into her lorgnette.

"Well, don't you look fancy," said an all too familiar voice.

Tylak had returned.

Jura stiffened and slowly leaned back in her seat. Everyone was cheering. Beshar didn't seem to notice the man who had seated himself behind her. But then again, neither had her *Arbe* stopped him. They must be distracted by the show. She'd have to remember to talk with them.

"What are *you* doing here?"

"I've come to collect." Tylak's voice was low and fierce.

"I don't have it."

He hit the back of her chair. "Wrong answer."

"You disappeared. This isn't entirely my fault. In fact, you left me unescorted to travel the city in the dead of the night. I could have been killed. I said I would help you get it. I promised, and I keep my promises." She kept her head forward, careful not to reveal anything in her face.

"I've had promises from your kind before," he grumbled.

What did that mean? Jura wondered over his words. She hadn't broken a promise to him. Well, not yet technically. *Did he mean that he'd had promises broken by a woman? By a member of the Thirteen?*

Beshar still hadn't noticed.

"We can meet later and I'll help you," she blushed. I'm in the middle of something right now."

She couldn't see his face, but his silence seemed to mean he was considering it. She felt him stand behind her.

"I'll find you another time."

He walked away and Jura relaxed. She'd been foolish to believe that just because Tylak had been out of sight he was gone for good. She would have to make good on her promise. Somehow. She pushed the thought out of her mind and focused on the present, reaching for Beshar's arm.

SEVENTEEN

TYLAK

Tylak *walked away but he* didn't leave. He went to the back of the room and stood against the wall, frowning down at his borrowed clothing. He'd taken the precaution of stealing some garb from the servant's quarters on his way into the arena, in case his invisibility slipped. He got more than one disapproving look from a servant, but no society person gave him a second glance.

He watched Jura's shoulders soften as she relaxed with the knowledge that he'd gone. *I really make her nervous*, he thought with a small smile. Not that he cared. She was a member of the Thirteen, daughter of the First no less. And anyone from the Thirteen was bad news. He watched as Jura reached for Beshar's arm and frowned when she smiled up at him. *What was her game?* She was nice looking enough, and young. If he didn't already know how annoying she was, he might give her a second glance. *Burn it all, most anyone would. So why was she flirting with the older, much larger councilman?*

She'd said she'd been in the middle of something. Did she mean her date or was there more to their outing than met the eye? What did Beshar have that she wanted? Did he have his birthstone? He watched the couple for a bit longer, trying to decide. She was definitely flirting with him. It was disgusting. Batting her eyelashes, tossing her braid. She wasn't even doing it right. He couldn't take his eyes of her. She was constantly squinting into that fancy eyeglass thing and occasionally her peal of laughter could be heard above the crowd.

"That's it. I'm going down there, tell her what I think of her behavior." The petulant voice carried up to him, and he turned toward the sound.

"You'll do no such thing. She's lowered herself by sitting among them, and she's already aligned herself to our house. You'll stay up here where you belong."

Tylak rolled his eyes. He should have known Jura would create problems by choosing to sit where she had. She probably hadn't even noticed what she was doing. The prime seats were the ones in the back on the raised dais, just underneath the balcony of the box belonging to the First, not down in front with the lower families. Jura should have been in her family's box. Indeed, that was where Tylak had gone looking for her first. He'd found the box empty and, frowning from the balcony, he'd seen her take her seat down in the second row beside Beshar. And Ash had been there, he thought feeling a pain shoot to his gut. Seeing Ash immediately brought out the loss of his brother. Jura kept odd company. It had to be some sort of ploy. Either she was more naïve than he thought, or she was some sort of political genius. He wondered what she was plotting.

"I'm not a little girl anymore." The voice sounded familiar and Tylak cocked his head, straining to hear. It was the same voice from before.

"I'm a woman now. The woman of the house." The voice deepened with confidence, and Tylak could no longer hear over the roar of the crowd. The preliminary show was ending. The crowd was excited and their screams rang in his ears.

He hadn't been back to the arena since the day his brother was taken. He could have sneaked in, like he had tonight, any number of times throughout the last few years. He'd never allowed himself. He'd gone back to the arena that fateful day. He'd banged on the gates until a harried admissions clerk came to the door. The clerk had frowned down at Tylak's tear-streaked face as he'd begged for the return of his young brother.

The clerk had shaken his head, "Go away. Your brother's gone." He'd ordered Tylak away from the building. Four men carried him away from the gates and beat him to a pulp. He had not returned until today.

The arena was just as he remembered it. Worse here in the private sanctum of the elite upper class. *At least the food was better*, he grinned, swiping a cheese filled fig from a passing tray. But the rich were selfish, conniving people. They'd do anything, even murder, to rise in rank among the Thirteen. And they were all so entitled. They didn't even think to set any guards outside the entry to their precious private box. Anyone could enter. It was as if the Thirteen knew no one would dare. *And even if they did*, Tylak thought scornfully to himself, *who would even notice?*

"This is no longer being discussed. The order is well in hand." The voice growled above the cheering crowd. Tylak smirked. It appeared the whining brat hadn't gotten her way.

He pulled a goblet of wine from another passing tray and drank deeply. The red wine was sweet and slightly chilled. Tylak had never had chilled wine before. He wondered how such a thing was even possible. The servant frowned down at his tray but if he noticed the missing wine he chose to ignore it.

The crowd had quieted down to an expectant hush, and Tylak watched a young woman excuse herself from the top row of the platformed dais. Her dark hair was piled atop her head, and she clenched her fist as she stomped off. Tylak watched her leave and turned his attention back to Jura. She leaned into Beshar, listening intently to whatever he was saying. After a moment she replied, gesturing her arms wildly. He wondered what she was excited about and leaned forward, squinting. *She's such a flaming distraction*, he scowled. He felt someone's eyes on him, and realized Ash was staring right at him, watching him watch Jura. *Burn it all, you've lost your concentration and been spotted.*

The Fire Dancer cocked his head to the side in silent question. Tylak did the first thing that came to mind, pointing at Jura and making a rude gesture with his hands. Ash looked horrified and stood up.

Tylak swallowed. He'd meant to look harmless, not dangerous. He had to disappear, fast.

He moved toward the door, jumping at the sound of the dragon horn. The battle was about to begin. He caught sight of Ash, still standing by his seat, staring at where Tylak had just been standing. Jura said something to him and the Fire Dancer returned to his seat, speaking in low tones to both Jura and Beshar. *Was he saying something about him?*

The dragon horn sounded again and the Fire Dancers tumbled out. Tylak watched them for a moment, caught up in memories of his brother. Sykk had loved this world so much, and now he was a part of it. Tylak could only hope his brother was still alive. He refused to think about the fact that

Fire Dancers died by the dozen, that these long-lived gladiators were few and far between.

The fact that Ash had survived long enough to retire was a thing of wonder. *He's probably amassed a fortune over the years*, Tylak thought. Though not one of the Thirteen, Ash was permitted as their equal in the arena. His wealth and fame made it so. Like all Dancers, Ash had once been slave born, and now he was conversing with Jura without a care in the world. *Ash would never have to sneak into the arena as I have,* Tylak thought bitterly and turned to leave. He'd gotten what information he could. He would have to return to the palace later to meet up with Jura. Hopefully, by then she would have his birthstone. After that, Tylak would leave and never come back. He was a fool to think she'd be able to help him find his brother. It was doubtful that she'd even be able to help locate his stone. It was time to let go of Sykk, to put the Republic behind him. The dragon gates rolled open and Tylak paused to watch the dragon enter the arena.

Most dragons stepped out cautiously, testing the air with their tongue before taking flight into the dome. After tiring from their flight circles and attracted by the brightly colored dancers, the dragon would land and the fight would begin.

This dragon was not like most dragons. He burst from his pen in a streak of brilliant blue and fire, rushing out and blowing flame at the same time. Only one of the dancers had the reflexes to leap to the side in time. The other didn't even let out a scream as he was burned to a crumpled heap of ashes. The crowd gasped and cheered. The second dancer was flustered and performed an intricate series of flips and twirls in an effort to stay in motion. The dragon roared, its bellow echoed throughout the arena, deep and rumbling in a way that sent chills down Tylak's spine.

The dancer flipped to the side and pushed aside the flame that the dragon sent at it, twirling his assegai as he did so. Perhaps this Dancer would prove champion. He seemed to have all the makings of one as he pushed aside another stream of fire. Tylak watched in admiration as the Dancer twirled around the sinuous monster. The red from the flames broke out in stark contrast against the shiny blue scales of the beast. Tylak couldn't tear his eyes away from the beautiful display of twisting, flashing colors.

The Dancer twirled and leapt into the air, assegai gleaming and poised to kill. The dragon pushed from the ground, snapping its wings back in a rush of air and sending dust up in a porous cloud that filled the stadium. The Dancer jumped up above the cloud of smoke. *No,* Tylak realized, *his body is wrong.* The Dancer was thrown and the dragon rose up, catching the Dancer between his giant jaw. He shook the Dancer's limp body and dropped it to the ground as he took flight, rushing high up in the air. He circled the dome, testing its strength with jets of fire that ricocheted off the glass. The crowd went wild, screaming out the dragon's name.

It's Beshar's dragon, Tylak realized, watching Jura give a whoop of delight and Ash clap enthusiastically. Several members of the Thirteen walked down to give their congratulations. The dragon still circled the arena. It would tire itself out eventually and return to the arena floor where its trainers would try to cover him and coax him back to his pen. Covering a dragon meant getting the giant chain muzzle around his head. Most dragons were very disagreeable to this process and many spectators lingered in the stands, hoping to catch a glimpse of more bloodshed. There were six trainers in the arena, probably because the chain muzzle was so heavy and any less they would be unable to lift it within enough time.

"You're in the way," said an annoyed voice. "Again."

Tylak looked up into the questioning eyes of a food runner. Tylak's garments clearly said that he was not upper class, and the man probably wondered why he was in their spectator box.

"I was just leaving," Tylak grinned, giving one last look over at Jura and Beshar who, like everyone else in the room, had also stood to leave.

"The dragon's name?" he asked the servant.

The servant let his eyes drift up to the circling blue dragon.

"Inferno."

Tylak cast one last look at Inferno, and then hurried out of the box, eager to leave the arena and disappear into the night.

EIGHTEEN

ASH

I t seemed he'd made a mistake in coming. Beshar did not look pleased to see him. In fact, when Ash had first made his presence, the Tenth had appeared annoyed. *Was he courting the First?* Ash shifted awkwardly in his seat. Last time he'd spoken with the council member, Beshar had seemed eager to discuss Ash's past achievements, praising the memory of his previous accomplishments. Ash had hoped that attending the fights today would afford him with more opportunity to discuss his future employment in the arena. Beshar had wanted no discussion. Instead, he found himself sitting across from the Lady of the First explaining the most rudimentary rules of Fire Dancing.

Just stand up now and walk away. As much as he wished he hadn't gotten himself into the situation, he saw no quick way out of it. He was Ash, the greatest Fire Dancer of his time, and he was already out-shadowed by others. The First had never even heard of him. He narrowed his eyes down at her and tuned in to what she was saying, interrupting her, "No, the Fire Dancers don't create fire. They can only manipulate existing fire." He sighed. "We can all feel the Everflame to a various degree. It's a presence that hums inside you. Some, Fire Dancers, can actually take control of that presence, that fire, and manipulate it the way they want."

She bit her lip, "So it's like mind control."

Ash frowned, he'd never thought of it that way, but it sounded right. He nodded.

"But you can't actually make fire?"

Ash thought about Timber, his control over the element was masterful and even though Ash would never admit it, if he believed someone could be capable of making fire it would be Timber. But people couldn't create fire, it came from the Everflame. *Had Timber really made his own Fire?*

"We leave that up to the dragons," Beshar slapped his hands enthusiastically, rubbing them together. The First leaned in toward him, flashing a beautiful smile.

She was flirting with Beshar. Ash had little experience with the opposite sex outside the Dancers of the arena, but the First was definitely flirting. *Why would the First flirt with Beshar?* He pushed the question out of his mind. There was no sense in wondering over the oddities of the Thirteen.

The preliminary fight was more of an exhibition than an actual battle. Two Dancers parried and twirled, tossing a flame of fire from one to the other. To the crowd it appeared as if the fire appeared from out of nowhere. But Ash knew of the hidden torches along the ring of the arena. He shared the secret with the First, an impish grin broke out in response to the knowledge.

It was fun to watch the Dancers from the eyes of the First. She bounced in her seat, excited as a child watching for the first time. She gasped out loud and cheered enthusiastically, all the while simpering beside Beshar. He wondered what she saw in him, but once again dismissed the thought. Who was he to question the attractions of a member of the Thirteen?

The first show ended, and Ash wondered if now was the proper time for his proposal. Beshar seemed no less distracted. His handkerchief fluttered out of his pocket as he repeatedly dabbed at his forehead. The First also appeared to be suffering from the heat because she called for more fanners. Ash never noticed the heat.

"That was amazing. They were beautiful." The First smiled at Ash, seeming to remember that he was there. "Is that what you used to do?"

"I can still dance with fire," he answered slowly, careful not to snap. She couldn't possibly know the pain her question evoked. And he *could* still manipulate fire. No one could ever take that away. He smiled tightly. "Though these old bones won't let me move quite so painlessly." He tapped his knee.

The First frowned sympathetically. "It must be very difficult, stepping down from a world that's been your entire life."

He stared at her light amber eyes, surprised by the compassion that rang in her voice. "It is."

"Don't depress the girl, Ash," Beshar laughed, but the sound was forced. The councilman smiled at the First. "He's a free man with plenty of water chips to live out the rest of his days however he pleases."

The First smiled at Ash and placed a hand on Beshar's arm. "Didn't you say you owned the dragon in this fight?"

Beshar smiled smugly, and Ash realized he was very confident with this one. "Inferno. Mean as they come. I expect you'll have an impressive display. Though the arena hardly brought out their finest." He smiled at the First. "I had hoped you would see Timber fight. He's quite the athlete. Wonderful to watch, though I dare say that didn't end so well for my dragon last time." He chuckled, "I'd hate to make the habit of training a new dragon for every fight."

Ash bit his tongue. Timber was all anyone ever talked about these days.

"Where do they keep the dragons?"

Ash realized the First was asking him and he gave her his attention. "The dragons? Well, that depends on if they belong to someone or if they belong to the arena. The councilman's Inferno is probably sitting in a holding pen." He leveled his eye on Beshar. "He probably has land outside the palace with some sort of containment for his dragons. I would imagine the councilman had him drugged for easy transportation. If they belong to the arena, they live under the arena in a network of catacombs. Every dragon has their own pen with an individual tunnel that leads to the arena."

"Catacombs? That's fascinating. Did you know that?" Jura seemed genuinely impressed as she directed her question at the councilman beside her. Ash was once again reminded that most people were completely unaware of the details that made up day-to-day life in the arena.

Beshar nodded, "Of course. I know everything."

The First poked Beshar in the arm. "And was that true what he said about your dragon? Did you have him drugged?"

The councilman nodded. "It's easiest. I feed all my dragons in their own transportable pen. On days that I bring them to the arena, I drug their food. It's a tranquilizer. Makes them very docile. It wears off in a day's time. By

159

then I've transported them to the arena. And I do own land outside the palace. The key is to be sure you have a good dragon trainer, someone your dragon can bond to. Once the dragon imprints with its trainer, he would never hurt him. And while the dragon is never completely domesticated, it's content to eat the food and live with its imprinted trainer. Though it's uncommon, Inferno is bound to me instead of a trainer." He smiled at the First. "I guess you could say I'm a dragon trainer now."

The First nodded her head enthusiastically, "How many dragons do you have, Beshar?"

He tightened his lips and wiped at his brow. "Trained and ready to fight in the arena? At the moment, just the one." He frowned at Ash. "Suppose I should be thankful Timber's not in the arena."

"He has a son training as a cadet," Ash heard himself saying and wondered why he shared the information.

"I know," Beshar smiled, surprising him. "I bought him."

The First dropped her gold glasses and fumbled for them on the floor. She stood quickly, dusting at the bottom of her robes.

"Did you say that you bought the Fire Dancer's son?" she asked, peering up at Beshar.

Beshar nodded. "It was a good investment. The boy has a solid bloodline, Timber being his father. The opportunity presented itself and I took it."

"How long will he train?" The First directed the question at Ash.

He shrugged. "It depends. I trained for eight years before I took to the arena for the first time, but I was a quick learner."

"Though not as quick as Timber's boy," Beshar boasted. "I project he'll have his naming day before his twelfth birthday."

A Fire Dancer left their slave name when they were chosen to be a cadet. From then on, they were simply referred to as cadet. It wasn't until a Dancer's entry into the arena that they were given their true name, their Fire Dancer name. To name a child at the age of twelve was unheard of.

"You can't be serious."

Beshar frowned up at him, "Very serious."

"I can't imagine that. A boy of twelve doing all of that," the First gestured her arms wildly. "Everything the dancers were doing earlier."

Beshar laughed. "He's only nine now. Come with me to the arena next week. You can watch him in the practice field."

The First smiled. "I'd love to."

Ash felt awkward in their presence. The councilman was in the middle of trying to woo the lady's affections, and Ash had come crashing in. No wonder Beshar had been so upset. Now wasn't the time for Ash to be unwanted company. But he couldn't leave now, it would appear strange, and it was his own fault for being so dense before. He would leave as soon as the match ended and approach Beshar another time. *Wait, no*, he reminded himself, *it has to be tonight.* If he didn't take advantage of tonight it could be months, a year, before he was granted another chance. *Burn his luck.*

He gazed off into the distance, trying not to listen, and caught sight of a long-haired man in the back of the box. A servant, his clothing seemed to suggest, and yet he didn't appear to be working. He appeared to be watching the First. He stared at the man, confirming it. The man hadn't take his eyes off her. Ash's fingers itched to reach an assegai that wasn't there. He had stopped wearing his last week and felt its absence. He made a vow to start wearing it again, burn anyone's opinion. Timber was sure to have words about it, but Ash found that he didn't care.

The man was still staring. Ash cocked his head and lifted his shoulder in question. *What do you want?*

The man gestured rudely at the First. *Disgusting.* He had just met the lady, but she was a member of the Thirteen, the First, and Ash would be a flaming fool if he would let some boy shame her. He was Ash Flame Dancer, greatest fire dancer of his time. He stood up.

The man was suddenly gone. Ash shook his head in wonder. *Impossible. Where did he go?* People didn't just disappear. Unless he was never there to begin with. Ash shook his head. He'd heard of a disease that fell upon the aging where their mind saw things that weren't really there. Surely he was too young for that?

The dragon horn sounded and he sighed. The fight was beginning. He settled into his seat, smiling when the First squealed in delight at the appearance of the dragon. Beshar had much to be proud of. Inferno truly was a monster of a beast. Massive, quick, and deadly. He felt no pang at the loss of the Fire Dancers. They enjoyed a death found in the arena. Gone in flashes of fire and smoke, deceased after battling something bigger, grander, greater than themselves. Their deaths were beautiful.

Everyone cheered at their passing. Ash included.

NINETEEN

JURA

J ura *hated to admit it,* but she loved the arena. The rush of the crowd, the anticipation of the dragon, and the magic of the fire display. She loved it all and it ended too quickly.

Afterword, Beshar deposited her in her awaiting litter and said he would call on her the following day. She'd failed. She had tried to secure an invitation to his quarters, but Beshar had seemed distracted by the details of bringing Inferno home and had called for her vehicle.

"May I see you tomorrow?"

"I would love that." She breathed the words, the way she had seen Amira do in front of her suitors.

Beshar didn't seem to notice. *Maybe you're not doing it right? Or maybe the Tenth just has no interest in me?* He nodded brusquely and helped her into the litter before walking away without so much as a backwards glance.

She expected the Shadow Dancer in her litter, but that didn't stop her from jumping in surprise.

It was a man this time. He lounged against her pillows, sipping on her flagon of wine. He wore a thin black mask that covered his eyes and nose. She managed to sit down across from him and raised a slender brow.

"Checking up on me?" She was proud when her voice came out cool and relaxed.

He smiled. His teeth were crooked. A pity, it took away from his handsomely sculpted chin.

"We expect a return on our investment."

Jura narrowed her eyes. "Your investment? That's laughable, considering you have yet to invest any knowledge to me. Who is responsible for my father's blood chain?"

"Nasty business those. I hear they're impossible to remove by anyone except the owner of the chain." He tsked and shook his head. "And I do apologize, Greatness, but you *are* an investment. Just because we haven't told you who to hold responsible for your father's predicament doesn't mean we haven't given you information. Learning Beshar's secrets will be helpful to you too." He cocked his head to the side. "What did you discover tonight?"

Jura gritted her teeth. "Beshar is very proud of his dragon. He imprinted it to himself rather than a trainer."

"Interesting but hardly worth taking note of."

"He's bought a new cadet. The son of Timber and only nine years old." Jura was losing confidence but she forced a smile.

The Dancer rolled his eyes. "Well, it seems you can pay attention at the arena. And while this isn't exactly common knowledge it certainly wasn't being kept a secret." He smiled again. "And I can't help but notice you're going home," he looked at her pointedly, "alone."She flinched. *I'm not even attracted to the Tenth, so why do I feel so rejected?*

"We're having dinner tomorrow." She lifted her chin. "A private meal in his chambers." The lie slipped off her tongue easily, surprising her. Well, there was no reason she couldn't make it true. She would just have to force an invitation. *You can do this.*

The Dancer kissed the air between them and let out a girly squeal.

She ignored his mockery and clasped her hands together. "I don't understand why I'm being asked to spy on him." She noticed how her knuckles turned white as she gripped her fingers. "Your league seems to make a habit of sneaking about and breaking into private rooms. Surely one of you could discover his secrets?"

She looked up, but the Shadow Dancer was gone. She sighed. Of course he'd disappeared. *I should demand they teach me this trick,* she thought to herself, relaxing against the pillows. Tomorrow was a full day. She had a luncheon with the Fifth. Beshar had insisted she attend. *Why has he taken such an interest in my game of politics? Perhaps he's noticed how terrible I am at it?* Whatever the case, she wished his interest hadn't been so invested in her skill in politics and was instead invested in an interest in her.

There has to be something he wants from me.

"I can help your Rank. My house can vote toward it on the next vote," she had suggested, but the councilman had laughed.

"I wouldn't want to be any number but the Tenth. Not so low as to feel unstable and without vote, yet not so high as to be overly noticed."

He was right to a degree. The houses below him were weak and struggled to hold their place, and any of the greater houses wouldn't worry over one with rank in the double digits. And he *did* seem to have a fair amount of power. Jura had noticed the way the other members of the Thirteen had fawned over him, though he'd insisted it was only her presence that had made them act so. Perhaps it was. She hadn't spent enough time out in society to know otherwise.

When father is better, I will stay involved. Take a more active role in politics. Be the true Lady of the First.

She'd enjoyed the tidbits of information Beshar had let slip about each of the members. She had never pictured herself as a gossip, but all those facts had been so *interesting.* She'd devoured his words like they were the script from one of her mystery novels. She now knew many details involving several of the houses' rise to power. Beshar had whispered of betrayal and backstabbing. She'd learned who was sleeping with who. Most shockingly, the lady of the Seventh was having an affair with the Lady of the Ninth. As a virgin who didn't even fully grasp the concept of what happened between a man and a woman, she wondered over the mechanics of two women. *Did everyone know everyone's secrets?* Beshar also knew that Zair had killed the previous Thirteenth. He'd known every detail of the family's murder. *Was it because Zair had told him or had the Tenth simply known? Did everyone know everyone's secrets? What if someone knew about father?*

The palanquin stuttered to a stop, and Jura felt it slowly sink to the ground. *Why have we stopped?* They couldn't have made it all the way to the palace yet. She sighed, eager to be home, and poked her head out from behind the curtained wall, annoyed by their delay.

She hadn't realized it was so dark outside. The moon was hidden and the only light came from the courtyard fire pit. It flickered against the clay walls of the square. She met the eyes of East, but of course he couldn't answer. She noticed that his hand sat ready on his scimitar. In fact, all of her *Arbe* stood ready.

She directed her question at one of Beshar's litter men, ignoring the sight of the man's oiled, rippling muscles.

The man smiled at her, bowing low, and Jura noted that even the top of his shaved head was oiled. "The litter up ahead. It's stopped. We are just making sure the roads are safe to continue." The man had a light rolling accent.

She squinted, trying to make out the litter's colors in the dim firelight. "It's the House of the Third. Continue. We will see if they need assistance."

She was hoisted back up without another word, and she gripped the cushions on either side of her to keep from toppling out. When they arrived beside the Third's palanquin, it was raised and once again continuing on its way. Jura frowned at the unfamiliar faces. The *Arbe* was definitely not Amira's. She nearly shrugged it off. It would make sense that Amira's father would make use of his own *Arbe* when he was out, and though she knew the faces of each of Amira's *Arbe*, she had hardly committed to memory the faces of the Third's.

She relaxed again against her pillows, ignoring the nagging feeling pulling at her gut. She would have to apologize to Amira in the morning. She should never have let herself listen to Beshar and ignored Amira at the Arena. Amira would be furious and was sure to feel slighted. Now she would have to plead for Amira's forgiveness. She liked to hold grudges and Jura was sure her friend found joy in Jura's apologies. *Perhaps I will throw a luncheon in her honor once things are back to normal.* Amira like to be fawned over.

Jura tried to settle back against the pillows, but she still had that strange feeling in her gut. What was this nagging anxiety and why wasn't it going away? Politics must be getting to her. She was as paranoid as any member of the Thirteen. Amira would get a laugh out of that. She was always saying Jura was too trusting, that she needed to be more cautious as a member of the First house.

Jura sat up in alarm. *Where* was *Amira's Arbe?* Even if Amira was with her father, she would still have her own *Arbe* with her. After all, Amira wouldn't even so much as use the privy without her *Arbe* in tow.

"Stop the litter," Jura shouted. She pushed back the voluminous curtains and cursed as they twisted about her tiny frame.

"Greatness?" One of Beshar's oiled men frowned back at her. She ignored him and reached for East. He looked down into her eyes.

"Something's wrong with House of the Third's palanquin. Amira should be in there but where is her *Arbe?* She *never* leaves without her *Arbe*."

Understanding dawned on his face. East and West took off at a run, scimitars drawn. North and South stepped in front of Jura and drew their swords.

At the same time a bloodcurdling scream erupted from the Third's litter, and Jura felt ice run through her veins. *Oh, please let Amira be all right.* She pushed herself out of the pillowed box, running toward the other palanquin, but she was grabbed by one of Beshar's men. She struggled against him.

"Let me go," she cried.

"You will stay," the man growled. "It's not safe."

She pushed against his oiled arms, but she slipped against them. His grip around her arm was like a vice. At least now she knew what the purpose of the oil was. She watched as her *Arbe* came upon the Third's litter, scimitars crashing.

It was dark, and Jura squinted into the night, cursing her bad vision.

She sagged in relief when she noticed a slender figure running toward her.

"Amira!" The oiled man let her go and she flew at her friend, wrapping her in a crushing embrace. "You're okay. Thank the Everflame, you're okay."

Amira sobbed into her hands. Her shoulders shook, and Jura had the fleeting thought that her friend even cried prettily.

"He's dead, he's dead, he's dead." She whispered it over and over.

She rubbed her friend's back. Jura's *Arbe* walked back toward her, blood dripping from their scimitars.

"Your father?" As soon as she asked the question, she saw an anguished Third drop to his knees between the two litters.

"Antar," Amira wailed, and Jura squeezed her friend tighter. "Our wine was poisoned. Father and I didn't drink any but, but…" Amira trailed off in tears.

She had never been close to Antar, but news of his sudden death was stunning and she swayed on her feet. Death was common in the Sand Sea, but she felt she would never become jaded to its presence. She swallowed the rush of bile that rose in her throat and tightened her grip on Amira. She had to remain strong for her friend.

"Where's your *Arbe*?" Jura heard herself asking. "I knew you were in trouble because I didn't see your *Arbe*." Amira looked up, the tears in her eyes made them sparkle. She stared at Jura in wonder.

"You saved my life."

TWENTY

ASH

He lingered behind Beshar as he said goodbye to the First. Ash was surprised when the councilman called for separate litters, but grateful. Now was his chance to talk to Beshar alone.

"Councilman. If I could have a word?"

Beshar turned around, his face one of anger, but he smoothed it into a smile when he saw Ash.

"Ash, hello again. You're still here?"

Ash wanted to grab Beshar by the throat and smash his face in, wipe that smug smile off the councilman's face, but that wouldn't solve his problem. He needed the voucher of a councilman to purchase new cadets. It was his last chance to work as a trainer this season. The houses that owned the Chosen had their own trainers and their own steady stream of Dancers from their slave population. Ash was a free man, but he still did not have the right to purchase a slave. Only a member of the Thirteen could do that. While

Ash would be a trainer to his new cadet, he could never own one of his own. A former slave himself, Ash wasn't permitted to own one of the Chosen. Freedom had its limitations.

"I wanted to speak with you about your cadet training."

Beshar shook his head. "I have only one cadet, and he's already being trained by the best."

Ash flinched. He clenched his fist tight by his side so he didn't do anything stupid.

"Why not another cadet? A new trainer? Have some friendly competition in your own training field. It will make Timber's cadet work harder and my cadet—"

"You have someone in mind?" Beshar interrupted, wiping at his brow. He stuffed his handkerchief into a pocket sewn into his sleeve.

"No, but tonight—"

"I know what tonight is." He clasped his hands behind his back as he paced. "You need the voucher from one of the Thirteen. And dare I say that I'm the only member of the Thirteen you've ever met?"

Ash didn't respond. What Beshar said was true. The only other member of the Thirteen he had ever known had been his last owner, Fajir, but he was long dead and his house was no longer one of the Thirteen.

"You need me to attend so that you may purchase an illegal slave for my house. And then you want me to, what, hire you on as the cadet's trainer? Never mind the extra cost to me and ignoring the fact that I already have a very promising cadet?" Beshar heaved a sigh and then shrugged his shoulders. "I'll do it."

"You will?" Ash couldn't keep the surprise from hitching his voice. He hadn't expected it to work out so easily.

"Yes, I'll escort you there. I will vouch for you and leave you with water chips, but I'm not staying for the auction."

♦

The auction was held an hour's trip outside of the city walls. Like many of the wealthy, Beshar owned a small carriage and a team of camels for distance travel that was unsuitable to a litter. Ash was grateful and enjoyed the comfort while he could. Beshar said he wasn't staying for the auction, which meant he and his new cadet would be walking home in the moonless night.

As if reading his thoughts, Beshar spoke up, "I'll send the carriage back for you and our new investment after I return to the city."

"Thank you, Councilman."

"Just watching my water. You'll ensure he settles into the arena…I assume you've done this before?"

"More than once," Ash lied. He'd always heard whispers of the night auction. Its very essence was taboo. Slave traders from Kitoi held the auction once a year. While it was not illegal to own slaves, it was illegal to purchase them within the Republic. Slaves from the Republic were chosen to their calling by God, marked by the Everflame. Ash was unsure how the slaves were chosen in other lands. The few cadets that came from the secret auction were almost always the most powerful, but they never seemed to live long. The cadets were always moody and rebellious. They came from distant places and didn't understand they had been chosen. They were reckless in the arena. They didn't care if they lived or died. They didn't understand the glory of being chosen because they could still remember their old lives, back when they had been free. Ash was free now, for all that word did for him.

The carriage jerked to a stop; they had arrived. Just outside the city limits a huge tent had hastily been erected in the dunes. The thin fabric stretched over several wooden poles and the material was thin enough to see the stars, had there been any. The night sky was full of clouds and the dunes were impossibly dark. The only light came from torches and a single fire pit lit within the tent. Ash hopped out of the carriage, forgetting his knees in his excitement. He was grateful for the soft sand that dulled the sting of his landing.

Beshar lumbered down awkwardly, helped out of the carriage by one of his oiled men. Beshar led him into the makeshift tent and stopped him in front of a small man with stooped shoulders. The man's long hair was pulled back by a leather cord.

"Udo." Beshar handed the man a small sack of water chips. He handed a much larger one to Ash, meeting his eye.

"Ash will purchase in my stead."

Udo nodded, pocketing his chips with a smile and pointing a finger toward the center of the tent.

Ash followed the direction to see a network of cages set up in the center.

Beshar turned away. "I have to leave now. I've done far too many favors for one day." He stopped and turned around to face Ash one last time. "You *have* done this before?"

Ash nodded, albeit a bit too enthusiastically, but Beshar seemed to buy it. Or he really was busy, because he faded from view and disappeared into the night.

The tent filled up quickly. For a secret auction, quite a few people seemed to know about it. He watched a few enter and noticed that they walked immediately to the center of the tent. *Right, to scout out their purchases.* Following suit, Ash walked toward them. He hoped he wasn't staring wide eyed, but he had never seen children in such horrible conditions. Yes, he had grown up a slave, but he had never been treated so badly.

There were over a dozen cages, some of them stacked on top of one another and none more than a few feet in diameter. Inside each was a dirty, frightened child. Ash's stomach clenched. This was horrible. He took a deep steadying breath.

"Not much of a display this year," a voice sniffed from behind him.

Ash turned around to see a well dressed woman, presumably in the Thirteen, smiling at him.

"You're Ash. I watched you when I was a little girl."

He nodded, embarrassed. It didn't feel right for him to be here. He had been so desperate for a way back into the arena, but he couldn't take it if this was the cost.

"So, what do you think?" she asked, leaning in toward him. She motioned a man over.

"Tamir, look who I've found. It's Ash Flame Dancer. He's going to help us pick our selections."

"Is that so?" Tamir called back as he sauntered over. His robes were brightly colored and made out of some sort of shiny fabric.

"I am Tamir, from the house of the Eleventh, and this is Fatima, the Twelfth."

Ash nodded politely. "I don't know that I was going to stay…"

Fatima frowned. "Not stay? You mean there's nothing here even worth purchasing? That's a pity." She shrugged her shoulders. "Udo won't like that. At least his cart will be empty without all those sniveling creatures."

"What happens to the children?"

Fatima cocked her head to the side. "The slaves? Well, if no one buys them I suppose he kills them. Or leaves them here. I've never really given it much thought. Tamir?"

"I'm sure he sells them all for something. Just because a cadet isn't found doesn't mean you haven't found a personal Torch."

Torches were cadets that failed out of arena training. Unable to fight in the arena, they worked at maintaining light, warmth, and cooking fires for their house. Though these slaves never achieved freedom, their lives were long and their end days were spent relaxing in the working halls and overseeing the newly trained house Torch.

"They all look fine. Pick whatever kind you want." Ash excused himself and walked away from the couple, breathing heavily. *It had been foolish to come here. Is this really what I wanted? To steal a child away from its home for my own purpose?* He felt someone's eyes on him and looked down into the bright blue eyes of one of the caged children. Her hair was a mess of curls crowding her tiny face. Wide eyes peered out at him, drawing him closer.

"Hello," he said softly.

The girl cocked her head to the side and scrunched up her nose.

"My name is Ash."

She shook her head.

"You don't have to tell me your name if you don't want to." He kept his voice low and even, her eyes stared back at him, wide and confused.

Understanding dawned on him. They were illegal slaves because they had been abducted from their own lands. She probably didn't speak their language. Sympathy rolled in his gut and once again Ash was sorry he had come.

Udo called for attention. The auction was starting. Udo stated the approximate age and suggested a bidding price as each slave was presented. A large fire pit stood center stage for any prospective Dancer to display their skill. Around the perimeter of the tent, several bored-looking Torches stood guard, ready to dispel any dangerous fire movement from a rebellious slave.

The first three were teenage girls. They held no skill with fire, yet they were sold quickly. Udo praised their beauty and virtue and sold each to the highest bidder. Concubines were always in demand. Next was a young boy. Ash watched him carefully. He was guessed to be around ten or eleven, and he had the gift of Fire Dancing. Ash put in a bid for him but his heart wasn't in it. He watched the boy move about the makeshift stage, catching the awkward turnout of the boy's feet. He conceded the bid to Fatima, who nodded to him graciously.

Another boy was presented, the same age but twice as big. He was strong, Ash thought, but his movements were slow and clumsy. He wasn't agile enough for the arena.

Udo continued to call out each of his bids, coaxing the slave in turn to circle the stage and forcing them to perform at his will. One boy declined to do anything. He sat at the center of the stage and refused to move. Udo boasted of his skill at Fire Dancing, but the boy wouldn't so much as make the torch flicker. Hoping to force a reaction, Udo asked his Torch to shoot fire at the boy. The boy didn't even scream as he was burned to a crisp.

The next two cadets were more than willing to show their skill at manipulating fire, but Ash dismissed them both for being too timid or clumsy.

Then Udo announced the tiny, blue-eyed beauty. Her cage was set on the stage, and Udo pushed her out. She stumbled out of the cage, glaring at Udo. He announced that she was a prospective Dancer, age six or seven.

Ash leaned forward in his seat. She was impossibly young. Could she really be displaying signs of the gift so early? She was small, but then most girls were. Her feet were shaped nicely and she had excellent posture, despite having just been cramped in the tiny cage. Though her hands were bound, she stood straight and tall as if unaware of the chains around her wrist and ankles.

"This one will need a heavy hand in training. She lacks discipline and does not speak the common tongue. She is our last item for auction."

Some people began to leave. They had made their purchases earlier, and seeing that the auction had nothing more to offer, they were content to head home.

"Don't let yourself miss this opportunity. This girl is a rare find. I'll start the bidding at 300."

"Why don't you show us what she can do?" Tamir called out. He had purchased the giant clumsy boy.

"Unfortunately, I had to drug her. She is very powerful." Udo explained. "But 300 water chips is a steal. She is worth ten times more."

The girl simply stood still, staring into the pit of the fire. Ash recognized the hungry look in her eyes. If she was as powerful as Udo said, the presence of the fire pit would be enough for her to cause serious damage. The fact that she was drugged was probably the only thing that kept Udo alive.

"I'll give you the 300." Ash heard himself say. The girl looked up at him and met his eyes. She looked from him to Udo.

"300. Would anyone like to bid for four?" Udo scanned the dispersing crowd and met Ash's eyes. "She's worth ten times as much in Kitoi."

Ash held his gaze. "But you didn't take her to Kitoi. You brought her here." His gaze slid to the girl who watched as he approached the stage. "If she's as powerful as you say—"

"She is. That's why she has her worth," Udo assured him.

"Then you must be keeping her fully drugged at all times? Kept out of reach of fire? Kitoi is a ways further. You must have stocked up on tranquilizers. Otherwise, how would you make it there? Alive? I can see the hatred she has for you burning in her eyes. I'll give you 400. She comes with me."

Udo smiled and reached greedily for the bag. "The Tenth will be quite pleased with your purchase. You will see." He handed the girl's chains to Ash.

Ash stared down, startled by their weight.

"Take these off of her." *I must be going crazy.* "She's drugged, right?" he asked, to silence Udo's protests.

Udo removed the chains from the girl, and though she swayed on her feet, she glared at Udo and spit on his boots.

He laughed. "She's your problem now."

TWENTY
ONE
BESHAR

There were *few people who* were truly gifted liars. It took someone with exceptional intelligence and reasoning to successfully lie to another. Beshar had learned the different tells: accelerated breathing, fidgeting, eye movement. Even something as imperceptible as shifting one's weight or leaning back. He had seen it all. Yes, most people were poor liars, and Ash was as terrible as they came. Beshar hadn't cared. The Dancer's request had been simple enough, and the councilman liked to bestow favors so that people would be in his debt. He liked to take chances and was never one to let an opportunity pass him by. He had little need for another cadet. His holdings already included his prize dragon, two in training, five Dancers, and his cadet. He smirked. Well, two cadets now. It didn't matter who Ash bought or if the cadet lasted through training, what mattered now was that

Ash owed him a favor. And Beshar did love his pets.

The ride back to the palace gates would take nearly an hour, but Beshar wasn't worried. He had plenty of time yet before his next appointment. *Perhaps I should have stayed for the auction,* he wondered for a moment before brushing aside the thought. He really couldn't abide those things. The slaves stunk, and the auction was full of his peers. As a member of the Thirteen, Beshar was expected to perform a certain number of social roles. He loathed the majority of them and forced himself to perform his expected duties with a smile on his face. He'd rather numb himself with wine, but was sure to always keep a clear head in the presence of the Thirteen. One had to keep their wits about them if they wanted to play the game and survive.

As they often did these days, his thoughts turned unbidden to Jura. Beshar loved puzzles and games of logic, and Jura was the biggest puzzle of all. She was, like everyone in the Thirteen, hiding something. The problem was, he had yet to figure out what. And though it was obvious that the girl was lying, she *was* terrible at it, he had yet to find anything under her timid demeanor. The real question was not a matter of discerning that she was hiding something. The more important question was why? The girl was clueless, or she wanted to appear that way. Beshar had yet to discover which. She wanted something from him. He knew her secret had something to do with her father's supposed illness. *But how do I fit into it all? What does she want?*

The fact that she hadn't come right out with her request showed that she was new to the game. Like most idiotic girls, she sought to purchase her information with her body. It was silly, really. The child was practically throwing herself at him. If it had been any other girl, Beshar would have gotten rid of her ages ago. But Jura was different. There was a desperation and hunger in her eyes that didn't fit her station.

It was common for young girls from wealthy families outside the Thirteen to prostitute themselves. They seemed to believe that Beshar would be so overcome by their sexual advances that he would become putty in their hands. It was a ridiculous notion. He rarely even had a need for the opposite sex, especially not the attentions of overzealous harlots found outside the Thirteen. But at least Beshar understood those women. They hungered for his power and station, and they reached for it the only way they knew how.

But Jura was in the house of the First. She was the only heir. Her bloodline was impeccable, and she was currently acting as First Interim. He couldn't imagine what she must want from him. He wasn't so foolish as to believe she was attracted to him. He was twice her age and outweighed her by at least two hundred pounds. And even if it was possible for someone like her to be attracted to his sort, it was clear that Jura wasn't. Revulsion was clear in her eyes every time she touched him. *And still, she reaches for me. Why?*

His carriage came to a stop and he sat up surprised. He had been so lost in his thoughts that he hadn't even noticed the passing time. One of his Samur opened the carriage door and assisted him down. One of twelve, the Samur cost him a fortune in water but they were worth every chip. Udo had acquired them for Beshar the night that he had achieved membership into the Thirteen. He'd been a merchant then, campaigning his membership by rubbing elbows with the Thirteen at the arena. He had always been a fan of the arena. He loved the excitement of battle, the thrill of the kill. Dragon, gladiator. It mattered not who won the fight, so long as blood was shed. And just as he had always loved the arena, he'd always known he was meant to be a member of the Thirteen.

He'd been young but cunning. Beshar had never been cocky and found that he detested arrogance in others. He'd known that achieving membership by combat was out of the question for him. He'd been large and out of shape even then. No, his ability was his mind. And so, he'd formed a plan. It took four years of acquiring the right favors, but eventually he'd found himself in the perfect position to make his move.

It was executed perfectly. Three houses were taken down in the span of a single night. Two had been feuding, Twelve and Eleven, as was often the case. Thirteen had been easy pickings. Thirteen was an ambitious man with a young wife, and it had been all too easy for Beshar to urge him to get involved. The families had murdered one another, at least that's what the Thirteen believed. Though Beshar had it on very good authority that the Thirteenth's wife had killed her husband after his involvement when he'd failed to become the Tenth. Beshar had been voted in the very next Session. Conveniently, he knew just who to suggest to fulfill the other Ranks. Beshar remembered the thrill of his past fondly and had enjoyed his position as the Tenth for over two decades.

He'd asked for the Samur that same week. He'd known there would be backlash from his sudden advancement. It was unheard of for a new member to join as the Tenth instead of at the bottom of the Ranks, and Beshar was prepared for the attacks of the scorned surviving families. Unlike the *Arbe* of the Glass Palace, the Samur were not chosen from slaves. Instead they were free men, citizens of Shrivo, a small nation outside of Kitoi that swore their lives to the art of battle. It was said that their god lived in another plane and that the Samur could only gain access to this plane through a glorious death. Otherwise, the Samur simply refused to die. This made them excellent warriors. A select few even had special skills that Beshar had found extremely helpful. And they were loyal. So long as Beshar gave them the freedom to worship as they wanted, they guarded him night and day. In that regard, they were like the slave *Arbe,* but more importantly, the Samur still had their tongues. The Thirteen often forgot to hold their tongues around bodyguards, believing them all mute, and there was no limit to the information Beshar had acquired from his.

He walked quickly to his rooms, hurrying through the glass halls in small shuffling steps. He only had three Samur with him. The lack of his full retinue made him nervous. *It's these flaming glass halls,* he thought with annoyance.

The towers of the Thirteen were all connected by a series of hallways that met at the Justice Dome. The thirteen halls spread in a circle around it. If anyone was found outside of their rooms, they were in full view of everyone else. It was dangerous being a member of the Thirteen. The palace design was meant to keep members safe from an ambush inside their own homes, but the lack of privacy made it hard for people to keep secrets. Several of the houses were moving among the halls, presumably in the direction of the Dome. Beshar ignored them and continued to the safety of his chambers.

He reached the privacy of his stone rooms and sent one of his Samur to see what the commotion in the halls was about. While the man was gone, Beshar set about changing his robes. He gazed with some longing at his wine collection but forced himself to wait, reminding himself that he needed a clear mind before his meeting. The Samur returned with the information that the son of the Third was dead, presumably poisoned on his way back from the arena. Beshar shook his head. Nasty business, that. *Who would kill the second child of the Third? Either someone had failed entirely, or this was the*

183

beginning of a very elaborate scheme. He smiled at the prospect.

Another Samur entered, bowing low in his customary way before speaking. "Dahr the Fourth awaiting permission to enter."

"*Arbe?*" Beshar asked, one could never be too careful.

"Just one, Councilman."

Beshar's Samur could more than handle a single *Arbe*. "Send him in."

Dahr entered, his long legs sweeping him across the room. He came to a stop in front of Beshar and scowled down at him. "Have you heard?"

Beshar smiled. "About the Third? Yes. What a pity. Antoine was it?"

"Antar," Dahr answered tightly, his dark eyes darted nervously across the room. "It appears the carriage wine reserve was poisoned."

Beshar frowned. A botched job then, someone had wanted to remove the House of the Third. "Who would destroy an entire supply of wine? It's a damn waste."

Dahr gawked at him. "I'm not here to discuss the flaming wine! What will I do? I'm the Fourth. They'll think I killed him."

"Didn't you?"

"No!" The man's face was shocked and angry.

Beshar shrugged. "I had to ask." He sat down on his chaise, stretching out his legs and yawning loudly. "Then why did you request a meeting? If not to devise a strategy plan."

Dahr once again looked nervously about the room. "I came to ask for a favor."

Eventually everyone came to him for favors. Beshar said nothing, but his heart leaped with the promise of a new pet. He motioned for a Samur to bring wine. Dahr sniffed it cautiously, causing Beshar to laugh. "It's not poisoned, Councilman." He took a sip from his goblet to set the man's mind at ease.

Seeing him drink, Dahr tilted his glass back and took several swallows, swiping at his mustache afterward.

"I saw your dragon in the arena tonight. He was spectacular."

Beshar smiled. Inferno was something he was quite proud of. The best dragon he'd seen in years. "Thank you. What was your favor?"

"I need a dragon." Dahr licked his bottom lip, and Beshar noticed it was stained from the wine. He motioned for a Samur to refill the Fourth's glass.

"I'm not breeding any at the moment. I can put you in touch with a contract trainer. He captures them wild, though I find their sort to—"

"I don't want to buy a new dragon. I want *your* dragon. I want Inferno."

Beshar deliberately set down his goblet and sat up in his chaise. "He's not for sale. Why do you want mine?"

"I saw him at the arena tonight. I admired him and thought I'd be hard pressed to find another so beautiful," Dahr said.

Beshar noticed that Dahr's bottom lip quivered and that he wrung his hands together so tightly that his fingers turned white. He was lying.

"He's not for sale," Beshar repeated.

Dahr let out a forced laugh. "Come now. Everything is for sale."

"Not this dragon." Beshar stood up. "If that was all, Councilman, the hour grows late and I'm sure you have much to do in preparation for tomorrow's accusations."

Dahr opened his mouth as if to say something but quickly closed it, turning on his heel and stomping out of the room.

Beshar watched him leave, waiting several moments before he allowed himself to once again lean back on his chaise. He reached for his goblet of wine and downed its contents, motioning for another glass. He didn't plan on leaving his chambers again for the rest of the night and he intended to get good and drunk.

TWENTY TWO

JURA

mira and her father rode back to the palace in Jura's litter. The ride was silent, save for Amira's occasional sniffles. The Third stared blankly at the floor. They arrived at the palace without any further incident, and Jura escorted them to the halls of the Third.

All three *Arbe* from the house of the Third were missing. Twelve men, gone.

Jura grabbed Amira's arm, preventing her from following her father into their rooms. "What do you think happened?"

Amira turned red-rimmed eyes up to Jura, lines of khol streaked down her cheeks and she shook her head. "I don't know. We left. My *Arbe* was there, and father's and Antar's held the litter. Antar immediately had a drink. I was pouting because you didn't come say hi to us, and father was talking me through it. I was so mad at you." She wiped her eyes. "Then Antar…he just sort of choked and grabbed at his throat and I knew," she sniffled. "I just knew." She shook her head. "I screamed, I think. I was scared and then the curtains opened, but it wasn't a face I knew. And then your *Arbe* was there and you saved us. This was the Fourth, it had to be."

"But how did four men overtake twelve?" Jura bit her bottom lip, not expecting an answer.

Amira pulled her close for another hug and sighed. "I'm exhausted. I don't know how I'll ever sleep knowing that whoever is responsible for Antar's death is still out there." She began to cry again. "Jura, someone tried to kill me."

"You two. Stay with her," she pointed at North and South. She looked up and met the disapproving eyes of East. Imperceptibly, he shook his head.

"Really?" Amira smiled and wiped at her eyes, "You would do this for me?"

"Certainly. I want you to rest easy. You've been through a terrible ordeal. And besides, I can just use father's *Arbe*." As soon as the words were out of her mouth, she wished she could shove them back in. She struggled not to make any facial emotions and hoped she hadn't flinched.

"Won't your father need his *Arbe*?"

Jura bit the inside of her cheek. She'd been foolish to hope Amira would let the comment slide. "Well, of course, but we can share. I'll sleep in the room adjoining The First's, and our men can watch us both."

Amira stared down at Jura, wiping away at her tears. "How is the First? Well enough to attend the vote? He hasn't made a public appearance all week. It's bad politics."

Jura swallowed. "He's fine. Doing very well now. I'm surprised he wasn't in attendance today."

Amira sniffed. "If he was, perhaps then there would be some action to justice being served. This was clearly the doing of the Fourth house, trying to make his move before the votes."

"We don't know for sure it was him. And your men are still missing. No bodies, no deaths."

Amira yawned loudly, "I'm exhausted. I'll see you tomorrow." Jura knew she was dismissed, and so she turned and left for her meeting with Markhim.

It was an impossibly long night. Jura was late for her meeting with Markhim. She was exhausted but she didn't dare cancel, not now when she needed his strength. She entered her private gardens and squinted in the dim lighting. The glass ceiling normally bathed the room in moonlight, but tonight was overcast and the only light came from a single torch resting in the doorway. Jura eyed the torch warily before snatching it into her hands. Fire was mostly harmless, but all fire was an indirect result of the Everflame and one could never be too careful when it came to gods and magic.

"Markhim?" It was far too dark and silent. The only sound came from the gentle tinkle from her tiny fountain and the soft breathing of her men beside her. She ignored the gentle hand on her forearm and tugged loose of her man so she could step further into the square gardens.

"Markhim? Are you here?" She ignored the panic rising in her chest and tightened her grip on the torch, swinging it back and forth to shine light in the various corners of the room. The firelight danced wildly and cast intimidating shadows over all her plants but there was no sign of Markhim.

"Where is he?" She asked no one in particular, but East answered her with a slow raise of his arm.

She stared after where he pointed and rushed to the colored parchment pinned to the thick vine of jasmine. The intense fragrance of the flowers filled her as she pulled the parchment loose, knocking several clusters of the starry white flowers to the ground. They fell to her feet and Jura joined them, kneeling on the cool stone floor.

Jura,

I've left the Republic. I'm never coming back. You had to know there could never be anything between us. I could never be with one of the Thirteen. Good-bye.

-Markhim

Jura read the note several times before it slipped between her flaccid fingers to join the flowers on the floor. Markhim had left the Republic? He'd left her with scarcely any explanation and not even an apology. *Shouldn't I be crying?* She felt achingly numb, as if the moment wasn't truly happening to her. After the night she'd had, all she had wanted to do was talk to Markhim, her confidante. Now he was gone and apparently never coming back. She left the parchment there on the floor and rose to her feet, grabbing onto East's proffered arm for support. She was suddenly so exhausted she could barely move. She only wanted to reach the comfort of her bed. Tomorrow was going to be another long day.

TWENTY THREE

TYLAK

Tylak *loved the night. So* many seemed to be frightened of it, afraid of the shadows and the creatures of the night. Tylak felt embraced by those same shadows. The darkness allowed him to blend in, to hide from those who might hurt him. Darkness was his ally.

He walked through the city streets, staying close to the clay walls of the various buildings, careful to avoid the flickering flames that illuminated each square. More than anything, he wanted to see Jura again. *Only to get my birthstone,* he told himself, *not because I want to see her.*

The air was dry and the heat clung to his clothing, warming his skin. He wished he hadn't chosen such a thick cloak. His clothing options were limited these days. He supposed he should be grateful for the heat of summer. The winter months were so cold a man could freeze to death without shelter.

Tylak had spent the last few nights sleeping in various door steps. He had to be careful not to get too close to the palace lest someone spotted him and returned him to his cell. Tylak didn't wish to tempt fate. He managed enough of that on his own.

He rounded the corner and found Peppik where he'd left him. The old man sat cross legged in an alley drawing circles in the sand with a long stick he'd sharpened to a point. He looked up at Tylak and grinned a gap-toothed smile.

Tylak handed him a piece of flat bread he'd managed to steal, and Peppik bit into it with relish.

Tylak watched him eat in silence.

"I didn't see anyone leave the building," Peppik offered, licking his fingers and swallowing hard.

Tylak narrowed his eyes. "You're sure? You were watching the entire time?"

Peppik nodded enthusiastically. "Of course. I didn't leave. I was here watching."

"Thank you," Tylak said. He sat down beside the older man and stared at the darkened building across the street.

Was anyone in there? He wondered if he'd had Peppik watching an empty building. He hoped not.

Peppik was still drawing his circles. His hand seemed to move of its own accord as he kept his eyes trained on the building.

"You can stop watching," Tylak said. "I'm going to go check it out myself."

Peppik nodded, turning his attention to his drawings in the sand. "They're inside. They watch too, waiting."

"Who's watching?" Tylak asked, but Peppik didn't answer, just continued drawing circles. Tylak stood back up, dusting the sand from his trousers.

"Will you be here when I get back?"

Peppik nodded, but he didn't look up. "Peppik will be wherever you need him to be."

Tylak frowned at him. Peppik often said odd things. He took a deep breath before darting across the street toward the darkened building.

It was square, with traditional clay walls and a low roof. There were windows, but they were closed up and covered with curtains. Tylak couldn't see any light shining from inside. The building was far away from the square, but shadows from the fire pit still flickered against its walls.

Tylak hoped his information was correct, that he hadn't hit yet another dead end. If he was right, the leader of the Shadow Dancers would be inside. He stepped in front of the door and took a deep breath, poised to open it when the door suddenly swung out at him. He leaped away and rolled to the side of the building, peering around its corner and praying he hadn't been spotted. A hooded figure exited, their cloak drawn tight around their shoulders as they walked briskly onto the street.

Tylak paused, unsure what to do next. *Follow the cloaked figure or rush inside the building?* He deliberated for another moment, then pushed to his feet with an inward moan and hurried after the figure.

They were headed in the direction of the palace, though they took the most inconvenient of routes to get there, darting in and out of alleyways and crossing the streets only to cross back at the next intersection. *Can he tell I'm following?*

As if in answer to his question, the hooded figure stopped and Tylak took his chance, pouncing at the figure and tackling him from behind.

The figure hit the dusty, unpaved street with a grunt. Tylak was amazed at how slender the figure was beneath him. He turned the figure around and stared into the startled brown eyes of a woman.

"You." He stood up abruptly, ignoring her outstretched hand for help up, and glared down at her.

"Tylak." The woman smiled, rising to her feet and wiping her hands on her robes.

"Denir. I should have recognized it was you. Trying to scratch a dragon's balls leads to less trouble."

"Dragon's ba… Is that any way to speak to your better?" She pouted.

"Better at what? Being a lying, deceitful cu—"

"Ouch," she interrupted. "Careful. I'll think you don't care."

"I don't," he sighed. He'd missed his chance at getting answers. By the time he got back to the building it would be empty. Yet another opportunity wasted at the hands of one of the Thirteen. He scowled at her.

She smiled, cocking her head to the side and raising a delicately arched brow. "Hmm. I thought we killed you."

He grunted. "You certainly tried. What are you doing out here?"

She looked around the empty street and motioned for him to follow her into a darkened alley. He did, but kept his hand on his dagger, just in case.

"Lovely night for a stroll, isn't it? I was just heading home. What are you doing? Besides attacking ladies in the street?"

"You're no lady."

"I'm Fifth of the Thirteen." Her voice was indignant but her smile widened. "I'm glad you're not dead."

"Are you? It didn't seem that way when you told the Light Guard you saw me stealing fire from the Everflame."

She shrugged. "I wasn't entirely sure the fool man would believe me. Who but Fire Dancers can steal fire? Besides, I can't help it if you've gotten sloppy."

"Why did you do it?" Tylak hoped she wouldn't hear the pain in his voice, couldn't stand it if she did.

"Why does a woman do anything? If you didn't know it was me in the street, then why did you attack me?" Understanding slowly dawned on her face and she laughed, a lyrical tinkling sound that sliced at his gut. He'd once loved that sound.

"Oh, you poor, stupid boy. Will you ever learn?"

"Apparently not," he sighed. "I don't suppose you know where they'll be next?"

Denir frowned, drawing her eyebrows together in concern. "Even if I did, why should I tell you? What do you want?"

"Information."

Her face smoothed into one of her charming smiles. "Perhaps I can help?"

Tylak snorted. "Doubtful. Besides, I've had enough help from you to last a lifetime."

She reached out a slender hand, cupping his face. He flinched at her touch.

"Do you really mean that?" she asked.

"More than I've ever meant anything in my life. I want nothing from you."

"You didn't always feel that way."

"You weren't always such a bitch."

Her hand fell to her side, and she looked so sad that Tylak almost felt bad for her. Almost.

"I am sorry, you know." Her deep brown eyes peered up at him, searching.

"For which part? The betrayal? That time you sold me out, or the time you had me killed?"

"For all of it." Her voice was soft and her eyes were far away. "You should leave the city, Tylak. Things are happening here. Things you know nothing about. The Republic isn't safe anymore."

"It was never safe for people like me. I'll take my chances."

She nodded. "I understand." She pulled her hood up, tugging it low to cover her pretty face and hide her flowing mahogany locks.

Tylak watched her go, hating the woman she was and remembering the man he had once been with her.

TWENTY
FOUR

JURA

S he went to her father's chambers. His *Arbe* was stationed outside his door. They looked at her questioningly. She motioned them all inside.

"I haven't discovered who's behind my father's blood chain. I have one more day. If this doesn't work, I'll have no choice but to reveal his situation to the Thirteen." She met the eyes of each of them. "I don't know what this will mean for our house. We may need added protection."

The men nodded.

She sent them out into the hall to guard her while she slept. Then she curled onto her father's bed and closed her eyes. She didn't want to think anymore. In seconds she was asleep.

She was awakened by a hand clamped over her mouth. She dug her nails into the hand and bucked wildly, hoping to make enough commotion to alert her men just outside the chamber. Whoever held on to her was much stronger than she was, and it became increasingly harder to breathe through her panic. Her eyes darted about the room, struggling to focus. If only there was some sort of weapon. On the far side of the room, a lone candle sat on her father's desk. It hadn't been there before. She blinked rapidly and eventually she was able to focus on the figure that held her pinned to her father's bed.

"I'm not going to hurt you. Don't scream." He removed his hand and she scurried back toward the wall, dragging the bed covers up to her chin.

"Don't scream," he repeated. He held up a halting hand but made no move to close the distance between them. "I only came to talk."

"Tylak? What are you doing here? My men are just outside."

How long had she been sleeping? Minutes? Hours? It felt like she'd only just placed her head on her pillow, yet the surge of adrenaline had her fully alert. Tylak, the dangerous, mysterious man involved with the Shadow Dancers had been watching her sleep. She drew her knees up to her chest, keeping a firm grip on the blanket just under her chin. *What if he saw me in my nightclothes?*

"How did you get past my *Arbe*?"

"I came in through the window." She glanced at the single window and saw that it was indeed wedged open. Jura was sure men were stationed just outside the window too. In fact, Markhim had complained of her father's snoring whenever he was stationed there. She shoved thoughts of her traitorous friend aside and focused on Tylak.

"How did you get past the palace guards?"

"I'm sneaky."

This was going nowhere. She sucked in another deep breath. "What do you want?"

He gestured to the bed. "May I?"

She didn't answer, so he took a seat at the foot of the bed. He was cleaner than when she'd last seen him, and he seemed to have changed his clothing, though it was hard to see in the dim lighting.

"Any luck with my birthstone?"

She gaped at him. "You really snuck into the palace in the middle of the night to ask me about your birthstone?"

He shrugged, "Sentimental value." He leaned back on his elbows and looked around the room, whistling softly. "So, this is how the other half lives. I've got to admit, I imagined your room somewhat less…masculine."

She stiffened. "This is my father's room."

His eyes widened. "You don't say?" He stroked his chin and Jura realized that it had recently been shaved smooth. She missed the look of scruff and bit her cheek. This man was a criminal. He'd broken into the palace. She had no business noticing such things.

"Where's the First?"

His question snapped her out of her reverie. "Excuse me?"

"Your father. You said this is his room."

"T-that's none of your business. He's working. Handling affairs of the Republic." She lifted her chin. "The affairs of the First do not need to be explained to one such as you."

His expression darkened. "Right, I'm nothing but a slave."

"You're a criminal."

"But what if I'm not?" He leaned forward. "Things aren't always what they seem." He shrugged. "But I think you know that. You're right. It's none of my business where you keep your father."

He knows. She bit her lip and stared at the door. If she shouted, her men would be at her side in a matter of seconds. Tylak watched her and said nothing. She lifted her chin.

"You shouldn't be in here. I don't have your birthstone."

"Because you never meant to help me?"

"I don't have it *yet*. I keep my promises." His eyes were so gray. She hadn't even known such a color was possible. The color wasn't pure gray, there were flecks of blue and—

"It's ocean blue."

"What is?"

"My birthstone. My mother always said the blue of the stone was the same color of the ocean. Maybe after I get my stone, I'll go see for myself. I've always wanted to see the ocean."

His eyes looked over her shoulder, but she knew there was nothing behind her except a stone wall. His mind was someplace else.

"Is your mother upset you lost the family stone?"

"My mother is dead." His eyes snapped to hers and he stood up, the bed groaned in protest at the sudden shift of weight.

She thought of her own mother in the garden, singing as she tended to her jasmine. Her father's face had been so grim when he'd come into her room to explain that his beloved, her mother, was gone. Gone forever. Yet another casualty of the Thirteen. She would give all the water in the world just to see her one more time.

"My mother is dead too. It doesn't stop hurting, does it?"

He stared at her for a long moment. It didn't seem like he would answer, but then he shook his head. "No, it doesn't." He crossed the room and reached for the lone candle, pausing at the open window that opened up to the courtyard and her mother's garden.

"I'm sorry I frightened you. After I get my stone, I'll leave. I promise."

He ducked through the window and was gone before she could reply. It was a long while before sleep found her again.

TWENTY
FIVE
JURA

The following morning Jura woke with the sun. She'd slept fitfully, tossed awake by dreams of nameless faces chasing her with bloody hands through glass halls. She sent for food, feeling ravenous and knowing her father was probably more so. Though he still refused to speak, he always ate with a fervor that startled her. She took three men with her to her chambers, East and West and one of her father's. She decided to name him Tomor. Like the other two, he was blissfully unaware he'd been named.

She fed her father. He *did* look better. *Perhaps he would sit still for a shave…*

He seemed content to just watch her while he ate. She sat down across from him, tracing her finger on the etching of the heavy rug that covered the stone floor. *If I remove his bindings, what will he do?* It'd seemed before he'd been intent on killing her, but now he was happy to sit and watch. She watched him back, and they had a silent breakfast. *It's almost like nothing has changed,* Jura thought with a wry smile as she finished the last of her meal. Her father stared at her, still chewing.

"I'm leaving now," she stood up and reached for the ladder. "I'll do whatever it takes, father. I'll find a way to get you back."

She left him in his tiny underground prison and left the hall with East and West, heading for the halls of the Third.

Amira met her in the courtyard just outside her halls.

"Are you going to the luncheon?" Her voice was flippant, and she took long strides that sent her gossamer outer robes flying out behind her. Jura cursed her short legs and hurried to catch up.

"You look like you're feeling better," Jura said. "How's your father?"

"The Third is handling the death of his only son in a manner that anyone would expect. I will be Third interim while he is in mourning."

"You...your father stepped down?" Jura asked, confused.

Amira stopped walking, looking down the length of her slender nose as she frowned down at Jura. "He hasn't stepped down. I'm acting as head of household, like any child would do for a father that is unwell." She drew in a shaky breath. "There's precedence for this. One can hardly expect a man to be in his right sense of mind following the death of a child. I will act in his stead while the Third is indisposed." Her lips turned up slightly at the word.

Jura forced her face to remain blank. The Thirteen would accept her without question. The death of a child was solid reason to step down. It also drew all the more attention to her own father's disappearance.

"The luncheon?" Amira reminded her friend, once again pumping her long legs.

Jura ran after her.

The luncheon was held by the Fifth. Denir was the last of her household and likely held the monthly luncheon as an excuse to display her obvious wealth. *And to watch,* Jura reminded herself as she and Amira walked in after Jura's *Arbe.* Amira had assured her that the Third was diligently working toward their safety, and that she was sure to have a replacement *Arbe* but could she please hold on to Jura's men just a tiny bit longer?

Jura had said yes of course, unable to say no to her friend. She was just glad she hadn't had to spend the majority of the morning apologizing for some unknown crime. Amira flitted around the room, speaking to everyone briefly and no one for any time at all. She would disappear for minutes at a time and then her trilling laugh would ring across the room and demand attention from all. She made Jura dizzy watching her.

"I see that you're once again letting her take control," A husky voice observed from behind.

Jura turned and stared into the amused face of Denir. The Fifth was in her mid-forties though her dark hair had not a streak of gray and her tanned skin was free from wrinkles. *I hope I look as young in twenty years,* Jura thought. She found it refreshing that she could stare at the Fifth from eye level. The woman was nearly as short as she was.

"I'm sorry?"

Denir nodded toward Amira who, at the moment, was laughing up at Beshar. "I was watching you yesterday."

"Beshar says you watch a lot," Jura answered.

The Fifth smiled. "So does he. It was nice seeing you at the arena. You looked so comfortable and grown up. You reminded me of your mother."

"You knew my mother?" People rarely spoke of her. When a person's life flame burned out, it was best to move forward and never look behind.

Denir nodded. "She was a lovely woman. You look so much like her." The Fifth's eyes looked far away. "We were friends, once. Like you," she flicked a hand in the direction of Amira, who still stood laughing with Beshar. "And that one." She glanced sideways at Jura from under sooty lashes. "Wasn't the Tenth your escort at the arena yesterday?"

For some reason Jura found herself blushing. "It's not like that. He's not a suitor or anything."

Denir arched a brow. "It isn't my business," she shrugged. "But, if you did have something with the Tenth," she leveled an eye at Jura, "some unfinished business that is, I would suggest staking your claim now before your curious friend steals your chance."

Jura bit her bottom lip. "What do you mean?"

"My lady First, everyone saw you two at the arena together." The Fifth cocked her head to the side. "Has the daughter of the Third ever given any attention to the Tenth before?"

Jura gritted her teeth. *Of course, why would Amira suddenly focus all her attention on the Tenth?*

It was something Amira often did, throwing herself at someone or something only after Jura expressed interest. Jura shouldn't be surprised that her friend sought to capture Beshar's affections, either out of curiosity of Jura's motives or simply because she could. Jura sighed and walked toward them.

Amira smiled at her approach. "There you are. I was just speaking with Beshar about how radiant you looked today."

Jura frowned at her.

"Isn't she beautiful? Jura, you're positively glowing." Amira stood between her and Beshar, smiling widely at both.

"The Tenth was just telling me about his wine collection. It's absolutely marvelous. He stores it in glass bottles and it keeps for years." She grinned at Beshar. "Jura loves wine."

Jura hardly touched the stuff but she smiled politely. *What was Amira's game?* She thought she'd have to fend off Amira's advances, not be embarrassed while Amira presented her to Beshar on a polished dinner platter.

The Tenth was staring at Amira, either enraptured by her beauty or trying to figure out her motives…or both.

"I had hoped Jura would accompany me to Inferno's training arena. She expressed such interest yesterday."

Amira wrinkled her nose, "Inferno?"

"His dragon," Jura answered without looking over at her. "And I would love to." She had to make her move tonight. "But perhaps dinner, tonight? You could show me your wine collection."

Beshar looked her over, evaluating her. "Indeed. Shall I send a litter?"

"No, thank you. I'll see you at the dinner hour."

Beshar wriggled his thumbs and then excused himself to greet Jabir, the Seventh.

Jura waited until he was out of earshot before whirling on her friend. "What was that about?"

"What do you mean?" Amira snatched a glass of wine from a passing tray and drank deeply. "Mmm, this is delicious. Try it." She thrust the goblet at Jura.

She took it, but only to avoid having it spill down the front of her robes. "You know what I'm talking about. Why did you say all that in front of Beshar?"

"The Tenth?" She snorted. "What? You like him. I was just helping you out. I know how awkward you can be. Are you going to drink that?" She reached for the goblet she'd given to Jura.

Jura sighed and handed it back to her. "How many of these have you had?"

Amira shrugged. "Not many. Just a few. You're so pretty."

"I have to get you home."

"No," Amira protested loudly. People looked over. "No," she squealed again. "Jura, no. We're having fun."

Jura smiled tightly, reaching for her friend's arm. "I think you've had enough fun. Let's go."

Velder approached and the disapproval on his face was enough to stop a lotus flower from blooming. "What's going on here?"

"We were just leaving," Jura said quickly.

Velder's face smoothed into one of concern. "I do hope the Lady of the Third is well?"

"Nothing a nap won't fix," Jura grunted. Amira had decided to lean all her body weight on her. She staggered under her limp friend.

"And your father?" Velder pressed on. "I have an urgent matter and I must speak with him."

"Councilman, you're in my way. Please step aside. I'll tell the First you wish to speak with him, and the First will see you when he has the time."

Velder was too surprised to do anything and stood frozen as Jura brushed by him and Amira giggled.

It wasn't easy convincing Amira to go to her chambers. She wouldn't release her hold on Jura, so she was forced to carry her friend through the halls and to her chamber door. The private chambers of the Third, just across from Amira's, stood open. Jura could see the Third sitting at his desk, poring over ledgers. He frowned at Jura and she quickly looked away.

"Take a nap," she ordered Amira. "You'll feel better after that."

"Are you going to do it?" Amira grabbed Jura's arm, her face intense.

"Do what?"

"You know. *It.* With Beshar." She narrowed her eyes and frowned down at Jura, wobbling slightly from side to side. "Or maybe you want to do it with your Light Guard? Markus or Marton or—" She hiccuped loudly.

Jura blushed. "I don't know what you're talking about." She shoved Amira inside her room and shut her door firmly behind her.

"Greatness—Amira, is she…"

Jura flinched when the Third placed a firm hand on her shoulder. She hadn't heard him approach. She intertwined her fingers and wriggled her thumbs then twisted her hands so that only her little fingers were interlocked and so that her thumbs pointed down to the ground, the traditional sign to show sympathy. "I'm so sorry for your loss."

Ahmar nodded grimly. Jura had thought him much too stern to waste water with tears, but his eyes were rimmed red all the same.

"Amira is just…tired. She'll feel better after some rest."

"This is a very troubling time for my family. I hope you'll look after her. She's been so different lately, and I worry…" He shook his head. "I should never have taken her offer to take interim power. I—please, look after my daughter."

Jura searched her mind for a reply, but the Third was already shuffling back to his study.

Jura felt lost. First the worry of her father, then Markhim's disappearance, and now the worry of her friend's family after the loss of Antar. On top of all that, the impeding evening loomed over her and with it the nagging question of whether or not she would lose the rest of her innocence. *I won't do it…right? If I can't even say* it, *then I definitely shouldn't do it. Sex. There, I said it. Well, in my head anyway.*

She was running out of time and tonight was her last chance. Beshar seemed to like her well enough, but he also seemed to know how to keep a secret. *How am I going to get him to divulge his? And why had Amira asked her about it? What does she know?* She walked the twisting glass hall in a daze, turning from her memory, and was surprised when she once again stood outside her own chambers. East opened the door and entered before her to do his usual surveillance sweep. He turned to her, his features surprised.

"What is it?" she asked, not expecting an answer. She pushed past him to see for herself.

Her bedroom was destroyed. Her bed was overturned. Her chests were empty, their contents strewn across the floor. And worse, much worse, her giant rug was thrown back and her trap door left open. *No, no, no.* She raced across her room and peered down into the blackness of the crawl space.

Her father was gone.

TWENTY SIX

KAY

*S*he sat straight up in bed, panicking that she was late for morning chores. *Mama is going to kill me,* she thought leaping from the bed. As soon as her feet hit the grainy sand floor she stopped. She wasn't home anymore, and Mama was dead, burned alive. She sat down heavily on the bed and stared at her surroundings. The effects of the drugs were gone. She nearly felt herself. She Breathed in the heat around her and produced a small spark of flame that danced along her fingertips. She extinguished the flame and let loose a heavy sigh of relief. Yes, the drugs were out of her system and the chains were gone, but she had no idea where she was.

She was in a large room. The walls appeared like they were made out of mud. Kay wrinkled her nose at the thought. She reached out and touched the walls with her fingertips. It was as hard as stone. The floors were dirty and the room was empty save for several beds that lined the walls. Every bed was empty.

Someone had left a small mug of water by her bed and she reached for it greedily, suddenly realizing that she was dying of thirst. The water was warm and stale, but she drank it anyway, gasping after and feeling refreshed. She was unchained, she wasn't drugged, and someone had left her water. She felt the safest she'd felt in days and allowed her mind to wander, swinging her legs as she sat and drank.

Mama and Daddy are dead. She hadn't been able to give it much thought since it had happened. The last thing she clearly remembered was Rumble dying in front of her, then she'd woken up to find herself chained, drugged, and left in that tiny cage, the kind that Daddy had built for the chickens. After her initial outburst, Udo had kept her heavily drugged. The rest of the trip had been a blur. She'd spent most of her time drifting in and out of consciousness, vaguely aware that she'd been in some sort of moving cart. Kay made sure she didn't cry. She tried to stay strong like Daddy would have wanted. She hadn't understood exactly where she'd been taken, but she understood the exchange of currency well enough to know that she had been sold.

The big man with the kind eyes had tried to speak to her. Though she didn't understand his words, his voice had been soft and gentle. She had just been happy to leave Udo.

The door at the end of the room opened and Kay crouched down on all fours, ready to leap from the bed. She Breathed in the heat, grateful that it was so hot in the room, but she didn't produce fire just yet.

The man entered, the big one with the kind eyes. He carried a tray and entered the room with slow measured steps. Kay watched him walk toward her with wide eyes.

He stopped just in front of her, setting the tray down on the bed beside her. He was mumbling soft words and staring into her eyes, and she wondered what he was saying and what he would do with her. He'd brought her food. She looked down at it and her belly growled loud enough to rival Rumble on his best day. The man laughed.

He pushed the tray closer to her and she reached for the flat, bread-like substance and stuffed it in her mouth. It was dry and nothing like mama's soft bread, but it was food and Kay hadn't eaten in days. Besides the flat bread stuff were tiny, purplish brown balls. She picked one up and looked at it questioningly.

"What is this?" she asked, knowing he couldn't answer.

"Fig," he responded, surprising her. He opened one of them to produce a fleshy red middle. With a shrug, she popped one in her mouth. It was slightly sweet, and she let the fruit roll around her mouth, testing its grains against her tongue.

"Fig," she repeated.

He smiled. Looking deep into her eyes, he pointed to the fig and repeated the word. Then he pointed to himself, thumping his hand against his chest.

"Ash."

Was that his name? She frowned over the word before repeating it to him. "Ash."

The man smiled. He appeared utterly delighted, Kay resisted the urge to roll her eyes. She'd repeated a word, not ridden a dragon.

The man was saying something else, but she couldn't understand his words, they were fast and clipped to her ears. *What language was this and where am I?* She knew there were several lands outside the borders of her home, but she'd never visited any of them. Mama had insisted that she was too young to go on any of Daddy's trips, no matter how she begged.

The man, Ash, stood up from his crouched position. Though the movement was abrupt, it didn't startle her. He didn't appear to want to hurt her, and Kay exhaled the heat she'd Breathed in, eating more of the figs and the flat bread. The man seemed content to watch her eat. After she'd finished, he stepped back toward the door, motioning for her to follow.

She followed him reluctantly. His strides were short and measured. Kay figured it was probably in deference to her tiny size. She had to jog to keep pace behind him. They walked down a series of hallways that led outside to a wide-open field of dirt. Kay wrinkled her nose. These people had an odd idea of what a field should look like. *Where was the grass? The wildflowers?*

The dirt field was empty save for a group of boys on the opposite side. They each held long sticks and twirled them about in unison. Kay watched with interest.

"Ash." Someone called out from across the field. Kay followed the sound of the voice and saw a man waving Ash over. Ash walked toward him, motioning that Kay should follow.

The two men spoke in animated tones. Kay ignored them, more interested in the athletic display from the group of boys than a conversation she couldn't follow.

The boys twirled and leapt in the air, occasionally throwing their sticks and spinning around those too. It was beautiful, and Kay wished she had a stick so that she could try too.

"Hello."

She'd been so mesmerized by the dancing boys that she hadn't heard the woman approach. She flinched, startled by her presence and the familiar language. She met the eyes of Ash who stood near, watching her intensely.

"Hello." She whispered, giving the woman a once over. She was tall and slender and wore pants that were cropped at her knees and a loose tunic that showed her bare, toned arms. Her hair was short and spiky. She smiled at Kay with blue eyes that reminded Kay of her mama. The woman had a jagged scar over one of her eyes, but Kay liked the way it looked. It made her appear brave instead of scary.

"My name is Kindle. What's yours?"

"Kay. How do you know my language?"

The woman's smile deepened. "I didn't always live here in the arena. I grew up just south of the wilds in La'Nor. That's near the river lands of Tirdrakor. My family were traveling merchants. What about you?"

Kay was careful in her response. Mama always said it was polite to answer a question but smart not to reveal more than you had to.

"I lived on a farm."

Kindle nodded. "It must be very hard for you, being so far away from them in such a strange place."

"My parents are dead." Kay heard herself answer bitterly and wished she could stuff the words back in her mouth.

Kindle's eyes were full of compassion. She knelt beside Kay so she could stare into her face at eye level. "I'm very sorry to hear that. You must miss them terribly."

Kay nodded.

"Ash is a friend of mine. He wants me to help you get used to your new life here. I'm a friend, okay, and I want to help you in any way I can. I can tell you anything you want to know."

Kay considered this. She would not accept that her life was here, wherever here was, yet she also knew that she wasn't strong enough to plan an escape. She needed to learn more about her surroundings. She needed to learn the language.

"Can you teach me his words? The one's that Ash speaks?"

Kindle stood up and smiled at Ash, saying something to him before answering. "Of course. I'd be happy to. And Ash would love that. But first, I need to ask you some questions." Kindle pointed over to the boys. "Do you see those boys over there? They're called cadets."

"Cadets." Kay repeated, trying out the new word.

"Yes, a cadet is what we call boys and girls when they come to this place to train. When they come here, to the arena. You're here because Ash is going to help you train."

Kay scratched her nose to keep it from scrunching up. Though she did like watching the boys perform their acrobatic dance, she could hardly see a reason why Ash would care if she learned how. She wondered if that was the entire reason she had been stolen from home. She had thought at first it was because of Daddy and the dragons, that it had something to do with the fact that she was special.

"Why does Ash want to teach me anything?"

"Kay, is there something different about you? Anything that makes you special? Maybe you have some sort of power?"

Kay could feel her heart beating hard in her chest. She clenched her fists together, trying to calm its wild thumping. *What would Daddy want me to do?* Daddy and Mama had always warned her about sharing her powers with anyone. Mama was worried, and Daddy had warned that it was smart to keep such things secret, only sharing within the family. She hadn't kept her secret with the bad man, and he had hurt Mama and Daddy and brought her here.

"I don't know what you mean."

Kindle shared a look with Ash, whispering something to him in his language. Ash shook his head, and Kindle threw her hands up in the air, shouting back at him. Ash said nothing, looking ashamed.

"You don't have to be afraid, Kay. No one will hurt you. You can tell me the truth. Do you know anything about dragons?"

Kay felt a funny feeling in her gut. She looked back at the dancing boys and then at Ash and Kindle. Ash's face looked worried, and Kindle's face was serious and intense. *I can't tell them anything. Maybe if they think I'm not special, they'll let me go.* She shook her head. Shrugged.

"The dragons live beyond the border of the wilds. Nobody goes there because dragons are dangerous." It was a safe answer, the right answer, but Kay hated lying, and the anxiety in the pit of her belly grew stronger.

"Kay, what do you know about fire?"

"It's hot."

"Is that all?" Kindle's voice was flat and her blue eyes no longer sparkled.

Kay nodded, forcing her breathing to stay slow and even. She realized she was Breathing in the heat and released her breath with clenched teeth.

Kindle laughed. It wasn't a nice sound. She laughed loudly, throwing her head back and shaking it. She spoke a few words to Ash, who begun to shake his head. His eyes were wide and disbelieving as he stared down at her.

216

Kay looked away, not wanting to meet his eyes, and pushed aside the feeling that she'd let him down. She'd made the right decision. Daddy and Mama would have wanted her to lie. She had to find a way to escape. She had to find a way back home. She ignored the nagging truth that she had no home, that to return back to her family's land meant returning to an empty house and a burned barn. *It doesn't matter,* she told herself. She didn't belong here. She would find a way back home, no matter the cost.

TWENTY SEVEN

JURA

"Shut the door." She barked out the order, pacing the length of her room. *Gone. He's really and truly gone.*

"You two. Search the palace halls. See if you can find him." Had he left on his own? Had she forgotten to latch the trapdoor? Had he made his way out and was now wandering the halls, forced to the bidding of his master? Or had someone else found him and spirited him away for their own purposes? She bit her bottom lip to keep from screaming out in frustration. *Think Jura, you can do this.*

There was a smart way to handle this. No one except her and her father's *Arbe* knew that he'd been held captive in her room. She continued to pace. *Tylak knows.* She pushed the thought aside. If he had anything to do with this, her father was truly gone. She was missing something, somehow. Either through Tylak or her *Arbe*, one of the Thirteen had learned where she was keeping her father. *Arbe* had no form of communicating. They couldn't speak. They couldn't write. *Could it all be a coincidence?*

Say someone entered her room looking for something. They tear the room apart and happen upon her trapdoor. Naturally, seeing the First inside they remove him from his prison. *But what would someone have gone to my room looking for?* She had nothing to hide except her father. No, whoever was responsible had gone looking for her father. It made sense really. She should have seen this coming. Whoever was responsible for her father's blood chain would get tired of waiting for results. It had been nearly two weeks. It was safe to assume that her father had yet to complete his tasks. It had to be someone in the council. They were all aware that her father was indisposed, and Jura had assured them that he was thriving in her care. Someone had known she was lying and someone had taken action to find him. *Who has him?*

She should never have gotten so complacent, so confident, that all would be fine. Her *Arbe* returned shaking their heads in disappointment. They hadn't found her father.

Wait. The men shook their heads. Sandstorms, but she was an idiot. Just because an *Arbe* couldn't speak or write didn't mean they couldn't communicate! There was body language. At the very least they could answer yes and no questions.

"None of you saw who did this?"

They all shook their heads, eyes downcast in shame. It was well within her right to kill them in punishment for being lax. She assured them she would not do so.

"Do you have any idea who might have done so? Any one I should suspect?"

Again, they shook their heads.

She tried another tactic. "Can you all talk?"

They stared at her with unblinking eyes.

"Is it possible for you to communicate with one another?"

They nodded, their heads bobbing slowly in unison. She felt chills run down the length of her spine.

"How is this possible?"

They stood unmoving. Then West slowly brought his hands together.

What is he trying to tell me? "I don't understand."

West pointed at Jura and brought an open hand to his chest, then he pointed to himself and splayed his fingers.

She shook her head, confused.

Frustrated, East pointed to a book then opened his hands together in the shape of an open book. Then he pointed to Jura again, slapping his chest.

"Are you saying you communicate with your hands?"

They nodded their heads.

"So, you *can* communicate with each other!" She narrowed her eyes. "That means you can communicate with other *Arbe*. Have you told anyone else about my father?"

They quickly shook their heads. West looked horrified.

"Then how did this happen?" she growled in frustration, sitting heavily on the floor. The *Arbe* stood unmoving before her.

"You don't know who did this?"

They shook their heads.

"And to your knowledge, none of the other *Arbe* know about this?"

Again, they shook their heads.

"But it is possible for you to communicate such a fact with another *Arbe*, if you so choose? You could find a way?"

They nodded.

She sighed deeply. Could they be trusted? Could she trust anyone? With Markhim gone, she suddenly wished she'd told Amira everything. She desperately wanted the strength from the support of a friend.

There was a knock at her door. Jura stood up in alarm.

She motioned for her *Arbe* to open the door.

Velder stood outside. His face quickly twisted into one of concern as he peered inside.

"Greatness, what—are you—is everything alright?"

Jura swallowed. "I'm fine. I was…looking for something." *What if Velder found out the Third and I were making a move for his Rank? Is he behind this?*

"Indeed?" His eyes swept across the room, taking in the overturned furniture and spilled contents of her chests.

"What did you want?" she asked.

"I've come from your father's chambers. I was hoping to gain an audience with the First. When I saw his *Arbe* outside your own chambers, I thought I might find him here with you. I have an urgent matter to discuss."

"Well, as you can see the First isn't here." She narrowed her eyes at him. *Was that the hint of a smile that played under his thin mustache?* Velder's own *Arbe* stood close around him, their faces still and impassive. She looked at them and then back to her own men, wondering if they had ever spoken to one another. *Stop it*, she ordered herself, dragging her thoughts back to Velder.

"What is it that you wished to discuss?"

"Private matters. Meant for the ears of the First alone."

"I am acting interim."

"You *were* acting interim." He smiled then, and the sight of it made her nauseous. "But it appears that your father is up and about and no longer indisposed. I suppose if I cannot track him down the matter will have to wait another day. Good day, daughter of the First."

She flinched. He'd dropped the honorific.

"I do hope you find what you were looking for."

TWENTY EIGHT

ASH

Beshar will kill me. Ash was a free man. It wasn't too late for him to disappear, take his savings and leave the city. He'd spent a small fortune on the girl only to find out he'd been duped. She was powerless. A little girl with a foreign mouth and no fire sense at all. He was in serious trouble.

"What are you going to do?" Kindle's voice was urgent, her large blue eyes narrowed in concern.

Ash shook his head, shrugging his shoulders in a helpless gesture. He looked down at the tiny, girl cadet who wasn't a cadet at all and sighed. *What do I do with her?*

"You said her name was Kay, right?"

Kindle nodded. The girl looked up at the mention of her name. She looked frightened.

"Tell her we have a problem."

Kindle frowned at him. "Why? What's the purpose of scaring a little girl?"

"She's already terrified and we're here arguing right in front of her in a language she doesn't understand. Explain to her that we have a problem."

Kindle sighed but sank down to her knee and spoke to the girl in quiet, serious tones.

Kay listened with solemn blue eyes and a trembling bottom lip.

Kindle stood up. "There. She's suitably terrified. Satisfied?" She stabbed her assegai into the dirt. "This is really messed up, you know that? She said her parents are dead, the slavers probably killed them in front of her for all we know. What are we going to do?"

"We?" Ash raised his brows in surprise.

"Well, unless you suddenly learn her language, I guess I'm sticking around as translator."

At her offer to stand by him, Ash felt much better. "Thank you."

His relief lasted for all of ten seconds before it faded away with Timber's presence.

"What are you doing on the practice field, old man? Come to watch me and my boy?" He grinned as he walked over, twirling his assegai with quick sturdy fingers. "Hello, little girl."

"What, no greeting for me?" Kindle smirked.

"I was talking to you." Timber winked at her. "Who's the cadet?"

"None of your concern." Ash growled. "And she's no cadet."

"Oh no? Then what's she doing here? She looks kinda like you, Kindle. This your kid?" He leered over at her. "What's your name, little girl?" He directed the question at Kay.

Kay looked up at Kindle with questioning eyes and stepped back away from Timber into Kindle's protective embrace.

"Yeah, she's mine. Her name is Kay and you can keep away from her." Kindle laid a hand on either of Kay's shoulders.

Timber grinned and Ash wanted to punch the smug look off his face. He clenched his fingers, forcing them to remain by his side.

"That's too bad, old man. I thought you were training a new cadet, trying to bring up some competition for my boy." His grin deepened. "Though I must say, I'm glad this isn't all you managed to dredge up. Pathetic excuse for a cadet if she was one. She's awful little. Sorry Kindle." He looked around, his gaze searching. "I guess your plans fell through." He shook his head in mock sadness, leveling an eye on Ash. "Looks like your life in the arena is over."

Ash took a step forward. If he slammed his fist with enough force at Timber, he could cause serious damage, give the man a collapsed sternum or a crushed windpipe. He slowly unclenched his fists and forced himself to draw deep, calming breaths.

"Shouldn't you be training your cadet?" Kindle's voice was low and threatening. She fingered the shaft of her assegai with narrowed eyes.

Timber shrugged. "Sure thing. I'll leave you kids alone."

He winked before sauntering off. Ash gritted his teeth while he watched him walk away.

"Cocky prick."

Kindle nodded her agreement. "He's always been that way. My first day as cadet was the day he had his naming day. They said he stabbed the dragon's heart as it reared up and the beast fell heavy as a chopped tree." She shook her head. "He's a magical sight in the arena but could use more than a few manners."

"I wish I could beat them into him." Ash sighed, his eyes falling down to Kay. Her small frame still trembled next to Kindle. "Have any ideas what to do with the girl?"

Kindle forced out a laugh. "You're the brains of this operation. Did you feed her? Timber was right about one thing, she is really little."

She changed languages and addressed Kay. Ash could tell she asked a question by the inflection in her tone. He raised his brow in question as the girl whispered her answer.

"Says she's seven years old." Kindle frowned. "Maybe she's just too young for the gift to have manifested?"

Ash shook his head. "I fed her. And no, I've been played is all. You should have seen her in that cage, Kindle. All hair and big blue eyes. The trader claimed he had to keep her drugged so she wouldn't use her power. I believed him, fool that I am. At least I got her out of there. Cadet or not, no child deserves to be treated that way."

"I'm glad you did. I'm sure she is too." She patted the girl's shoulders.

Kay's attention was back on the boy cadets in the sparring field. Timber was leading them through parry sequences, the tip of his assegai flashed in the sun as he twirled it over his head.

A bugle sounded, announcing the entrance of one of the Thirteen. Ash sucked in a breath, praying that it wasn't Beshar. He wasn't ready yet and needed to come up with a plan before Beshar demanded a cadet or his money back. The Everflame ignored his prayer.

Beshar walked onto the dirt field, accompanied by his usual company of oiled bodyguards. Ash watched as the councilman stopped to talk with Timber. The two exchanged greetings. Something Timber said caused the councilman to let out a shout of laughter that echoed across the field.

"At least he's in a good mood," Kindle observed.

Ash sent her a dubious stare.

"What?" she asked innocently. "It's better than him walking in angry."

Timber had the boys perform an attack sequence, and Beshar watched for several minutes. Apparently satisfied, he patted Timber on the shoulder before spotting Ash and heading toward them.

Here we go, Ash thought. He inhaled a deep breath, and Kay looked up at him in curiosity. He shook his head in silent warning.

"Ash. Happy to see you've an early start. Is this my cadet?" He looked Kay up and down, frowning at her cowering form. "Kinda small, isn't she? Don't be frightened, girl. You belong to my house now. We're winners in the arena. Stand proud."

"She doesn't speak our language." Ash said stiffly, wondering what to say next. *Should I just blurt out that she's ungifted? How would Beshar respond to his wasted coin?*

Beshar actually smiled. "Of course. Drakori, is it?" He directed a question at the girl in a foreign and clipped tongue.

Kindle's eyes widened, and she looked at Ash in alarm. Beshar spoke the girl's language. *I'm a dead man.*

Kay actually laughed and responded to the councilman with a slight smile.

Ash attempted to swallow his tongue.

Beshar bellowed a laugh and slapped Ash hard on the back. "Fiery little chit

227

that one. I've never had a female gladiator before." He smiled, considering it. "I like it." He looked about the training field, seemingly satisfied. "Get some meat and muscle on those tiny bones, Ash. I have faith that she'll deliver once in the arena?"

Ash felt like his tongue was growing larger in his mouth.

"Councilman, there's something you should know—"

He was interrupted by a cheerful Kindle. "I'm helping him train her. Working as translator." She squeezed Ash's shoulder in warning.

Beshar narrowed his eyes at them both. "I'll not pay for two trainers."

"That's okay," Kindle answered, still smiling. "Ash promised to pay me out of his own wages."

"That's right," Ash quickly agreed. He didn't dare look over at Kindle.

Beshar nodded. "Well, I only stopped by to check on my latest investment. I'll expect a thorough display of her skill next week after she's had time to settle in." He shot another glance toward Kay, who stared at him with wide blue eyes. He nodded at her in satisfaction and then left the arena, his oiled men in tow.

Ash exhaled loudly, watching him leave.

"What was that about?" He asked Kindle, frowning down at her.

"Just buying you time." She shrugged. "I can't believe he speaks Drakori."

"What did he say to her? What did she say to him? To make him laugh?"

The corner of Kindle's lips turned up, and she smoothed back Kay's riotous curls from her face. "He told Kay that he was very excited to meet her but that he was surprised she was so small. She told him that she was surprised men could grow to be so large."

Ash inhaled a breath so fast that he choked on it. He stared at the girls with wide eyes. "She called him fat and he laughed?"

Kindle smiled, "I guess he did. Maybe he liked her cheekiness?"

Ash shook his head in wonder. "Well, we've bought ourselves some time at least. We have a week to figure out a plan."

"Do you think that will give us enough time?" Kindle wondered out loud.

Ash could only shake his head. It wouldn't be enough time. No amount of time would be. He was in need of a miracle.

TWENTY NINE

JURA

*S*he didn't know how long the person stood knocking at her door before she recognized the sound for what it was. She met the concerned gaze of one of her men and flicked a wrist toward the door. She'd spent the rest of the morning looking for her father and had come back to her room to restore it to order and think. She'd laid down on her bed and had lost herself in her thoughts. Her father had disappeared without a trace.

The door opened and Amira appeared, her hair slightly mussed and her breath still reeking of wine. Once again, she wasn't wearing any makeup, and Jura was struck by how vulnerable her friend looked without it. Also, she was wearing simple cotton robes in place of her customary dress. Jura had never seen her friend in such a bedraggled state.

"You look like I feel." Jura acknowledged.

"I came to apologize," Amira said. She sat on the edge of Jura's bed and frowned down at her friend. "I think I'll stay away from wine for a bit." She reached for Jura's slipper-encased foot, giving it a tug. Jura sat up, hugging a pillow to her chest.

"I know why I feel bad. Want to tell me what's bothering you?" Amira patted her foot.

More than anything in the world, she wanted to open up to Amira and tell her what was going on. She opened her mouth but stopped herself at a disapproving look from East. *Did I imagine that or is he telling me to keep quiet?* She shook her head.

"You don't have to apologize, Amira. I can't imagine what you're going through. Your father's worried about you. We both are. Losing your brother so suddenly…it must be very difficult."

Amira nodded. "Yes, it's hard. I'm surprised to hear father even noticed. He won't come out of his study. I could use some cheering up, though. I suppose we both could. You sure you can't tell me what's got you so upset?"

"It's nothing," Jura sighed. "Really, just the stress of the week I suppose."

"I could see that. I thought you were going to say you were upset because your guard left."

"What? How did you know he left?"

Amira shrugged. "I haven't seen him around, that's all. Where did he go?"

Jura sighed. "I wish I knew. Just forget about him. It was just a stupid crush." *And maybe one day I'll convince myself of that.*

"I wish you were going to be in the council meeting with me tomorrow. Not that I'm unhappy your father is feeling better, but I had hoped—"

"Where did you hear that?" Jura leaned close to her friend, her heart leaping to her throat. "Did you see him?"

"No, I didn't see him. But Velder came calling to speak with father. He said it was a matter of importance. He requests a meeting with the first three houses. I don't think he was too happy that I'm acting as interim Third."

Jura let out a small laugh. "He wouldn't tell you anything either, huh?"

"I wish he hadn't," Amira frowned. "It's bad news, Jura. I wish I could tell you, but Velder said it wasn't to be discussed outside the heads of the first three families." She sighed dramatically and fell back against the bed. "Honestly, I don't know how you did it. It's only been a day and already I'm more stressed out than I've ever been. Don't worry, though. I won't have any more to drink."

"What's going on? What doesn't Velder want anyone to know?"

Amira shook her head violently, causing her thick braid to fall over her shoulder. "Jura, you mustn't ask me again. I really can't tell you." She frowned over at her. "Besides, we all have our secrets, don't we?"

Jura stared at Amira, resisting the urge to scream in frustration. She had been keeping many secrets from her friend, and she probably deserved this bit of payback. She just wished that Amira didn't seem to be enjoying it so much.

"Yes, I suppose we do. And you don't have to apologize for anything."

Amira suddenly giggled. "You know, I don't remember how I got to my room. I'm assuming you?"

Jura smiled back. "You were pretty intoxicated. I had to carry you."

Amira's eyes widened. "You didn't."

"It wasn't easy," Jura admitted. You're not fat but you're far from light."

Amira tossed a pillow at Jura's face. "I remember talking to you and Beshar."

Jura laughed. "Oh, you did. You practically propositioned him for me."

232

"No," Amira's eyes widened.

"Oh, yes. We're having dinner in his apartments."

"Did you—that is, do you…" She trailed off, seemingly at a loss for words. "Do you really like him, Jura?"

"I do." Jura answered carefully, picking over her words. "He's very… interesting."

Amira seemed to consider this. "What are you going to wear?"

Jura thought of her wardrobe. She needed to wear something sexy, and her entire wardrobe was anything but.

"I have no idea." *I'm in way over my head.*

Amira laughed, "Well, we don't have much time to figure it out. You have less than an hour before the dinner hour."

Jura jumped up from the bed startled. *Was it really so late?* The entire day had been a disaster. She felt a fool for even continuing through with her dinner plans. *Father is missing. What good will come from a seduction attempt? What good is knowing who's responsible for father's blood chain when he's missing? And where in the sandstorm is he?*

Amira was saying something, and Jura focused her attention back to their conversation.

"…and if we had more time we could do it."

"Do what?" Jura asked blankly. She had to stop zoning out.

"Take in one of my gowns. They'd never fit you as is. You'd look like a little girl playing dress up. I've never seen anyone as short as you."

"The Fifth is." Jura mumbled defensively.

Amira brightened. "That's a great idea!"

"What is?"

233

"Borrowing a dress from the Fifth. She has hundreds. I don't think I've ever seen her repeat one." She sighed wistfully. "I wonder what it's like to be so rich and in total control of your own fortune? Father never lets me have enough dresses."

"I'm not asking the Fifth to borrow a dress." Jura frowned at the idea.

"Why not? Come on, Jura, it's the perfect idea. You can't wear your tunic and robes on a dinner date, no matter how nice they are. You need a dress and she has plenty in your size." She jumped off the bed and pulled at her arm. "We're asking her. It's final."

"No, I don't think—"

"It's the best idea you've had in ages. Come one, we're running out of time."

Jura allowed herself to be dragged from the room. Her *Arbe* quickly fell in place beside them.

"Isn't it odd what your father's doing?"

"What do you mean?" Jura concentrated on walking and keeping her breathing calm and even.

"Wandering about the palace without his *Arbe*. It makes no sense."

Sandstorms. Amira was right. People would question it. *And was he simply just wandering about the palace?* The glass halls were empty save for the girls. If her father was meandering through the halls, surely someone would have spotted him.

"The First has always believed in taking care of himself." Jura replied with the vaguest answer she could think of.

Amira nodded, taking a sharp left in the direction of the Fifth's apartments. "You're right, of course. Who would dare to challenge the First?"

Who indeed.

They arrived at the door to the Fifth's apartments. No men stood guard, and Amira sniffed at the lack of security.

The Fifth answered the door herself. She wore a black silk dressing robe that fell to the ground in soft waves about her tiny frame. Her hair was unbound and hung in a straight waterfall down her back. Her tired eyes widened in curiosity at the girls.

"Daughters of the First and Third. What an interesting surprise. Please, do come in." She opened the door wide, and Jura heard Amira mutter about the Fifth's trust as they walked inside.

Though smaller than her own halls and apartments, the Fifth's were lavishly decorated and screamed of her wealth. Marbled pillars were spaced throughout the room and the tiles of the walls were lined with gold. Jura had a sinking realization that it was actual gold, probably shipped from Kitoi. Thick lush carpeting covered the stone floor, and on the far side of the room, a jade statue of a child spitting water from its mouth into a tiny pool full of the precious liquid. Jura gaped at the wealth. She'd never seen anything so ostentatious in her life.

The Fifth took a seat on a soft, plush chaise and gestured for them to do the same.

"What can I do for you girls?" Her voice was curious; her eyes shrewd and questioning.

Jura suddenly felt very foolish for coming to see her.

"The daughter of the First needs a favor." Amira said, lifting her chin and sounding haughty. Trust Amira to remind a woman twice her age that she was lower than herself in Rank.

Unfazed, the Fifth raised her brow. "Does she?" She smiled a bit, looking to Jura.

Amira nodded. "Yes. She needs a dress."

"I can ask for my own favor," Jura muttered to Amira, and the Fifth smiled wider.

"My lady Fifth—" Jura began.

"Please, call me Denir." Her voice was low and husky, and she stared at Jura with direct eyes that made her blush uncomfortably.

"Denir," she repeated. "I was hoping to borrow a dress."

The Fifth widened her eyes and Jura hurried to explain.

"I don't really own one, you see, and I have a dinner date."

Understanding dawned on Denir's face, and she stood from her chaise, motioning forward a handmaiden that Jura hadn't noticed.

"Of course," Denir said smoothly. "Something in a jewel tone, I imagine, to compliment your complexion." She gestured for the girls to follow her into the adjoining chamber. The room was dominated by a massive bed that took up most of the room and a large wooden armoire that took up the rest of the space.

"Thank you." Jura said awkwardly as the handmaiden began pulling gowns out from the Fifth's armoire.

Amira eyed the gowns critically, pointing out a deep blue sapphire. "That one." She held out an expectant hand, and, amused, Denir nodded for her handmaiden to place it in Amira's outstretched arm. Amira held the gown up against Jura's slender frame. Jura frowned at the gown's plunging neckline. The dress was everything she needed it to be, and she was terrified of it.

"Ohh, I love this," Amira squealed in excitement and pushed past the handmaiden to reach into Denir's armoire. She pulled out a long, gold chain that held a deep blue stone.

"Is this a birthstone? It matches the dress perfectly. You simply must let Jura borrow it."

Denir stood up quickly. Her arm snaked out and snatched the stone and its delicate chain from Amira's fingers.

"That's not yours to loan."

Embarrassed, Jura shot a warning glance to her friend. "Of course not, my lady Fifth." She glared at Amira. "What are you doing?"

Nonplussed Amira shrugged. "What? It's just a necklace. It's not even really her birthstone." Amira looked pointedly at the red stone that hung from Denir's neck. The Fifth tucked the red stone back under her dressing gown and shoved the other one in her pocket.

"It's not my birthstone. But the necklace has sentimental value. The stone was my mother's."

Horrified, Jura nodded. "Of course. Amira was just being presumptuous. Thank you, my lady. The dress is lovely."

Denir stared from one girl to the other; her face unreadable. "You're quite welcome. You girls had best be along now. You wouldn't want to miss your dinner."

She ushered the girls to her door, and Jura thanked her again, still embarrassed by Amira's display. Once outside the Fifth's apartments and back in the glass halls, Jura frowned at her friend.

"That was rude, asking to borrow someone's birthstone simply isn't done."

"It wasn't her stone." Amira said pointedly, refusing to be chastised. "Besides, it matched the dress perfectly. The ocean blue looks great with the sapphire."

Jura stopped in her tracks and turned to stare up at her friend in wonder.

"What did you just say?"

"That it matched the dress. Which it did." Amira frowned down at the sapphire dress she still clutched and handed it over to Jura.

Jura took the dress, remembering the words of Tylak.

"No, not that part. The part about the color of the stone."

"What? Ocean blue? It's a lovely color."

"You've never been to the ocean."

"Oh, Jura. Don't pretend you've never seen the painting in our salon. That stone was the same color."

Right. A coincidence maybe? Jura doubted it.

THIRTY

JURA

The gown was somewhat loose on her bosom, but Amira's handmaiden was able to pin it back easily. Afterward, Jura had to admit it fit perfectly.

"You look gorgeous," Amira sighed, pushing Jura's shoulders so she would take a step back and allow Amira to examine her figure.

Jura frowned at her image in the looking glass. Her hair was captured in a loose braid that hung over her shoulder and provided some coverage from the plunging neckline of the dress. If Jura's bosom was more impressive, the neckline would barely be able to contain them. She couldn't believe that the Fifth had actually worn the gown in public. The blue silk complemented her tan skin and dark brown hair and clung to her skin in a way that was teasing and soft. Her cheeks were red, flushed from embarrassment. She spun in a slow circle, blushing at the way the dress belled out and exposed her ankles. It was a perfect dress for seduction. Jura immediately wanted to take it off.

"Are you sure it's not too much?" She pulled the fabric away from her skin to scowl down at it.

Amira rolled her eyes. "It's perfect. It's what everyone wears in Kitoi. In fact," she leered down at Jura's chest and wriggled her eyebrows. "It might not be enough."

Mortified, Jura crossed her arms over her chest. "I can't do this."

"I was only teasing, Jura." Amira pulled her arms down and smiled at her friend. "Truly, you look beautiful. Beshar won't be able to resist you. No one could." She grinned. "The only question now is why would you ever choose the fat, rotting body of the Tenth when you could have any man you wanted?"

Jura shook her head, refusing to answer. "I better get going."

"Of course." Amira nodded enthusiastically. "I wouldn't want you to be late." She frowned, looking unsure before blurting out, "Leave some of your men with me? Please? I should have an *Arbe* of my own again by tomorrow, but I'm much too frightened to go without one. Dahr is still out there. He probably wants to finish what he's started."

"Absolutely." She indicated for East and West to stay behind, deciding to keep North and South with her this time. "You really feel it was the Fourth?"

"Who else would it have been?" Amira shivered and shook her head. "I'm speaking out against him at council session tomorrow. I'm voting for him to be brought down. I wish you were going to be there. I'm not sure I can convince your father to back my vote. Maybe you could talk to him before the meeting?"

Jura nodded absently, distracted by the idea. Would her father attend the session or would his absence become public knowledge?

She said her goodbyes once again and began the long walk down the east halls on her way to the Tenth's apartments. North and South followed her. North looked particularly ready and kept his hand rested on his scimitar. She knew she'd reached the private halls of the Tenth when she saw the presence of his oiled men. She fought the growing anxiety in the pit of her belly. *It's not too late to run,* she told herself. Yet, inexplicably her feet continued forward. Two of his oiled men, they really all looked the same and she wondered how he told them apart, swung open the large, imposing double doors to his private apartments. Jura stepped inside.

She was immediately greeted by the crisp smells of saffron and roasted fowl. Her mouth began to water. As always, her nerves only served to make her more ravenous. She stared at the opulence of his rooms, wondering at his vast wealth. Why, Beshar appeared to have even more money than the Fifth. His carpets were thick and luxurious, and intricate tapestries lined the walls. But what was most shocking was that Beshar had an actual body of water in his salon. A tiny pool full of fish. They swam about the glass box flashing a variety of colors. The idea of owning water that wasn't used as drinking water was outrageous. The only time Jura had seen a fish was in a drawing in a book. She couldn't believe Beshar kept a reserve of water simply for the creatures to swim around in his home. Any riches found in her own home paled in comparison to those she'd found in the towers of the Fifth and Tenth. *How's such a thing even possible?*

"Hello! Jura, my dear, you look stunning." Beshar's robust greeting snapped her attention back to thoughts of seduction. He reached for her cloak and pulled her further inside.

She blushed furiously and forced herself to lean into his touch. She could do this. She *would* do this.

"May I offer you some wine?"

"Yes, please." She took the offered goblet without a moment's hesitation and took a deep gulp, ignoring the burning sting of the alcohol.

Beshar stared at her, his expression amused. "Yes, it's an excellent vintage. It comes from my own vineyard, west of here in Tirdrakor."

"Near the wilds?" she asked, choking down more wine. She'd barely tasted it.

Beshar hid a chuckle behind his handkerchief and refilled her glass. "Yes. Just outside the wilds, actually. Have you ever been?"

She shook her head, taking another swallow. This time she noted the fruity and slightly acidic accents of the chilled wine. She took another sip, savoring the feeling on her tongue. It really was quite good.

"Father would never approve of me traveling."

Beshar tsked. Waving an arm for the dining table to be set, he ushered her to a seat, his hand lightly pushing against the small of her back. She wondered at the delicate size of his fingers when he was so large.

"That's a pity. One can never truly broaden their knowledge until they have traveled to exotic places. New experiences bring new knowledge."

She nodded, taking her seat and swallowing more wine. *You should slow down,* she told herself. It would do no good to be so drunk she couldn't complete her mission. She shivered. Did she really want to do anything sober? She took another swallow and pushed the glass out of her reach.

"It smells delicious in here. I'm starved."

"Excellent, my lady. Then we shall feast." He ordered the first course to be brought out, figs and dates stuffed with creamy goat cheese and smoked meat. It was delicious, and he paired it with a chilled white wine that sparkled and fizzed against her nose. Jura found that she liked it better than the red.

"Is this from your vineyard too?" she asked, enjoying the way the bubbles rolled along her tongue. She was beginning to feel incredibly relaxed, and she bit into a stuffed fig with relish.

"No. I bring this in from Friize. Do you like it?"

She nodded. "It's delicious. Where is Friize?" She tried out the foreign word. It sounded strange coming from her lips.

"Northeast of here. A small country near the edge. "

"So far away? Do you travel there often?" She wondered at the idea. A trip like that would take several weeks.

"Not so often as I used to. I have men to travel there for me now."

Of course, she thought to herself. He probably didn't have to leave the Republic for anything. Her father was well traveled from the misadventures of his youth, though he never spoke to her of any of his journeys. And all of his traveling had come to a stop when Jura's mother had died. Even after all these years, the pain of her death was still as sharp as ever. Jura took another swallow of the sparkling wine, enjoying its numbing effects.

The next course brought out a clear soup that held floating mushrooms sliced paper thin. She loved the flavors and remarked upon the dish.

"My chef is quite excellent." He waved for the main course. Jura was reluctant to give up her soup but excited for the roasted fowl.

The skin was crisp and the meat was juicy. The flavors sank into her tongue with a soft sigh.

"This is wonderful. No wonder you're so fat," she murmured before she could stop the words from springing from her lips. She immediately wished she'd kept her mouth shut and choked on her bite. "Oh! I'm so sorry. I didn't mean—"

He waved off her apology with a dismissive hand and a stern shake of his head.

"Not to worry, my dear. I'm well aware of my physical stature." He shrugged. "I would blame Yemekk, but the truth is I've always been rather large. I'm glad you're enjoying dinner but do save room for dessert."

Dessert proved to be a fattened brown bread of some sort with a smooth topping in a deeper brown. It smelled heavenly, but she raised a brow, curious as to the food's origins.

"It's cake." He offered. "Layered chocolate cake with chocolate frosting." He cut into it and pushed some toward her on a silvered plate.

She sliced into it and placed a small bite in her mouth, immediately moaning in delight. "This. Is. Amazing. Chocolate, you say?"

He nodded, cutting himself a much larger piece. "One of my greatest weaknesses, I'm afraid. Also from Friize. It's cultivated from a plant called cocoa and—"

"Why don't we all live in Friize?" she interrupted, finishing the rest of her cake despite her full belly groaning in protest.

He laughed and signaled that the plates be cleared. "I'll have some wrapped up for you to take home."

She nodded her thanks and took a small sip from her refilled goblet of wine. She no longer felt the heady effects of the wine and instead felt sleepy and content.

"I think I've eaten entirely too much," she remarked, patting her flat belly.

"Would you enjoy an after dinner smoke?" Not waiting for a response, he signaled for a tall hookah to be set on the table. Within moments, he had his Torch light the instrument, setting forth a pungent odor of dried flowers and fruity smoke.

Jura had never smoked before but tried it out, assuming she would like it as much as the new foods. She was wrong. She choked on the smoke and took a huge swallow of wine to get the horrid taste from her mouth.

"That was awful," she choked out between her fits of coughing.

Beshar smiled at her, amusement twinkling in his eye. "It's an acquired taste."

"Why would anyone want to acquire such a taste?" She watched as he declined a refill on his wine and motioned for her own to be refilled. She took a hesitant sip, beginning to feel a slight tingle in her toes. *Was it from the wine or the smoke? You didn't even check the glass for signs of poison. …He wouldn't. Would he?* Purposefully she set her wine down. She had come here with a purpose. She scooted her chair closer to him, feeling the smoke settle into her hair and dress. Denir wouldn't care for her dress to come back so smelly. Beshar watched her with interested eyes.

"The effect of the smoke can be a heady experience. People like to lose themselves to it." He exhaled a long line of smoke and set the hookah aside, gazing deep into her eyes.

She trailed her finger down the length of his arm. *Should I try to kiss him?* She'd never kissed a boy before, not even Markhim, and now she was here, prepared to do so much more. She stared at Beshar's lips, trying to imagine her own pressed against them. He seemed nice enough, but she hesitated, still unsure if she should continue on her path. She didn't have a choice. She leaned forward and licked her lips.

"Why did you come here?"

The question surprised her, and she stared down at her fingers, which still sat lightly on his arm. *Was I doing it wrong?* She'd thought she was making her intentions quite obvious.

She reached for his face. "I think you know why," she whispered. She tried to make her voice husky. *Was it husky or just scratchy from the smoke?*

He caught her hand and slowly brought it down to her lap. He released her, staring at her intensely. "I know what you're trying to do. What I want to know, is why?"

"I-I like you," she stammered.

"Do you?" Abruptly he stood up, moving with surprising speed despite his large frame. He pulled her toward him, crushing her chest to his own. He felt soft and warm, and his lips were mushy and wet. His breath reeked and tasted of wine and dusty flowers. She struggled not to gag against him. Just as abruptly, he pushed her away. She fell back against her chair, breathing hard and trying to calm her frazzled nerves. She forced herself not to wipe away his touch.

"The disgust is still in your eyes, my lady First, so I will ask again. What do you want? Why did you come here? What purpose does your attempt at seduction serve?" His eyes were angry and stared into hers, but he didn't move toward her. Instead, he took a sip from his wine and kept his eyes trained on her face, waiting for an answer.

"I was trying to seduce you," she admitted softly, her mind racing for a reason to give him.

"Why?" He repeated.

"I need you. I need your help."

"Why?"

If she told him the truth, it would all be over before it started. Perhaps it was time to admit that it already *was* over. She had failed. *Why wasn't I a better actress? How could I have let him see through my attempts at seduction? I've failed. Failed father and the family name. What will the Shadow Dancers do now?*

"You have something I need," she said slowly.

"Damn you woman, tell me what game you play at or so help me I—"

"Master, silence. We are not alone."

The interruption came from one of his oiled men. Beshar and Jura turned to him in surprise.

Beshar stood up, grabbing at the knife that was still imbedded in the cake.

"Where?" His face was alert. His eyes searched the room wildly, and Jura trembled.

"What's happening?" she whispered her thoughts aloud, stepping closer to Beshar despite the fact that he held the knife in a ready hand.

He pulled her close and several of his oiled bodyguards flanked around them. North and South stepped closer.

"We know you're here, assassin," Beshar called out, "Show yourself."

Assassin? Jura felt both hot and cold. She wished she too had a knife to clutch, or at the very least her whip. Despite the presence of their men, Jura was frightened. She gazed about the room, taking in the various corners and curtains. *Where could anyone hide?* The room appeared empty, and yet Beshar and his men seemed to know someone was there. No one moved a muscle, and the tension caused Jura to break out into a sweat.

"I don't see anyone here. How can you be sure?" she whispered to Beshar, still unsure what was happening.

"The Samur have varying and unique talents. Some of them can sense when magic is being used. Someone is bending firelight." Beshar turned in a slow circle, pulling Jura close.

"Bending fire…what are you talking about?" She was so confused. One of Beshar's men suddenly leaped toward an empty spot in the room, tackling a figure that had seemingly appeared out of nowhere. The Samur wrestled until yanking the figure to his feet. A Samur grabbed each arm and held him tight.

The figure was dressed entirely in black and had a black silk mask hiding his face. A Shadow Dancer.

Jura stared in shock. So that was how they were always disappearing from sight. They used some sort of magic. *Are Beshar's men somehow immune to such magic? Is that why the Shadow Dancers enlisted my services?*

Tossing the knife to the table, Beshar walked forward and stopped in front of the masked Dancer.

"Explain yourself before my men end your life."

He ripped the mask from the man's face, and Jura gasped. It was Tylak.

THIRTY ONE
TYLAK

He was in trouble. He'd spent the entire morning convincing himself that he needed to break into the palace. It had seemed a fantastic idea. Jura was there. Not that he'd gone to see Jura because that was just silly, but she *was* in the palace and she *was* helping him get his birthstone. And he needed his birthstone. He'd arrived just before sunset, hovering outside her stone chambers while she'd gotten ready for her date. He'd almost followed her and her chatty friend inside to watch them get ready, but had stopped himself just outside in her halls. Spying on her while she got ready just felt wrong and well, creepy. So he'd patiently, very patiently, waited. *Why did girls take so long to get dressed?* She'd finally emerged from her chambers looking stunning in her blue dress. Tylak had had to force himself to concentrate so he wouldn't blow his cover.

It wasn't easy. He'd overheard that she was going to meet Beshar for dinner in his private chambers. Tylak should have been thrilled at the idea. He assumed Beshar had his birthstone. That's what Jura had alluded to at the arena in any case. He felt that if he followed her to the man's chambers, he could ensure he got his stone back.

He was surprised that Jura's choice of outfit had bothered him so much. She was a nice looking girl, and he was a man after all. And he had *maybe* noticed her full lips that almost always drew into a pout when she wasn't nibbling on the bottom one. And, yeah, maybe when he got close enough he noticed that her hair smelled like jasmine. But that didn't mean anything. Wait, what was he mad about again? Oh right, the dress. She hardly needed to parade about in a dress that hugged her curves and accentuated her tan glowing skin and…he shook his head. He wasn't concentrating enough. If he didn't focus on bending the firelight, he would be seen and then he'd be in real trouble.

He'd followed her into the chambers of the Tenth, though the door had shut so quickly he'd been unable to sneak inside. Disappointed, he'd paced the length of the hall for some time until he'd gotten the clever idea of going around the outside and climbing into the Tenth's chambers through his open courtyard window. Walking around the halls and along the stone walls of the palace had been easy enough. The palace guards were stationed around the gates of the palace. Their job was to keep people from getting in. It was up to the palace member's *Arbe* to keep people inside the palace safe. It was actually a security issue, not that he was complaining.

Beshar didn't have an *Arbe*. Instead his oiled men were positioned about the room, some lounging and some acting as servants. Tylak had paid them as much attention as he would pay to any person's *Arbe*, which was little. He was reckless while he was bending firelight.

Similar to manipulating fire itself, bending firelight was just that. Tylak, and people like him, had the ability to draw in the heat of the fire and use the temperature gradient to bend the rays of firelight. Once heated, light bends away from an object. If a person is the object, they are able to guide rays of light around themselves, much like a rock diverting water in a stream. Manipulating firelight in this specific way, Tylak was able to render himself invisible. And when Tylak was invisible, he felt unstoppable. Well, he had in any case. Now he wasn't so sure. Somewhere during the course of the evening he'd made a terrible mistake in judgment. *How had Beshar's men been alerted to my presence?*

Careful to heed Beshar's warning, and partially because his men were holding him locked in place, Tylak stood straight and still, pasting an impassive expression on his face.

"Tylak?" Jura questioned. Her lips had dropped open to form a tiny pink O, and she stared at him with wide eyes.

"You know this man?" Beshar asked, frowning as she moved toward them. He held up a halting hand. "Best to not get any closer, my lady First. We don't know his intentions."

Jura ignored him and stepped close, jabbing a finger into his chest. "What are you doing here? Where is my father? And how did you do...whatever it is you did?"

She was cute when she was angry. She glared up at him, and Tylak noticed her nostrils flared slightly with each heaving breath. He was careful not to look down at her chest. Damn that dress. Those curves of hers were never revealed in her robes.

"Councilman, if you could call off your men." Tylak looked pointedly from one oiled man to the other, each held his bicep in a vice-like two handed grip. *How did they know I was here?*

"Not a chance." Beshar's eyes narrowed as he scrutinized the details of Tylak's face. "You were supposed to be executed nearly a week ago. The Interim First gave the command. Explain yourself." He made a small gesture, and Jura was grabbed as well. She muttered out a protest but held still as the men grabbed her arms. "You both will."

Her men started forward, but Jura told them to stand down. They held their hands on their scimitars, their expressions anguished.

"Did she hire you?" Beshar asked him.

"Hire me?" Tylak raised his eyebrows in surprise. "Hardly. I work alone. I came here for what's mine."

Jura looked up at him in surprise but said nothing. He smiled at her smugly. *That's right. I don't need you.*

Beshar wrinkled his brow. "For what's yours? My dear boy, why would I have anything that belongs to you? Why would I want anything of yours?"

Tylak ignored the insult. "Who knows why the Thirteen does anything they do?" He tried to shrug, but it was difficult with the men holding him so tightly.

Jura was muttering something under her breath.

He looked over at her and caught her heated glare.

"You lying scumbag," she hissed. "Where's my father?"

He blew her a kiss. She growled, there was really no other word for it, and tried to lunge at him but was held back by her captor.

"Your father?" Beshar sat heavily onto his chaise. "If you don't tell me what's going on, immediately, I'm going to kill you both."

Jura grew quiet and looked at Beshar with wide eyes. "You wouldn't."

"Try me. Now who would like to explain?"

Jura sighed. "I came to seduce information out of you. The Prince of Shadows put me up to it. He said you have a secret and if I were to figure it out, he would help me with information on my father." She jerked her head toward Tylak. "I don't know what he's doing here. I released him in exchange for taking me to the Shadow Dancers. I thought since he had stolen the Everflame, he must be a member of the Shadow Dancers. Seems I was right about that. He's working for them and he's kidnapped my father. He can't be trusted."

Tylak flinched. "I only came for what's mine." He repeated. "And why would I have your father?"

"You knew where I was keeping him. Don't deny it. Where is he?"

Beshar rose from his chaise and poured himself a glass of wine. He drank deeply, refilling his cup before settling back down in his chaise. He motioned for their release.

Jura immediately sat down, breathing hard and rubbing at her wrists.

Tylak watched her with interest. His eyes going from her to Beshar.

Beshar took another slow deliberate pull from his goblet. "Jura, is the First family in some kind of trouble?"

She nodded, tears were beginning to form in her eyes.

"I see. And this Shadow Dancer? What about him?

"I came for my birthstone." Tylak grunted out with clenched teeth. Trust the councilman to talk about him like he wasn't even there. "*Jura* was

253

helping me get it."

The councilman raised his eyebrow and wiped at his forehead with a handkerchief. "I see. And you two think I have it?"

"No," Jura said at the same time Tylak answered, "Yes". He looked at her in surprise.

"He doesn't have it," Jura explained. "Denir does."

He felt the realization stab his gut. Of course. He couldn't wait to get his hands on the bitch.

"The Fifth?" The councilman asked, still working the situation out. "Now that's interesting. What does she have to do with any of this?"

Jura shrugged.

"We were lovers," Tylak answered. Jura looked over at him sharply. "It was a long time ago," he explained.

She looked away. *Was it his imagination or did this bit of information appear to upset her?*

"I don't have your father, Jura," Tylak said.

Jura studied her hands and refused to look at him.

The councilman stuffed his handkerchief back up his sleeve and rose from his chaise, pacing the length of his apartment and only pausing to take sips from his wine. He stopped in front of Tylak and stared at him for a moment before smiling.

"Young Shadow Dancer, I do believe we can help each other."

"I'm not a Shadow Dancer. And I don't need your help."

Beshar smiled at him and the sight of it made the hairs on his neck stand. "Oh, but that's where you're wrong. You owe me your life. I will give it to you and return your birthstone to you. Meet me here tomorrow afternoon.

In exchange, you will owe me a small favor. Then you will be free to live the rest of that life however you see fit. Go now. I suggest you heed my words."

He turned away from him, and Tylak knew that he was dismissed. Beshar turned to address Jura, but Tylak bent the light around him and quickly left through the window that he'd come in.

THIRTY
TWO

JURA

Jura *watched Tylak disappear, quite* literally. She stared for several moments at the empty spot where he'd stood just seconds before.

"How do they do that?" she finally breathed out in wonder.

"They bend the light around them, altering what your eyes can perceive." Beshar waved his hand in a dismissive gesture. "Please, have a seat. We have much to discuss." He waved one of his Samur over. "Would you like another glass of wine?"

She took the goblet and drank from it wordlessly, sitting down on the chaise beside him.

"Would you really have killed me?" she finally asked, unable to stand another moment's silence.

Beshar took another sip of his wine. "Oh, most assuredly. Though I see now that it isn't necessary."

She choked on her swallow.

"You are a remarkably naïve child."

She stiffened. "I don't think I'm so naïve."

"It wasn't a question." He patted her arm. "Don't worry. I'm going to help you."

"In exchange for a favor." She heard the flatness in her tone.

"Naturally, my dear. It's how this world works."

Her world was collapsing around her. "What do you want?"

"We'll get to that in due time. For now, let's discuss what you want, since it would seem your affections toward me were somewhat artificial in their manufacture." He stared at her in interest.

She took a deep breath. *You've shared this much with him. What would be the point in hiding more? And there is still the problem of father. He's missing. Who's to say that he will appear before tomorrow's meeting? What then?*

"It's my father," she started, choosing over her words carefully. "He's been ill."

Beshar said nothing, simply stared at her, waiting for her to go on.

"It's no natural illness. Something…someone is responsible."

"What kind of illness?"

"A blood chain." She waited for the shock to register on his face. *Where were the outraged protests? The disbelief at their existence?*

Beshar took another sip from his wine. "Please continue. I've had quite a fair amount of wine, and I won't have my wits about me much longer."

"You aren't shocked?" This wasn't the reaction she'd expected. At the very least, she'd expected some sort of surprise…or any facial expression.

Beshar stared back at her, his face bland and emotionless. "They're not even supposed to exist. They were all destroyed! Where would someone even acquire such magic?"

"I would get them from Kitoi," Beshar answered. He continued when she stared at him, "And you don't think you're naïve? My lady, the issue of where they came from is not the problem. You should be asking yourself who put them on him?" He shook his head. "I assume you've been keeping him in a safe place?"

"I was. He was in my trapdoor storage room—"

"Your wine cellar?" Beshar interrupted.

She swallowed. "My wine cellar, yes. He was in there but—"

"Where is he now?"

She struggled to blink back the tears. "I don't know. Earlier today, after the luncheon, I got back to my room and he was…gone."

"He'd left?"

"I think he was taken. My room was destroyed but nothing was missing except him. I questioned his *Arbe*, but they didn't seem to see anyone. When Tylak appeared, I thought maybe he…but no, I don't think it was the Shadow Dancers."

"How did you get mixed up with the Shadow Dancers? They're dangerous. You sh—"

"I was desperate. I thought they could help me."

Beshar rolled his goblet between his hands, staring into the glass as though it would provide him with answers. "You went to them for help, and they sent you to me." He nodded as if everything made sense. Jura was still as lost as ever.

"So, the Shadow Dancers, this Tylak fellow, and I'm assuming your *Arbe* all know that the First has been imprisoned."

She drew in a shaky breath. "Yes."

"But we're assuming, for the moment, that none of these parties are responsible for your father's current whereabouts."

"I think it was Velder."

"Of course you do." Beshar sighed. "It wasn't him."

"What is that supposed to mean? Of course I do? And who else would it be?" She was getting tired of Beshar's cocky attitude.

"Well it's only natural that you would assume the Second to be responsible for any foul play. You think he's next in line, so he's the natural suspect. But what would his true motive be? And to take things further, I happen to know for a fact that Velder is not responsible."

"Well, if it's not him, then who?"

"Ahh," Beshar smiled at her. "Now that is the question you should be asking."

She bit her bottom lip in frustration. "I still think it's Velder. He seems very suspicious."

"Suspicious in what way?"

"Well, the way he talks to me. I get the feeling that he's hiding something. Plus, I don't like the way he looks at me sometimes."

Beshar rolled his eyes.

"It *could* be him," she insisted.

"I can assure you it's not him."

"How can you be sure? You can't really know that. It could be him," Jura repeated.

Beshar's smile widened. "My lady First, I know it's not him because I know everything the Second does and have for some time." He held out his arm and pulled up the sleeve of his robe. Dangling from his wrist was a tiny gold and silver chain. A master blood chain.

"You…" She shook her head, trying to find the right words.

"Yes, my lady First. Velder is completely my servant. He's been wearing my blood chain for the last seven years."

THIRTY THREE

JURA

"You can't be serious." She shook her head, as if her mere denial of it would somehow force it all to be a lie. She took another heavy swallow from her goblet, ignoring the searing sting as the alcohol made its way down her throat.

Beshar pulled the sleeve of his robe back down so that it covered his wrist and took another dainty sip from his own glass. "I'm very serious. Naturally, it's not something I've shared with another. I imagine my secret is safe with you, providing I keep your own?"

She nodded.

"Excellent. So now, who do you propose is responsible for your own predicament?"

She lifted her shoulders in a hopeless gesture. "I haven't the slightest idea.

Honestly, I suppose anyone could merit from having control of the First."

"Indeed. We need to think deeper. What was the first thing you witnessed the First do that was out of character?"

"He tried to kill me."

His goblet stopped halfway up its flight to his lips. He blinked at her for several seconds before placing it into the hands of a waiting Samur. He leaned forward. "Tried to kill you? How?"

"Does that matter?" She let out a wild laugh. The flood of information was driving her crazy.

"Of course it does."

"He was trying to stab me. My bodyguard stopped him."

"Where was your *Arbe*?"

"I'd never felt the need for one before. Akkim had always been more than sufficient." The corners of North's lips curled up in a smirk in response to her comment.

"What did he use?"

She frowned up at him, blinking back tears. "What?"

"What did he use to try and stab you with?"

"I don't know. A spear, I think?"

"A spear or an assegai?"

She shook her head. "I don't know. I don't even know the difference between the two. Why would it matter between one or the other?"

Beshar leaned back in his chaise, crossing his feet at the ankles and frowning thoughtfully. "Well, whoever wanted you killed clearly didn't care that the council saw you murdered. There are any number of ways to make your death appear accidental, but choosing to murder you outright, that makes a statement. And to not use the preferred scimitar of the First says something more. If it was an assegai, then the villain wanted the council to believe the attack had come from the arena. But if it was a spear, the attack could have been from anyone, perhaps even another country. Do you recall what the weapon looked like?"

"I don't think it was an assegai, though it might have been. It was definitely some sort of spear. I never gave it any thought. It happened so quickly. But, maybe if I saw such a weapon again…" She caught her bottom lip between her teeth and chewed thoughtfully.

Beshar waved a Samur forward, whispering orders that sent the muscled man scurrying with a flick of his wrist.

"Have you noticed any odd behavior from any of the Thirteen?"

Jura shook her head, once again cursing her own introverted nature. If only she'd participated more in politics, then she would have some basis for comparison. But outside of her interactions with the Second and the Third houses, she was woefully ignorant on any personalities of the other ten. In fact, she'd be hard pressed to name every member. Once again, she was aware that she had allowed herself to get into this mess entirely based on her own actions.

"I can't think of any. But then, I barely know anyone." *Amira.* She pushed the thought from her head as soon as she had it. Amira was her best friend, and yet she had been behaving inconsistently ever since her return from Kitoi. The Third would stand to gain much if he formed an alliance with the First to bring down the Second and then seized power from the weak Interim daughter. It would be the perfect coup, and yet the thought was outrageous…as outrageous as Beshar in control of Veldar for the last seven years. Could Beshar really be trusted? What if the master chain wasn't controlling Velder after all? Beshar could lie to her face and she would be none the wiser.

The Tenth studied her intently, and she forced a wan smile. "This is all so overwhelming. I don't know who to trust. For all I know, you could be a suspect."

Beshar nodded, seemingly unsurprised.

"But you knew I'd think that...I suppose I have to trust you. I haven't told anyone, not even Amira, and she's my best friend...Thank you, this has been so hard, going through all of this alone." She had to hope that he believed her, believed that she trusted him completely. Maybe he was trustworthy. Maybe he really could help her, but she would keep her guard up, just in case.

"Oh, don't worry, Greatness. I'm sure you'll find a way to repay the favor."

"Why did you do it? With Velder, I mean."

Beshar smiled. "How could I not? The opportunity presented itself, and I always take opportunities when one comes my way."

"So how does it work? Can you make him do anything? Is he himself at all or is he just a mindless puppet?" Jura leaned forward, desperate for answers.

Beshar opened his mouth to reply but stopped when two of his Samur entered the room carrying bundles of sticks in various sizes. *No, not sticks,* Jura realized. The men carried different assortments of weapons.

She gasped. "What a marvelous idea."

The Samur lay the weapons on the floor between her and Beshar, stretching them out one after the other along the stretch of his thick floor rug. Jura watched them place each weapon down and then stood up, walking along the line of weapons and pausing before any that looked familiar. She'd never known there could be so many different weapons. She stopped in front of one, a long stick that split slightly at the end into three narrow points that intersected close to their tips. With a shaking hand, she reached for the weapon, remembering the hungry look in her father's eyes, the deep red of Akkim's blood.

"This one." She held the weapon in front of her for several moments before thrusting it away from her.

Beshar gripped it with steady fingers and peered deep into her eyes. "This one?" He raised his eyebrows. "You're sure?"

"Absolutely," she said with a shudder. "This is the one."

"Interesting." Beshar stood up, pacing the length of the room once again.

"What?" Jura whispered, following him with her eyes and swallowing back a rising feeling of panic. "What is it?"

"It's a trishula. It's foreign."

"Foreign? Foreign how? Where did it come from?"

He turned the weapon in his hands for several seconds as if mesmerized by its twisting movement. "The trishula is the official weapon of the sea people. Either the Wave Master has broken the alliance or someone in the council went through a lot of trouble to make it seem that way."

THIRTY
FOUR

BESHAR

His head was pounding. The feeling was familiar and expected, considering the amount of wine he had consumed the night before. Still, he sat up with a groan and gingerly brought a hand to his temple. It was going to be a very long day.

He had sent Jura home after their discovery of the trishula. Shocked and disappointed that she had allowed her friend the use of half her *Arbe*, he had insisted that Jura take the offered protection of three of his Samur. He hoped he'd scared her enough to accept the gravity of the situation. Something big was happening in the Republic. And amid the conspiracy of the First, the Prince of Shadows had sent Jura after him. It wouldn't be long now before his desperation sent him into an outright attack. The events were somehow connected.

He moaned and reached a grateful arm out for the offered laudanum and washed it down with a swig from an open wine bottle. He hadn't finished it the night before. A pity; it would turn. He then summoned for his robes and dressed with slow precise movements, still waiting for his headache to dissipate.

Today the council would convene. They would have their monthly vote on house Rank. It was of utmost importance to show strength to the fellow council members. Yet he was hungover and the house of the First would have no member present.

"Perhaps I should just go to the meeting," Jura had suggested in his doorway. She had lingered in her departure, though Beshar had been unsure why.

"They'll be expecting that."

Her amber eyes had widened, appearing more gold than brown, and she had twisted her slender fingers in an anxious gesture.

"But we don't know who he is…" She'd frowned at the ground, nibbling on her bottom lip. "My house will have no one to represent them at the session."

"I'll take care of it," he'd assured her. "Trust me."

And it seemed she did. She had left, and he finished their bottle of wine and opened another before slipping into blissful unconsciousness. Now, he wondered where his confidence had come from. He planned to defend the house of the First. He hoped that when the time came, the words would flow to him and his argument would be eloquent and persuasive. He should have been more forthcoming with the girl. If he'd told her everything he knew… well, there was no point on chastising himself on what he should have said. All he could do was trust that he had made the best decisions for the moment. He had to believe that the actions he'd taken and the secrets he'd chosen to keep would be enough. The girl was right not to trust him. She shouldn't trust anyone.

It was a strange sensation to care about someone other than himself. Perhaps it was the trusting way Jura had smiled at him when he'd told her he would take care of things, or perhaps the way she appeared so small and vulnerable, so trusting and naïve. He refused to let her down. She needed the safety net of her Rank, and Beshar intended to do everything in his power to see that she had it. It was impossible to vote out the First. Well, he shouldn't say impossible. In order to out vote the First, every member of the council would have to vote against the house. The First himself held three votes, which Beshar equaled with his own vote and that of Velder's. That was nearly half the council votes there. Surely he could count on the alliance from the Third and some votes from the lesser houses…Still, Beshar was nervous. And he was never nervous.

Then, of course, despite the more pressing problem of the imminent council meeting was the fact that a war was brewing. *Was someone in the Thirteen trying to make it appear as though the Tri-Alliance was broken? And if so, why? What could they have to gain?* Beshar liked puzzles, but this one was frustrating. The answers seemed to slip through his fingers like loose grains of sand, and he couldn't shake the suspicion that somehow everything was connected. He only needed to discover how.

His headache somewhat abated, he headed for the hall, signaling eight of his Samur to accompany him. The men were unnecessary. It was entirely uncivilized to attack a house on voting day, but Beshar knew most of the council would approve his show of strength. He and his men walked the length of the glass halls, and though the images were somewhat distorted through the glass, he was able to spot several members of the Thirteen also headed to the meeting.

He reached the center hall and was surprised to find Jura waiting outside the large imposing doors of the Dome. He frowned at her. Her presence only forced her house to appear vulnerable. She smiled at his approach.

"What are you doing here?" he hissed, grabbing her elbow and forcing her to walk away from the doors and back toward her own hall.

"I couldn't help it." The tone of her voice was low and fervent. He could practically smell the desperation wafting off of her. *This is bad.*

"You need to go," he whispered, smiling at Denir as she passed by. The Fifth raised a brow before breezing inside the Dome. He turned his focus back to Jura. "I told you I would take care of everything and I will. You just have to trust me."

She shook her head, pulling her arm from his grasp but staying close in case anyone noticed. To members of the Thirteen, they appeared as close friends, whispering to one another.

"I don't know how you expect me to do that. There's so much going on that I don't understand. I didn't ask for any of this, you know. You want me to trust you. And I want to, I really do, but how can I trust anyone when I know someone here is responsible for my father's blood chain? When you yourself have a blood chain on Velder."

The Second walked by, his alarmed glance at the two of them mirrored Beshar's expression before it smoothed into a blank canvas and he disappeared into the dome.

"Lower your voice!" Beshar's eyes darted around, but no one was near them. Still he leaned closer and whispered, "I know you're scared, Greatness. You have every right to be. But you are strong and you will get through this."

Her skin turned white and she shook her head, eyes wide, "My father."

"We will find out who's responsible for his chain and then we will find him."

"No," she whispered, shaking her head with urgency. "Beshar, my father."

He realized she was looking behind him and he pivoted tightly on his heel only to come face to face with the First himself.

"Beshar," the First greeted him with narrow eyes that glared down at him.

Beshar lowered his eyes and dipped the customary bow, wriggling his thumbs in greeting. "Greatness, how wonderful to see you out and about." He forced himself to keep his eyes on the ground and away from Jura, though he could feel her trembling beside him. "I trust you're feeling better?"

"Oh, entirely. I feel like a new man." He smiled tightly. "Jura, there you are, cowering behind this behemoth of a man. Is that any way to greet your father?"

THIRTY
FIVE
ASH

"**W**hat are you reading?"

He dragged his eyes away from the tome and flashed Kindle a warm smile. The Fire Dancer leaned against his door frame, twirling her assegai with deft fingers.

"It's the Chronicles. I find myself constantly drawn to them. Perhaps because soon I will find my own name along its pages. There were so many of them, decades and centuries dead, and the only thing that remains of them is a name in a book. Maybe a sentence or two if they're one of the lucky ones."

Her eyes were full of sympathy and she leaned her weapon against the wall, not waiting for permission to enter before strolling in and sitting on the edge of his bed. She perched against its thin frame and stared at him like a watchful bird.

"Where's Kay?"

He pointed to a corner of the room where the young girl sat huddled in a blanket, reading a picture book that Kindle had left with her the day before.

Spotting her, Kindle's eyes softened and she appeared, well, motherly. Life in the arena made it near impossible for one to have a family. He wondered if Kindle felt loss from the fact that she would probably never be a mother.

"She's been reading that thing non-stop since you gave it to her." It had been a good idea. Found in the library, it was a picture dictionary designed for teaching young cadets to read. Though as a whole the slave race was not taught to read, all cadets and those training for the life of a Torch were taught after they were chosen. It had been a simple matter for Kindle to write the words in Drakori beside their counterpart in the language of the Republic. Kay proved to be an excellent reader in her own language, and she'd seemed delighted when Kindle had gifted her the book of simple translations.

Kay sparkled whenever Kindle was around, but had yet to acknowledge his presence, except to offer a smile in thanks for a meal. Otherwise, she'd spent her time reading. Kindle had arranged to come for a language lesson before her sparring practice.

"Hi, Kay," Kindle called out loudly, capturing the girl's attention.

Kay leapt to her feet, grinning while she threw herself into Kindle's waiting arms.

Well, that friendship certainly hadn't taken long, Ash thought wryly. He watched the girls exchange greetings in the guttural clipped tones of Drakori for a moment before once again losing himself in the book. His father had been a Fire Dancer, and Ash liked to look at his father's name, though he never felt the sting of remorse. He'd never known the man. He had been

272

conceived while his father was on leave, perhaps he even had a brother or sister, though Ash had never bothered to do any research to find out. His father's career had ended early, after just two seasons in the arena, which meant that his father had died nearly fifty years ago. His record was spotty at best and already forgotten by everyone except Ash himself, and he only held on to the memory of an idea. With a sigh, he closed the heavy book and pushed it aside, leaning back in his chair.

What was the purpose of it all? They were chosen by the Everflame and the only glory in death was found in a rush of smoke and flames. And yet, he wondered. …Staring at Kay, he found himself questioning what the honor of dying early and leaving a child fatherless was? He'd never wondered at his father for so long before, and he pushed the thoughts aside.

Idly, he opened another book he'd brought from the arena library, one that documented the dragon legends, and flipped its weathered pages. It wasn't as interesting as the book documenting the Dancers. There had been many dragons, and the book served as more of a ledger, simply stating the dragon's name and owner, how many matches won, and who had felled the beast at its end. He flipped several pages, skimming entries before he noticed a pattern. When the dragon was owned by one of the Thirteen, the dragon's lineage was described: the dragon's birth weight, his sire and dame, as well as any transfer of ownership and trainer. The dragons listed as belonging to the arena held no such information. Instead, these dragons simply had the name of the dragon and the name of the Dancer credited for his death. *Interesting. Why not include the other information? Did all arena dragons come from the same breeding pair?*

"Kindle?" he called out, not taking his eyes from the book.

"Yes?" She sounded distracted and annoyed, most likely he'd interrupted her.

"Where do the arena dragons come from?"

She muttered something in Drakori before heading toward him. "What?"

"The dragons," he repeated, flipping pages and searching for a discrepancy in his theory.

"If you're going to interrupt our lesson, the least you could do is look up at me and stop mumbling."

Sheepishly, he raised his eyes until they met her scowling blue ones. He smiled. "Sorry. Where do the arena dragons come from? I've never heard any mention of our breeding program. No whisper of where our breeding facilities are located. And this book doesn't mention any of it."

She shrugged. "I dunno. I never gave it any thought. We must have some sort of land outside the city. I guess everything happens there."

He was unconvinced. "Yeah. I suppose so." He sat up tall, stretching his aching arms above his head. Used to be he only felt such aching muscles after a long day in the training field, now it seemed a few hours in the chair were enough to do him in.

"How's the lesson?"

"It would go better if we weren't interrupted by the ramblings of an old man." There was no sting in her catty remark, and her eyes twinkled.

He swatted at her, but his heart wasn't in it and she moved easily out of his reach. He was aware of Kay's watchful eyes.

"Come over here, girl. Show me what you've learned."

"We've only been practicing the alphabet," Kindle warned. "Though I've a feeling she's learning quickly." She waved Kay over, and the girl moved toward them in that graceful floating way of hers. Once again, Ash was struck with the sad thought that Kay would have made a wonderful Dancer.

"Well," Ash said once she was close, "tell me something in the Republic's tongue."

Kindle said something in Drakori, and Kay stared at her for a moment before turning her solemn blue eyes up to Ash.

Without a trace of an accent, the girl whispered, "I want to go home."

THIRTY SIX

JURA

"**F**ather." *She met his eyes,* counting to herself in an effort to slow her racing heart. *One, two, three, four—*

"Velder mentioned you were spending much of your free time in the company of the Tenth," her father stated, watching her carefully.

She glanced toward Beshar and met the nearly imperceptible shake of his head. *Of course, her father's chain master didn't know about Velder's own blood chain. If Velder didn't say anything, who did?*

"Yes," she said slowly. "The Tenth and I have sparked up quite the friendship during your illness."

The First smiled. Her father never smiled, preferring instead to always appear stoic and strong. The sight of him smiling now made her knees shake.

"Yes. About my illness, I can't thank you enough for taking care of me.

You've done the Republic a great service."

"Yes, father. You've always taught me to do what's right."

"So, I have." He looked from one to the other. "It seems you've also taken an interest in politics. I do hope that was because of my own influence and not that of your new friend?"

"Yes, father. I did my best to keep control of our Rank."

"Did you?" His dark brown eyes stared deep into her own and she clenched her fist so she wouldn't shudder.

"Greatness, if I may suggest, we had best take our leave. The session starts now." Beshar had whipped out his handkerchief and was wiping the line of sweat at his brow.

Her father frowned at the Tenth. "The session starts when I want it to." He looked back at Jura and smiled. "But you are correct, we should go inside. Jura, would you care to join us?"

Jura wished she'd been able to decipher more how blood chains worked the night before. Perhaps then she'd better understand just what her father's chain master was up to. "You've never wanted my presence before." Each word seemed to fight its way out of her mouth.

"Ahh, yes. But that was before you proved you had a head for politics. Come, sit beside me. You will benefit from further lessons."

The First extended his arm, and Jura took it wordlessly, allowing herself to be pulled inside. Beshar followed after them.

The Thirteen were already seated along their long stone table. Beshar was quick to take his seat, and she noticed that several of the Thirteen muttered at her entrance. During session, only the Thirteen voting members were permitted in the hall. Jura's presence was unprecedented and a huge faux pas.

Jura's eyes desperately sought out Amira, sitting in for her father. Jura sent her a worried glance, but the corners of Amira's lips merely turned up in a smile.

Velder hurriedly grabbed a chair from the far side of the dome. He set it up on the dais beside her father's glass throne and called the meeting to order. She watched Beshar as Velder spoke, but could see nothing that gave any indication of his blood chain. Citizens were called in, and Jura watched as her father passed judgment to each without hesitation. Her father once again seemed himself. It was as if the last week and a half had all been some terrible dream.

The First had worn the ceremonial robes. They all did. It was a voting day for Rank, but this time Jura didn't notice that her clothing was out of place. She was distracted and stared at her father's wrist. It was covered by the thick wool of his robe. If she hadn't known any better, she would never even believe the blood chain was there. When the last citizen was sentenced, Velder announced the vote for Rank. Fatima and Tamir exchanged nervous glances. They had a say in the judgment of the people and the Republic's politics, but not when it came to their own Rank.

Jura felt her breath catch in her throat. Her father was back now and showed no signs of weakness. *Was it enough? Was her family's position secure?* She scanned the faces of the Thirteen, wondering what would be decided. …Wait, there were only twelve. The seat beside Fatima sat empty. How had she not noticed it before? She counted once again, realizing that the Thirteenth was missing. The twitchy little man named Zair. She thought back to the night that she'd met him at the arena. He had disappeared after their brief encounter. Had he been murdered then? She shuddered at the thought.

Velder, or should she say Beshar, was speaking. And though she stared at Velder's thin mouth, she couldn't hear any of his words over the buzzing in her ears.

"Jura, what do you think?"

She jumped, meeting her father's eyes in embarrassment. "I'm sorry?"

"Merchant Ledair has made a motion to join the council as the Thirteenth. Shall we vote him in?"

So, Zair truly was gone. "Yes, father."

"Why?"

Why what? Why allow the man to join? "Is there a reason he shouldn't join?"

Her father stared at her. His dark eyes squinting and thoughtful. Suddenly he smiled, "You must always think before you allow someone to join. What are his holdings? Who has he aligned himself to?" He nodded. "We will second Ledair's motion." The First called out to the council. "Does anyone else agree?"

Ledair was voted in, and it was decreed that he would be alerted to move into the apartments of the Thirteenth after the meeting. It was hard for Jura to believe the lives of two men had changed so drastically in the course of one meeting. Ledair was suddenly one of the elite Thirteen, and Zair's household now belonged to him. Zair was probably dead, his body most likely burned to ash days ago.

"The house of the Third would like to make a motion." The voice was Amira's, and Jura turned to her in surprise. *What was she doing?*

Velder stroked his thin mustache, probably to distract his trembling hands. Jura noticed that Beshar was wiping at his brow. *Were their movements somehow connected through their blood chains?*

"Speak, Third. This session is still open."

Surely Amira wouldn't try to make a move for Second? Surely she didn't still plan to ask that her house be moved forward in Rank? Her father had yet to recover. He hadn't made a social appearance since the death of his son.

"The House of the Third would like for the Fourth to face judgment for crimes against their own."

Jura shook her head at her friend. This wasn't the way things should be done.

"What crimes have I committed?" Dahr stood up, his chair scraping against the stone floor.

"You killed my brother." Amira's voice was soft and her eyes sparkled with hatred. She also stood up and her height placed her nearly nose to nose with the Fourth. "You tried to kill my entire family. You made a move to poison my house in hopes that you could become Third. Don't try to deny it."

Dahr's face went pale, and he shook his head so furiously that his eyes seemed to rattle in his head. "N-no. No, it isn't true." "My lady Third, perhaps you shoul—"

Beshar was interrupted by Amira, "Tenth, you would do well to hold your tongue. I don't recall asking the opinion of the lower council."

Velder spoke up. "The house of the Third has made some serious accusations."

"I second the motion." The low and husky voice came from the Fifth. She stood up, nodding her head in deference to Amira. "I'll admit that the council will turn a blind eye on murder when one is aiming to increase their rank, but the botched attempt of the Fourth only proves his incompetence."

As the Fifth, Denir would rise in rank at Dahr's absence. All of the lesser council members would. Jura swallowed. No one would speak up in the Fourth's defense because his absence would work in everyone's favor.

"But I didn't do it. You must believe me." Dahr turned away from Amira and cast pleading eyes up toward the glass throne. "I—I have information." He thrust a shaking finger at Denir, waving it at her nose. "The Fifth knows! She knows what's happening. There is a conspiracy. The arena. Don't do this, Denir." His fingers gripped the shoulders of the Fifth. She jerked away from him. Dahr shook his head wildly and clasped his hands together as he lifted his desperate face up toward the dais.

"Please, your Greatness. I beg of you. Please! The ar—"

Her father held up a hand for silence. "The council has spoken. Dahr, speaker of the House of the Fourth, your home has been stripped of all rank. You no longer hold the position of the Fourth."

Dahr let out a low moan. Jura's breath made a small, whistling sound as she sucked it in between clenched teeth. Her father didn't even mean to listen to the defense of the Fourth. The man hadn't even had a fair chance.

Her father raised his palm again. "The council will vote in a new Thirteenth at the next meeting. Now, if there are no other motions this session wil—"

"I want him dead." Amira's voice was flat and cold. Jura hardly recognized it as the flippant lilting voice of her friend.

The First frowned, considering this. "Jura," he said softly. "What would you do?"

Why is he asking me? "He's already been stripped of his rank. What would his death prove?"

The First tilted his head to the side and raised his brows. "You would

281

grant him mercy?"

She stared at Dahr. The man had slumped back into his seat and held his head in his hands, sobbing quietly. Only a week ago, she had sat in her father's chair and sentenced Tylak to his death. But that had been different. She had been pressured. Her family's Rank and the safety of the Republic was at stake. But this…this was petty revenge, nothing more. The defense of the Fourth should at least be heard out.

"There's no proof he even committed this crime."

Her father shook his head, almost sadly, and tsked. "Ah, Jura. I give you so many chances, and still you continue to disappoint me. Now that we have taken all that Dahr has, he has nothing to lose. And a man who has nothing to lose is a dangerous one, remember that. Amira is right in demanding his death. Your friend is strong. You are weak." He turned back toward the council and addressed them in his booming voice.

"The request of the Third is granted. Dahr will be held in the dungeons until the next execution day."

Dahr fainted in his chair.

Jura watched as his body slumped to the ground. No one made a move to help him, though palace guards arrived within moments to haul him to his feet and out of the hall. She didn't dare look at Amira. She couldn't stand to look into the smiling face of her friend who had just committed murder.

THIRTY
SEVEN

JURA

ather is a monster. They're all a bunch of monsters. Bitter bile rose in
her throat, and she choked it back, breathing heavily. She watched as
Dahr was escorted from the room, and her father rose from his seat
in the glass throne to speak with other members of the council. *Get up,* she
ordered herself. *Get up and go to your rooms.* Her feet remained planted to the
stone floor, and she didn't rise from her chair.

I can't even blame the blood chain, she thought desperately. If she was truly
being honest with herself, her father acted the same way he always had. She
once again questioned if her father was even still wearing the cursed thing.

"Are you alright?"

She looked up at the concerned voice and tried to smile at Beshar. He
stood before her, a frown etched into his pale round features.

"I will be," she murmured. *Why was the room spinning?* She took a deep breath, "I'm fine."

Beshar fished around in his pocket and handed her a handkerchief.

She stared at it.

"It's fresh."

With a slight smile, she took it and wiped at her face. The heady perfume from the cloth assailed her nostrils. She handed it back, wrinkling her nose.

"It's lavender and aldehyde." At her look of confusion, he went on. "It's a calming agent." He pushed the handkerchief back at her. "Take a deep breath of it. You'll feel better."

Grateful, she did as she was told.

"Am I interrupting something?" The voice was Amira's. Beshar stiffened at her approach.

"Not at all," Beshar straightened up and inclined his head toward them both. "I was just leaving. I'm late for a meeting with the Fifth." He met Amira's eyes. "Excuse me, the Fourth."

Jura watched him leave, already feeling the effects of the calming oil. She dragged her eyes up to Amira's, frightened of what she might see.

"Are you alright?" Amira asked. *She looks the same. How could she look the same? How could she be so calm knowing she'd sent a man to his death?*

"Better now." Jura stood up, stuffing Beshar's handkerchief up the sleeve of her robe.

"I was thinking I would throw a luncheon," Amira said.

Jura stared at her blankly. *I want to slap her.* The thought shocked her, and she clenched her fist. She'd never felt violence toward her friend before. "Why?"

"Whatever do you mean? Who knows how long father will allow me to act as his interim. I have to take advantage of the freedom while I can."

"Like ordering executions?"

Amira lifted her chin, a small smile turning up the corners of her full red lips. "Oh, so that's what this is about. I told you I would seek revenge. He killed my brother, Jura. He would have killed us all. Doesn't that mean anything to you? I could have died!"

"There's no proof that it was him." Amira was right. She had almost died. Yet the threat to her friend wasn't enough to erase the memory of the terror in Dahr's eyes as he pleaded for his freedom. Without evidence of Dahr's foul play, she refused to believe he deserved execution. She wanted to hear the full story of his defense.

"Oh, stop being so naïve. Of course it was him. Who else would benefit from the removal of my house?"

"Everyone," Jura answered softly. *Wasn't that what had just happened?* Ledair had just been voted in this morning and was already moved into the rank of the Twelfth.

"I see," Amira pulled a pout. "Does this mean you won't attend?"

"I—" She stood up, dismayed that the room still seemed to be spinning. *Must be from all the wine the night before.* "I think I need a nap."

"I have a new *Arbe*. I'll send your men back to you before the luncheon starts. That way you'll have a full escort before you attend." She reached out her hand and placed it on Jura's shoulder.

Amira's fingers were icy cold and bit through the pale cloth of her robe. Jura flinched and pulled away. "Thank you. I'll see you later."

"Goodbye, Jura." Amira called after her. "Don't do anything foolish."

Jura hurried away, before her father, Amira, or anyone else could stop her.

She breathed in the familiar scent of her room. The smell of jasmine and dusty leather comforted her. She walked to her bookshelf and opened up a book at random, burying her nose in its leather bindings, not caring how foolish she must look to her remaining *Arbe*.

The smell of books had always relaxed her. She sat heavily on her bed, longing for the days when she had hidden away from politics and lived through her books. Books were safe; books were simple. When she was caught up in a good book she could live any life she wanted. She didn't have to worry about being too small or weak. If things became too scary, she could simply close the book and walk away. It was easy to open another. Easy to bury herself in any story she wanted. She wished desperately that she could close the book on the hellish story she was living now.

She didn't even know what she was doing anymore. Her father remained enslaved by the blood chain. At least she thought he did. She couldn't even really be sure. And then there was the way she left things off with the Shadow Dancers. She'd never given them the information they'd requested, and she doubted that they would simply go away just because her father had reappeared. She began flipping through the pages of the book, not reading anything but comforted by the familiar gesture. She had to be missing some important clue.

Her father's chain master had to be one of the Thirteen. It wasn't Beshar. *It can't be Beshar,* she whispered to herself, more so because she desperately wanted to believe it was true. He was the only one of the Thirteen that she had entrusted with her secret, and he genuinely seemed to want to help. But then again, he was already a chain master to Velder. Who was to say that he wasn't controlling her father as well? What if the master chain he'd shown her was her father's after all, and Velder wasn't even imprisoned? Her stomach rolled at the thought, and she pushed away the idea. No, she had to trust him. She wanted to trust him desperately, needed someone to place that trust.

So, if it wasn't the Second or the Tenth, well Ninth now, who did that leave? It wasn't Dahr, obviously, or the previous Thirteenth, murdered men couldn't control chains. Perhaps it could be the newly voted merchant Ledair, though she doubted it. He would have had few, if any, opportunities to get close to her father. It could be Denir. The woman seemed ruthless enough, though Jura wondered what she would have hoped to gain by commanding the First when she was already the richest of any council member. Could the woman really just be that power hungry?

She dismissed Geedar the Sixth, well now Fifth. He had enough going on with his wife's pregnancy and infidelity...But who was the father of her child anyway? If father was responsible, perhaps Geedar would have wanted revenge? The scenario was wild and unlikely. Though she suspected her father wasn't abstinent, she assumed he found his pleasures outside of the Thirteen. She pushed away the image of her father finding pleasures anywhere, what a disturbing thought, and again went through the list of the remaining members. It was so complicated. She could barely keep everyone's name and Rank straight, much less worry over their possible motives.

Oh, and then there was the detail of the trishula. Somehow, the Sea King was involved. Or someone from his kingdom. Or someone in the Thirteen wanted it to look that way. Whoever was responsible, the fact remained that someone very much wanted to start an all out war. And she'd helped it along by not listening to the Sea King. Overwhelmed, she let out a groan and threw herself back against her pillows.

"Rough day?"

She bit back a scream and scowled at the intruder.

Tylak appeared at her bedside, dressed in his customary black clothing, only this time a long dagger hung at his hip and his birthstone hung low on his chest. He'd pulled back his hair too. The long, dark locks were captured with a leather cord at the base of his neck. She noticed that his birthstone brought out the blue in his eyes and her scowl deepened.

She waved off North and South as the men came running from across the room. Her *Arbe* held quick reflexes but were no match for people who appeared magically out of thin air. She sent them outside to guard her chamber door and turned to face Tylak.

"I would prefer you didn't do that." She lifted her chin and sat as tall as she could in her bed. At least from the raised mattress she was able to stare into his intense gray eyes. She glared at him. "How long have you been in here?"

"Long enough to see that you've got a lot on your mind…and you really like the smell of books."

She threw a pillow at him.

He sidestepped it easily, grinning at her. "Want to talk about it?"

"With you?"

"Sure." He sat down beside her and she stiffened. She'd never had a man sit on her bed before, especially not one so young and good looking. *Stop it,* she ordered herself. *This man is a dangerous criminal. Shouldn't that make me feel worried instead of warm and melty? Sandstorms, melty is not even a word.*

"I see you've got your birthstone back," she said. She tried to focus on the stone, but that meant she was staring at his chest. *His hard, muscled chest. What is wrong with me?* She looked away and focused on her hands.

"Yes. I retrieved it this morning."

"Beshar didn't waste any time."

"I didn't get it from Beshar. I went into Denir's apartments and retrieved it myself while you were all in your little rich people meeting this morning. What do you do in there anyway? Argue over who has the most water?"

She rolled her eyes. She'd forgotten how insufferable he could be. It made it easier to look at him without blushing. "The council meeting is the sole source of government in the Republic. Without a council the citizens would—"

"Think for themselves?"

She frowned. "It would be anarchy."

Tylak nodded, considering this. "You're right. I know when someone wants to be a baker but the square already has one it's perfectly acceptable to murder the poor man, never mind the fact that he's a wife and five children."

"That's not—" She closed her mouth. *He was right of course. What argument did she have against him?* Just moments before she had been questioning that very rule of her society, he was right to mock it. "You're right."

"I am? Well now, that was easy wasn't it? Say it again. Tylak, you're amazing. So smart and right about everything." He'd raised his voice into a squeaky falsetto and batted his eyelashes at her.

"I do not sound like that!" she laughed.

"Sure you do. At least when you're talking to Beshar, anyway. What's with you two? I wouldn't have thought he's your type."

"He's not."

"That's right. Because you already have a lover. What was his name again? Markuri?"

"Markhim." Jura shook her head. "And he's not my lover. He… he's not anything."

"Ah, so if not Beshar or Markhim, then who—"

"Why the interest in my love life? I have more important things on my mind."

"Exactly. Important things that I've managed to take off your mind." He grinned and scooted closer.

"You—I…What are you doing here?" He was very good at making her nervous.

He seemed disappointed but he stood back up, his face becoming serious and stern. "I wanted to make sure you're all right. We had a deal. You return me to my birthstone; I help you with your father…"

"My father. You knew I had him in my cellar?"

"I found him the other night when I searched your room."

"You searched my room?"

"I was looking for my birthstone." He held up a hand in protest when her expression darkened.

"I didn't touch him, though. I saw him down there, but I left him down there. I'm sorry he's missing."

"He's not. Not anymore."

"That's good news, isn't it?"

She crossed her arms over her chest.

"Well…I got my stone so I wanted to make sure you didn't need anything else before I left."

"You're leaving?" The thought of his absence caused a sudden unexplainable ache in her gut. "Where are you going?"

He shook his head. "I can't stay here anymore. Too many painful memories of a life I need to leave behind." He smiled, but it was forced. "Besides, I'm a wanted man, remember?"

"Oh," she continued to study her hands.

"If I didn't know better, I'd say you were upset." He lifted up her chin so that she met his eyes. "I'm not leaving until I know I did right by you. A deal is a deal. So, want to tell me what's upsetting you? You can start with why you were keeping your father locked in a hole in your room."

"It's complicated." She sighed. She shouldn't trust this man and yet, he'd never lied to her. "Have you ever heard of a blood chain?"

She told him everything. Her concerns about her father, Beshar's involvement, her deal with the Shadow Dancers, and her worries over a brewing war and the pending execution of Dahr. When she was finally finished, she was surprised to find herself crying.

Tylak reached for her hand and clasped it tightly between his.

"It's okay. We can fix all that."

She stared down at her hand in his and snatched it out of his grasp. His hands had been warm and strong. He didn't move when she pulled away, and a part of her wished that he had forced her hand to remain in his, that he would pull her into his arms and hold her close. She shook her head at the thought. Her emotions toward him were conflicted. She knew nothing about him, and yet with every moment in his presence she saw another side of him.

Dark and brooding, dangerous and mysterious, sensitive and wounded. And now he was full of optimism and offering help.

"You do realize what you just said, don't you?" She smiled up at him.

He grinned back. "Sure. I mean, you might not be able to finish everything by the day's end, but we'll do what we can."

"We?"

He shrugged, "I can put off leaving for another day or so."

She shook her head.

"I guess first off we need to head to the dungeons," he said.

"The dungeons? For Dahr?"

"Why not? You busted me out of there. I assumed this was something you liked to do for fun. You know, the hobbies of a bored rich girl."

She was caught between the urge to leap into his arms or punch the smirk off his face. She did neither, standing up and crossing her arms over her chest.

"You'll have to leave so I can change."

"Done." He disappeared from sight.

"Tylak…"

"What? I'm not here."

The voice came from beside her, and she couldn't help but smile. "Not funny. You'll use the door and wait for me in the hall. Now show yourself so I can be sure you've really left the room."

He reappeared by the door and winked at her as he opened it. "Well don't you just suck the fun out of everything."

She threw another pillow and it bounced off the closing door.

THIRTY
EIGHT
TYLAK

He *waited patiently in the* hall, wondering just what he had managed to get himself into. He'd meant to go to Jura to say his goodbyes. Instead, he'd somehow convinced her he would stick around and help fix all her problems like some damn hero from a flaming children's story. And he'd actually meant it. Sandstorms.

She stumbled out into the hall, looking relieved when he appeared beside her.

"I'll never get used to that," she said, staring at him in wide-eyed wonder.

"Stay close. I can make you invisible too. Easiest way to walk around these glass halls. But stay quiet until we get to the dungeons. We're invisible, not soundproof. Are you—" He paused, frowning at her. "Where are your spectacles? Won't you need them? You know, to see?"

"I left them in the room. They're only for reading anyway. I can see perfectly fine without them. Mostly I just leave them on because it's easier than spending time looking for them. Also, I read a lot." She sounded defensive. "Shouldn't we get going?"

Right. She *was* defensive. She looked cute with her glasses, but she was stunning without them. He wished she was wearing them. He needed to concentrate. "So long as you can see." He muttered. "Stay close."

She huddled closer and he bent the torchlight around them. Manipulating the light around two people wasn't impossible but required more concentration than usual, which wasn't easy with her so close. She was soft and little and her customary scent of Jasmine wafted up to him in pleasant puffs that wasn't at all assaulting in the way some girls wore perfume. He swallowed and did his best to ignore all that.

Because she had to remain close, he slowed his pace to match her tiny strides. The dungeons were located directly underneath the palace and were accessed by descending a staircase in the judgment hall. He was grateful that her halls led directly to the center tower. Though they didn't run into anyone, he could see several people walking about in neighboring halls. What was the purpose of these damn glass hallways anyway? They afforded no privacy and would give little security if the palace was ever attacked. Flaming rich people.

As they neared the center hall, he could feel Jura tremble in anticipation. He again questioned if he'd been completely sane when he'd agreed to stay and help. Now that he'd acquired his stone, he should have sprinted out of town while he still had the chance. Use the time to regroup and plan before he used it to get Sykk. Denir was likely to be furious when she discovered he'd gotten his stone back. She'd probably taken it in hopes of luring him into her chambers, more than likely to provoke a confrontation of some sort. Of course, that had been before their meeting in the city the other night, when he'd gone out to confront the Shadow Dancers.

He fought a sigh and hugged Jura close as a council member and their *Arbe* brushed by them. It was appalling, the practice of cutting out men's tongues and enslaving them to serve as your protectors. He warred with the idea, hating that Jura participated in such practice but grateful that she had the protection. She seemed to trust them implicitly, ordering her men to stay behind and leaving with him without a second thought. And she would need the protection, especially now that she'd botched her deal with the Shadow Dancers. Tylak knew from experience that Jura should expect a nasty retaliation.

He tightened his grip on Jura, swearing to himself that he wouldn't let them hurt her. Once they descended into the dungeon halls he relaxed, releasing the captured light and breathing regularly.

Jura beamed up at him. "That was amazing. Can you teach me how to do it?"

He chuckled. "It's not that easy. It's like Fire Dancing. It's a gift. You're either chosen for it or you're not. I'm sorry. I wish I could teach you. Just believe me when I tell you it's not worth the trouble."

She seemed disappointed but accepted his answer. She no longer needed to, but she remained close to him. He liked that.

He didn't like being back in the dungeons. He'd forgotten how awful the smell was. The rusty water and filth of those that lived above dripped around them. Unlike the halls above, the dungeon was constructed of heavy stone. Without Jura's guidance, he would have been utterly lost.

"How do you keep all these turns straight?" he asked as she once again pulled him opposite of the direction he'd been headed.

"It's a direct copy of the palace halls. In a way, I grew up down here," she answered, taking another sharp turn. "And when I forget, I pick one at random."

He sincerely hoped she was joking. Torches were scarce in the dungeon, making the halls dark and foreboding. There wasn't enough firelight for him to bend light around them, so it was a good thing the dungeon halls were deserted.

Probably because of the frequent executions, the dungeon held few occupants. Each prisoner was locked in a stone room. There wasn't a need for more than one or two guards at a time. Much like their last time in the dungeon halls together, Jura was intense and withdrawn, lost in her own thoughts. They walked in comfortable silence until she grabbed his arm. He looked down at her to find her raise a finger to her lips.

"Guard," she called out, stepping toward the torchlight.

He wished she had waited before making their presence known. There was enough torch light here that he could have bent it around them. He wasn't surprised though, all women were impatient.

The dozing guard jumped in his skin and, embarrassed, bowed low in front of her. "My lady First, a thousand apologies. I wasn't expecting any members of the council."

"So, in the absence of a council member you are lax in your duties?"

"No, of course not. I was just…that is to say—"

"Please, save your excuses. I'll let your shoddy guard skills slide if you'll give me privacy."

"My lady?"

"I need to speak with former councilman Dahr. Alone."

The guard anxiously wrung his hands. "I can't have anyone disappearing, my lady. His Greatness specified that Dahr was to remain locked up in his cell until his execution."

"I see. So, you're questioning my authority?"

The guard paled further. "Never, my lady the First. Err, your Greatness. That is…it's just, the last time you were in here—"

Tylak groaned, this bumbling idiot would never be convinced. He stepped up beside the man and clocked him soundly in the head. He fell in a crumpled heap to the floor at their feet. Tylak grinned at Jura.

"Why'd you do that?" Her voice was annoyed.

Damn. He thought she'd be pleased. Flaming women. There was just no pleasing them.

He shrugged. "It was faster." He held up his hands in a defensive gesture. "But don't worry. I respect your authority."

She laughed and he smiled, enjoying the sound of it. He knelt down beside the fallen guard, rummaging in the man's pockets for his keys to the cell. Triumphant, he stood and tossed the keys toward her outstretched hand.

They fell on the floor.

He choked back a laugh and bent to retrieve them, careful to place them in her hand.

"I'm a terrible catch." She took the keys, turning away from him.

"Oh, you aren't so bad," he heard himself say. Great, now he was outwardly flirting with her. She didn't seem to notice as she concentrated on finding the correct key for the locked cell.

"My lady the First? Is that you?" A man, presumably the councilman they'd come for, came to the door of the cell. He stared at them in wonder. "What are you doing here?"

"We came to help you escape," she mumbled under her breath and tried another key.

Tylak swore that she was mumbling curses.

"Thank you, thank you! I didn't do it, you know. I didn't poison the Third."

"That's good to know," Tylak quipped coming forward. "If you'd confessed, she'd probably leave you in there."

"Got it." The key turned in the lock with a loud click. Jura stepped back, a satisfied smile on her face and the councilman swung the door open.

He fell to his knees in gratitude, kissing at the bottom of Jura's robe.

"Really, it's nothing. Please, rise. We have to get you out of the city." She looked at Tylak, embarrassed.

Tylak stretched out his hand to help the man up. He took it with trembling fingers, and Tylak hauled the man up to his feet. When his face met Tylak's, he turned pale white and pulled his hand away, pointing a finger at him in wonder.

"You…"

Great, the man recognized him as the fire stealing convict. "Don't worry, I'm harmless. Seems like Jura makes a habit of setting prisoners free."

"But…How are you here? And in this form? I thought Beshar had you. I tried to set you free. I tried to go back for you." His eyes were wild and he clutched at Tylak's chest. "Is it the stone? Is that what set you free? I looked for it. I wanted to help you, Sykk. I wa—"

The councilman fell to his knees, clutching at his chest. It took Tylak several moments before he registered that the man had been stabbed. A dagger protruded from his chest and he choked as blood gurgled in his throat. The man had said Sykk. He'd said his brother's name! He dropped to his knees beside the councilman, shaking his shoulders.

"How do you know my brother? How do you know Sykk?"

"I'm s-sorry Sykk…" He coughed up more blood. "I nev…." His eyes closed. *No. Burn it all, no! He'd been ready to leave town. He'd given up on finding his brother. How could this be happening?*

He looked around wildly, searching for the source of the dagger and found himself looking into the smiling face of a Shadow Dancer.

THIRTY
NINE
JURA

I t was all happening so fast. One minute, she was standing there smiling
and laughing to herself over Dahr's gratitude. The councilman was
babbling, clutching at Tylak's chest and speaking so quickly that his
words tumbled over one another. She couldn't understand what he said.
Then, she'd watched as a dagger plunged into his chest. She looked up to
see five masked men dressed in the dark clothing of Shadow Dancers come
around the corner. *Had they been followed? What were they doing here? And
why had they killed Dahr? Had they even meant to kill Dahr or had the councilman
just gotten in the way?*

All too fast, the men had her and Tylak surrounded. Tylak knelt beside
Dahr. He screamed and tried to staunch the steady flow of blood pumping
out of the man's chest. The Shadow Dancers moved closer. They weren't

here to talk. Each of the men held a long, wicked dagger similar to Tylak's.

Wildly, she whirled in a circle, trying to take it all in. They were in serious danger. They were going to die. It was happening here and now, and there was nothing she could do about it. It was too fast.

Time slowed down.

She felt her heartbeat, slow and steady in her chest, as one of the Dancers reached for her. She easily sidestepped his grasp. *Why was he moving so slowly?* She was grateful, because it allowed her to turn her attention to the next. He came at her from behind. She saw him coming, just as slowly as the first. She ducked low, causing the man to grasp at nothing but air. She came up at the man's side, kicking her leg out like Akkim had taught her, hitting his knee. He cried out in pain. When he fell low, she kicked again, hitting him square in the chest. He fell all too easily.

Another man lunged at her from her right. She turned to her left knowing that her action would cause the man to run headfirst into the stone wall behind her. She watched him fall to the ground with the lazy descent of a falling feather. She turned back toward the first man who was poised and ready to throw his dagger at her. *Why was he taking so long to aim?* She watched him take aim for several heartbeats. Watched him slowly release the dagger toward her. Saw the dagger would hit her in the heart if she didn't move. She fell to the ground, sweeping her leg out as she did so, and knocked another Dancer's legs out from under him. She twirled around as another Dancer threw yet another dagger, this one coming for her face. It was easy to grab as it floated toward her. She caught it in the air and plunged it into the man's chest. The first Dancer, the one that had too slowly thrown his dagger, stared at her for several moments, his face frozen in shock. While he wasn't moving, she rushed at him, throwing all of her weight low at his legs and tackling him to the ground. He lay still. She leapt back to her feet and pivoted tight on her heel to avoid getting punched by another Dancer. The Dancer's movements were sluggish and heavy, and she easily dodged his blows. The man growled, clearly frustrated that his fist connected with nothing but air. Jura wondered how it was that everyone appeared so stagnant.

Tylak had finally found his feet and was locked in battle with a Dancer. Their movements also seemed slow. Jura watched as Tylak swung a lethargic arm toward the man's face, his skin pushed back as Tylak made contact. Another Dancer was coming for her. She could *feel* him behind her. She rolled sideways, easily dodging yet another dagger thrown at her. She picked up the dagger and held it to the man's face, breathing hard.

Tylak slowly walked toward her. *Why were his movements so unhurried?*

"How." The word was long and drawn out. *Why was he moving so slowly?* "Are." The registry of his voice was low. "You." He took another step, and she marveled at the way each fiber of hair on his head seemed to move in deliberate synchronization with him.

"Doing this?" He suddenly sounded normal. He closed the distance between them at a normal pace.

"What's happening," she demanded. *Had he done something? It was as if Tylak had slowed down time around her. How was he able to do such a thing?*

"That's what I was going to ask you. How did you learn to fight like that?" He was staring at her, eyes wide and confused.

"Fight like...I didn't...I..." She looked around dazed, realizing that four of the Dancers lay still. Were they dead? The fifth Dancer lay beside her, she still held a dagger pressed to his throat. She blinked up at Tylak in wonder.

Jura was going to be sick.

"Okay, take it easy." Tylak knelt beside her, peeling her fingers from the dagger one by one. "That's it," he murmured. "Deep breaths now, everything is fine."

She sat down heavily, grateful that the stone floor felt so cool against her thin clothing. Her skin was burning, and she struggled to catch her breath.

Tylak held the dagger up to the Dancer's throat. The man stared at them with hatred in his eyes.

"What are you waiting for? Go ahead. Kill me." The Dancer didn't struggle under Tylak's blade. If anything, he pressed himself closer to it, causing a tiny drop of blood to form under his chin.

Tylak held the blade steady. "Not without answers."

"You think I'll talk?" The Shadow Dancer laughed. "You're more foolish than I thought."

"The councilman. Why did you kill him? Was it because of what he was saying? Why don't you want me to find my brother?"

The man said nothing, and Tylak moved with lightning speed, slicing off one of the Dancer's ears. The man screamed in pain.

Jura swallowed down the rush of bile. *Tylak just sliced off that man's ear. He cut off his ear. The man had no ear!* She panted short, shallow breaths in an effort to control her nausea.

"Why did you kill the councilman?" Tylak asked.

The man whimpered and Tylak moved the dagger to his other ear.

"No, please no," the man shouted, his voice pleading and irregularly pitched.

"Tell me," Tylak growled.

"It wasn't meant for the councilman. Jo has always had bad aim. We were meant to kill her. Kill the girl and whoever gets in the way."

"The councilman knew about my brother. How do you explain that?" Tylak pressed the blade further, drawing blood from the man's still intact ear.

"I don't know. I don't know." He sniffled. "I didn't even know you would be with her. We were told to watch her. That she might come down to the dungeons. We waited in the halls. When we saw you come down, we attacked. We don't ask questions. The money was offered, so we took it. It was supposed to be easy. She's just a stupid girl."

"Why would the Prince of Shadows want Jura dead? Was it because of their deal?"

"It wasn't the Prince." The dancer moaned, squinting up at them through the blood that flowed into his eyes.

"Who is she?" He turned toward Jura, his eyes wild and his face covered in blood. "How did you do that? Move so fast? Who are you?"

She stared back at him, trembling. Assassins. The chain master had hired assassins.

"If it wasn't the Prince, then who sent you?" Tylak demanded.

The man began trembling violently. Blood red foam poured out of his mouth, and his eyes bulged. The shaking stopped. The man fell limp in Tylak's arms.

Tylak laid the man down and pulled Jura into his arms. She fell into them, sobbing. "The other men…"

"Shh, it's alright. They're all gone."

"But the men—–"

"Shh…they're dead. You're safe now.

"I killed them, didn't I?"

"Well, I got one. And this one killed himself. Poison, to keep from talking. I think I should get the credit though. So officially, I got two."

His joke didn't make her feel better. She moaned and buried her face in his chest, feeling the hot tears flow down her face. He held her for several minutes, rubbing his large hand down the length of her back until her sobbing quieted down to sniffles.

"We need to get you out of the palace. It's not safe."

"No."

"Jura, you can't stay here. This person isn't going to stop. They want you dead."

"I said no." She pushed against his chest and stared up at him. "If I leave now, I'll be leaving everyone in danger. My father, Amira, everyone. I have to stay. I have to find out who's responsible. The Republic has to be warned."

"All right," he said slowly. "I'll take you back to your rooms. But I don't want you going anywhere without your bodyguards until we find out who's responsible. And I'm staying with you."

She nodded, suddenly feeling tired. She'd wished she'd just taken a nap after all. Maybe then Dahr would still be alive.

"How did you do it?" she asked him as the two made their way back to the upper halls of the palace.

"Do what?" He still had his arm draped over her shoulders. She snuggled closer, enjoying the way he made her feel safe.

"How did you slow down time for me so I could fight? And if that's something all Shadow Dancers could do, how come they didn't do it too?"

"Jura, I have no idea what you're talking about." He stopped walking and turned her around so that she faced him. He frowned down at her. "I don't know what happened back there, how you managed to fight like you did, but you did that all on your own."

FORTY

ASH

"I wish I could take you there, Kay, I really do. But didn't you say your parents were gone? I know you can't easily forget the life you left behind, but you have to accept the fact that your old life is in your past. This is your home now." Ash looked to Kindle. She translated the words to Drakori, her voice low and reasoning as she reached out a comforting hand to the child.

"I want to go home," Kay repeated, her chin lifted stubbornly and Ash sighed. *How could he reason with a child?*

"I know. Why don't you two come with me to the sparring arena? I bet Kay would enjoy it. And you both could use some fresh air." Kindle's voice dripped with optimism, and Ash felt himself warming to the idea. It would be nice to get out of his tiny room.

"That sounds like a wonderful idea. Kay, get your boots on." Despite the fact that she wasn't truly a cadet, Ash had outfitted her as one, partly because he had no access to children's clothing and partly because he wanted her to keep up appearances in case Beshar decided to make another unannounced visit. Though the councilman had said he wouldn't be back for a week's time, Ash knew better than to trust the word of one of the Thirteen.

He'd spoken the words in the language of the Republic, but Kay sullenly rose and begun to tug on her boots, proving once again that she was quick to learn. Flames, but it was such a shame she wasn't gifted.

Once Kay had slid on her boots, the trio made their way out to the sands of the practice field. The twin fields were already full. The cadets working lines in one while the Dancers sparred with each other in the other. As they neared the field for the Dancers, Kindle began to bounce in excitement. Ash grinned, he remembered the feeling well. Outside of the days spent in the actual arena, there was nothing better than testing out your strengths and skills against your fellow Dancers.

Kindle mumbled several phrases to Kay, bringing a smile to the girl's face. Ash was once again grateful that Kindle spoke her language. He'd be lost without her assistance.

Sending a wink his way, Kindle trotted out into the field.

"She's sparring against Flint today," Ash said. Kay looked up at him with her wide blue eyes. She couldn't understand him he knew, but he continued anyway, feeling that it couldn't hurt. "Flint's all right as far as Dancers go. It's his third season in the arena, so he's made it farther than half of us anyway." He grinned. Kay continued to watch him. "He's not as good as I was of course, but I was a special case. In any case, Flint manages to hold his own."

Kindle adjusted her leather blade cover at the tip of her assegai. Unlike cadets who used training poles, the Dancers in the sparring field tended to use their actual assegai during sparring practice. It was best to simulate an arena fight as closely as possible. That way there were no surprises in the actual arena. The bladed tips of the assegai were covered with a leather pouch that dulled the blade from cutting but still left it capable to hurt an opponent something fierce.

Kindle's expression was hard and ready. Though she often looked amused, she was always deadly serious in the arena.

"Don't worry. He's not better than Kindle."

Kay's eyes sparkled in recognition of her friend's name.

"That's right. She may be little but she's fast as lightning and she really knows her stuff. It's Kindle's fifth year in the arena. That's rare for most Dancers, but especially a woman. Something to be proud of for sure. She's had some close calls but she always seems to make it out all right. Speaking of close calls, she had one just a few weeks ago. A dragon's tail caught her good. Knocked her right out."

Ash wasn't sure if it was his imagination, but Kay seemed worried by his words. He hurried to explain. "Don't worry. She's healed up all right. She's making another appearance in the arena this week's end, so that just proves that she's got a clean bill of health. The arena council doesn't let weak Dancers compete."

Kay yawned. He must be boring her. He continued anyway. "The arena council is different from the Thirteen. The Thirteen is our government, but the arena council is just five people. Not one of them are a member of the Thirteen. But here, those people are the ones that matter. They make all the decisions regarding life in the arena."

He frowned. If he was curious, he could easily petition the council for information on where arena dragons came from. Since there wasn't a book describing it in the arena library, maybe he could write one up. The thought amused him. Ash the great Fire Dancer deduced to nothing more than a library historian. Most likely, the arena council would be frustrated he'd petitioned for something so trivial.

"Okay, good. She's all limbered up. See how she holds her assegai. It's loose in her hand. You can't have a stiff wrist because you have to be prepared for movement. The assegai is an extension of the Dancer itself. A stiff wrist means a stiff Dancer, and you have to be fluid if you want to win. Also, you have to be prepared to thrust or throw the assegai, and you can't do that if you're holding on too tightly."

Flint and Kindle began to circle one another, testing each other with simple thrusts and twirls as they made their way around the arena.

Flint attacked, rushing forward and twirling his assegai over his head and then slashing it down toward Kindle's side. She parried the blow easily, knocking his assegai off course with her own and thrusting her's back toward Flint.

Kay grabbed Ash's hand in concern.

"It's okay. It's just practice. Remember what I said about their blades being covered? Kindle's way better than him, anyway."

"Unfortunately for Flint, you're telling the truth."

Burn that man. For someone so large, Timber had an easy way of sneaking up on him. Kay snuggled closer to Ash.

"Timber, I would say it's nice to see you."

"I'm amazed you can still see. Don't most people your age wear spectacles?"

"You're hilarious. It's a wonder that I'm ever bored in your presence. And yet, here we are." He turned his attention back toward the fight.

Kindle was gaining on her opponent, eating up the ground between them with confident steps and a twirling assegai. In a last ditch effort, Flint leapt toward her, assegai pointed downward. Kindle stepped into the attack, deflecting the blow with an armored arm and hitting Flint sharply on the back with her assegai. He fell to the ground and she pointed it at his neck in a mock kill blow.

Kay smiled and Ash shouted out congratulations. He tried to ignore the slow mocking clap of Timber beside him.

"Excellent showing, Kindle. Now that you're warmed up, perhaps you'd like some real competition. That is, if you're not too tired?" Timber drawled out, wrapping the leather cover over his own assegai.

Kindle helped Flint to his feet and frowned over in their direction, chest heaving.

"You want to spar?" she called out between breaths.

Timber sauntered toward her. "That's what I was aiming for, yes."

Ash noticed that Kay had begun to tremble beside him.

"Don't worry, little one. It's still just practice." But he felt his heart rate quicken as Timber got ever closer.

Not waiting for the two to tap weapons, Timber launched into his attack, setting Kindle on immediate defense as she struggled to parry his flurry of blows.

"Ash," a familiar voice called out across the field.

Perfect. This day keeps getting better. Annoyed, Ash pasted on a smile and waved at the councilman. Beshar waddled over, picking his way delicately across the sands and fanning at his face.

"I've had a dreadful morning," he said once he got closer. "Thought a trip to the arena would brighten my day." He patted Kay on her head and spoke to her in Drakori. She smiled back up at him.

"How's my new cadet?"

"Well, we haven't had too much time in the practice fields," Ash said carefully, distracted by the movements of Kindle and Timber. *Didn't Timber realize this was practice? Why's he attacking so fiercely?*

"So, you thought to have her watch two Dancers practice?"

Ash swallowed. "Well, I thought—"

"Excellent idea," Beshar interrupted, wiping at his brow. "Timber is the best there is, and Kindle is a fine example of what a female Dancer can do."

Timber pulled a flame from one of the torches that bordered the practice field and sent it straight toward Kindle. Kindle caught the flame, awkwardly rolling it in her arms before shooting it up toward the sky.

"She's certainly got an eye for the flame," Beshar commented.

"Yes," Ash frowned. Most sparring matches didn't include flame throwing unless it was planned ahead. "Kindle is really something."

"I was referring to our young cadet."

Ash looked down at Kay who stood mesmerized as Timber threw yet another flame at Kindle. This time Kindle was ready and caught it, twirling it around her body before shooting it back toward Timber. Kay watched the movement of the flame with hungry blue eyes. Beshar was right. She did have an eye for the flame.

If only she was gifted.

Beshar spoke again in Drakori to Kay, and she looked up at Ash in confusion before mumbling her reply.

Beshar stood up slowly. His face was deadly serious as he turned toward

Ash. "Do you want to explain this to me before I lose my temper? And I must warn you, I've already had a very bad morning."

Ash swallowed. "Explain what? My lord Tenth—"

"It's Ninth actually. And I think you know exactly what I need explained. I've asked our newly acquired, very expensive I might add, cadet here if she was excited to show me her skills at Fire Dancing. Imagine my surprise when she responded that she has no such skills. So, I will ask again, and think carefully on your answer, why do I have a cadet who can't manipulate fire?"

FORTY
ONE
JURA

They made their way through empty halls back to the First Tower. She wondered at their emptiness and then remembered that everyone was probably at Amira's luncheon.

"They're all at Amira's," she stated.

Tylak frowned down at her. The two had been traveling in silence, and Tylak was probably wondering at her sudden outburst.

"The council. Everyone." She felt numb inside. *Have I really just killed people? Really and truly killed them?* "She's having a luncheon. Maybe I should go."

"Like hell you will," Tylak's voice was a low growl.

"Excuse you?"

"You heard me. Someone just tried to have you killed. The person responsible is probably at the flaming luncheon now, gloating as we speak.

I'm taking you back to your room. You're going to stay in there, surrounded by your *Arbe*. Then *I'm* going to the luncheon to see what I can learn. Alone. Also, I need to find Beshar. He won't be happy with me after I stood him up, but we need one of his men, the kind that can detect when someone's bending firelight. I'm keeping you safe."

She wanted to argue with him, but it felt nice to have someone on her side. Instead, she snuggled close beside him. They walked the rest of the way without saying another word.

He stopped, hesitating in front of her chamber door. "Where are your men?"

"Inside I guess." She pushed open the door to her room, but Tylak slid in front of her to enter the room before she did.

The room was empty.

"This is strange, right?" He circled the room, slashing his dagger at the air wildly. He did this around the perimeter of the room. *He must be searching for Shadow Dancers,* Jura realized, though he looked ridiculous.

"It's more than strange," she answered, carefully stepping in behind him. "My men should be here. All four of them. Amira said she would send the rest of my *Arbe* back before the luncheon."

"Amira? Who's that?"

"My friend, she's the daughter of the Third."

"Why does she have your men?" Tylak pressed his lips together in a firm thin line. He stuffed his dagger back into its sheath.

"Hers have all disappeared. Murdered we suppose. After the night her family was poisoned. That's what Dahr was imprisoned for. Amira felt unsafe, so I gave her two of my men."

"When there are assassins coming after you?"

"Well, to be fair, I didn't know I had assassins coming after me then. But we did know that someone had tried to kill Amira." He was right of course. She had been acting First Interim and there had already been at least one attempt at her life. It was foolish to grant Amira the use of half her *Arbe*, but that's what friendship was all about. She refused to feel bad for helping Amira. She lifted her chin. "She was frightened. I was only trying to help."

"You…You gave away half of your men? Dragon's breath, woman! You should thank the Everflame you've managed to stay alive this long. You're defenseless without them."

"Thanks." She rolled her eyes. "Do you think something awful has happened to them?"

"Well, I don't think they're off having a tea party."

She sighed. "Right. So, what do we do now?"

"I'm taking you to Beshar's apartments. You can wait there."

"Can't I just go to Amira's?"

He stared at her as if she'd grown another head.

"What?" she asked, biting her bottom lip.

"Don't do that," he snapped. "It's distracting." His thumb pulled down at the skin beneath her bottom lip, releasing it. "And I mean this in the nicest way possible Jura, but you're an idiot."

She jerked away from him.

"That was unnecessarily rude." She pouted. *Just when she was really starting to like the man…*

"Stop acting like a child and I'll explain."

"And I'm not an idiot." She stuck her bottom lip out further and then realized she was behaving exactly as a child and sucked it back in, narrowing her eyes up at him.

"Let's think about what we know. Your friend asks for two of your men. Someone tried to have you killed. They're one of the Thirteen. Now all of your men are missing after said friend promised to return them. Meanwhile, all of the Thirteen are also at friend's house. A perfect alibi. Do you see a pattern here?"

"You think Amira is responsible for all this? That's insane. She can be petty but she would never... I refuse to believe it."

Tylak shrugged. "Suit yourself, but I'm not taking you to her house."

"Ahmar. Her father. I never would have thought it possible, but he travels frequently, more so even than Beshar. He would have had access to Kitoi, assuming he got the blood chain from there. And he and my father are close. He would have had plenty of opportunities to put the blood chain on him."

"Great, so they're both suspect. I'll say it again. I'm taking you to Beshar's. End of story."

"But that still doesn't explain who attacked their house. Or who's behind the start of this war."

"No, it doesn't. But it does reiterate the fact that you people are all crazy, and I was right to stay away from your kind."

"You think I'm crazy?"

He laughed. "More than you know." He kissed the tip of her nose.

The contact of his lips on her skin sent shivers down her spine, and she stared up at him in wonder. "Why did you do that?" She couldn't take her eyes off his lips. She licked her own. *Kissing him would probably be nothing like her kiss with Beshar.*

"Dragon fire, woman. You really are a child. Come on. I'm taking you to Beshar and then I'm going to see what I can learn."

"We'll have to pass by the halls of the Third on our way to Beshar, assuming he hasn't moved into the Ninth tower yet, which I highly doubt."

"Good thing we'll be invisible, huh?"

She frowned. "If we'll both be invisible, why can't I just go with you to the luncheon?"

"Damnation woman. I'm trying to keep you safe!" He raked a hand through his long hair.

She liked it when it was pushed back from his face. Although when it fell in front of his eyes, that was nice too. She shook her head.

"I appreciate it, you wanting to keep me safe. But as you saw back in the dungeons, I'm perfectly capable of looking out for myself," she sniffed.

"You can't explain what happened back there. How can you be so sure you'll be able to do it again?"

"How can you be sure that I won't?"

He sighed loudly. She smiled. She knew she was wearing him down.

"I'll stay right beside you, quiet as a desert rat. We'll poke around a bit and see what we can learn. It will be easy."

He smiled. "Oh no, you don't. I'm a fast learner, and I've come to learn that nothing's ever easy with you."

FORTY
TWO

KAY

The practice field was actually really neat. Kay still thought the deserted and barren sands were a funny way to describe a field, but she liked to watch the cadets practice with their sticks. She was excited to see Kindle practice like the boys. She'd spent the last two days learning as much of their language as she could, but Ash's words were hard to form and they didn't roll off her tongue as easily as they should. Still, she felt that she was learning quickly and could pick up one in every few words that he said.

Ash reminded her of her daddy. He was big and strong, and his eyes always had a smile in them when he looked at her. Though she didn't understand much of what he said, his voice was always soft and comforting. And Kindle was nice too. She was nothing like her mama. Mama was small and soft and smelled like freshly baked bread. Kindle was tall and lean with spiky hair and rough hands, but her face wore an easy smile. Kay liked that. She liked both of them, but still she resolved to get home.

I don't belong here, she thought sullenly, standing beside Ash in the hot sun. There was no breeze here, no flowers. She missed her cat and the silly clucking chickens. She missed Rumble. As always, the thought of him and her parents hurt her belly. She Breathed in the heat around her until the feeling passed. She Breathed often. Though she never produced a flame, she liked to know that she could still Breathe. It made her feel safe. She touched a hand to her earrings, the only thing she had from home, and let out her breath, feeling calm once again. Daddy had given her the earrings two years before for her fifth birthday. They looked like rubies, the kind of stones that Daddy said were the color of Rumble but really weren't. Daddy had made the earrings out of a stone he wore around his neck, he said that wearing them meant that she was wearing a part of her family. The earrings reminded her that she had been loved. They reminded her of home. *This isn't permanent,* she reminded herself. *I will get home.*

Ash spoke to her as he often did. He didn't seem to care that she couldn't understand anything he said. Kay didn't mind. She liked the low rumble of his voice. It reminded her of Daddy whenever he explained the proper care of dragons, and she was content to stand beside him. She was strong again. She no longer felt aches in her muscles or a stabbing hunger in her belly. The water here was yucky, but she was never thirsty. Maybe other little girls would be happy here, but not her. *I still need to go home.* She hoped the dragons had all been able to find food. Most of them had imprinted to Daddy. *With no one there to feed them, would they stay?*

Kindle started fighting. She tried not to worry that Kindle would get hurt. She noticed that they had covered the blades of their weapons. And though the blows they sent toward each other looked serious, none of them looked like they were really hurting her. Kay was glad. She didn't want anything bad to happen to Kindle.

Ash seemed to enjoy their fight. He kept talking, but his voice had taken on an excited edge instead of the patient explanatory one he'd used before. Ash liked fighting. She wondered why he no longer fought if he liked it so much. Maybe it was because he had hurt his knees. She noticed that he would rub them sometimes, much the same way that Daddy rubbed at his lower back. After long days in the barn, Daddy would ask Kay to walk on his back. She delighted in doing so. It was fun, and Daddy always promised that her feet made his back feel better. She should offer to walk across Ash's knees. Maybe her feet could make him feel better too.

The fight finished. Kay was pretty sure that Kindle had won because she had her stick pointed at the bad guy's throat. Kay cheered loudly. She liked when the good guys won. Kindle was one of the good guys because she was so nice. She felt Ash stiffen beside her and frowned as she watched the tall man approach. He was special too. She had seen him moving fire with the boys, but he wasn't as special as her or Daddy. Kay didn't like him. He was a bad guy. She could tell that Ash didn't like him either. If he tried anything, she'd burn off his eyebrows. He didn't look at her, and she smiled to herself, grateful that she was so small.

It's good to be small. Maybe no one will notice when I run away, she thought to herself. The bad guy stomped toward Kindle He wanted a fight and Kay felt her tummy twist in circles. She didn't want Kindle to fight another bad guy. She didn't like to watch her fight, even though she was really good at it.

Ash called out across the arena, and she watched with interest as the fat man approached. He walked slow. Kay giggled at the way his body shifted from side to side as he made his way toward them. *He walks just like a duck.*

Ash was serious when he greeted him, so Kay tried to be serious too.

"Hello, my little hellion. I hope you're staying out of trouble." The fat man patted her on the head, and she smiled at him. She didn't know why Ash didn't like him. He was one of the good guys. She could tell.

"Hello, sir." She decided to be polite. Mama would have swatted her bottom good for calling the man fat last time. Mama said she could never tell someone they were fat, ugly, or stupid. She didn't understand why it was so bad. It was the truth and Mama also said she shouldn't lie.

Ash and the fat man begun to talk, so she turned her attention back to Kindle and the bad guy. The fight was getting intense. The bad guy moved the flames from the surrounding torches and threw them at Kindle. She was able to catch them and throw them back. Kay was surprised. Kindle had never mentioned that she was special too. She watched the two of them throw flames and poke their sticks at one another. It was terrifying and amazing at the same time. Maybe Ash had saved Kay because he wanted her to be special like Kindle. She thought about this, turning the idea over in her head. She liked that phrase. Daddy said it often, and she always pictured the word doing cartwheels in her brain. I-d-e-a. That spelled idea and—the fat man was speaking to her again. She focused on what he was saying.

"—fire dancing? I bet you're excited to show me your own skills with the flame. When can I expect a demonstration?"

Demonstration? Kay thought it over. She thought the word meant showing someone how to do something. *Did the fat man want her to show him how to do what Kindle was doing? Impossible.* The fat man had no fire sense, she could tell. She shook her head and frowned up at Ash. She hadn't told Ash what she could do, so she had better not show the fat man how special she was.

"I'm sorry, sir. I don't know how to demonstrate fire tossing." *There.* She was pretty proud of herself. Not only had she used the new word in a sentence, she also hadn't lied. Well, not exactly anyway. She really didn't know how to demonstrate how she was special. She just was. And she had called the fat man sir, so she had been polite too. Mama would have been proud.

For some reason, her answer made the fat man angry. His voice was loud and quick and he was frowning a lot. *Was he angry at Ash?* Kay hoped she hadn't gotten her friend in trouble. Maybe the fat man was Ash's boss. Ash put his hands in the air and spoke quickly. He looked worried.

There was a loud pop to her right. Kay turned her head in time to see a ball of flame hit Kindle in the chest. Her friend fell backwards, landing on her back and breathing hard. Kay was worried. She knew that Kindle wore a chest plate made of dragon scales. Dragon scales were fire proof, but what if the bad guy's fire had hit her someplace else? *What if she burned like Mama?* Kay Breathed in heat.

The bad guy wasn't playing fair. He and Kindle had been tossing flames back and forth at each other using the fire from the torches. Now the bad guy was moving multiple flames at a time, spitting them out at Kindle in short rapid bursts. He was throwing the fire too fast for Kindle to keep up. Kay knew that Kindle wasn't as special as she was because if she was, she would just Breathe in the flames the bad guy tossed at her. Kay twisted her hands together, wondering if she should try to help.

Ash and the fat man were arguing now, she ignored them and Breathed in more heat. Kindle and her opponent both had power, but neither of them were as special as she was.

The bad guy shot another tiny ball of fire toward Kindle. She managed to catch this one, but just barely.

I won't let him hurt her.

Kay Breathed in more heat. There was so much of it. There were torches all around. The sun was a giant ball of fire above her and the sands were hot below. There was heat everywhere. She sucked it all in. She'd forgotten how glorious it felt to Breathe so deeply. The world grew bright around her. She felt big and strong like Daddy. She was ready to show the bad guy what it really meant to be special.

She was ready to give him a demonstration.

The bad guy sent another flame up into his hand. Kay Breathed it in too before exploding a giant wall of flame out toward the bad guy. She wouldn't hurt him. Mama and Daddy would never approve. But she would make sure he couldn't hurt Kindle.

The flame wall encircled the bad guy, towering over him and blocking him off from Kindle. Kay thrust out her arms, Breathing in more heat and adding it toward her already massive flame wall. The bad guy stumbled back, falling on his butt and turning to stare at Kay in wonder.

They all were. Feeling dozens of eyes on her, Kay Breathed out and extinguished the flame, panting softly. Everyone in the field was staring at her. Ash's mouth was hanging open, and the fat man seemed very happy. He was the only one who seemed happy. Everyone else just stared.

She cast her eyes toward the ground. *Uh oh. I think I did a bad thing.*

FORTY THREE

JURA

"*This is a bad idea,*" Tylak whispered in her ear.

"I thought we had to stay quiet."

He frowned at her. The two huddled against a stone wall in the Third's banquet room. Tylak had explained that it was easier to bend firelight the closer he was to the source of light, so the two had stayed against the walls bearing torches.

Jura tired of waiting. It had been nearly two weeks since the discovery of her father's blood chain. She finally felt close to exposing the mystery. But instead of action, she stood paralyzed against a wall. As much as she didn't want to admit the Third could be behind everything, she dismissed Tylak's argument that it was Amira. That thought was ridiculous and she was excited to finally have some answers.

Soon, everything will be over. She could feel it in her gut.

The luncheon had begun to die down. The guests had clearly all eaten. The men were lounging in the high-backed leather chairs of the Third's smoke room, passing around hookahs and sipping on sweetened fermented cactus juice.

Most of the ladies had already retired. Although Denir and Fatima stood whispering in serious conversation.

"We should get closer to them," Jura murmured, eyeballing a tray laden with sweetened delicacies meant to be enjoyed after one's meal. Flames, but she was starved. She reached out a hand and Tylak slapped it down.

"Are you trying to get us caught?" His voice darkened in warning.

"Sorry." She rubbed at her slapped hand and popped half a tart in her mouth. It was delicious. "We can't just stand here all afternoon. We'll never get any information that way."

His look suggested that he wished to strangle her, but he pulled her forward toward Denir and Fatima.

The Eleventh was leaning toward the Fourth, speaking in earnest tones. "The child is absolutely power hungry. I know I'll think twice before angering this family."

Denir yawned before a lazy smile played across her lips. "I think she's frightened. It's natural for her to assert herself after being granted interim power. At least she's doing a better job of it than the daughter of the First. Justir is lucky to still have his seat after leaving her in charge."

Jura ground her teeth and threw her tart at Denir's rump. Tylak shot her a warning glance. She smiled back sweetly.

Denir brushed the crumbs away, confusion written on her face as she tried to find the source of the attack.

"That's another thing. What was that mysterious illness of his? He certainly seems back to his old self now." Fatima gestured across the room. Jura and Denir both turned to stare at the First who stood with his back to them in the smoke room. The First neither drank nor smoke, choosing instead to listen to the conversation around him.

Amira sauntered toward the women, a large smile pasted on her face. Her face was done up. Her eyelids heavily lined and her lips painted red, but she still wore the ceremonial robes from the earlier council session. The robes formed and flowed around her. They fit perfectly and gave her a regal look that was a far cry from the way Jura drowned in them.

"Ladies, I hope you're enjoying yourselves?"

"Of course. Your luncheon was positively divine," Fatima gushed.

Denir nodded and lifted her wine glass slightly. "We were just speaking about you. Quite the impressive display. I believe I may have misjudged you before. Clearly you have a real future in politics."

Amira lifted a glass of chilled wine from a passing tray and sipped delicately. "People often underestimate a pretty face."

Denir smiled. "I couldn't agree more. I'm surprised the daughter of the First is not in attendance. I thought you two were thick as honey."

"And still are. Poor thing has taken to her rooms for a much needed nap. I think the morning session took a lot out of her," Amira responded.

"Yes, today's session was quite—" Fatima was interrupted by Denir.

"Intense." Denir finished for her.

Amira cocked her head to the side. "Intense? Whatever do you mean?"

"It's not every meeting that nearly the entire council moves up in Rank,"

Fatima offered. "In fact, I can't recall a time this has ever happened before."

"They say there's a first time for everything." Amira smiled. "If you two will excuse me, I must make my rounds."

She floated away and Jura watched her leave. Fatima began speaking about the wine selection. Jura pulled at Tylak's arm. They'd discovered everything worth knowing here.

The two stayed close to the wall and walked around the perimeter of the room, Jura directed them toward the private chambers of the Third. Amira was sometimes strange and she had always been a spoiled rich girl, but despite her snobbery Jura refused to believe that her friend would ever do anything to hurt her. Amira was her best friend. Her sister in every way except blood. It was time to find Amira's father and prove to everyone that he was behind her father's blood chain.

Leaving the main room, Jura pulled Tylak along the deserted hallway that led to the private chambers of the Third. They found him in his study, hunched over his desk engrossed in his reading. She started forward but Tylak pulled her back into the hall, shaking his head. He leaned close so he could whisper in her ear.

"Be careful, there's not much light in there."

"I have to get closer to him. I have to see what he's reading. It could be the proof we need to expose everything." She pulled against his grasp, but he held tight, refusing to budge.

"Looks like just a book to me. How will that prove anything?"

She tried to keep the annoyance out of her voice. "He's reading a book from Kitoi," she hissed back. "Look at the way it's bound. It's stitched with horse hair. We use dragon bone and camel. The book proves that he's brought back articles from Kitoi. A blood chain could have just as easily been one such item." She squinted at the words on the cover of the book. "If only I could read the cover."

"Xao Shin, The Five Elements and Properties of Blood."

She stared up at Tylak in wonder. "I didn't know you could read."

"Of course I can, how many times do I have to tell you I'm not a slave." He stiffened and pulled Jura close against him. "We have company."

Amira stomped past them and came to a quick stop in front of her father. She tapped her foot impatiently until she had his attention.

The Third jumped in alarm and slowly set the book down, an uneasy smile spreading across his face. "Amira dear, I didn't hear you come in."

"Not surprising, father, considering how engrossed you were in your reading."

"I'll admit the book has a curious title. I found myself drawn to it."

Amira crossed her arms. "Yes, I suppose the magnetic pull from it was such that you felt you had to remove it from my room."

Jura felt goosebumps form along the length of her arms. This was wrong. Amira didn't talk this way, and Amira couldn't be forced to read anything, not even her studies. In all their years of being friends, Jura had never seen her friend so much as glance at a book, never mind own one.

The Third also appeared nervous. He closed the book and handed it to her with trembling hands. "Well, you can have it back." When Amira reached for the book, her father grabbed her hand, snaking his hand out quick as a viper and holding her wrist tight. He pulled up the sleeve of her robe to expose a tiny dangling chain.

Jura choked back a gasp.

The Third released Amira and fell back as though he'd been slapped, staring up at his daughter in wonder.

"No. That can't be," he whispered.

"What is it, father?"

Jura couldn't see Amira's expression because her back was to her, but she could hear the smile in her voice.

"A master blood chain," the Third whispered. Jura strained to hear. "You're wearing a master chain."

"Of course it is. Did you think *I* was being controlled?" she laughed.

Tylak's grip on her arm tightened.

"How…What…Who—"

"Where and why?" Amira giggled. "Let's see, what shall I answer first? I'm controlling the First, have been ever since we returned to the Palace. Ever since you dragged your precious daughter to Kitoi with the thought of deepening your pockets. And what a fortuitous trip that was. Sorry about your son. I know what it means to lose your boy, but we needed Dahr dead. And Antar's death was a handy way to accomplish this."

"Amira—"

"Is in Kitoi where you left her, foolish man. Don't worry, she's still very much alive, which is more than I can say for you."

"*Arbe!*" The Third's voice had taken on a desperate quality.

"They won't come. We've gotten rid of them. And Jura's. Just like we intend to get rid of anyone else that stands in our way. We are everywhere. You can't stop us."

He stood quickly in his chair, reaching for the dagger strapped to his waist. Before he could unsheathe his weapon, Amira leapt over the desk, her fingers reaching for his throat.

Her body *changed*. Jura felt her knees buckle and would have fallen if Tylak hadn't held her from behind. No longer Amira, but a tall, slim, hairless creature with tightly stretched, gray skin and unnaturally long arms choked the life from the Third. The Third flailed his arms, desperate to gain hold of his assailant, when the creature suddenly bit into the Third's neck and drank deeply.

It's drinking his blood! Jura was going to be sick. She felt herself be lifted from the ground, but barely registered the fact that Tylak was carrying her down the hall and away from the horror filled room. Her friend was behind her father's blood chains. Her friend was replaced by a blood sucking monster. The Third was dying. He was probably dead. This was wrong. Everything was wrong. She couldn't see anything. Didn't want to see anything. There was so much red, and then the world went blissfully black.

FORTY FOUR

BESHAR

The day had a less than wonderful start, but what a finish. It was the most glorious day ever. He'd been in a horrible mood when he'd left Denir's chambers. First to watch poor Dahr's sentencing. The man was innocent, any fool could see that. And then to waste his one chance at blackmailing Denir. He'd managed to bully her into giving him the boy's birthstone, but when they'd gone to retrieve it they'd discovered that the damned Shadow Dancer had already broken in and retrieved it himself.

He'd been furious. He was just getting ready to wring Ash's thick neck, well order someone else to do it in any case, when the little cadet had dazzled them all. What a spectacular display. She was amazing. It was inspiring. She was worth every drop Ash had paid for her ten times over. He was beside himself with joy. Not only did he own the most spectacular dragon, but he now owned the top two cadets in the arena. He was unstoppable.

He'd wanted her to show her amazing skill again, but the poor child had been overwhelmed and exhausted. Kindle had stood over her glaring at him until he'd backed away. He'd made do with slapping Ash enthusiastically on the back before leaving the arena.

He was stopped by two men wearing the loose red tunics of the arena council. He frowned. If the council wanted to raise membership dues again, he'd have words with them.

"Beshar. Quite the display in the sands today." Tommon smiled at him. He was a tall elderly gentleman with thick white hair that hung loose and flowed to his shoulders. His black eyes were dark and beady like a rat's. Though in polite society Beshar outranked them, such laws didn't apply to life in the arena. The council called him by his first name as was their right. Still, it irked him.

"Thank you, gentlemen." He stepped forward to move past them, but the two moved closer together, blocking his way.

"Was there something else?"

"We're concerned about your cadet's training." Viktor crossed his arms over his chest. He was a short man, barrel chested with ruddy cheeks and thinning hair.

No need to question which cadet they meant.

"We feel she'd be better suited with a certified arena trainer," added Tommon.

Beshar's defenses immediately flared up. He didn't like sharing his toys. He stared from one man to the other. "Ash Fire Dancer has more than proven his skill in the arena. And you've never questioned my choice in trainers before." He raised his eyebrows.

"Naturally, the council agrees with you. Ash was an exemplary gladiator and surely a talented trainer. But don't you suppose, given that this specific cadet is so vastly talented, that she would be best served directly under the supervision of the arena council?" Viktor's voice dropped an octave, and he leaned forward cracking his knuckles.

Was this a threat? Beshar didn't care. "No." He smiled. "Actually, gentlemen, I feel that my cadet is exactly where she needs to be."

"Cadets can grow expensive. Surely it's more rewarding to own a dragon than to pay toward a gladiator's freedom?" Tommon smiled, holding up a halting hand to Beshar's chest. "What if we could offer you an arena dragon that would match the ferocity of your Inferno?"

Beshar frowned down at the hand in disgust until Tommon dropped the offensive appendage down by his side.

"If you're offering a trade, I cannot accept. This discussion is over. You must excuse me. I have pressing issues at the Palace." He didn't, but he couldn't stand to continue this boring conversation for another minute longer. He shoved his way past the men and called for his litter. Likely he'd made enemies with the council. *What did it matter?* he thought with a sly smile. Let them double his dues. He could more than afford it now. *I'm having the best day ever.*

He arrived back in the palace and entered his rooms through his private entrance from the courtyard, choosing to avoid the main halls. He didn't need a confrontation from one of the Thirteen to spoil his day. He pushed open his doors and found Jura and her Shadow Dancer waiting in his salon. He scowled. Sometimes there was just no escape.

"Jura, to what do I owe this pleasure?" He frowned at the Shadow Dancer. "You, get out." He called for wine and a Samur brought a goblet quickly.

"We need your help," Jura's face was pale. She seemed in danger of uploading the contents of her stomach on his expensive rug.

He frowned and handed her his goblet, urging her to drink. He gestured for another for himself. The Shadow Dancer could go thirsty.

"Where have you been all afternoon? My father has called an emergency session."

"That's not what's bothering you." That much was clear. Something was very wrong. It was all over her face.

"The session will start quickly and there isn't much time to explain." She looked at the Shadow Dancer, and Beshar frowned when the man squeezed her shoulder in a gesture of comfort.

"We're leaving the Republic." Jura took a deep gulp from her wine and drew in a shaky breath. "Not long before you returned, the Third raced into his dining hall claiming to have found an assassin in his chambers. An assassin from the Sea Kingdom. He was like a crazed man, screaming through the halls before he ran back into his own room. Amira found him, dead in his room, stabbed with a trishula. There was no evidence of any break in and no assassin was found."

"So the people of the sea really are attacking?"

The Shadow Dancer and Jura exchanged a look.

"We don't believe the person who made these claims was actually the Third. Just like Amira isn't really Amira."

"Isn't really...what are you saying?"

"I saw Amira. She's wearing my father's master chain. Only it isn't Amira, not really. I don't know what it was. It was gray and tall, unnaturally tall, with skin stretched tight and abnormally long arms. That's what killed the Third. It killed him...and then it drank his blood."

Beshar felt very cold. He set his wine glass down and rubbed at his arms.

"*Alttaw'am*," he whispered. "I didn't think such creatures actually existed. They use blood magic. Dangerous stuff."

"You know what this is?" The Shadow Dancer looked relieved. "Then, you know how to stop it?"

Beshar shook his head and threw up his hands in a helpless gesture. "I don't know much. Only that by ingesting the blood of their victim, they're able to walk in their skin. They're only copies though. If something were to happen to the original, the same would happen to the creature. They're bound by their victim's blood. And if the original dies they can no longer wear their form."

"That would explain why it's staying in Amira's form. She's still alive out there. We have to save her. We have to stop this from becoming a war." Jura's voice broke. She took another sip from her glass. Her hands shook so violently it was a wonder she wasn't wearing any wine.

"What's blood magic?" The Shadow Dancer frowned. "I thought there was only Fire and Water?"

Beshar sighed audibly so the Dancer would see his annoyance. "There are five kinds of magic, actually. Fire, Water, Earth, Air, and Blood. But you didn't come here for a lesson on magics. What can I do to help?"

"We're going to Kitoi," Jura said. He was surprised by the vehemence in her voice. Jura had never sounded so passionate. Her eyes sparkled dangerously. "Amira—that creature—thinks I'm dead. We have to use this to our advantage. We'll need water and one of your men, the kind that can detect when someone's bending firelight."

"Kitoi? Jura you can't be serious." When he'd offered his help, he thought it would mean he would help her find a place to hide, not assist her on a suicide mission. He had to talk her out of it. "It's too dangerous, you don't even know who is behind all this. *Alttaw'am*...I don't know much about them. I've heard they're mindless creatures. It's only doing the bidding of its master. Stay here, tell the council what you've discovered—"

"And put my father in further danger? You yourself know how easy it is to place someone in blood chains. Who can we trust? No, not with so many lives at stake. I have to take advantage of the fact that whoever is behind this thinks I'm dead. They think they're getting away with everything. I have to send a message to the Sea King, I have to save Amira. I can do this, if you'll help me."

"I'll help in any way I can." The words were out of his mouth before he gave it any thought. He was surprised by the ferocity in which he meant them.

They left shortly after, Jura and the Shadow Dancer, with two of his best men. He'd wanted to give her more, but the Shadow Dancer had reasoned that they were better off with a smaller party. He saw the wisdom in the boy's words and wished them good luck. They were going to need it. After their departure, he hurriedly dressed for the emergency session. He was about to leave when Kenjiro shoved him down into his chaise and stepped in front of him.

The head of his Samur whirled around in a tight circle. But before he could pinpoint the source of his distress, one of his Samur brothers fell to the ground, clutching at a wound on his stomach.

Adham, the Prince of Shadows, stepped over the fallen man and smiled a wicked smile. He wore his customary black clothing but he was unmasked. Beshar knew the Prince would never allow anyone to see his face and live to see another day. He wiped the blade of his dagger clean. The Prince had come with the intent to kill him.

"Beshar. You're a hard man to reach."

"And you're not as handsome as I thought you'd be. No wonder you always wear a mask."

Adham's face was scarred and mottled pink and white, a stark contrast to the brown skin of his arms.

The Prince smiled tightly. His teeth were very white.

"The result of a tragic run in with a Fire Dancer, I'm afraid."

"If you play with fire…" Beshar rose to his feet, but he made no motion to move from behind Kenjiro. The man would give his life in protection of Beshar and he would allow it. He had no intention of dying this day. He had quite a few Samur at his disposal, they more than outnumbered the Prince, but Adham was capable of making himself invisible. Though Kenjiro could sense when one was bending firelight, the deadly Dancer would remain invisible to him.

Kenjiro flexed his arms but remained very still, waiting for Beshar's command.

"You've gone through a lot of trouble for this meeting, my Prince."

"There's no need for such formalities. Please, call me Adham."

Beshar smiled. "Adham. I'd offer you wine but I have very expensive tastes. I prefer to share only with those I consider a friend."

"Am I not a friend?"

"Certainly not. Enough of these games. I have a session to get to and you'll have me arrive late. What do you want?"

Adham's eyes widened. "Brave words from a man armed only with his *Arbe*."

So the Prince didn't know of his Samur. Beshar still had the advantage. He took a single step forward so that he stood at Kenjiro's side.

"I'm waiting."

Adham laughed. "I thought to let you live after I acquired my information, but now I don't think I will. Your insolence is insulting. You play a dangerous game in the arena."

"The arena? That's what this is about? You can't be serious. I thought this was your own agenda. What do you want? Have I caused someone to lose their chips in a bet?"

Adham stared at him for several moments. He twirled the point of his dagger on the palm of his hand. "You really don't know, do you? Your dragon, he—what is your man doing?"

Adham stared at Kenjiro. The Samur pressed his palms together and held them just over his chest. He stomped on the floor muttering in his native tongue. Beshar had never seen any of his Samur do such a prayer. He too watched in interest.

Kenjiro's mutterings grew louder as the rhythm of his stomping quickened. He fell into a frenzied state, shouting and pounding his feet into the stone floor. One by one his brothers joined in. Soon the sound was deafening. Their shouts echoed off the stone walls. Beshar resisted the urge to bring his hands up to cover his ears.

Adham started forward, but the ground split open in front of him and he stumbled to his knees.

"What's happening? Beshar, wha—"

His words were cut off when a massive hole ripped open and the stone floor crumpled around him. The Prince of Shadows fell into the hole. The Prince's hands scraped against the walls as he scrambled to escape the shallow fissure.

"Beshar, you fool! You can't stop this. You don't even know what you're involved in. This doesn't stop with me. The Queen will have her revenge. Let me out of here. We can help each other." His fingers clawed at the dirt and crumpled stone.

The room fell to silence as the Samur abruptly stopped.

Beshar stepped forward, peering down at the captured Prince of Shadows. He'd never seen Earth magic at work before. The results were fascinating. His men had just caused the ground to rip open. The trick was beyond useful.

"Good work, Kenjiro. I'll have…" His voice faltered as he looked into Kenjiros eyes. They were entirely black. The whites of his eyes had disappeared. He and the other Samur marched forward in unison. They dropped to their knees at the edge of the freshly formed pit. The Samur formed a circle around its edge. When the last man fell to his knees, they once again began to chant.

Adham screamed. A viscous liquid rose up from the bottom of the pit and began to cover the body of the Prince. The man's screams tore through him, and his body twitched and jerked under the attack of the oily substance. He didn't stop screaming through the choking fluid until the oil rose to the top of the pit and the Prince disappeared into its depths.

Kenjiro reached into the pit and began to wipe the oil all over his body. His men joined him. Beshar could only watch as the men covered themselves in the liquid. When they finished, the oil in the pit sank back into the ground. There was nothing left of the Prince of Shadows.

The ground rumbled beneath them. The hole was filled and the split formed back together. In a matter of moments, the stone floor appeared as it always had. There was no proof of the gaping hole that had existed only seconds before.

Beshar was not a man who was easily astonished. He sat heavily in his chaise. It seemed the wonders of this day would never cease.

"Master," Kenjiro placed a large warm hand on Beshar's shoulder. Though the hand was glistening with oil, it didn't leave a mark on his robe. "You must attend your meeting."

FORTY
FIVE
JURA

They had to hurry. It was difficult because they had to leave the palace unseen. To do that, Tylak had to bend light around four people at once. The foursome huddled close together and Tylak became covered in sweat as he concentrated.

"We should get a torch."

The suggestion came from one of Beshar's men, and Jura was startled at his voice. She'd forgotten they could speak. He was right of course. If they had a torch, they could move freely, without the worry of staying close to walls that bore torches. But how would they ensure that it stayed lit?

"The Everflame." She motioned for the men to follow her. She led them in the direction of the center tower.

The Everflame sat in a massive bowl of stone. It was inextinguishable. It was constant. The flame was said to have burned since the beginning of time, eternal and watchful. The flame provided their livelihood, a tangible god and vehicle for their prayers. They climbed up the narrow stone steps that led to its home. Once they reached the top, Tylak gasped and fell to his knees.

"It's incredible."

"Haven't you seen it before?" Jura wished that she had a quill and paper to burn a quick prayer before their departure. She whispered one anyway in hopes that the Everflame would heed her words and grant them safety.

"I told you. I didn't steal from the Everflame. I've never stolen fire."

Jura bit her lip and stared at the flame. *How could they take some with them?*

"Come with me." She pulled at Tylak's hand and the men scurried behind them.

She led them back into the hall. Jura pulled a torch from one of the braces against the glass wall. They made their way back to the Everflame. This time Tylak wasted no time in snatching the torch from her hands. He tore a piece of his cloak and smothered the flame, stomping on it for good measure. Once the flame had sputtered out, he held the torch to the Everflame.

It ignited easily, their very own piece of the Everflame. The firelight from the Everflame seemed to give him more power, or perhaps the thrill of the theft had given him confidence. Whatever the case, Tylak bent the light easily around them. They ran down the stone stairway, but Jura stopped them before they could head in the direction of the palace exit. She had to know what was happening in the council session. It was her last chance to glean any information.

Tylak and the two Samur followed her to the Justice Dome. She paused before entering. Tylak's expression was hard and ready, so she pushed forward. Last time she had attended a council meeting, she had felt invisible. This time she truly was. Once they entered the Dome, they moved to the far side and pressed their backs into the glass wall. Everyone was in attendance except for Beshar. The session would start at any moment.

He was the last to arrive. He took his seat in the Ninth chair, looking harried and more frazzled than she'd ever seen him. He cast a surprised look at the end of the stone table. Jura followed his gaze and noticed Ledair already occupied the seat of the Twelfth. She wondered who would be voted in as the Thirteenth, and then chided herself for worrying over something so trivial with everything else that was going on.

Beshar must have been too distracted to call the session to order, because Amira stood and called its beginning. She sent a curious glance in Velder's direction.

Her father sat tall in his glass throne and stared at the members of the council, his expression stern and foreboding.

"We were recently contacted by the Sea King, urging us to enter a war against the peoples of Kitoi. The Sea King claimed that the peoples of Kitoi were in breach of our contract alliance." The First held up a sheet of parchment.

"I have here an envoy from Kitoi that states just the opposite." He scanned the faces of the council members. Everyone waited in silence. "As many of you know, I was indisposed this past week and unable to stand as your First. What you did not know was that my illness came from an attempt on my life. It is now my belief that I was poisoned by the portion of fresh water granted to me by the sea peoples. This attempt at my life, in conjunction with the most recent departure of the Third, has led me to believe that we the Republic must take action."

All of the council members began to nod. Beshar looked troubled. Jura bit the inside of her cheek to keep from crying out. *It's happening.*

"We must find and fulfill the position of the Thirteenth with all due haste. Fill it with someone who has the constitution to handle the days ahead. In light of the recent misfortunes handed to her, the young daughter of the Third has handled herself admirably. I motion that she be inducted as full ranking member as the Third of the Thirteen."

"I second the motion," Fatima said, bobbing her head.

The majority of the council knocked the table in agreement.

Jura trembled. Now, more than ever, she realized exactly what was at stake. She was going to Kitoi to stop a war. She stared up at the man who used to be her father and closed her eyes against his words.

"It is decreed that Amira the Third is a full member with all the benefits her Rank deserves. We will reconvene at the week's end to vote in a suitable candidate for our Thirteenth. We must remain strong and unified as a council. We will show the Sea King his mistake in attacking the full strength of the Republic. The Sea King has asked that we go to war, and that is exactly what we will do."

END OF BOOK ONE

ACKNOWLEDGMENTS

First and most of all, the biggest thank you to my husband for leaving me in the woods of Alabama and forcing me to write. Without you, Robert, my book would still be a distant dream. I love you. To my parents for always believing in me and supporting my decision to be a writer. To my sister, my alpha and best friend: I can never repay you for all the hours you spent on the phone with me, listening to my insecurities and helping me fill plot holes. Melody, thank you for your honesty, Ignited is actually good because of you. Thank you, Cayce, for holding me accountable. Chelsea, for all the times you gave me a listening ear and for all the free editing! To the rest of my family and friends, my network of people who worked behind the scenes, Olivia and Leah, and my team at RadiantTeen, THANK YOU.

ABOUT THE AUTHOR

 Alexis Marrero Deese is an avid reader of young adult and fantasy. Her favorite authors include Brandon Sanderson and Orson Scott Card. She graduated from the University of South Florida with a Bachelor's Degree in Creative Writing and a sun tan she misses dearly since her move to north Georgia. She has a passion for cooking, spends entirely too much time on Pinterest, and is a self-proclaimed dog training expert for her family's legion of dogs.

FOR MORE INFORMATION, VISIT:

WWW.AMDEESE.COM

END OF THE BORDER WARS
YEAR 1341: JOSPER

He didn't know he was already a dead man. Josper watched the foreigner with interest. The dead man walking cast furtive glances over his shoulder, his quick steps and hunched posture did little to hide the fact that he carried a large satchel in his arms. Josper snorted. Anyone from around here knew not to bring packages through these parts; one was liable to have their clothes stolen off their own back.

"Who are we watching?" The whisper came from Josper's side but he didn't flinch at the sudden presence of his friend, Bard.

"Some poor fool about to get robbed." Josper raised an eyebrow. "I haven't decided yet if I'll intervene. What are you doing out here?"

"Business." Bard grinned back, his white teeth appeared to glow in the dark of the night.

Josper rolled his eyes. Business meant patrolling the streets for poor fellows such as the easy target in the alley just below. Crime was rampant in the city proper and the majority of the King's local army was used to escort and protect the water cart shipments. These days, in the northern borders and in the central cities surrounding the Everflame, water was increasingly difficult to come by. Perhaps that was why so many men turned to a life of crime. They lacked hope.

CPSIA information can be obtained
at www.ICGtesting.com
Printed in the USA
LVOW11s1808120418

573254LV00002B/549/P